Conversations with
Aurangzeb

Celebrating
30 Years of Publishing
in India

Praise for *Conversations with Aurangzeb*

'Wry Tamil humour is a distinct form of telling a story; there is something uncomplicated and good-natured about it. I am glad English readers are going to get a feel of it. If you know Tamil, you'd think you're reading Tamil, and if you don't know Tamil you would think you're reading your mother tongue. Also, who would have thought Aurangzeb could be so entertaining.'

— MANU JOSEPH

'Comprehensively irreverent, this genre-bending, sparklingly witty novel fuses history with the wryness of our own times. Bringing together a long-dead Mughal emperor and the impulses of the Instagram generation, it throws the reader headlong into a marriage of parody with social commentary. I was, in succession, befuddled, amused, alarmed, but always also spellbound.'

— MANU PILLAI

Conversations with
Aurangzeb

~ A NOVEL ~

CHARU NIVEDITA

Translated from the Tamil by
NANDINI KRISHNAN

HarperCollins *Publishers* India

First published in India by HarperCollins *Publishers* 2023
4th Floor, Tower A, Building No. 10, DLF Cyber City,
DLF Phase II, Gurugram, Haryana – 122002
www.harpercollins.co.in

2 4 6 8 10 9 7 5 3 1

Originally published in Tamil as *Naan Thaan Aurangzeb* by
Zero Degree Publishing, Chennai © Charu Nivedita 2022
This English translation © Nandini Krishnan 2023
Translator's note © Nandini Krishnan 2023

P-ISBN: 978-93-5699-392-1
E-ISBN: 978-93-5699-394-5

Typeset in 11.5/16 Adobe Caslon Pro at
Manipal Technologies Limited, Manipal

Printed and bound at
Manipal Technologies Limited, Manipal

This book is produced from independently certified FSC® paper to ensure
responsible forest management.

Contents

Translator's Note

My acquaintance with Mr Charu Nivedita began sometime in 2008, when I picked up the English translation of his *Zero Degree* from Madras Terrace House, the cafe–bookshop–boutique that housed Blaft Publications.

Hanif Kureishi said in a recent tweet, 'Art should not be safe or complacent; it should frighten, alarm and make us want to throw the book across the room.'

Zero Degree did exactly that. I then read the Tamil version, which was even more savage. It frightened and alarmed me so much I doubted I'd want to be in the same room as its author. It also struck me that some works were perhaps genuinely untranslatable.

It would be eleven years before I found myself in the same room as Mr Charu Nivedita. I had gone to watch a staging of Mr Indira Parthasarathy's play *Aurangzeb* by Theatre Nisha at the Alliance Française de Madras. I ran into Mr Charu Nivedita's Tamil publishers, Gayathri R. and Ramjee Narasiman, who introduced me to the man. He was rather less strident than I expected. He spoke in a clear, but not loud, voice, and his first question to me was, 'I believe you have a lot of animals?' His second question was, 'You're the one who translated Perumal Murugan's latest novel, right?'

His reputation had preceded him. The Tamil literary world is divided into his fans and his haters. Labels like 'pornographic', 'misogynist' and 'no convictions' were bandied about by the haters, most of whom are regular panellists at literature festivals. Of these, I found the last most interesting. If one was believed to have 'no convictions' about any political issue, it essentially meant one had found favour neither with the chest-thumping right wing nor with the self-proclaimed liberals. That's someone I don't mind finding myself in a room with. And he had a lot of cats. Two reasons to like him, I thought.

A year later, Ramjee called to ask whether I would consider translating a novel-in-progress. Within ten minutes, Mr Charu Nivedita had called me. He had written about twenty thousand words of a novel on Aurangzeb. He expected to end it at about thirty-five thousand words. Would I consider translating it speculatively, he asked. I said yes. And then we spoke about cats for half an hour before he said my reputation had preceded me too. He had heard I was abrasive, arrogant, short-tempered, sarcastic, contemptuous of political correctness, dismissive of opinions that were not in line with my own, adoring of animals, irritated by human adults, very irritated by human children, and vegan – all of which I believe are true, and for the first nine of which he could forgive the tenth.

This literary partnership could be fun, we thought.

When the chapters came in, I realized it made little sense to translate them. The milieu, the in-jokes, the rhythm of the sentences, the puns, were all meant for Tamilians. They would be lost on an audience that did not speak the language, and a straightforward translation would do it no justice. The book would have to be rewritten in English.

The Tamil novel ran to a hundred and forty-five thousand words over the next two years. The English novel is about a third shorter but has entire sections that one will not find in the Tamil version. Some of these have been written by Mr Charu Nivedita and others by me. We saw it as a collaborative exercise in creating a work, a groundbreaking book that would reflect on the process of translation, publishing, editing, sales, fandom, controversy, hate, censorship, and awards – the life cycle of a novel.

To me, this is not a new genre so much as defiance of all genre. Our editor Rahul Soni suggested we might call it a 'transcreation'. While I like the word, I don't know if any label will sit easily on the novel. When three characters as deranged as the three of us – Aurangzeb, the writer and I – are involved in birthing a novel, it is only to be expected that the book will be deranged too.

I do hope it alarms, frightens, and makes you want to throw it across the room. It is rather heavy, though, so I also hope you choose a worthy target to aim it at.

– Nandini Krishnan

Be in this world as though you were a stranger or a wayfarer
And count yourself as among the people of the graves.
— *Prophet Muhammad*
(in his advice to Abu Dharr, from Makarim al-Akhlaq, 12:5)

How to Begin a Novel

The writer did want to begin his novel with a more interesting, perhaps more titillating, sentence than 'Before writing this novel, the writer was doing his research for another one he was all set to write – about the Catholic nun Catarina de San Juan.' The writer has a reputation for titillation, you see.

Having written eleven chapters and four prologues – the writer had, like normal people, begun with a Prologue 1 rather than a Prologue 0 – he decided to send the manuscript to his friend Baahubilli, who said…

Wait. You haven't been introduced to Baahubilli yet. She is the translator of this work into English, Nandini Krishnan.

Now, what would one expect a writer and his translator friend to discuss? Perhaps which of his creations should be translated next? Perhaps an interesting novel one of them has read? But the writer and Baahubilli speak almost exclusively about cats. The writer takes care of twenty cats, and the translator takes care of sixty.

Every time the writer calls her, the translator misses his call and then returns it, always opening with, 'Sorry, I couldn't answer because my cats were sitting on my arms.' The writer thought she was lying, until one morning, he received a WhatsApp video call from a kitten who looked suspiciously at him. Then, he saw an arm move from under the kitten and his translator's sleepy face look into the phone. 'Oh, sorry, you were my last dialled number, and my cat called you.'

That was when he named her 'Baahubilli'.

For every hundred hours the writer has spoken to Baahubilli, ninety-nine have been spent discussing their cats. For every ten encounters they have in person, nine are at their vet's clinic.

The writer has often had dreams in which he and Baahubilli have intense literary discussions for hours together. They go like this:

Baahubilli: Miaow-miaow.

The writer: Miaow.

Baahubilli: Miaow?

The writer: Miaow! Miaow, miaow, miaow, *miaow*.

All is fair in dreams and fiction. Just as it was justified for a novel to begin with Gregor Samsa waking from sleep to find himself transformed into an insect, it may be justified for the writer to fall asleep and find himself transformed into a cat.

It's quite incredible, isn't it, that through all the miaowing, the two of them have managed to produce a novel that weighs about as much as two cats?

Why, even when Baahubilli was going to call the writer to discuss the editor's feedback on the first draft of the manuscript, they ended up talking about cats.

'Catappa,' she said – because, naturally, that's Baahubilli's name for the writer – 'a sweet little cat has come home. She is heavily pregnant, could deliver any time now.'

'Oh. What did you do?'

'What could I do, Catappa? I bribed her with food and brought her to the safety of my home.'

'How many kittens do they usually have?'

'Four.'

'So now, you have sixty plus four?'

'No, Catappa. Five. You're forgetting the mother cat.'

That night, Baahubilli made another appearance in Catappa's – tchah, the writer's – dreams. The two of them had a novel-length conversation, comprising a single word: 'Miaow'.

But this is not why the writer began this chapter. He was going to tell you about Baahubilli's feedback.

Having written eleven chapters and four prologues, the writer decided to send the manuscript to his friend Baahubilli, who said, 'I was just wondering ... perhaps you should begin your novel with something that will pull readers in, a sentence that would make them pick this novel in a bookshop, or order it after reading an excerpt? You know, Manu Joseph's *The Illicit Happiness of Other People* has this opening sentence I simply love: "Ousep Chacko, according to Mariamma Chacko, is the kind of man who has to be killed at the end of a story." How can you *not* buy a book that begins like that, you know? And then there's your friend Tarun Tejpal. His *Valley of Masks* begins with: "It is not a long story. Some men would tell it in the time it takes to drink a glass of bittersweet ferment. And then there are those who would tell it in such detail that barrels would be drained dry and they would not arrive at its end." You're already interested. I'm wondering, what is the story? If it isn't long, is it short? And then there is humour. And before you can recover, he offers this up: "I know the Wafadars will find me. I know they will show me no mercy, for mercy is flab." You know he is going to die. And you want him to tell the story before he dies. The sense of urgency, the curiosity he incites … Why, you couldn't stop talking about it when you recommended the book to me. Isn't that how you should begin your novel too?'

The writer felt she had a point. And so, he inserted a Prologue 0 before Prologue 1.

But what was he to put in there?

Having written autofiction all his life, the writer suddenly felt he had reached a dead end. You must know that Jean Genet wrote *A Thief's Journal* having done his primary research by pursuing the vocation of his character. Who wouldn't want to read a thief's journal? Genet became an overnight sensation.

Later, at a literary meet, he ran into a socialite – as one tends to at festivals of literature, except, given the era during which they met, one ought to refer to her as a member of the bourgeoisie – who advised him, unsolicited (as people one encounters at festivals of literature tend to do), 'Monsieur, please don't give up your first profession. If you do, you would be denying your readers novels as exciting as *A Thief's Journal.*'

Genet is said to have replied, 'I used to have the freedom to be a thief, undetected and unrecognized, for as long as I was insignificant. Now, that might be rather difficult.'

The story could be apocryphal.

But the point this writer of autofiction is trying to make is this: even if he hadn't become an overnight sensation like Genet, he had attained a degree of fame over the decades. Now that his daily activities can so easily be fodder for the tabloids, he finds himself unable to write autofiction.

Let me give you an example. He and his woman friend – a girl and a friend, but not a girlfriend, let's be clear – had gone to the pub 10 Downing Street. She was twenty-five years old, and he sixty-five. But, as you must know, a writer published in the West has always remained an attractive companion to women much younger than he. Besides, he was considered broad-minded by dint of the subjects he chose.

This was during a phase of his life when he was teetotal. He had been going through an emotional crisis, having realized that the output of his contemporaries was ten or twenty times that of his own. He had then arrived at the conclusion that he was losing most of his time to soirées and decided to stop drinking.

I must interrupt this narrative to tell you that his going off alcohol did not in any way increase his output. The time he wasted drinking with his friends continued to be wasted with those very same friends, only without alcohol. To be precise, without the writer drinking, but while watching those friends drink. Oh my God. He had never put himself through something quite as traumatic before and hasn't since. It was the closest he had come to hara-kiri, to give his drunk friends company while remaining sober himself. This was what drove him to drink again. But on the evening we find him at the pub, his sobriety was to rescue him from a grave fate.

His woman friend drank. He didn't. Having downed three pegs, she said, 'Let's go to the dance floor.' Three pegs will do that to you. Dance was everything to him. But when he danced, he was reminded of what another woman friend had told him: 'You look like those villagers shaani midhuchufying' – making cow dung cakes – 'when you dance.' She had found it so funny she'd repeated it several times. The writer had put it down to this woman friend being a salsa dancer. What was dance, anyway? Did one have to be an Uday Shankar to dance? Music elicited a response from one's consciousness, and that translated into movements of the body. One *moved* to music. That was all.

But that day, on the dance floor, he found that neither his mind nor his body responded to the music. His woman friend was a good sort. 'You dance well,' she said. Well, thank you for the certification. And he thought of the salsa dancer.

That's a tangent. What I wanted to tell you was that a *photojournalist* – that's what photographers for the tabloids call themselves these days – had taken a picture of them dancing.

'Saar, what a scoop! You're a lucky soul ... you live like a film star, Saar!' said the photojournalist, practically jumping with joy, presumably on the writer's behalf.

The writer's heart stopped. Aiyo. A scoop. Of this kind. In a newspaper. Of that kind.

This was no France. And he was no Michel Houellebecq. A film star's image might be enhanced by an outing on the dance floor with a girl a few decades younger than he. So might a French writer's. The literary world in India, though, was another matter. He would go from human to hashtag. A writer, they felt, must be a Tiruvalluvar, spouting either philosophy or revolution. The writer often had requests from parents on the day of Saraswati Pooja, asking him to guide the hands of their children as they wrote their first letters on grain. And now here he was, drunk-dancing with a young girl. He would be not just a hashtag, but one attached to the word 'paedophile'.

But being sober that day, he was able to speak to the photojournalist and convince him to delete the photograph he had captured, even as his woman friend slurred, 'What's the big deal, let them publish the photo, what are you scared of?' She'd had three more pegs in the interim, and six pegs will do that to you.

Under the circumstances, the writer could no longer keep to the autofiction genre. Right. Allow him to cast modesty aside and tell you plainly: his wife had become a fan of his writing. End of story. So he couldn't quit his profession either. Which is why our writer turned to history. He'd dare anyone to say a word against him now. 'If you have a problem,' he'd tell them, 'go speak to Ashoka and Aurangzeb.' Which was how he arrived at the subject of Catarina de San Juan. You might ask who this Catarina was. She was born in 1606, in the palace of … turn the page, won't you?

The Novel that Wasn't

Before writing this novel, the writer was doing his research for another one he was all set to write – about the Catholic nun Catarina de San Juan. You might ask who this Catarina was. She was born in 1606, in the palace of Agra, as Shah Jahan's first cousin. Her given name was Mirra. She was raised in the same palace as Shah Jahan. Perhaps around 1617 – when she was ten or eleven years old – she was kidnapped by Portuguese sailors and sold into slavery. Her buyer was a trader from Mexico. She converted to Catholicism in Mexico and adopted the name Catarina to suit the newfound faith. Soon after, she joined a convent as a novice. Having performed several miracles in her lifetime, she was and remains highly regarded as a saint and Mother in Mexico. The Jesuit priest Alonso Ramos has written a three-volume biography of Catarina de San Juan.

In the early seventeenth century, at the time Catarina was being raised in the Mughal palace, Hindustan was the prime example of tolerance across the world. The Italian explorer Niccolao Manucci writes that traders and travellers were bound by law to wear the colour green in order to enter Turkey. They were obliged to speak with bowed heads. Meeting the eyes of one's interlocutor could have one sentenced to flogging, and an argument to amputation. That was the Turkey of the time. Whereas Hindustan was quite like a metropolitan city of our contemporary world. And I'm talking not just about the capitals of its constituent kingdoms, but of all Hindustan. Foreign traders and explorers visited, stayed, left and returned. The land was so rich as to incite the jealousy of the entire world, and countries like Persia were waiting with bated breath for a chance to loot it. This prosperity was the reason for Mahmud of Ghazni's repeated forays from across the Hindu Kush mountains. (Manucci writes that the senior bodyguards at Shah Jahan's palace would carry batons made entirely of gold, while their subordinates would carry batons of silver.)

The peaceful coexistence of religions in Hindustan allowed several Catholic priests to ensconce themselves in the good books of the royal family. This may have been among the reasons for Aurangzeb's fanatic adherence to the tenets of Islam, and his putting his brother Dara Shikoh to death. In one of his letters, Aurangzeb worries that if Dara were to mount the throne, he would hand over all of Hindustan to the priests.

While the three volumes written by Alonso Ramos were handy research material for the writer's intended novel on Catarina, being a priest did tend to colour Ramos's writing with his beliefs. He states that Catarina's very birth was owed to the grace of Mother Mary. Her parents, having remained childless for twenty years, took the advice of one of the palace's resident priests and prayed to the Virgin Mary. Ramos credits the birth of Mirra to this act. Well, that's as may be. But the writer needed

documentary evidence to verify certain facts about her life. He
wasn't able to find this anywhere. Everyone who had written
about Catarina has used Alonso Ramos's biography as his or her
primary source.

It was then that a friend of this writer's mentioned an Aghori
who could speak to Akbar's spirit. In fact, he could summon into
his body the spirit of anyone with whom one wished to speak.
And then it would be the spirit and not the Aghori who spoke to
the interlocutor. Every now and again, he would call the spirit of
Akbar for the entertainment of his friends.

'What if there's some golmaal in all of this, how can one be
sure it is Akbar who is speaking?' the writer asked.

'Come and see for yourself,' the friend said.

The Aghori has asked that the writer not give out any details
about him, and therefore it would not be right to speak about the
Aghori or even his town either in this novel or in any other forum.
So, it is asked of the readers not to pester either the writer or the
publishers for such details about the Aghori. At times, letters of
this nature have caused the writer great distress. 'I've had scabies
for twenty years, and don't remember when I last slept through the
night. Please do give me the address of the siddhar about whom
you had written.' How can the soft-hearted writer deal with such
a request? The siddhar, for his part, has asked that no one be made
privy to his whereabouts. This is the sort of awkward situation in
which the writer often finds himself. So, I ask that nobody write
to ask for the Aghori's address. Please.

~

There were ten people in that room. In a corner, incense sticks
had been lit. The aroma of attar wafted through the air. A tinny
recording of a woman's mellifluous voice singing a ghazal played

from an iPod in another corner. On a slightly raised platform
cushioned by a quilt sat the Aghori, eyes closed. Everyone else was
seated on a jamakaalam on the floor. The writer had taken pains to
ensure that the spirit felt at home and had tailored the ambience
to suit the purpose.

It was indeed Akbar who spoke. Without a doubt. Because,
the friend said, the Aghori didn't know a word of Farsi. His
connection with North India had given him some knowledge of
broken Hindi, but he wasn't well versed in Urdu, let alone Farsi.
And Akbar's spirit held forth in poetic Farsi, occasionally peppered
with Hindawi.

Once the seance was over, the writer spoke to his friend and
the Aghori. He wondered if it might not be a good idea to ask
Shah Jahan himself for anecdotes about Catarina's early years for
his novel. The Aghori acquiesced and a date was set for the seance.

But it was obvious, even before the spirit had announced his
name, that it was not Shah Jahan who had entered the Aghori's
body. Shah Jahan was passionate about music. He was an
accomplished singer. His voice is said to have mesmerized anyone
who heard him. Keeping this in mind, the writer had taken the
precaution of playing a khayal in Raga Yaman by Kishori Amonkar.

However, when the spirit spoke, they all heard, 'Fie on you
all! Stop that bleeding music at once, I command you!'

At first, they looked around the room for Shashi Tharoor – the
voice or, to be more specific, the accent and wording had suggested
he might have made a sudden appearance. Not the order. While
Shashi Tharoor's interest in music or lack thereof isn't known to
the writer, he could not think of anyone else who might say 'fie'.

The confusion cleared when the spirit that had manifested
itself in the Aghori announced its name.

'I, Alamgir, born Aurangzeb, have come before you.'

Fresh confusion, however. The writer did not think Aurangzeb knew English, let alone the words 'fie' and 'bleeding'.

The spirit looked at him through the Aghori's eyes. 'I know English well, and some French too. But we shall cross that bridge when it presents itself. We have a long journey together.'

Which brought the writer to the more pertinent issue: Why had Aurangzeb arrived in Shah Jahan's stead, and what was this journey they were to embark on, crossing bridges at the former's will?

Even before the writer could ask, Aurangzeb took it upon himself to explain. This is the gist of what he said in an elaborate monologue:

There is much misinformation in history about Aurangzeb. In the belief that by telling a writer his true story these errors may be corrected, he had told his father he would go in his stead. Aurangzeb then launched into details that would leave the writer stunned. Quite naturally. He made assertions to the contrary of everything the writer had read about the Mughal empire. And cited historical evidence for each of these.

The first curveball was this: The court astrologer had been a Brahmin, the spirit said and then offered proof.

'Two score and ten pages of the commencement of the *Akbarnama* are dedicated to Padishah Akbar's horoscope, did you not see?' he asked. 'It is said we did not suffer Hindus in our court. It is said more of me than of my predecessors. That I forced conversions. Stuff and nonsense! Why, I built temples for the Hindus and even had endowments bestowed upon them for their maintenance.'

When the writer set out to verify his citations, they did appear – for the most part – to be true. The evidence taken into

consideration comprised largely the writings of European voyagers
and histories of Aurangzeb's era written after his death. They had
not been commissioned of writers hired for the purpose, unlike
the histories of certain other emperors. They were written when
Aurangzeb was no longer alive.[1]

Anyhow, the appearance of the wrong spirit was a bolt from
the blue, which prompted the writer to put the novel he had

---

1 As Aurangzeb himself said in the course of one of the seances, he cannot
   be boxed in by a single adjective, or even a short series of compatible
   adjectives. Because, in his eighty-nine-year-long life – and forty-nine-
   year-long reign – he did not always act in the same manner. Because he
   was not always the same person. His beliefs changed over time. He could
   hardly be described as predictable. His personality is complex, and he is
   not an easy man to decode.
       In a letter written to his son Azam Shah in 1704, Aurangzeb says,
   'How could you fire a Muslim official in order to replace him with a
   Hindu?' In 1672, he had issued an order that his governors remove
   all Hindu officials from their posts and replace them with Muslims.
   But this order could not be implemented. Since they were not able to
   find qualified Muslims for the posts required, they were often given to
   underqualified officials by virtue of their being Muslim. Despite this,
   several states could not find enough Muslims with any qualification that
   could pass for being suitable, and therefore Aurangzeb's order remained
   unfulfilled. This has been documented by Khafi Khan in his *Muntakhab-
   al Lubab*, published by Maulvi Kabir al-Din Ahmed in Calcutta between
   1768 and 1774.
       Most works of history about the Mughals use Khafi Khan's tome as
   a reference. The reason for this is that Khafi Khan, after serving briefly
   in Aurangzeb's court, worked for the latter's descendants. Since his
   manuscript could not have been read by Aurangzeb, we may assume that
   it was written with independence. And therefore, we must conclude that,
   contrary to Aurangzeb's assertions to the writer, Hindus and Muslims
   were not treated equally. However, it is true that he built temples for
   Hindus and that there were more Hindus than Muslims in his army.

planned on the back-burner and write Aurangzeb's story instead of Catarina's.

Permit me a diversion here. At this point, the writer couldn't help thinking, 'Ada paavi, it was bad enough that you kept your father under house arrest when he was alive. Even after having passed into the spirit world, must you be a usurper?'

It struck him, even as the thought crossed his mind, that Aurangzeb looked right into his eyes and gave him a sardonic smile. He might have imagined it. Or Aurangzeb might have heard him think. No, that was impossible. Or was it? The spirit *had* made a reference to his knowledge of English earlier. Well, that might have been because the writer must have looked evidently taken aback.

Right, so I was saying: This bolt from the blue prompted the writer to put the novel he had planned on the back-burner and write Aurangzeb's story as his spirit told it.

And now another dilemma presented itself to the writer. If he were to simply write the story of a spirit as the latter told it, how could the authenticity of the book be established? There was only one way to go about this. He would report what the spirit said, in its words. But he would also add a commentary with historical evidence and secondary sources that may prove or disprove those assertions.

To maintain his fidelity to the spirit's words, the writer thought it would be a good idea to record Aurangzeb's testimony. But Aurangzeb refused to allow this. Apparently, it was not acceptable in their world – the world of spirits – to leave behind corporeal evidence. The writer couldn't find any logic in this. But he was mollified when Aurangzeb said he had no objection to notes being made on paper.

The writer was also moved to make one more request.

'Huzoor, I ask that you speak in Urdu. Your English is too complex for this century. I'm not very fluent, and if one goes by the national bestseller lists in India, our readers are even worse. I understand some Hindi, and I will bring along a translator in any case, so I can make notes that I can understand. You told me yourself that you have been misunderstood over the centuries. You were speaking figuratively, I'm sure, but you will be literally misunderstood if you use words like *fie*.'

The spirit smiled and nodded. Our story shall commence shortly, he seemed to say.

~

In the meanwhile, the writer would like to introduce you to those sources of his who *did* leave corporeal evidence behind.

All Mughal rulers, Aurangzeb included, had given Brahmin astrologers positions of importance in court. Pandit Chandrabhan Brahman served as the royal astrologer, court poet and munshi from the late 1620s to 1663 – under both Shah Jahan and Aurangzeb, and possibly under Akbar and Jahangir before them – without compromising on his Brahmin identity. When Shah Jahan took ill, his duties were taken over by his son Dara Shikoh, whom Pandit Chandrabhan Brahman served as munshi.

Despite being Brahmin, Pandit Chandrabhan was India's leading poet and prose stylist in Farsi. His works remain objects of deep study for Farsi scholars. He is said to have brought innovations in style that persisted for centuries after his time. For all this, Farsi was not his first language. It was an acquired one. Let us reflect, for a moment, on what a rare treasure the autobiography of a Brahmin who occupied a position of importance in Aurangzeb's court and documented it in prose is.

François Bernier (1620–88), who served as the royal physician in the courts of Shah Jahan and later Aurangzeb, has also written a travelogue.

Yet another book has been penned by Niccolao Manucci (1638–1717). He left his home in Venice in 1656, aged eighteen, and came to India, which would be his home for fifty-four years. Manucci claimed to be a medical practitioner, but his only real success seems to have been curing one of Shah Alam's[2] wives of an earache. He wore many other hats, from artillery man to diplomat. He had, at some point, become close to the European assistants of Shah Jahan and Aurangzeb, which allowed him access to the Mughal courts. His observations have been documented in a four-part history. The first of these is about Aurangzeb's rule. He writes that everything he has recorded is an eyewitness account. 'I haven't documented anything that I have not seen or lived,' he says.

The writer used several other books as references and has listed them in an appendix at the end of this account – which, because of the fact that he must rely on the testimony of a spirit for most of its course, he has decided to call a novel.

There is one last thing the writer would like to emphasize. Just as François Bernier writes in his travelogue, this writer too would like the reader to note: 'I won't say this history is entirely accurate. But I can promise it has fewer errors than those written by others.'

---

2   The Shah Alam referred to here is the first of his name. He was the second son of Aurangzeb, and also known as Muhammad Mu'azzam. He would be crowned king in Delhi in 1707 and serve as Bahadur Shah I until he was put to death in 1712.

Languages, Titles & Stray Dogs

He (Aurangzeb) is that truly great king who makes it the chief business of his life to govern his subjects with equity and impartiality.

– FRANÇOIS BERNIER, French physician who
spent eight years at Aurangzeb's court

I was sent into the world by Providence to live and labour, not for myself but for others.

– AURANGZEB

[It is] the obligation imposed upon a sovereign, in seasons of difficulty and danger, to hazard his life and, if necessary, to die sword in hand, in defence of the people committed to his care.

– AURANGZEB

DISCLAIMER(S):

The views expressed in this story by the spirit of Aurangzeb are those of the former emperor, and the writer is in no way responsible for them.

Although the writer is not the slightest bit in agreement with many of those views, he cannot undertake to argue with Aurangzeb on these matters. He is an emperor. And that too, a spirit. A blow could close the writer's account for good, and there will be little point in screaming *Amma* or *Aaya* after that. This was why the writer chose not to engage in debate or argument, and instead, held his peace and listened to the spirit. Moreover, you must already be aware that Aurangzeb could neither be enough of an expert in democracy nor a twenty-first-century intellectual, and it would be foolish of the writer to aspire to such debate.

We cannot hold the Aghori through whom the writer interacted with Aurangzeb's spirit responsible for the latter's views either. Other than the fact that a ruler named Aurangzeb once existed, the Aghori who played medium was not aware of anything of the emperor's life. Once the spirit finished its oration, the Aghori could not even remember what it had said.

~

Aurangzeb spoke to the writer in a mix of several languages. Apparently, he knew many and was prone to using them. Here is what the spirit had to say about this:

'Honourable Katib,[3] I was most well versed in Rekhta. Before we reached these shores, our future subjects spoke in the Hindawi tongue. Rekhta was a melange of Hindawi with our native Farsi. I do know English, as must be evident from the fact that I speak it to you now. It has become the common tongue in the spirit world. It appears to have several versions over the centuries, and I am rather intrigued by it. It might be the one I have had most

3   Arabic for 'writer'.

opportunity to speak since my death, but I believe that might be a hindrance to your ambition with this work and it would suit you best that I switch to Urdu?'

The writer nodded.

'Very well. I knew some French too when I was alive. My brother Dara Shikoh's personal physician François Bernier passed on to me after Dara's death.' The writer thought he detected a smile at this point. 'If you had troubled yourself to read Bernier's travelogues, the false image of Alamgir fostered by history would have disappeared. Would you prefer that we speak French?'

'Let us stay with Urdu, Huzoor,' the writer said. 'I write in Tamil, but I can understand Hindi. The story of my acquaintance with languages is a long one.

'Until I heard the spirit of Emperor Akbar, I had been under the impression that those of you who have been liberated from your bodies' – the writer was hesitant to use the word 'spirits' and found a workaround – 'could speak just about any language. Because, once the atma leaves the body' – aha, this is a better word than 'spirit' – 'it is no longer bound by the confines of the world. It is us corporeal beings who must bend over backwards to learn a language. It appears very few people have an aptitude for language. The rest of us run and hide the moment we're introduced to the grammar of a new language, Huzoor. And then, the grammar of languages like German and Sanskrit could drive one mad.

'Why, Tamil has the same effect. It gives the impression of being a sadhu. But the moment a newcomer approaches it, the language turns Dracula and chases him away. Let me give you an example, Huzoor. If I had to teach a Hungarian or a Russian a sentence to explain the verb *po* – go – how would I go about it?

Why don't you give it a try with me, it won't cost you anything, will it?

*Naangal naalvarum netru cinemaavukku **ponom**.*

– The four of us **went** to the cinema yesterday.

*Naangal naalvarum naalai cinemaavukku **povom**.*

– The four of us **will go** to the cinema tomorrow.

*Avalum avanum netru cinemaavukku **poyikkondirundhapodhu** oru rowdy aval kaiyaippiditthu izhuththaan.*

– When she and he **were going** to the cinema yesterday, a rowdy caught her by the hand and pulled her close.

*Indha death certificate vaanga engengo **poga** vendiyirukkiradhu.*

– One **has to go** here and there to get this death certificate.

*Enge **pogiraai**?*

– Where **are you going**?

*Ipoodhu **pogaippogiraaya**, illayaa?*

– **Are you going to go** or not, now?

'*Ponom, povom, poyikkondirundhapodhu, poga vendiyirukkiradhu, pogiraai, poga, pogiraayaa* … went, will go, were going, has to go, going, are you going to, to go … the person who came to learn the language will be driven to end it all with poison within a day. All right, let's say for the sake of argument that the Russian manages to learn all this by heart. If he's asked, "*Nee naalai cinemaavukku **povaaya**?*" – "**Will you go** to the cinema tomorrow?" – that will be the end of the story. *Po* is a verb. And look what games Tamil grammar plays with this little verb. It was in this way that the German language once made me take to my heels.'

'Don't you, who are so well read, know the reason for your struggle with languages, Honourable Katib? Dyslexia. The reason

I know this is that it was because of this condition that Padishah Akbar remained illiterate. You might have dyslexia too.'

'Adada, if only I had met Huzoor earlier, I could have freed myself from the worst emotional trauma I've been subject to. Because, except for Tamil, the grammar of any language that I learn makes me want to hunt out either poison or a rope to make a noose and put myself out of my misery ... right, why did this subject come up? Aanh ... since you're in an atma state' – how easily flattery comes to one's tongue – 'and I was under the impression that atmas are omnipotent, I'd figured you would speak to me in Tamil.'

'No, Honourable Katib, I might have turned into a spirit, but I cannot turn into Padishah Akbar.'

'Do forgive the interruption, Huzoor. But may I know what the connection between Padishah Akbar and Tamil is?'

'It was one of Padishah Akbar's greatest dreams to cross the Vindhyas and conquer your land. He would often sigh that he had been unable to do what Krishna Deva Raya had. Thankfully, he gave up once he realized he couldn't do it. I wonder what would have happened if he had refused to give up. His Majesty Giti Sitani Firdaus Makani Babur Padishah Ghazi[4] did not get into that dangerous game either. If he had, Mughal rule would

---

4 Aurangzeb often made the writer's life even more stressful by switching to titles instead of names for his ancestors. Sometimes, he was so kind as to include the ancestor's given name. At others, he was not. When they got to know each other better, the dead emperor would sometimes spare the writer the trouble of keeping up with elaborate titles and simply say 'Babur' or 'Humayun'. The writer learnt a few things from the seances, among which are these facts: Giti Sitani means 'He who rules the world'; Firdaus Makani is a posthumous title, meaning 'He who resides in heaven'. Ghazi is an honorific title given to a Muslim warrior who fights infidels.

have died with him. Krishna Deva Raya's terrible army would
have crushed that of Firdaus Makani with all the fuss of ridding
oneself of an annoying mosquito. Arsh Ashyani[5] Padishah Akbar's
desire to conquer the Tamil land was not so much lust for land as
for language and culture. Although he could not read, he would
have books read out to him. He was an illiterate scholar. Someone
had introduced him to Tamil music. He wanted to listen to it all
the time. That was why he wanted to bring the Tamil land under
his rule. He wanted to see this tribe of people who'd had trade
links with the Greeks right from the era of Ashoka. I've heard
him say this often, with my own ears. I find it quite interesting,
Honourable Katib, that the far south of India and the northern
reaches of Kashmir have somehow always evaded Delhi, right
from the beginning of time, through our era, to your present
day. Two thousand three hundred years ago, the army from
Pataliputra failed to capture Kumarimunai. And in your modern
times, Chakravarti Rajagopalachari, Arignar Anna, Kalaignar
Karunanidhi and Puratchiththalaivi Jayalalithaa have got your
Delhi to dance to their tunes, haven't they?'

Showing some consideration for the fact that neither English
nor Urdu was the writer's native language and that he might
be further hindered in note taking by his probable dyslexia,
Aurangzeb spoke fairly slowly, with pauses in between. There
were times when an emotional outburst would see him switch
to Farsi. Having lost out on the content of one such torrent, the
writer decided to take Rizwan, a student of Farsi literature who
also had some knowledge of Arabic and was fluent in Urdu, with

5   Akbar's posthumous title, which means 'He who lives in the world
    of gods'.

him to the seances. He did not dare ask Aurangzeb's spirit to translate for him.

But he envied the emperor's felicity with languages. If it was the writer's destiny to be unable to pick up any language but his own, could he not have been born in a different place? Like France or Spain, which accorded writers a place of dignity in society? Why, one need not go that far. His neighbouring state Karnataka would have done. It is the state which most celebrates its writers. Bengal and Kerala are no match for Karnataka. Tamil Nadu, of course, has writers on par with stray dogs.

~

This conversation took place over twelve seances, each of which typically lasted between six and eight hours. Aurangzeb would sometimes close his eyes for a while and sink into silence. The writer would be quiet too, so as not to intrude into this silence. It would be with a sudden and Shakespearean 'Lend me your ear, Honourable Katib!' that Aurangzeb resumed his narrative, but he did for the most part acquiesce to the writer's request that he speak in Urdu.

Each seance would begin with a recitation of the seven Makki[6] verses of the al-Fatiha. But, in consideration of the length of the novel, the writer has only cited this in the beginning. At the first seance, when Aurangzeb finished his recitation and began to speak, the writer did something.

Now, there is a certain way in which Mughal emperors must be greeted. One must place the back of one's right hand against

---

6 There are two types of revelations in the al-Quran – Makki surahs that were sent before the Prophet migrated to Medina, and Madani surahs which were sent after his migration.

the ground, and bend a whole hundred and eighty degrees from the hip so that one's torso is pressed against one's legs, and touch one's head to the palm of the right hand. This is called Uttanasana in yoga. The writer got to know of this from Niccolao Manucci, who writes that this was how he first greeted Padishah Shah Jahan. And so, the writer did the same for Aurangzeb.

Upon observing the writer perform this elaborate contortion, Aurangzeb burst out laughing.

'Why, the Honourable Katib's actions do stir old memories! However, unless it be the health benefits that tempt him, the Honourable Katib need feel no obligation to bow in this manner to a dead emperor. I believe this is the era of *democracy* – what a word, what an idea. The people are the kings, and the ministers are their servants … so I've heard. I hope we shan't go as far as that, but let it not be asked of you to relive the mores of my period.'

'Do forgive the interruption, Huzoor. Although what you say is true on paper, the reality is rather different. The ministers would find it hard to greet their leaders as I did just now because their paunches would get in the way, so they go all the way down to the floor and fall at the feet of their chiefs. Once, because access to the precious feet of a certain female politician was blocked by the table behind which she was seated, a minister crawled on all fours to work his way under the table and reach his target. And so, while we may call it by another name, the form of governance can hardly be said to have changed over these centuries.'

~

Through the eight hours of the first seance, Aurangzeb never partook of anything but water. This moved the writer to ask, sometime during the second seance, 'Would you like some kabuli,[7] Huzoor?'

Having laughed so hard he had to clutch his sides, Aurangzeb said, 'I see you have read in some detail all the missives I wrote my sons. It was in one of those that I'd mentioned my fondness for kabuli. A sentence does not a life illustrate, Honourable Katib. While I'm something of a connoisseur of food, I'm not a big eater. Doers don't indulge in such sensory pleasures; that is the folly of the dreamer. It was my pragmatism of body and mind that enabled me to live four score and nine years and rule for two score and nine.' After a moment's thought, he added, 'The reign of Padishah Akbar, too, lasted two score and nine years. But when his father – Jahanbani Jannat Ashyani[8] Humayun – passed away and Padishah Akbar ascended the throne, he was only fourteen. Until he attained majority, it was Bairam Khan who ran the kingdom as regent, wasn't it?'

'Since you're a connoisseur, Huzoor, perhaps you would allow us to have some mango juice brought for you?'

After another hearty laugh, Aurangzeb said, 'You're some khiladi, Honourable Katib. My entire dynasty is slave to that fruit. Giti Sitani Firdaus Makani was the only one who made no time for such pleasures. But our ties with mango began with Jahanbani Jannat Ashyani. Even when he had to flee from Delhi to Kabul, he made arrangements for baskets upon baskets of mangoes to greet him on arrival at his refuge. Did you know that

---

7   Biryani made from rice, mutton, basil leaves, chickpea, dried apricot, almond and curd.

8   Jahanbani means 'The person who rules the world' and Jannat Ashyani means 'He who lives in heaven'.

there were one lakh mango trees in Padishah Akbar's orchard? In fact, the emperor[9] once had me kept under house arrest – yes, I am familiar with the term, since I have conversed with some of your ... servants? politicians? ... who have passed into the spirit world. He had me kept under house arrest over an issue that had to do with mangoes, would you believe it?'

'Huzoor, forgive the interruption. But my readers' chief problem in following your narrative – aside from your switching to English so very often, when they can barely spell "Shakespeare" let alone understand his language – is the fact that you say "Giti Sitani Firdaus Makani" and "Jahanbani Jannat Ashyani" and "Arsh Ashyani". How are we to remember all these titles? I must warn you that unless you help us out here, no one will read your story.'

---

9 Through the course of these conversations, Aurangzeb would typically refer to Shah Jahan as 'the emperor'.

Treason & Tooth Powder

'If the Honourable Katib would suffer me to tell him the story of the emperor keeping me under house arrest over mangoes, I will respond to his query in due time.'

The writer nodded. The spirit switched from English to Urdu.

'Once, a consignment of imampasand mangoes was sent me from Bhagnagar.[10] I ought to have rightly sent a few baskets of those to the emperor. But I had never tasted mangoes of that variety before. It was my first time, and I was so taken by the deliciousness of the fruit that I retained all the baskets. Yes, I do admit it was wrong. And foolish. A housefly could barely sneak from one room of the palace to another without the emperor hearing of it. He saw fit to punish me, but it was all rather convenient, to be locked in with imampasand mangoes. Well worth a term of house arrest. If this is the season for

---

10 Bhagnagar is a former name of Hyderabad. Muhammad Quli Qutb Shah had built the city and named it Bhagyanagar after his wife Bhagyamati. This was corrupted over time to Bhagnagar, and in the era of the Nizam, the name of the city was changed to Hyderabad.

imampasand mangoes in this city, please do have some sent here, Honourable Katib!'

Fortunately, since it was summer, there was no shortage of Imampasand mangoes. At each seance, the writer would have the fruit peeled and cut into small pieces and presented as finger food on a porcelain plate, complete with a toothpick for the spirit to help itself.

'You've turned me into a firangi.[11] I suppose that's just as well,' said Aurangzeb, and reached out to taste it. The writer had thought to keep a glass of water handy. He and Rizwan ate with Aurangzeb.

'Entire epochs have passed and wrought so very many changes, and yet the impampasand alone remains the same ... Well, all right, to answer your query on the subject of titles. In our Mughal dynasty, it is customary to refer to an emperor by his title rather than his name. Giti Sitani Firdaus Makani refers to Padishah Babur; Jahanbani Jannat Ashyani to Padishah Babur's son Padishah Humayun. And Arsh Ashyani to Padishah Akbar. You could have noted this from the *Akbarnama*, surely, Honourable Katib? Unless you learn these three titles by heart, you will find it rather hard to follow my story.

'Now, you had asked me how one was to remember all this. Good question. Given that I was to speak to you, I'd armed myself with some knowledge of you and your land. Let's say a worker of

---

11 The word 'firangi' has an interesting etymology. Its roots are in the Arabic word 'firanj'. In the Middle Ages, the Muslim Arabs would refer to European Christians as firanj. The reason for this was that most European visitors to Arab countries were Frenchmen. Farsi borrowed the term from Arabic to refer to all Europeans. And this was the word Aurangzeb consistently used. He never specified the country from which his European acquaintances came. To him, they were all firangis.

the Dravida Munnetra Kazhagam were to speak of its late chief, the Honourable Tiru Karunanidhi. Would he refer to him as *Karunanidhi*? However many times he had to use his name, he would say *Kalaignar*,[12] would he not? Under such circumstances, how can I be expected to refer to my forefathers by name? Besides, Giti Sitani Firdaus Makani has already once said, "The people of Hindustan know no respect. Their speech and demeanour know no propriety."'

'That's true, Shahenshah. It appears there is great compatibility between the Mughal dynasty and our Tamil Nadu as far as titles are concerned. No one should refer to emperors by name. I know. Which is why Abu'l-Fazl says "His Majesty Giti Sitani Firdaus Makani" throughout the *Akbarnama*. He has explained this in some detail right at the beginning. But it is rather annoying to read shortened forms like H.M.G.S.F.M. and H.M.J.J.A. You must not take this as a criticism of Abu'l-Fazl. I would say the *Akbarnama* is a rare epic among the prose books that I have read. Although I could only access it through an English translation of the original Farsi, the depth and poetry of its narrative is apparent even in translation. That said, it is unfair on the reader to be burdened with having to decode H.M.G.S.F.M. and H.M.J.J.A., isn't it?

'But Your Highness has it right, Huzoor. Not just Kalaignar, but other political chiefs and even film stars are not referred to by name. We only refer to them with titles such as Arignar, Kalaignar, Navalar, Perasiriyar, Sindhanaichchirpi, Puratchiththalaivar, Puratchiththalaivi, Captain, Thalapathi … I beg your pardon,

---

12 Tamil for 'artist'. It is the honorific given to the former chief minister of Tamil Nadu, Karunanidhi.

Huzoor. I see that these titles have bewildered you. Allow me to translate them for you:

Arignar – Scholar

Kalaignar – Artist

Navalar – Tongue-strong

Perasiriyar – Professor

Sindhanaichchirpi – Sculptor of Thought

Puratchiththalaivar – Leader of the Revolution

Puratchiththalaivi – Leaderess of the Revolution

Captain – Well, this needs no translation

Thalapathi – General

'Moreover, since cinema and politics cannot be separated in our land, I ask that you listen to this list of titles from both streams, Huzoor – Nadigar Thilagam, Navarasa Nayagan, Kaadhal Mannan, Puratchiththamizhan, Puratchiththalapathi, Ilaya Thalapathi, Power Star, Vaigai Puyal, Thala, Kavipperarasar, Ulaga Nayagan[13] … I beg your pardon again, Huzoor. I forget you cannot understand Tamil.

Nadigar Thilagam – Actors' Icon

Navarasa Nayagan – Nine-rasa Hero

Kaadhal Mannan – Love King

Puratchiththamizhan – Revolutionary Tamilian

Puratchiththalapathi – Revolutionary General

13 Honorific bestowed by Tamil Nadu's film audience – and one of his directors – upon Kamal Haasan.

Ilaya Thalapathi – Young General

Power Star – Umm, I'll google him for you, Huzoor

Vaigai Puyal – Vaigai Storm

Thala – Head

Kavipperarasar – Poet Emperor

Ulaga Nayagan – Global Hero

'See, Huzoor, they have even appropriated your title Alamgir. You're Alamgir, aren't you? Which means Ulaga Nayagan, he who rules the world. What's even more bizarre is the man looks quite like you too!'

'Honourable Katib, your titular names refer to inquilab and captain and general rather often. Now that this idiotic fad called democracy has taken over the world and shaken the very foundations of rule, how is there place for revolutionaries and generals? Perhaps it is the war heroes who have defended your nation against Pakistan and China and Bangladesh and won laurels for their role who find acceptance in cinema and politics? Right, in that case, I'll allow that the title Thalapathi makes some sense. But how can you have inquilab in a democracy?'

'Huzoor, you're the hero of this novel. But then, the questions you ask demand elaborate answers. If I supply them, you will be relegated to the role of a supporting character, and I will be the chief storyteller. This would not do justice to the title of this novel. And so let me try to keep my answers brief.

'There's an actor who is referred to as Nadigar Thilagam. He is the one who has embodied eight of the nine rasas for an entire generation – veera (bravery or heroism), hasya (humour), karuna (pathos), raudra (rage), bhayanaka (terror), bibhatsa (disgust),

adbhuta (wonder) and shanta (peace). And the subjects under
his purview were compassion, affection, philosophy, sacrifice,
patriotism, etc. What I mean to say is, we Tamilians accord more
respect to the simulacrum of reality rather than to reality itself. It
is my belief that Tamil cinema would have been a field of great
interest to the sociologist Jean Baudrillard and the philosopher
Gilles Deleuze. It's a pity they didn't know that, somewhere in
the south of India, a field suited to their ideas existed.

'And here's another thing – we'd rather watch someone
experience something than go through it ourselves. I suppose you
might call us Tamilians "voyeurs" in that sense. For instance, while
none of us can be moved to do a damned thing for our nation, all
we have to do is watch our Nadigar Thilagam play the eponymous
characters of *Veerappandi Kattabomman* or *Kappalottiya Thamizhan*
to feel like heroes of the freedom struggle against the British. We
revel in the sentiments the films seek to stir in us. For one, there's
veeram – courage. For another, there's tyagam – sacrifice. And
underlying both is the sense of patriotism. One involves going
to war for the defence of the nation. The other, a sacrifice for the
nation. But, in real life, let's say one of my children wanted to join
the army, I'm going to snap, "Idiot! Have you lost your mind?"
and then follow it up with advice: "Why doesn't it occur to you to
move to America and earn in dollars?"

'Then, there's Puratchiththalaivar – Leader of the Revolution.
He is the manifestation of all our revolutionary emotions. In our
country, a sanitation worker earns a monthly salary of Rs 7,000.
But the average middle-class professional earns Rs 70,000 at
the start of his career. Many earn in lakhs. Now, how can the
sanitation worker afford to send his children to school? What will
his children grow up to become? You can imagine. The person

who said all this must change is Karl Marx. You must have heard of him? He was born after your period, but likely continues his oratory in the spirit world. He came up with new ideas like *All men are equal* – and no one must surandafy anyone else.'

'Forgive me, Honourable Katib, but what is "surandafy"?'

'Oh, that's quite simple, Huzoor. All men are created equal, and there is no such thing as hierarchy, and therefore no one should live off another's labour.'

'But then, surely, no one would work? And the entire world would come to a standstill?'

'No, Huzoor. I'm afraid my explanation wasn't clear. One can work. In fact, one must work. But then the concept of employer and employee will not exist. There will be a supervisory body to assign various tasks to various people and give them all equal salaries.'

'Why, Honourable Katib, that is exactly what I did. I taxed my subjects and used the money to put in place the infrastructure they needed. I didn't take any of these funds for myself. I lived off the earnings I made from selling the prayer caps that I embroidered myself, didn't I?'

'But then, no one could oppose you without having his eyes dug out or being trampled by an elephant or having his head chopped off ... Karl Marx says that is inhuman.'

'Then he must have been an idiot. What must one do with antisocial elements if not put them to death? A man who does away with antisocial elements is inhuman, is it? What does this nincompoop have to say in response to my question? Perhaps I should speak to his spirit about this.'

'Let's not get into all that, Huzoor. It strikes me that Karl Marx has become rather obsolete. So, rather than waste precious

time on analysis and debate around his opinions or on consulting
him directly, if you could use the hours we have to tell us your
story, both my readers and I would be grateful.'

'That's all very well, Honourable Katib. But you were the one
who wove Karl Marx and revolutionary heroes into the thread of
our interaction, in response to a simple question of mine. Have
you finished your oratory, then?'

'Uh ... yes, Huzoor, do forgive me. I was explaining why our
Puratchiththalaivar earned his title. In the film *Nadodi Mannan*,
he takes his entire theory of governance from *The Communist
Manifesto* without ever alluding to its author Karl Marx. Any
mention of Marxism would have had him disappeared or finished
off in an encounter. And so, without using the man's name, he
used all his ideas in an election manifesto.'

'Encounter, finished off, disappeared ... I'm not sure I
understand the import of these words in the manner in which you
employ them, Honourable Katib.'

'It's quite simple, Huzoor. You're an emperor. You could have
a man beheaded and the offending head stuck on a pole in the
city centre as a warning to other prospective revolutionaries. Since
that isn't quite feasible in a democracy, one has to have the police
chase the man, claim he tried to attack them and that they had to
kill him in self-defence, and finish him off quite laboriously. As
evidence of the accused shooting at them, the cops might have
to draw a scratch on their faces with a fingernail. Their own will
do – their own fingernails, I mean.'

'While I am not quite at sea with your terms any more, I'm
afraid the contents of *The Communist Manifesto* elude me. Which
of its ideas did your Puratchiththalaivar promise to implement?'

'Land will go to the man who tills it.'

'Injustice! Iniquity! Insubordination! Why, this is anarchy! All the land belongs to the emperor, surely?'

'Forgive me, Huzoor. What you say would hold in a monarchy. But we live in a republic. That said, while we've named ourselves a republic, we can be said to be ruled by monarchs. Landowners – zamindars – are small kings. Nawabs are of slightly greater importance. There's an entire ladder of hierarchy. Our Puratchiththalaivar promised to destroy this system and give land to the labourers in his *Nadodi Mannan*.'

'High treason! A subject who speaks thus ought rightly to have been beheaded and had his head displayed on a pole!'

'No, Huzoor. I've explained this already, haven't I? All that isn't feasible in a democracy, because the "subject" is in fact a "citizen". We didn't behead our Puratchiththalaivar. We voted him in on merit of his promises.'

'Aiyo!' the spirit had brought some Tamil flavour into the conversation now. 'What did the traitor do? Did he slice up the land and give away the parcels as promised?'

'Huzoor, sometimes you display better comedic brilliance than our Vaigai Puyal[14] himself. Yes, Puratchiththalaivar came to power. And no, he didn't give away parcels of land for free. Instead, he gave school students tooth powder. And slippers. And the noon meal. A nutritious noon meal.'

'Why, was it not the habit of your students to cleanse their teeth before the traitor turned king?'

---

14 Titular name of Tamil film comedian Vadivelu.

PROLOGUE 4

Of Love & the Leader of
the Revolution

It may have been only a little over three centuries since Aurangzeb passed away in 1707, but there is much about our world that struck his spirit as bizarre and incomprehensible. It is the period which is a problem: 1700–2000. If he had died in 1300 and the writer had met his spirit in 1600, he would not have sensed such an enormous gap between himself and the writer. It must be understood by the reader that Aurangzeb's question about the tooth powder distributed to students was not sarcastic but posed in all seriousness.

'Why, was it not the habit of your students to cleanse their teeth before the traitor turned king?'

'You're not aware of the poverty that has stricken our nation, Huzoor. Those of us to whom even tooth powder is a luxury item would use ash and brick dust to clean our teeth. Why, I did this myself until I was about twenty years old. But this is not why Puratchiththalaivar earned his title. It was his revolutionary dialogue in *Nadodi Mannan*: "The land belongs to the man who tills it." That's all we needed to hear. To say it is enough. One doesn't have to implement it. We're happy with the illusion. To use Baudrillard's terminology, hyperreal images, in this case divorced from reality.

'The ninth rasa is sringara. Romance. It was Puratchiththalaivar who was destined to embody this rasa. There is a film called *Ananda Jyoti*. The film features this ammaal called Devika, a barrel of a woman if ever there was one. But our entire land was slave to her smile, to that perfect row of teeth. I've never seen such pearly whites on anyone else, Huzoor, not until the Hindi actress Priyanka Chopra entered the field. If only I had been an emperor, I would have willed the entire empire to Priyanka Chopra.'

'One need not go quite as far as that, Honourable Katib. When one is the scion of an empire, one's subjects are one's slaves, and one has little need to curry favour with a slave. This reminds me of an incident that occurred during the emperor's rule. The Italian explorer Niccolao Manucci had arrived at the court of the emperor for the first time. It was the month of July, 1656. To use your modern political terminology, it was a panchayat of sorts. Manucci's firangi patron had passed away unexpectedly. In our empire, the belongings of the dead were the charge of the treasury – by which I mean, the property of the king. Citing this rule, two firangis claiming to be royal officials came to take possession of Manucci's and his patron's belongings and stole them from under his nose with this ruse. Manucci brought his complaint to the emperor. The two firangis were caught. Manucci's belongings were returned. Manucci had gone to meet our wazir over this. Because Manucci had medical training and was a foreigner, the wazir wanted to retain him in his household. Manucci had no interest in this. At the time, this was how the conversation between the wazir and Manucci went:

'"As a Christian, I cannot stay with you in your palace." That was Manucci.

'No one had ever, until that moment, refused to accede to a request of the wazir to his face, let alone a dandiprat, albeit a firangi dandiprat.'

'"Don't you know you're slave to the emperor?" That was the wazir.

'"No European has ever been, or will ever be, slave to anyone." With that salvo, and without so much as bothering to take leave of the wazir, Manucci got on his horse and left.

'When the wazir had finished giving us the account, I told him: "One who lives in Hindustan shall nary comprehend a firangi. And a firangi shall nary comprehend a Hindustani."

'Honourable Katib, I narrate to you this story to illustrate that, as a padishah, you would commit folly in willing your empire to … what is the name of this…'

'Priyanka Chopra, Huzoor…'

'Hanh … Priyanka Chopra … a firangi, I presume?'

'No, Shahenshah … she's one of us.'

'Well, in that case, we need not worry so much. But even so, it would be folly to give away a kingdom to a woman. If she does please you excessively, you might crown her queen of a demesne. For even with the royal title, she remains slave to the emperor. If you were to wear an emperor's shoes, Honourable Katib, you would know that grand zamindars and wealthy men and ministers and minor kings will line up to offer their daughters to you in marriage. To give you an example, as recognition of his having taken over the leadership of Ghazi, the head of the Yusufzai[15] clan asked that Firdaus Makani Padishah Babur marry his daughter Bibi Mubarika. Kings who have been vanquished in war give their daughters in marriage as a form of peace accord. It's a terrible pity that such things are not possible in a democracy ... isn't it?'

'They just occur under different names, Huzoor. But, to finish what I was saying, we would sit in a crowd and watch films in a tent cinema. The rasas would play out in the dark, and we were enamoured by those shadows and illusions. Puratchiththalaivar and Devika Ammal. The reason I say "Ammal" is ... well, to understand, you should watch the film *Kalangarai Vilakkam*. Starring this Kannada paingili – how do I explain this word to you, well, let's say, "the prettiest bird you could imagine" – called Saroja Devi. Adadaa ... her gait is unparalleled. No woman in the world before or since could emulate it. The way she walks ... there's a song called "Kaatru Vaanga Ponen" in that film. At the beginning of the song, as the Kannadatththuppaingili sashays down the stairs in a salwar kameez, the camera follows her from behind and drinks in the bounty ... ada ... adaa ... do forgive me, Huzoor ... I feel rather awkward, to speak thus in the presence of an emperor...'

'Speak, by all means ... I'm not the man I used to be. If I had a chance to live again, I would choose to live in a hut with a thatched roof, where I could sit all day and write poems every day of my life...'

Aurangzeb, a poet? What would he write about, Saroja Devi walking down the stairs to meet Puratchiththalaivar? But if the writer allowed himself to get into yet another thread, there would be no time to finish his own story, let alone the emperor's.

---

15 A Pashto-speaking tribe of Afghanistan.

Ulaga Nayagan

'Right. So, to sum it all up, from romance to mourning, we live all our emotions through shadow play on a screen,' the writer said. 'Nadigar Thilagam cries for us. Puratchiththalaivar fights for us. What else does a man need? There's one other thing I simply have to tell you, Huzoor. I don't think anyone in our land has ever kissed. Because Ulaga Nayagan has this USP – whoever the heroine, he is bound to kiss her. This should not come as a surprise. Why should it surprise us that the hero of a film kisses its heroine? But when Ulaga Nayagan embarks on a kiss, the cinema breaks into whistles and hoots, the sound of a thousand unrealized orgasms. They whistle when Jackie Chan jumps from a fifty-foot height, and they whistle when Ulaga Nayagan kisses a woman … this would mean, then, that Ulaga Nayagan has achieved a rare feat, would it not?'

'Honourable Katib, with every utterance of yours that turns my mind to your Ulaga Nayagan's kisses, my skin crawls. When I gave myself the title of Ulaga Nayagan – Alamgir – I meant for it to signify "He who has conquered the world". For such a tragic fate to have befallen that title in three hundred years … if I had known then what I know now, I would have chosen a different title for myself.'

It so happened that, at that very moment, someone texted the writer. Although he had taken the precaution of putting his phone on silent mode, the screen lit up through his light linen trousers. Aurangzeb's eyes darted to the pocket in which the writer had kept his phone.

'What is that? May I see it?' Aurangzeb asked, his curiosity piqued by the sudden appearance of light through cloth.

'By all means, Huzoor. But … I do feel rather hesitant. Someone might have gone and sent me a Sunny Leone video on WhatsApp. I don't have friends of that inclination, but then I've been caught and trapped in a couple of WhatsApp groups. No one can elude that fate. Well, an emperor could. There's nothing an emperor cannot do. But the writer's stature is not quite that of an emperor, is it? One of the groups of which I'm a member is named Arignar Peravai – assembly of scholars. Please don't let the name scare you. We discuss the nuances of ancient Tamil literature. The group admin is the corporation commissioner of our city. He had nothing to do with the group or its inception. His friends started it and made him a group admin. His link with ancient Tamil works is that he is passionate about literature. He holds me in some regard. That's why I was added to the group. The depth of the *Tirukkural*, the beauty of the *Kambaramayanam*, the names of the ninety-nine flowers that find a place in the *Kurinjipaattu* … some three dozen texts and treatises piled up every day and burdened my iPhone so much that, one fine day, I was moved to slip out of the group.

'The next minute ... no, the next second, one of the group admins called me.

'"What is this, Writer Saar, what have you gone and done? ... What happened?" he asked me.

'I gave him a detailed explanation. But he was in no mood to listen.

'"No, Writer Saar, all this is by no means acceptable to us. Why, just yesterday Commissioner Saar was speaking about you. He said it is a matter of great pride for our group for Writer Saar to be in it. How will I explain your exit to him? I'm going to add you back to the group."

'What could I say? And here's another thing. You're an emperor. These are matters which would not even have touched your consciousness. Once, the drain on Santhome High Road had overflowed and sewage was coursing through the road with all the force of a canal. The stench turned my stomach. You could complain until kingdom come and no one would do a damned thing about it. I waited for a week. Then, I could take it no longer and phoned the commissioner. Within five minutes, a team from the corporation was there. But if the common man were to file a hundred complaints, he would get no response. When I told my friend Kokkarakko about this, he said, "Ada po ya, you're a good-for-nothing. If the corporation commissioner is a friend, you should have got yourself some contract-geentract, tender-vender. Instead, you're boasting about having set the gutter right. What can one do with you?" The truth is, I have no clue – not up to this moment – what link the corporation commissioner has to contracts and tenders, Huzoor.'

'Honourable Katib, while I'm no Padishah Akbar, I did hold some writers in high regard and was privy to their lives. I've encountered the same problem with them. They would bleat in my chambers, "Shahenshah, the roof of my house is leaking." What was the Shahenshah to do about a leaking roof? Had they asked for tangible recompense, I might have been able to offer them the succour they sought. But your lot make strange namoonas.

'There was this poet who kept moaning about how impoverished he was. I, in my largesse, decided to make him a minor king and gave him a demesne to rule. As his first royal act, he wrote me a missive refusing to pay his taxes and declaring himself the head of an independent land. "This is our national flag, this is our national emblem, we ask you to recognize our sovereignty" and so on. Naturally, I had no choice but to have him arrested and dragged to Delhi's Chandni Chowk to be trampled by an elephant. His foolishness condemned his wife and children to lives of slavery. A terrible pity, for he was quite a wonderful poet. An act of charity turned into a loss for literature. Not one, not two, but an entire legion of poets has met its end at the feet of elephants for their inability to receive generosity. And yet your textbooks say that Aurangzeb killed poets while Padishah Akbar was an exemplary patron … we shall come to that in due course … you were speaking about Sunny Leone? Who is this mohtarma?'

'Sunny Leone is…' – the writer could not say the words. Who knew what powers the spirit had? What if Aurangzeb were to summon the ghost of an imperial elephant and have him trampled for speaking of adult films?

'Forgive me, Huzoor,' he said. 'I'm afraid to talk about all this. It is a bit too early in our acquaintance for talk of sex.'

'Hmm … is that all? If I were to punish sexual sins, I would have to start with Emperor Arsh Ashyani and Emperor Jahangir.

Their harems were teeming with women. In fact, Emperor Arsh Ashyani had more women than horses, didn't he?'

Incredibly enough, the text the writer had received turned out to be rather fortuitous. His artist friend had sent across her portrait of Aurangzeb, commissioned for the cover of the Tamil version of this novel. It was aesthetically pleasing. More importantly, it looked quite authentically like Aurangzeb.

Showing Aurangzeb the portrait, the writer said:

'Just as our historians have depicted you with so little accuracy, our artists too have produced portraits that do you little justice.

The moment one says "Aurangzeb" – I beg your forgiveness for using your name, Huzoor, but I have no other option here – they draw a frail old man with a beard and the appearance of having starved for a month. I had given the designer of this novel's cover special instructions to make you as handsome as you were. Please do not take this for flattery. Of the six Mughal emperors, you were the most handsome. There's a certain feminine quality, a sense of the effete, in portraits of your father. We've done a similar thing with a one-hundred-and-thirty-three-foot statue of our Tiruvalluvar, sculpted him like a woman dancing Bharatanatyam, and parked him at Kanyakumari. I have no problem with anyone's sexual orientation or self-identification, but it seems wrong to me to impose our agenda on historical figures.'

'Sexual orientation? Self-identification? What are these things, Honourable Katib?'

'Let's not go there, Huzoor. If I start off on this, the novel will take a different direction, and I will end up not hearing your story. You might have come to this world where democracy is the norm, but I shouldn't take liberties with you. Right, what I was going to say was, of the six Mughal emperors, you're the one who best marries elegance, allure and authority. Although I can only hear your voice through this medium and have no way of seeing your face, I *have* seen portraits that were commissioned in your time with you as the live model.'

'Is that all you have to say about my appearance, Honourable Katib? Had I been a man of flesh and blood, I would have believed you. But I'm a spirit. It seems to slip your memory every now and again that I can read your mind.'

And Aurangzeb gave the writer a penetrating look that made the latter's hair stand on end.

'You must forgive me, Huzoor. It is my principle to avoid criticising elders, at least to their faces. The thing is, your face – to be specific, your eyes – your eyes have some guile, a certain craftiness about them. I'd forgotten this detail when I spoke to the artist. It was only after she sent me the portrait that I realized her version of your eyes had them brimming with compassion. Aaha, I'd made a mistake. I asked her to make the change. Well, let that rest for now. I haven't quite finished this matter of titles, Huzoor.

'In our land, titles are not the exclusive inheritance of politicians and film stars. Spiritual leaders are not exempt from this honour. Our gurunaadar[16] Tiruvalluvar has divided human experience into three sections – aram (piety), porul (polity) and inbam (pleasure). You might consider spirituality, politics and cinema as aram, porul and inbam respectively. Spiritual leaders took offence that, while the other two were accorded titles, they had been left out, and went on the warpath. And so, we bestowed titles upon them too.

'Once, when a reporter addressed one such spiritual gentleman as "Saar" instead of using his title "Sadhguru", the latter cursed him and the reporter caught the coronavirus and just about escaped death, Huzoor. Then, because a reporter addressed an actor whose title is "Thala" by his name followed by "Saar" – for instance, if I were to say "Aurangzeb Saar" (forgive me, Huzoor) – the actor boycotted interview requests from that newspaper for two years.'

Despite the writer's best effects to distract him, Aurangzeb stubbornly returned to the subject of sexual orientation, and so the writer was forced to explain in some detail, only for the emperor to respond:

---

16 Teacher and guide.

'Ah, is that all, Honourable Katib? There is little call for you to squirm. Shah Alam, who reigned in the last days of the Mughal empire, had imposed what you speak about on a boy. He had Ghulam Qadir castrated to serve as his ubnah.[17] But I shall tell you that story some other time. The things you speak of were not alien to our era. The difference is, back then, they were involuntary, and now it appears the ubnahs do so of their own volition.'

Before the writer could interrupt, Aurangzeb waved a firm hand in the air and said, 'Anyway, all we have spoken of is haram, and best left out of our future parleys.'

~

The writer had been feeling rather guilty about his abandonment of the novel which had initiated these conversations.

'Please forgive me, Shahenshah, but there's something I've been meaning to ask you for a while. As you know, it was your father whom I sought to meet. And you know the reason, too. I wish to speak to Emperor Shah Jahan about the facts of the kidnapping from the Agra palace and sale into slavery of Catarina de San Juan. Because Catarina ... well, I should say Mirra, since that was her given name ... Mirra was born in the year 1617. She is technically Shahenshah's aunt. A cousin of the emperor. Shahenshah was born in the year 1618. When Mirra was kidnapped, Your Highness was around ten years old. Do you remember the incident, even vaguely? Would the Shahenshah deign to speak about what happened as he recalls it?'

'I remember it all very well, Honourable Katib. It was this incident that forced the emperor's hand. Several thousand

---

17 Catamite.

Portuguese were massacred by his armies, with all the fuss of crushing as many bedbugs, over the next five years. Your historians write of that massacre as the one deed that stained the rule of the Honourable Firdaus Ashyani Shah Jahan Ghazi. But I call this stain by another name – a rosette to his memory. Not much love was lost between the emperor and his successor, but if there was one royal order of my father's I admire, it was this. To arrive at this point, I must tell a long tale, one I must commence from the disembarking of Vasco da Gama upon these shores. Have patience, Honourable Katib, for I have asked that you lend your ears to *my* story. Yet, you have troubled yourself to ask, and I must therefore respond to the question.

'Fourteen years before Mirra was abducted, that is to say, in the year 1613, the Hajj-bound *Rahimi* was captured by the Portuguese. The firangis call it "The Great Hajj Ship". The pilgrimage ship had left from the port of Surat, carrying hundreds of pilgrims and one lakh rupees. The ship was owned by Mariam-uz-Zamani. Her name must ring a bell? The Rajput wife of my great-grandfather, Padishah Akbar, and the mother of Emperor Jahangir and thus mother to every subject of the swathe of land he ruled. You must know this was fifteen years before the commencement of my father's rule, and Emperor Jahangir was on the throne. Frantic missives were dispatched from the palace to the Portuguese authorities, only to be ignored. The emperor's mother had been scorned, and it was a slight not to be borne. The emperor ordered the seizure of Daman from the scoundrels. All the Portuguese residents of his domain were apprehended, their churches closed. Your freedom struggle waxed eloquent on the firangis' lust for imperialism and colonization; the seeds of that lust were sown when the *Rahimi* was captured.'

And then the spirit said in English: 'I conjure you, Honourable Katib, to ready yourself to hear the memories of an emperor rather than demand of him what you might find in books of history.'

~

Once Aurangzeb has said the word, particularly in a language the writer finds challenging, there is little for us to do but plunge into the novel with no further ado or interruption.

Except … the writer has a question. If any among Aurangzeb's opinions were to be considered controversial or seditious, who is to be held responsible for those views? He has put in the right disclaimers early on, but will hashtags and high courts defer to disclaimers? Since it will be difficult to determine whose intellectual property this story is, the writer has decided to censor some of Aurangzeb's views himself.

He doesn't see any other option. Because the writer finds he isn't particularly keen on going to prison or being lynched over the views of another man – that too, a man who died three hundred and fourteen years ago. That doesn't merit his being seen as a coward. The writer would be happy to martyr his life over his own views. However, it strikes him as a tad insane to do so for those of a spirit. Therefore, do keep in mind that Aurangzeb's views are mildly mediated before being let loose among you.

As already stated earlier, the Aghori was seated on a platform, his legs tucked beneath him. At this point, his right leg was folded over his left. There were times when the right leg would dangle free, and others when the left leg would be folded and the right placed perpendicular to it so that his right hand may rest on the leg. Bolsters had been provided for him to lean against. The writer had thus far laboured under the notion that Mughal emperors sat on thrones like our Chozha kings, their legs outstretched in macho poses. That is how cinema has portrayed them, after all. The Aghori's posture, while being contradictory to modern cinema, was in line with Niccolao Manucci's description of his surprise upon seeing Shah Jahan seated in this manner. There was little chance of European royals assuming such postures. Having struggled for centuries to fold their legs, they have finally found the means to padmasana courtesy of yoga workshops organized by our corporate godmen.

Thus, we finally come to the end of our prologues. Let's hear Aurangzeb's story, straight from the horse's mouth.

CHAPTER I

'What I Hold Most Dear'

In the name of Allah, the most compassionate, the most merciful.
All praise be to Allah, Lord of the worlds,
the most beneficent, the most merciful,
sovereign of the Day of Recompense.
You alone we worship, and You alone we ask for help.
Guide us along the straight path,
the way of those upon whom You have bestowed Your grace,
not of those who have earned Your anger,
nor those who are astray.

SURAH AL-FATIHA, AL-QURAN

~

The writer feels it would be rather cumbersome to use quotation marks at this point. And so, having quoted Aurangzeb reciting the Surah al-Fatiha, the writer will now let you hear the spirit speak directly, except when the writer sees fit to interrupt with thought, word or deed, in which case he will use a section break.

51

And thus it spake – wait a minute, the writer and his translator have got carried away with the formality of the late emperor's English. We will defer to modernity now and say, 'Thus it spoke', or rather 'Aurangzeb said'.

~

AURANGZEB SAID:

As Abu'l-Fazl writes in the beginning of his *Akbarnama,* 'In the observatory of the mind the moon of speech rises, and sets through the tongue and the ear.'

And thus I begin my story as I know it, as I feel it.

My naissance was on a day that by modern calculation is 24 October 1618, in the town of Dahod. Hight Muhi-ud-din Muhammad Aurangzeb, cadet son of Emperor Shah Jahan and Begum Mumtaz Mahal, I became Alamgir.

(The writer interrupted to ask, 'The town of Dahod, Shahenshah?')

Yes, situated exactly between Gujarat's Godhra – aah, does this town need an introduction in your era? – and Madhya Pradesh's Ratlam. Although these regions were known by other names in my time and in the time of the firangis, I speak to you in the present time, and therefore shall use the names familiar to you.

My cultural roots are in Turkey, and by ethnicity, I am Mongol. As you know, His Majesty Giti Sitani Firdaus Makani Zahir-ud-din Muhammad, also known as Padishah Babur Ghazi, could trace his ancestors to Taimur on his paternal side and Genghis Khan on his maternal. You might also know that 'Mughal' is Farsi for 'Mongol'. Thus a man who claims we are aliens or invaders is but a mooncalf, for it is Asian blood that runs in our veins, for we have closer links with you than your precious Aryans, for although His Majesty Giti Sitani Firdaus Makani writes that Mongols are not to be trusted and detested them in his lifetime, the truth must be told and the truth is as I have said it.

Ask what I have accomplished that I hold most dear, and I would not tell you it was having ruled for two score and nine years, although no Mughal emperor has reigned as long. Today, you would fain prop up a politician and claim he is India. But for two score and nine – not one, not two, not six, not nine, but two score and nine – years, one would scarce deny that Alamgir was Hindustan and Hindustan was Alamgir. Why, my legacy may be traced even in the framing of your societal and governmental norms. Forsooth, my empire stretched from Ghazni in modern-day Afghanistan in the west to Chatgaon in today's Bangladesh in the east, from Kashmir in the north to Karnataka in the south.

('How will I remember all this English?' the writer wondered, and to his relief, the spirit switched immediately to Urdu.)

I remain the only emperor to have ruled over fifteen crore subjects across such a vast swathe of land. No one before me, and until the firangis came, no one after me had brought such expansive territory under his banner. ('And for all that, you weren't able to cross Karnataka to conquer our land,' the writer thought to himself, only for Aurangzeb to broach the subject the very next moment.)

You appear to have forgotten that I am a spirit, Honourable Katib, and capable of reading minds. If I'm being honest, I cannot tell why we were not able to conquer your land. Perhaps you would care to consult your historians and researchers and tell me their opinion on the subject? Not Ashoka, not Samudragupta, not Harshavardhana, none of your celebrated emperors had under his purview an empire the size of an ocean. I remain the one man, dead or alive, to have claim to the title of sole monarch and master of such a number of subjects. Yet, it is not the accomplishment I hold most dear.

It is true that my grandfather and his grandfather lost decades of their lives to wine and women, Honourable Katib. To live ninety years was no mean accomplishment in those times, albeit that I lived a clean life, immune to the sensual pleasures of mattresses and the sensory delights of palaces. An accomplishment, yes. And yet, not the one I hold most dear.

It is true, too, that there lived no man richer than I in the entire world. My treasury pulsated with unparalleled gems and invaluable stones. The Kohinoor, at which all the peoples of all the lands known and unknown marvelled, was in my possession. Not the accomplishment I hold most dear, Honourable Katib, as you can tell from my having slept on bare floors and lived off an income from stitching prayer caps.

It is true, too, that I lived as a sentry, chosen by Allah to look after his land. Ah, I see I must explain. My forefathers took the world for their oyster, tearing it apart to garb themselves in pearls. The elders in the palace spoke in awe and wonder of Padishah Akbar's habit of forgoing meat three days of the week. He would live like the Hindus, eating only vegetables. His frugality was coated in luxury, Honourable Katib, for the vegetables were grown in a separate garden and nourished on rose water rather than plain water, for it was his belief that this would augment their fragrance when cooked. Emperors! My frugality was real, Honourable Katib, for I knew the world was the Lord's bounty, and I His servant on earth. Ninety years of a servant's life, too, are not what I hold most dear.

What then, you wonder. It was this, Honourable Katib. It was that I became a hafiz when I was but a child, and could carry the al-Quran in my heart and soul everywhere I was and everywhere I went. Now that, that is an accomplishment I hold most dear.

The Holy Book was the reason for my every victory. It taught me ever so much. Do you know which quality is considered the greatest by the Book? Fearlessness. For when Allah is by us, what must one fear?

I will never forget that day. It was 28 May 1633 – going by your modern calendar, of course. I was fifteen years old. The emperor was watching a fight between two imperial war elephants, as was his wont, at the Agra Fort on the banks of the Yamuna. I, who had no knowledge of this sport, was riding my horse at breakneck speed into the fort, when I found myself face to face with an elephant intoxicated in its victory. Thinking I was bent on attack, the elephant charged at me, a boy of fifteen on a horse... As the elephant charged at the lone boy on the horse in its path, if a smidgen of doubt or fear had arisen in the heart of that lone boy, the history of the Mughal empire, and therefore the history of all of you who came after, would have been written very differently.

Without the slightest whiff of apprehension, I gave my horse the signal. If I had panicked, my horse would have gone into a frenzy. I touched him, and conveyed my intentions with my hands and feet. He understood. All this happened in the blink of an eye. I aimed my spear between the elephant's eyes. At that very moment, the elephant attacked my horse with his tusks. I jumped off my saddle in the nick of time, and stood ready for combat, sword in hand. Blood gushed from the spot where my spear had pierced the war elephant. The roar of the public came to my ears as the cheers of supporters.

How will I put into words the kashf-ur-roohi I felt at that moment, as I stood before the elephant, sword in hand? A revelation of the soul, of the spirit. Perhaps as a sort of spiritual ecstasy? Yes ... that roohi would stay with me all my life. The elephant did not attack me. Instead, he began to retreat. That remains a puzzle to me. Why did he not attack me? What was the tiny sword in my hand to his strength? What was it that made him retreat? It may be that when one faces death head-on, without fear, without doubt, it disappears like dew in the heat of the sun.

That day, the emperor rewarded my display of courage with my weight in gold.

And yet, I know what your history books say about this Aurangzeb, what your children read about me ... the man who killed his brothers, the religious fanatic, etc. etc...

Do you know what the problem is? Marketing. What? Does it surprise you that I use contemporary English terms? I'm more at home using the English of my time and the century after, but I've been interacting with a younger lot of spirits over the past few decades, and I've picked up some English from them too. They call each other 'dude', which sounds quite silly to me. Some even say 'bro'. Which sounds like half a word. Well, I suppose it *is* a third of a word. Right, so what I was saying about marketing is this: the kingpin of marketing was Ashoka. A real khiladi. Even today, your children read that Emperor Ashoka planted trees. Why? Because for every four trees he planted, he would have forty stupas erected with inscriptions in four different languages to the effect that Ashoka planted trees. And those stupas have lasted centuries, as has his reputation.

Do you know under whose rule the roads were best designed and maintained, from the time of the Indus Valley civilization until now? Ours. It's not I who affirm this, but Bernier who does. He writes that travel across Indian roads was far faster than across European ones. The only danger one faced was dacoity. What can emperors do about greed? The rulers of the land continue to fail, from monarchy to democracy. Evading tax and customs duties on gold and silver coins, melting gold ornaments and selling them off, mixing copper into gold and passing them off as pure gold coins for sale … is there anything you people don't do? Having consigned the gods to stone in buildings and stowed them away, you pay obeisance only to money, don't you?

(At this point, the writer took his right hand to his heart as if to ask, 'What are you saying, Shahenshah?')

Ada, what is this, Honourable Katib, you appear to be such an innocent? That's what they were doing. I had stringent punishments for them, of course.

Emperor Ashoka too, like me, followed another religion. It was, in fact, his religion that pushed Hinduism and its original values aside, wasn't it? And yet, you have quite shamelessly made his pillar your national emblem.

You know what this labelling is like?

Let's say there's been a rape in a town. A little child. The town is on the boil. The criminal can't be found. And therefore, a random fool has to be disposed of in an 'encounter' and labelled the criminal, right? That will cool the place down. Now, just take this to macrocosmic proportions, and you'll know why Alamgir has been called the chief enemy of Hindus. Someone had to be blamed. Aurangzeb became the scapegoat. Because, of all the Mughal emperors, he was the only one who remained loyal to the path into which he was born. He's the only one not to have had a harem as large as the royal stables, not to have cavorted with women. He's the only one who lived as simply as the most marginalized of his subjects. And so, he became the ideal candidate on whom to place the blame.

I had to wait three centuries and fourteen years to tell my story. For as long as one is flesh and blood, one is able to bear pain and sorrow. One has, at the very least, eyes to cry with. But do you know just how hard it is to bear the burden of blame when one is a spirit, Honourable Katib? Crores upon crores of people, generation after generation, century after century, say over and over again that it was Aurangzeb who forced conversions on Hindus. I have heard so many of them for so long and so often that I wonder whether I really did do this. I didn't do anything of the sort, didn't force conversions, didn't do a damned thing. Back in our day, we didn't give much thought to things like this. My only oversight was this – I didn't market myself like Ashoka did. I should have thought to erect a few pillars in every town, saying Alamgir did this and Alamgir did that. Having failed to do that, I am now saddled with the villain's role in various histories.

The reason I have pushed the emperor aside and possessed the medium in his stead is to break some of these myths that have been propagated about me. You might think it is modern-day politicians who are the culprits. You're wrong. It was your progressive Jawaharlal Nehru who started it all. He writes, 'Aurangzeb tried to put back the clock, and in this attempt stopped it and broke it up.' And not just that. Apparently, it was because I gave Islam too much importance that I could not rule, and that was why the Mughal empire collapsed. Nehru said that too. May God save him. Aah. I have heard he is an atheist. Is he not? This is how they talk, with no temperance in their tongues and no

conscience to their pens. What did I do that was so wrong? Did
I command that everyone convert en masse? No! As my religion
commanded, I prayed five times a day. I lived a simple life. I kept
the roza during Ramzan. Was that wrong?

And there's another thing. You know how the Mughal
and Rajput lineages mixed. My great-grandfather Emperor
Akbar's wife Mariam-uz-Zamani was a Rajput princess. So my
grandfather Jahangir was half Rajput. And his son, my father, was
a step ahead. He was three-quarters Rajput. His mother Princess
Manavati Baiji Lal Sahiba, posthumously Taj Bibi Bilqis Makani,
and his paternal grandmother were Rajputanis. Thus, we're more
Rajput than Mughal, are we not?

Right, that's as may be. You know why I have been slandered
so much? The world has only ever valued pomp and pageantry.
Those were never part of my life. Honourable Katib, answer this
one question: Have you seen the tomb of His Majesty Jahanbani
Jannat Ashyani?

(The writer was caught off guard. Whose posthumous title
was that, now? When the spirit spoke again, there was a hint of
annoyance in its voice.)

What is this, Honourable Katib, are you ever confused
over who is your Kalaignar, or Navalar or Perasiriyar or
Puratchiththalaivar or Ulaga Nayagan? And for all that, there is
no lyricism to your titles. They're flat. Each of our titles is a poem
in itself. And I have only mentioned three of them to you. Are
they so very difficult to remember? You might at least have had
the courtesy to note them down on a piece of paper. His Majesty
Giti Sitani Firdaus Makani – such music in those words – refers
to Padishah Babur Ghazi. His Majesty Jahanbani Jannat Ashyani

– such rhythm in those syllables – refers to Padishah Humayun. Arsh Ashyani – Padishah Akbar. Period.

(The writer looked up in surprise and said, 'Ah! Shahenshah, did you just say "period"?')

Well, I do have to adapt to the contemporary manner of speech when I use English, don't I, in order to market myself to your readers if nothing else? Right. Now, please answer my question.

('Why, Shahenshah, of course I have. It is among Delhi's artistic wonders!' said the writer.)

Yes. That tomb, near the Nizamuddin Dargah and on the banks of the Yamuna, was designed by Persian architects. It was the very first time red sandstone had been used in Hindustan. You must have seen my father's tomb too. There can't be a single Hindustani who hasn't. It has found its place among the wonders of the world. Honourable Katib, do you know where my tomb is?

(The writer guiltily shook his head no.)

There is no call for you to feel guilty. It was my intention that it be so. I didn't want to leave behind any corporeal traces in this world. The people here aren't worthy of it. Or perhaps I am not worthy of it.

When I died in 1707, I was buried according to the orders I had left behind, as a commoner would be. A burial pit, dug from mud, and a mound over my body, open to the skies. That was all. In death, as in life, I eschewed pomp. What surprises me is that without a show of splendour, one can't be accorded a hero's place in your textbooks. One is forced to wear the veil of the villain. Perhaps it was because it was reinforced so much in childhood lessons that Aurangzeb forced conversions on Hindus, but you yourself – Honourable Katib, you who must know to go beyond the book – have once referred to me in this context, do you remember?

(The writer said, 'Oh my God. Huzoor, it is true that I have laboured under this illusion too, because I was never interested enough in history to go beyond what the textbook said. But then, the incident to which Shahenshah refers … I'm afraid I don't recall when it happened, or…?')

2016. I can tell you the month and date and time too, if you wish. But these details might irritate your readers, which is why I choose to leave them out in the rest of my story too. You were part of a drunken crowd engaged in debate. A Hindutvavadi was with you. In a drunken stupor, you told him, 'If Aurangzeb had forced your ancestors to convert to Islam, now you'd be embracing another extremist philosophy against Hindutva, wouldn't you?' Do you remember now? I have never, ever engaged myself in such things as forced conversions.

I will give you an example. It was during the holy month of Ramzan. My soldiers and I had laid siege to the Satara Fort. We had caught thirteen rebels. Of them, four were Muslim and nine were Hindus. I asked the court to decide what punishment must be accorded to them. The qazi was Muhammad Akram. Once the investigation and interrogation were finished, the qazi gave his verdict – the nine kafirs could be pardoned and released if they converted to Islam; the four Muslims must be put to death. I changed the verdict. I was fasting at the time. Everyone was equal before the law. And therefore, I sentenced all of them to beheading. All their heads were to be brought to me before I broke my fast.

CHAPTER 2

Heroes & Villains

EMPEROR AURANGZEB CONTINUED TO SPEAK:

As I had ordered, the thirteen heads were brought to me, and it was only after seeing them that I broke my fast. It is my belief that the sovereignty of a government is determined by adalat. What should be the basis of adalat? Tell me yourself, Honourable Katib. (The writer said, 'We refer to "adalat" as "needi" in Tamil. Justice. Justice has its bases in "nyaayam" and "dharmam": in reason and rightness.)

Exactly. In Islam, 'akhlaq' and 'adab'. Throughout my long life, those two words were my rooh.

My oldest brother Dara Shikoh lived among dreams and illusions. That was why he began to fear me too. Fear spawns suspicion. He was suspicious of everyone around him. If such a man were to rule such an enormous swathe of land, can you imagine what would have come to pass? Along with crossing over himself, he would have drawn you all, bit by bit, to the firangis' religion. It was religious belief that carved a rift between him and me. He would rant that all was one, every religion was the same. His chant was 'Majma ul Bahrain'. The confluence of two seas, apparently. What foolishness! What idiocy. How can the idea of no-God-but-God meet the idea of God being in everything? Any man who says 'You and I are one' is dangerous.

My opinion is: You are different. I am different. But let us try to live with each other. This is the principle I followed throughout my half-century rule. Is that wrong? Do you know what people want? They are happy to be fed morsels of poison, as long as those morsels are dipped in honey. Bitter truths are unwelcome. Lies that bear the semblance of truth are ideal.

~

At this point, Aurangzeb stopped speaking. He became still and sank into silence. Two or three minutes passed. Had he left the Aghori's body, the writer wondered. But it was not quite like Aurangzeb to leave without so much as a goodbye. Perhaps they should wait a bit longer. The writer sat quietly. It was five minutes before Aurangzeb spoke again.

~

AND HE SAID:

You must bear with me, Honourable Katib. Upon reflection, it strikes me that my speech might have been rather too riddled with emotion. Nehru wasn't the sole culprit in casting me as the villain of the piece. Some historians are to blame too, and particularly firangi ones. It wasn't the enmity of a day or two, you see. It was the residual hatred of centuries upon centuries of waging a Holy

War that they took out on one man. Their grouse against me was that I remained a true Muslim all my life, honest and loyal to my faith. Unlike Arsh Ashyani Padishah Akbar, I didn't stick a finger in every pie. If I had, they would have spared me the title.

Once the firangis had pronounced it, what more did Indians need? What the white man says is gospel truth to you, isn't it? Aurangzeb killed thousands of Hindus, he razed thousands of temples. And if your children read this over and over and over again in their textbooks, what else could happen but that the calumny against me would be canonized as truth?

We Mughal emperors kept fastidious records of everything we did every single day of our rule, every verdict we passed, every ordinance we signed into law. Records were maintained so meticulously that you could look up how many times the emperor coughed or sneezed on a given day. This didn't strike me as the best use of public funds, which is why I terminated this particular practice. But what happened in my court was duly noted. Under such circumstances, could they not even take the trouble to go through historical records?

Let me give you an example. Do you know what the emperor's daily itinerary was? My father would wake as early as four in the morning. You might as well have set your clock by when he rose. You know who clocks remind me of? Your Nehru. What a terrible man he was! Why should he have slandered me without so much as reading about me?

Well, so the emperor would do his ablutions in the Abshar-i-Taufeeq and then pray with his courtiers. After prayer, he would read the Quran for some time. Soon after, the court musicians would begin their morning session. The public would gather outside the walls of the palace, on the banks of the

Yamuna. After sunrise, the emperor would make an appearance at the Jharokha-i-Darshan. This was to show the public that their monarch was in good health. There were Brahmins who would not have their breakfast until they had ascertained for themselves that this was the case. It was because of these Brahmins that I put a stop to the darshan. God alone is worthy of our worship. As a true Muslim, I couldn't bear the thought of someone keeping a fast for a human being, emperor though he be. I stopped the balcony appearances.

It was acts like these that distanced me from the people, I think. As you said yourself, it is not actions but appearances – forgive the pun – that strike a chord with people.

The emperor would be at the Diwan-i-Aam by ten in the morning. His officials would brief him about the latest goings-on in their various departments.

Bernier writes that it was from the Diwan-i-Aam's naqqar khana that he first heard the blast of twelve trumpets, shocking his European ears. But once he got used to it, what had initially seemed a foghorn turned into a symphony. He would listen to it from the terrace of his house at night. It was, as you say in Sanskrit, 'sunaadam'.

Next, the emperor had to be at the Diwan-i-Khas. One must be a poet to describe the Diwan-i-Khas. The gigantic pillars and golden awnings were carved and painted by the world's most sought-after artists. Nowadays, you have machines to cool the air artificially. You should have seen our palace. You wouldn't feel the slightest effect of the summer's heat. The height of the halls, the capacity of the stones to regulate temperature, and the architectural brilliance of the construction ensured that the air would be naturally cooled.

On the raised platform in the middle of the sabha was a throne for the emperor, flanked by slightly less grand seats for his sons. A poet has written of the Diwan-i-Khas:

Agar firdaus bar roo-e zameen ast,
Hameen ast-o hameen ast-o hameen ast

If there be such a thing as heaven on earth
It is this, it is this, it is this.

Do you know who it was who wrote these immortal lines? Everyone thinks it was Amir Khusrau. But it was, in fact, Saad Ullah Khan Allami. The 'Allami' was a title bestowed on him for his erudition. I know only of two people to whom the title was given. One was Abu'l-Fazl. The other was Saad Ullah Khan Allami. Did you know he affected my life greatly? He served as the emperor's prime minister for ten years. The emperor sent me with him twice to conquer Kandahar. Both our attempts were unsuccessful, but I would hardly call them wasted journeys because I learned ever so much from him.

Once, I was praying with him and some of his friends. When we had finished, we noticed that Saad Ullah Khan remained in position, his arms raised to the sky. He did not bring them down.

Finally, one of his friends asked him, 'What are you asking of Allah?'

And he replied, 'I asked him for the largesse of allowing me to live out my life as a straightforward man, one who can look himself in the mirror and meet his own eyes.'

He converted from Hinduism. Bernier often described Saad Ullah Khan to me as Asia's greatest politician. The reason

Saad Ullah Khan made such an impression on me was that straightforwardness and fairness of character had become such rare qualities in my time. When he was forty-seven, he was poisoned to death. I was, in a way, responsible for that myself.

The reason was that every time there was discussion on whom the emperor should appoint his successor, Saad Ullah Khan would put forward my name. He was so close to the emperor he had no reason to hold back from voicing a view contrary to the emperor's own.

This was the reason for his death too. Driven by fear that the emperor would listen to Saad Ullah Khan's suggestion, Dara Shikoh plotted to have him killed. Dara Shikoh was rather skilled at poisoning people. The physician would not be able to trace it. Gut-wrenching pain in the stomach one moment, and the target was gone the next. This is why the emperor began to fear and suspect Dara Shikoh – would a man who had so easily killed his father's closest friend hesitate to kill his father?

My hatred of Dara was rooted in strong reason, Honourable Katib.

Let me get back to the Diwan-i-Khas. There would be a khwajasara on either side of the emperor, wielding a peacock-feather fan. It was less for air circulation than to drive away flies. The umaras,[18] kings, and messengers from other empires would stand, arms folded, some distance from the emperor. The mansabdars[19] and rulers of lower standing would be further away.

---

18 Bernier writes that the umaras, high-ranking noblemen of the court, were the pillars of the Mughal empire.

19 Military commanders and other high-ranking officials in the mansabdari system founded by Akbar. Their salaries were assigned according to the sizes of their military units or mansabs, usually determined by the number of horses. The salaries ranged from 100 to 60,000 rupees per

Furthest away were the civilians waiting to meet the emperor. No distinctions were made among them – rich and poor, trader and sweeper, clothed and unclothed, anyone who wanted to speak of his grievances or meet the emperor for anything else stood with the rest. The emperor would hear out his subjects and have their issues addressed right away. This would go on until two in the afternoon, when we had to break for prayer.

Then the emperor would go to Azad Burj to meet his ministers.

At four in the afternoon, he would return to the Diwan-i-Aam and resume his royal duties. There would be music and dance concerts, interactions with various explorers about their adventures, and so on.

After the evening prayer, the emperor would retire to his private chambers. He would read until midnight. When he was settling down to sleep, the azan for the fajr would begin to sound from the minarets of the mosques.

You can look up evidence to attest to each of these things.[20] So well was the day documented. And yet, such calumny against me!

(The writer now said, 'Forgive the interruption, Shahenshah, but you mentioned the word "khwajasara". I assume this refers to the court eunuchs? We call them "transgender" these days?')

Yes, as you should know, Honourable Katib. You did, after all, grow up in Nagore, where Shahul Hameed Kadhir Wali Ganjasawai rests.

('We say "kosa", actually,' the writer said.)

---

month at the time. Going by the price of gold in Aurangzeb's time, this would work out to a range of 5,00,000 to 30,00,00,000 rupees a month today, although a monthly salary of thirty crore rupees seems a bit much for a government official.

20 The writer has referred to Abu'l-Fazl's *The History of Akbar*, edited and translated by Wheeler M. Thackston, to verify the spirit's account.

Well, that's a corruption, actually. In Farsi, 'khwaja' means God. Anyway, to get back to what I was saying, it was my understanding of human nature and of all my subjects as ingrates that prompted me to decide I'd be better off erased from their collective memory. My grave doesn't even have a roof over it, let alone a monument. And yet, they decided to name a road in Delhi after me. And then rename it. Your current government's decision, of course, to call it Dr A.P.J. Abdul Kalam Road. And thus they carry on Nehru's tradition of villainizing me, opposite faction though they claim to represent. Ya Allah! And look, they're such wonderful, broad-minded souls, eh? Because they have no religious prejudice, you see. One Muslim name replaced by another. How very secular. What clowns!

And who is this hero of theirs, Abdul Kalam? He erased all trace of his religion and lived like a Hindu. That's why the man's death inspired every taxi driver and auto driver in India to hang a portrait of his in their vehicles, and garland it and light incense sticks for it every day. The least he could have done was confess that his favourite food was beef biry … well, not even that, mutton biryani. Of all things, he turned vegetarian. Was he simply vegetarian, I wonder, or a no-onion-no-garlic case? Or worse, vegan? By the way, Honourable Katib, I've been wondering – what is this mafia that claims it is a sin to drink even the milk of cows and goats? I believe this is a popular trend in the West now. What is this world coming to? I wonder if your religion had it right, and it is indeed Kali Yuga.

~

The writer had to put a stop to the conversation about vegetarianism. The reason was one of the most important people in his literary career – Baahubilli.

'Forgive what I am about to say, Alamgir,' he said. 'But please let us not talk of this. You must permit me to edit out what you have said about veganism before I send this manuscript to my translator and friend Baahubilli. She is a militant vegan, and God knows how this conversation will affect the translation. Let's avoid all conflict.'

'Oh, is that so?' Aurangzeb said. 'Then why don't you bring your friend, this Mohtarma Baahubilli, to our next seance? Let me hear her point of view. I've told you, I'm a changed man. Do remember you're speaking to the man I was after nine decades in the world, not the emperor who led his army to war. Who knows, perhaps this sahiba's arguments will convince me to turn vegan. Allahu Akbar.'

'Huzoor, I must tell you it's a bit much to refer to Baahubilli as "mohtarma" and "sahiba". She is much, much younger than you. From what I know of her, this show of excessive courtesy will embarrass her.'

'But, Honourable Katib, surely you have read in the *Baburnama* that Giti Sitani Firdaus Makani Padishah Babur Ghazi believed the people of Hindustan were incapable of respectful speech. That is so true. Even in the twenty-first century, you lot fall far behind the Arabs. You're savages by comparison, really. You've written of how people from Coimbatore consider Chennai a rude place. Chennaivasis go right to *nee, vaa, po*, using the singular to address an interlocutor, instead of the respectful plural. I remember reading in one of your pieces of travel writing that a woman at Muscat airport addressed you as "Baba", which means "father". You won't find such courtesy in India.

'America is in a league of its own, of course. They'll want to know how much a tola of respect costs. The reason for this loss of courtesy is the English language, with its one second-person singular pronoun, irrespective of the addressee's age – *you*. Look at French, Spanish, any other language. As far as this slave is concerned, it's a disgrace to say "you". In your Tamil, you say "neenga" as the respectful plural. It should rightly be "thaangal". Your speech is a tad more polished than those of your countrymen because you come from Nagore, whose tongue is laced with the Arabic influence, and therefore its culture draws from the Arabic culture too.'

'All that's fair enough, Shahenshah,' the writer said, 'but it appears to me that while Mughal tradition emphasizes respect in speech and address, it is somewhat lacking in practice, what with all the beheadings and elephant tramplings and blindings, sometimes of emperor fathers by aspiring-emperor sons. For as long as they're alive, it appears their heads are in danger of separation from their bodies. But once they're dead, they're entombed in grand edifices that find themselves among the world's architectural wonders.'

At this, Aurangzeb threw his head back and laughed.

'Right, you do have a point, Honourable Katib. We'll get to this issue as we get deeper into my story. Now, you know I was the richest man alive in my time. But did I enjoy that wealth? I lived as your Gandhi said one should – I gave it all back to my subjects, didn't I? Do you know how much money I had at the time of my death? Three hundred rupees. Most of the treasury had been emptied to fund wars. It was the prayer caps I stitched and the Qurans I hand-wrote that served as my source of income. Yet, I'm the villain. And this Abdul Kalam, who cast his religion aside, is a hero. Perhaps it is my humble grave that's done it – perhaps the public thinks a man who doesn't erect a monument over his own body must be as worthless as rubbish on the streets. I ought to have done that, oughtn't I? Along with a few commissioned hagiographies? If only I'd done those things, not just Delhi, but every city in Hindustan would have a road named after me, as you do with Gandhi.

'Yes, I hear what you're thinking. It *is* true that I demolished a few important Hindu temples in Kashi. But we were at war. It was customary for the victors to demolish the houses and prayer halls of the losers. I couldn't go against such an important custom, could I? But here's a fact – let's assume I demolished fifty temples. I built five thousand. And unlike your contemporary celebrities who plant trees for the photo-op and then never bother to return to water that poor sapling, I ensured the temples had an income and an endowment for maintenance. Yet, I'm a villain because the public needs one – a man to worship, and a man to slander. I'm the latter, the receptacle of hate. Hate is their kriyashakti, you see, their mooladhara, their pranakini. I'm the victim of their need to hate.' The writer wishes to state here that he has edited some of Aurangzeb's first-person references. The emperor never used the pronoun 'I'. When he referred to himself, it would be as 'this slave', 'this sinner', 'this worm' or 'this lowlife'. But this would read rather tediously. The writer was tempted for a time to title his work *Conversations with a Lowlife* or *Conversations with a Worm*, but better sense prevailed. He has also chosen to 'I' some of the slaves and worms and sinners and lowlifes. This humble ... tchah sorry, I ... I ask that you forgive the artistic licence.

Having spoken of hate, Aurangzeb had lapsed into silence for a bit, and then startled the writer by closing his eyes and breaking into song. After about thirty seconds, he paused, and the writer gathered his wits about him. 'Shahenshah ... I thought you did not like music?' he ventured.

Aurangzeb looked at him with seeming surprise and then laughed. 'Music? But it must sound like music to you. It is the purest of its kind, after all. I was singing the Surah al-Baqarah Ayat 22, which goes:

> *Allazee ja'ala lakumul arda*
> *firaashanw wassamaaa'a binaaa*
> *'anw wa anzala minassamaaa'i*
> *maaa'an fa akhraja bihee minas*
> *samaraati rizqal lakum falaa*
> *taj'aloo lillaahi andaadanw wa*
> *antum ta'lamoon.*

'If it were not for this hatred driving the world, would we forget the God who made this earth our bed and the sky a canopy, and sent down from this canopy rain that would foster fruits on the earth-bed?

'Let me tell you the story of Allah's she-camel, of the Prophet Saleh, alayhi salam. It is the story of just how much hatred can fester in a people. You can still visit this cursed place if you go to Saudi Arabia today, but one is not permitted to spend the night. The fallout of this hatred culminated in divine retribution that one can still sense.

'Let me take you two thousand and five hundred years ago, two hundred and fifty miles to the north-west of Medina, to al-Hijr, where the Thamud lived. They were a resourceful, strong and intelligent people. They carved homes into the mountainside and dug wells in the deserts. They grew prosperous from making their habitat on the trade route between Arabia and Syria. The Thamud were tyrannical, oppressive and arrogant. They were idol worshippers, with no taqwa, no piety or faith in the One God. And it was to this tribe that Allah sent Saleh Nabi, a descendant of none less than Nuh Nabi – whom you may know of as Noah.

In his fortieth year, Saleh Nabi received the Message of God through the angel Jibreel. When he told his people of the Message, they dismissed him as insane. Yet, he persisted in spreading the Message of God among the Thamud. He found few takers for monotheism. The Thamud would challenge him at every step, despite the many miracles he performed. They then made a demand of Saleh Nabi – if he was indeed a prophet, he must make a pregnant camel with a black forehead and white body and long hair appear from within the mountain and whelp at once a calf that looked exactly like her.

'Saleh, alayhi salam, asked: "If Allah makes this camel appear as you have described, will you place your faith in the Message and accept the One God?"

"'Yes," they said. "But the camel must yield milk which is more intoxicating than alcohol and sweeter than honey."

"'If that happens," asked Saleh Nabi, "will you place your faith in the Message and accept the One God?"

"'Yes," they said. "But this milk must be cool in summer and sizzling in winter."

"'If that happens," asked Saleh Nabi, "will you place your faith in the Message and accept the One God?"

"'Yes," they said, and went on to add more conditions. The milk must cure the sick man, and make the poor man rich. The camel must not graze where their cattle did. Saleh Nabi agreed to all their quite atrocious demands, and asked for just two promises in return – no one must harm the camel; they must share the well with the camel, so that they would draw water on one day and she would drink water on the second. They must not interrupt her while she had her water.

'Once the two parties had reached an understanding, the mountainside split and a she-camel emerged, a hundred and twenty feet long, a hundred feet wide and fifty feet tall. She whelped at once, yielding a calf who looked exactly like her. Upon seeing this miracle, most of the Thamud were convinced, but the temple priests – afraid that this would put paid to their livelihoods – claimed this was black magic. Saleh Nabi said they could all do as they wished; whether they accepted the One God or not, they would prosper as long as the she-camel was well. The day she was harmed, they would perish.

'All went well for some time. The she-camel would stand outside each house in turn, and the people would bring out vessels for her milk. Thanks to the sale of dairy – milk, curd, butter and ghee – the entire clan prospered. And yet, they found space for hate. They began to resent the she-camel. Some hated her because she represented Allah's greatness, and some hated her because she had access to pasture; some hated her because they had to forgo a day at the well, and some hated her for no reason at all. One fine day, some of the Thamud attacked the she-camel as she was drinking water and killed her. They cooked her meat and invited the entire clan to partake of it. The camel calf disappeared into the mountain from which the mother had emerged. Allahu Akbar. Saleh Nabi cried tears of blood.

'"You have invited the wrath of God," he said. "You have challenged him to war. In four days, you will perish. Tomorrow, your faces will turn yellow. The next day, they will turn red. The day after, they will turn black, and on the next day, you will die."

'And that was exactly how the Thamud perished. The mountain still stands, but the fools have made a tourist site of it. People take photographs and buy souvenirs, as if it were a wonder and not a curse. They have made a monument of hate.

'Look at Hindustan now. People hate others for worshipping a particular god, and for not worshipping another. People hate others for speaking a particular language, and for not speaking another. Why, in your state, people are wearing T-shirts that read *Hindi theriyadhu, poda*, as if ignorance were a matter of pride. When all else is well, it is hate that drives us.'

~

When one of the writer's friends had reached this point in the novel, she called him and said, 'What is this, you've gone and scored an own goal in this Hindi matter? You speak Hindi fluently yourself and pepper your sentences with "behenchod" even while talking to people who can't understand either word. And yet, you've been writing against the imposition of Hindi for decades. Now that the novel is going to be read by non-Tamils, you've gone all pro-Hindi?'

The writer said, 'Look, I'm against the *imposition* of Hindi, not against Hindi itself. I'm against any sort of imposition. I know Hindi because when my father told me I should never learn that language, I went and promptly registered for a beginners' course at the Hindi Prachar Sabha. And when the central government seeks to impose Hindi on us, I oppose it. Now, please let me continue the novel.'

~

UNAWARE OF THE INTERRUPTION, AURANGZEB WENT ON:

It was hate that drove my sins too, wasn't it? I lived a life without hate for all of sixteen years. The rest of my life was a series of sins, including fratricide. But if I hadn't killed my brothers, they would have killed me and each other too.

I'm not the only one, you know. The history of Indian royalty is a legacy of fratricide. Take for instance your Ashoka, one of the hundred and one sons of Bindusara, who had sixteen wives to give him those heirs, only for one to kill ninety-nine others. The only brother he spared was Dishya, for no reason other than they were born of the same womb. Bindusara wanted his oldest son, Sushiman, to ascend to the throne after him. Sushiman was satrap of Takshashila, and Ashoka satrap of Ujjaini. But when there was an uprising in Takshashila, Sushiman proved incapable, and Bindusara had to send Ashoka to put it down, which he did. He had proven deserving of the throne, and the ministers were for it too. But his father was not. Do you know that it was only four years after Bindusara died that Ashoka was crowned king? Do you know why? Because it took him four years to kill his brothers and their supporters, one by one. He did it all by his own hand too. Over five hundred beheadings for each dead brother, carried out by his own hand. But his brothers did not all die by the sword. Sushiman was killed when he was entering the fort of Pataliputra to complete the last rites of his father. The crown prince was on the drawbridge, when hot oil was poured on him from above, followed by a flare so that he was burnt alive. Can you imagine such hate, for one's own brother? This man, filled with all this hate, is a hero. A hero who went on to embrace and spread the message of peace. History's heroes, you see, Honourable Katib, are illusory, bereft of any connection to reality. The heroes spew as much venom and hate as the villains.

CHAPTER 3

Mongolian Wolves &
Old Men's Wives

AURANGZEB SAID:

You know, Honourable Katib, the last two years of my life, my dreams were haunted by rolling heads. Heads that rolled when Firdaus Makani Padishah Babur was in power, heads that rolled at my behest.

Firdaus Makani, too, is much maligned – the Muslim who invaded Hindustan to establish Mughal rule, the emperor who killed Hindus. Those are misconceptions. An emperor's duty is to protect his subjects, and the only way he can do that is through vigilant and powerful governance, which mandates in turn that some heads – heads that are screwed on wrong – must roll.

The most effective way to thwart attacks from one's neighbouring kingdoms is to induce fear in their rulers. Do you know why my ancestor Genghis Khan, who swallowed China whole, never invaded India? China had an enormous army, but numbers mean nothing. The soldiers were fonder of whorehouses than warfare. In 1221, Genghis Khan chased down Jalaladdin Mangburni to the Indus river and annexed Khwarazm but did not venture beyond. The reason was Iltutmish, the great Mamluk king. A hundred years – and countless attempts at conquest, all of which failed.

When the Mughals eventually came to India, they had to surmount several barriers – the height of the Himalayas for one, the narrowness of the Khyber Pass for another. And once we were in power, the French and Dutch and British and Portuguese had to wait hundreds of years for our influence to wane.

And do you know why we were so powerful? Because it wasn't the norm for the oldest son to take the throne. The most deserving son did. And I will tell you what marked me out as the most deserving son – the incident with the elephant. It marked me forever as a warrior, a braveheart.

This was immortalized in watercolour by the court artist Govardhan, and it is the painting which sealed my fate and that of this land. The stoic expression on my face, the face of a teenage boy. The terror in my father's eyes, as he watches an elephant charge at his offspring. Two others run to my rescue, their horses rearing. One is my brother Shah Shuja, older than me and younger than Dara Shikoh. The other is the emperor's general Raja Jai Singh, who has his men set off firecrackers to scare the elephant. One boy alone, wearing royal finery, baulks in fear and reins in his horse. That boy is Dara Shikoh.

If Dara had looked at the painting closely, he might have poisoned Govardhan too. Govardhan spared him the trouble by dying in his forty-fifth year. But the painting shows us, nearly half a millennium later, what a coward my brother was. The reason he was the way he was is my father. The emperor loved him too much, and was so protective of him that Dara didn't stand a chance at being a true warrior.

Let me explain. Do you remember your young friend who accompanied you to the Jaipur Literature Festival? He would wake at eight in the morning and drink into the afternoon. And then eat. And then nap. And then wake and drink again until three in the morning. He would read. And write poetry. You once told him you would like to live like he does. And he asked, 'Why don't you?' And you said, 'Because I would die in months.' He asked you, 'What is there in the world that one must live for?' He died in months. How old was he, thirty?

Was it for this pointless existence that Allah gave us these bodies? He gave them to us so we would work all day and sleep the sleep of the just, so we would eat only as much as we need to survive and drive temptation from the body and mind through prayer.

Do you know why Genghis Khan could conquer the world? The wolves of Mongolia. They're the reason the Mongolian horse is so swift. His army was much smaller than that of China, his weapons less sophisticated, and yet he won wars because of his horses.

I was a Mongolian horse, you see, chased by my own wolves. This body and mind knew hurt and sorrow and deprivation and privation. To me, my father was the emperor. To Dara, he was 'Shah Baba'. So, you see, it wasn't I who killed Dara, it was our father. Dara was fit to be a poet and an intellectual, not an emperor. Battlefields were not meant for him. Whereas I spent every day of every month of every year from the ages of sixteen to thirty-eight on the battlefield. He felt he was entitled to the throne by dint of being the oldest prince. He learnt the skills, he had his training and his regimen – exercise, breakfast, rest, exercise, lunch, siesta, exercise, dinner, sleep – but I was thrown into the deep end, and I learnt how to swim. He was a Chinese horse, disciplined by training. I was a Mongolian horse, driven by wolves.

The more the emperor sought to remove me from the palace and royal comfort, the more accomplished a warrior I became. The closer he kept Dara to the seat of power, the further he pushed him away from his inheritance. Dara would not have made a strong king, you see.

And history has told us what happens when the king is not strong enough. Look at the events of 15 December 1398 – the invasion of Delhi by the army of Amir Taimur. Taimur had no sooner entered Delhi than the sultan, Naseeruddin Mahmood Shah Tughlaq, fled for his life. The armies of Taimur had camped on the banks of the Yamuna. They already had fifty thousand captives with them. Most of them were idol-worshipping Hindus, but there were thousands of Muslims among them too. Amir Taimur ordered them all killed. Do you know what the al-Kafirun surah of the Holy Quran says?

Oh, you disbelievers, you kafirs,
neither do I worship that which you worship,
nor do you worship He whom I do.
I will never worship what you worship,
nor will you ever worship He Whom I do.
To you be your religion, and to me mine.

Despite the Quran preaching that one should live and let live, Taimur had marched on Hindustan saying he was going to kill all idol worshippers. I believe he was fooling himself. His spies had

told him what a weakling this Tughlaq was. And also how rich
his khazana was. All of India was buried under gold and diamonds
and precious gems, they must have said. The temples are filled with
statues of gold, and no one will stop us from emptying them, the
spies would have said. And so Taimur left on his conquest, with
his religion for company.

With the sultan having abandoned his people, Taimur said
anyone who wanted to escape with his life would have to pay
blood money. Those who paid were spared for three days. And
then the army swarmed into homes. Hindus burnt their daughters
alive and jumped into the flames themselves. The soldiers killed
anyone whom they found alive. By the end of the month, a
hundred thousand people had been killed. Not even Taimur's
generals could hold the rampaging soldiers back. One couldn't
find a woman, even a girl, a child, who hadn't been raped. One
couldn't see the roads for the heads and limbs and torsos that were
piled on each other. The sky was hidden by flocks of carrion birds,
and dogs climbed over the decomposing bodies, tearing the flesh
apart. And yet the soldiers looked for life they could snuff out, and
when they found it, they would yell, 'Call your gods to your rescue!
I'm going to kill you, let's see if they can stand up to me!' When
they had had their fill, and Taimur had swept up all the gold and
diamonds and gems he could find, they left. And for two months
after, not a human soul roamed the streets of Delhi. They left only
corpses in their wake.

Do you know why this did not happen in my time? Because
I killed the three weaklings who would have let it happen – my
brothers.

When the Mughal empire went into decline, this very history
repeated itself. The Persian king Nader Shah began his march to

Delhi in 1738 – what an unfortunate city your current capital is! Has any city ever been ravaged as repeatedly as it has? And yet it has managed to stay standing, to recover after each blow.

In the three-hundred-odd years since Taimur's conquest, the city was back to its splendour, ripe for Nader Shah's rout. Nader Shah had been victorious in Kandahar, but the war had wiped his treasury clean. Naturally, he needed an excuse, and he claimed that the Mughal king Muhammad Shah had been providing succour and shelter to Afghan rebels, who had been causing unrest in the eastern territories. He sent messengers to Muhammad Shah, demanding an explanation.

When the answer proved unsatisfactory, he had his excuse. Kandahar to Karnal, via Ghazni and Kabul and Jalalabad and Jamrud and Peshawar and Attock and Lahore and Sirhind and Ambala and Asimabad. He clashed with the Mughal armies at Karnal. On 20 March 1739, Muhammad Shah surrendered, along with the keys to the Red Fort and his treasury.

Nader Shah sat down on Emperor Shah Jahan's renowned Peacock Throne and let his voice echo through the Diwan-i-Khas, his eyes blazing from victory. This might have been the moment the East India Company realized just how weak the Mughal empire had become, and also that it would be no mean feat to rule over Hindustan themselves. It was also the moment new coins were minted with the conqueror's face on them, and the prayers at the Jama Masjid were said in the name of the conqueror.

Nader Shah had no intention of staying behind to rule this land. All he wanted was the treasury, and all the money he could collect from the people. And so, like governments do these days, he increased the taxes. He imposed GST, your goods and services tax. But the traders at Chandni Chowk flouted his orders and sold their goods at the usual low rates. Nader Shah sent his soldiers there the moment he got wind of this. A war of words ensued, and then turned into a fistfight, and then turned into a bloodbath.

As news reached other markets, the traders set upon the soldiers in the vicinity. As is common in times like these, someone set off a rumour – that a female bodyguard at the Red Fort had killed Nader Shah. This boosted the morale of the civilians, and they attacked the soldiers with fresh gusto.

The next day – 22 March 1739 – would be the blackest day in the history of Delhi. You speak of Jallianwala Bagh. That was nothing compared to what happened in Delhi that day. Nader Shah and his armies had not rid themselves of their bloodlust. And here was an opportunity. The conqueror marched to Chandni Chowk with his entire army. He got off at the Sunehri Masjid in Roshan-ud-Daulah and gave the soldiers his command. This was not verbal. He simply pulled his sword from his scabbard and waved it in the air. This meant: *Go forth and be brutal. There will be no questions.*

Guns and swords were used against unarmed civilians. Ironically, it was Holi that day. Where jets of coloured water should have run, streams of human blood would flow. Chandni Chowk, Dariba Kalan, Fatehpuri, Hauz Qazi, Johri Bazar, Lahori Gate, Ajmeri Gate, Kabuli Gate … you've seen during your Delhi years how crowded these places can get, haven't you? Back in 1739, there were two million people in Delhi, more than Paris and London combined. The soldiers of Nader Shah fired at crowds, broke into homes, and looted shops. The lives of men were snuffed, the honour of women was violated, and the skulls of children smashed against walls.

It was the Devil that took over Delhi that day. No building that could be set on fire was left standing; but each was first stripped bare, every paisa and every knick-knack taken by the soldiers.

All this was chronicled by Anand Ram Mukhlis, who witnessed the events of the day and miraculously lived to tell the tale. It took eight days to put out the fires in the city, and weeks to clear the bodies from the streets. Six hours. Six hours was all it took for a hundred thousand bodies to fall.

Poor Muhammad Shah, he was like Dara Shikoh. He ought to have been a poet, not a ruler. He fell on his knees and begged Nader Shah to stop the massacre. Do what you want to me, he said, but spare my people. Nader Shah consented, under one condition. He must be paid a hundred crore rupees. Muhammad Shah agreed. The killings stopped. But the looting and the raping went on.

How did Muhammad Shah, who had just been relieved of his treasury, find the hundred crore rupees? It was decided that the citizens would have to pay the money; each family was worth so much. And in the blink of an eye, people lost their entire inheritance. The ground beneath their feet, the roof over their heads. All gone. The ones left alive drank poison.

As for Nader Shah, he packed everything he could lay his hands on into his caravan. The Peacock Throne, with its Kohinoor diamond and Taimur ruby. It is said seven hundred elephants and four thousand camels and twelve thousand horses were needed to transport the war bounty. If one were to adjust for inflation, this would be worth ninety-two thousand crore rupees today. The conquerors left Delhi in the first week of May. Once he reached

Persia, Nader Shah declared that he would not tax his people for three years. The treasury was overflowing.

Not long after, he lost something far more precious than his loot – his mind. Convinced that his son Reza Qoli Mirza was conspiring to kill him, he ordered the boy imprisoned and had his eyes gouged out. He went on to kill most of his courtiers. In January 1747, as he was crossing the Dasht-e Lut desert with his army, he ordered random people whom his eyes fell upon tortured and executed; the victims included some of his soldiers, and even his generals. The ones left standing decided he must be killed. Nader Shah, who had guessed their intentions, then flashed his sword at anyone who approached him.

You see, Nader Shah had not inherited the throne. You would call him 'lumpen', Honourable Katib. You know how some of your politicians pride themselves on having sold vegetables from pushcarts or served tea in stalls? Nader Shah was just your regular rowdy who joined the army and rose in the ranks and eventually usurped the throne. Lust for money, lust for power, lust for blood. Lust drove him.

But to get back to that black period in Delhi, you know what hurts me most? My name was spoken at the wedding of Muhammad Shah's daughter to Nader Shah's grandson. Yes, she was part of the war bounty. Muhammad Shah had to speak the names of his last seven ancestors, and all of us Mughal emperors were humiliated that day, starting with Firdaus Makani. When the maulvi turned to Nader Shah and asked him to recite his ancestry, this lout replied: 'I am the son of the sword and the grandson of the sword and the great and great-great and great-great-great and great-great-great-great and great-great-great-great-great-grandson of the sword.' In the Mughal tradition, our swords are given names too. But this haramzada couldn't name his father, let alone his sword.

(There was a heavy pause, and the writer didn't dare intrude on the spirit's silence.)

Honourable Katib, we've digressed a fair bit from our original thesis – the fact that the greatest villain in the history of Hindustan was Emperor Ashoka. His only reason for invading Kalinga, which at the time had the closest form of government to your democracy, was to establish his sovereignty. And because that unfortunate Kalinga was as powerful as the Mauryan empire, it was a pyrrhic war, with over fifty thousand lives lost on either side. And another two hundred thousand lives lost to starvation and the aftermath of war. A hundred and fifty thousand people – perhaps the only survivors of that bloodbath – were taken prisoner by Ashoka. If what that chakravarti of yours said in his stupas, of his having a change of heart after being brought to his knees by the horrors of war, were true, he ought to have released those prisoners, oughtn't he? Why didn't he, then? And even after he purportedly embraced ahimsa, he had thousands of Shramanas and Ajivikas killed. I don't speak a word without evidence. You will find proof of what I have said in the *Ashokavadana*. You will find that no less than eighteen thousand Ajivikas were put to death by him in a single day in the region you now call Bengal. It might have been the first instance of ... what do you call it, ethnic cleansing? Or communal genocide? All this after his conversion to Buddhism.

Once, a Shramana artist had created a portrait in which Tathagata stood with his head bowed before a Tirthankara. Blasphemy, cried Ashoka, and had the artist and his family burnt alive in their own home. And he didn't stop there. He announced a bounty of one gold coin for every Shramana head that rolled. The treasury gave away bags of gold coins. Ya Allah!

As a spirit, I have the ability to scan the entire contents of a library and upload it in my brain, Honourable Katib. It is research, and not rancour, that fuels this outpouring. If any man were to take issue with what I have said, I would direct him to the *Mahavamsa*, the *Dipavamsa*, the *Ashokavadana* and those ubiquitous stupas. And, of course, the *Tripitaka* – the *Sutta*, the *Vinaya* and the *Abhidhamma*. And that man would agree that the image of Ashoka you all have inherited has nothing at all to do with the emperor himself; it is a fiction divorced from all reality.

Honourable Katib, the Kalinga War began and ended within seven years of Ashoka ascending the throne. His reign would go on for a further three decades. The Sanatana Marg – which the Mauryas called the 'Brahmin religion' – has never seen the sort of deterioration it did at that time in any other period of history; nor have Brahmins been hated and sidelined as much, your Dravida movement of the twentieth century included. The only reason for the survival of the Sanatana Marg was that the Mauryan empire died with Ashoka. And yet, all you Hindus name your sons after Ashoka. You'll find an Ashok or an Ashokan on every street of every city. Talk about satanic worship.

They speak of *my* religious fervour, but such was Ashoka's missionary zeal to spread Buddhism that the khazana was empty at the time of his death. I left an empty treasury too, but that was because I spent it all on war – yes, I admit, an error, an unforgivable one. But not so grave nor so unforgivable an error as to donate it all to Buddhist organizations, surely! Rivers of gold flowed into those. Thankfully, with his death, Kalinga rose again, and Buddhism was exported to other countries, leaving Hindustan to go back to the Brahmin religion.

For that matter, if it hadn't been for Nehru and his westernized, fake intellectual cronies, Ashoka would have remained a nebulous historical figure. Nehru needed a hero for the New India, and they created 'Ashoka the Great'. And he had a readymade counterpart in 'Aurangzeb the Evil', this slave who abolished all the marketing initiatives of the Mughal empire, calling it wasteful expense. I stopped my balcony darshans because the public saw me as a God, and no one should be seen as God but God Himself. All my wazirs begged me not to stop it, for this was a tradition fostered since the time of Jahanbani Jannat Ashyani. They were afraid people would assume I was ill if I stopped these appearances, and crime would go up. Quite like riots break out in your era every time a politician – or a film star – dies. 'Let them try committing crimes,' I said. 'I want every criminal's head pinned on a stake in the town centre, and then let me see who says the emperor is ill.' That shut them up. The treasury was dedicated to the comfort of the citizens, and my time was dedicated to the service of Allah and his greatest creation, humanity.

And then I dealt yet another blow to the marketing department of the Mughal empire. I asked that they stop writing the history of each emperor. What do you read in Inayat Khan's *Shahjahannama* or Abdul Hameed Lahori's *Padishahnama*? Stories of war, stories of rampaging armies, stories of souls rescued from idol worship and set on the right path to God … hagiographies to the emperor, commissioned by the emperor himself from writers who would oblige him. Quite like the history of your Puratchiththalaivi written by her party men. Even the *Akbarnama*, with its lyricism and philosophical nuance, is no exception.

The one account that stands out is the *Baburnama*, because it was written by Firdaus Makani himself. And how? Since the age of twelve, he had never observed Ramzan in the same place twice. He was always on the road and spent all his days on the battlefield. And so his diary reads like a thriller and a confessional all at once. He speaks so very openly of things people hesitate to even think about ... is that why his work is so celebrated by firangis, I wonder?

When he was seventeen, he was married for the first time. He writes of how he felt no attraction to his bride, Ayesha Sultan Begum. His mother would have to force him to visit the begum's bedchamber once a month. And yet, he writes: 'I discovered in myself a strange inclination – no, a mad infatuation – for a boy in the camp's bazaar, his name Baburi being apposite. Until then, I had no inclination of love and desire for anyone, by hearsay or experience ... From time to time, Baburi appeared before me. But out of modesty and bashfulness, I could never look directly at him. How, then, could I make conversation with him? In my joy and agitation, I could not even thank him for coming. How was it possible for me to reproach him for going away from me? What power had I to command him to be of service to me? One day, during that period of desire and passion, when I was walking with my companions along a lane and suddenly saw him face to face, I got into such a state of confusion that I almost lost my senses. To look straight at him or string words together was impossible. With a hundred torments and shames, I moved on ... In that maelstrom of desire and passion, and under the stress of youthful folly, I used to wander, bareheaded and barefoot, through streets and lanes, orchards and vineyards. I showed civility neither to friends nor to strangers, took no care of myself or others.'[21]

---

21 This is an excerpt from *The Babur-nama*, translated by Annette Susannah Beveridge.

He has written poems about the boy. Which emperor could write so frankly? But what stuns me most about this work was the fact that Firdaus Makani found the time to write during his evenings on the battlefield and nights in deserts. Other than the *Baburnama*, every other biography is bakwaas, and taxpayer money ought not to have been wasted on this. My brother Dara Shikoh, of course, would have encouraged the practice. Why, his bride Nadira's trousseau at the time was worth eight lakh rupees – adjusting for inflation, that would be a hundred and twenty crore rupees today. On clothes. Not even your Puratchiththalaivi could have raked up comparable wedding expenses, eh?

Would anyone name his son after me, I wonder? And yet, you people are so besotted with the man who was the true enemy of Hinduism, Ashoka. The widest road in your capital has been named in his honour, as has your government's five-star hotel. Why, your national emblem has been designed in his honour.

You speak of his ahimsa. Well, it was true there was no great war after Kalinga. But then, his satraps were demons. Ashoka was so busy coating Buddhist viharas in gold and taxing his subjects when the treasury was empty that he allowed everyone a free hand. Why, Honourable Katib, your own novel-in-progress *Ashoka* speaks of how the kingdom was pretty much ruled by his young, gold-digging wife Tishyaraksha. For all his Buddhist leanings, the man decided to marry in his sixty-eighth year. The nubile Tishyaraksha was, perhaps naturally, attracted to her husband's son Kunala. Your Bollywood has churned out this story often enough. Poor Kunala was something of an ascetic and intellectual, and made the mistake of telling Tishyaraksha when she solicited his attentions that she was his mother. *Mother.* Talk about a woman scorned. Need I tell you what happened next?

She accused him of conspiring to overthrow his father and had him blinded by decree of that very father. And so the son of the emperor, the heir apparent, was made to wander the streets as a blind beggar. Tishyaraksha was your typical sociopath, you know. For no apparent reason, she ensured the Bodhi tree her royal husband worshipped withered and died by pouring toxins into the soil. And Ashoka the Great had no clue. What a – excuse my French – dumb fuck.

And yet he excelled at marketing. You know what this reminds me of? I heard recently, only some decades ago, about your Indira Gandhi's 'time capsule'. She was fool enough to bury it in the Red Fort, where it was prematurely unearthed, making her more laughingstock than legend. Ashoka was a tad cleverer, you see. His time capsules were not so much buried as erected, and in places that the people who could call him out would never visit. And his deeds were etched into metal, so they didn't dissolve in urine. Not bad for a dumb fuck.

CHAPTER 4

Of Plunderers & Conquerors

AURANGZEB SAID:

Honourable Katib, you know I was the sovereign ruler of the most expansive empire in history after Ashoka's, but I never decreed that my subjects should fall in line with my own religious beliefs, did I? The majority of this servant's subjects believed in idol worship. I find it quite blasphemous, and yet I felt I had no right to interfere. What's more, I even built temples for them. My most trusted assistant was a Brahmin. Most of my generals were Rajputs.

And yet, my name has been erased from your roads as well as from your lists of baby names. Ashok, Ashokan, Ashoka ... the hero of marketing, whose reign was documented by sycophants and mercenaries.

In order to make this appearance and speak to you openly so I may right the calumny, I familiarized myself with all the history that has passed after me, down to the contemporary events of your time. And here's what I found. There is one man more wretched than Ashoka, a man who ought rightly to be enemy to all humankind. Taimur – an ancestor of mine, but there can be no doubt he was a butcher.

And yet, a child who was arguably your media's favourite celebrity until he grew out of his cherubic chubbiness shares this illustrious gentleman's name. Why, I once heard a news anchor begging his father to get Taimur to blow a kiss to her audience.

It made me wonder how this child's namesake would have reacted if someone had asked him to blow a kiss to a television audience. The only kiss he knew, I believe, was the kiss of death.

I've told you, Honourable Katib, akhlaq and adab are my very soul, far dearer to me than regard for my ancestors. It is not I who speak of Taimur as a butcher, but his own autobiography that stands testimony to his deeds and his opinions. He writes with great pride: 'Maulana Naseer-ud-din Omar had never hurt a fly in his life. And yet, following my orders that day, he killed fifteen Hindus with his bare hands.'

It is estimated that Taimur killed about seventeen million people in his lifetime. That was an entire five per cent of the world population at the time. And with little discretion too. He was such an ignoramus, he didn't know that not all of Hindustan's population was Hindu. He punished Hindus and Muslims both for the crime of living on this land where idols were worshipped.

I come from a line of bloodthirsty kings. They speak of fratricide, but filicide was not uncommon in my line. Worse, the fathers were happy to maim their sons. Take Jahangir, for instance. His father, Padishah Akbar, was in constant conflict with him because Jahangir had become slave to alcohol and afeem. To say nothing of women. He had over twenty wives. Unlike his father's, they were not war bounty or strategic alliances. He had so many mistresses, you'd wonder how he managed to visit them all. Jahangir's own son Khusrau was a far cry from *his* father, though. His mother was Rani Manbhawati Bai, daughter of Raja Bhagwant Das of Amer, whose sister Mariam-uz-Zamani – known to you perhaps as Jodha Bai – was Arsh Ashyani Padishah Akbar's chief consort and mother to Jahangir. Khusrau was a saint for all practical purposes.

Jahangir aspired to his father's throne even when Akbar was alive. Akbar himself was keen that Khusrau should ascend the throne. The court was divided. Jahangir and Khusrau turned enemies, and this hurt Manbhawati Bai so much that she killed herself by consuming opium. It was Jahangir's grief in widowerhood that melted his father's heart and saw him ascend to the throne. One of his first acts as emperor was to have Khusrau blinded. When his courtiers, who had seen the prince grow from infancy, begged Jahangir to have mercy on his own son, he is believed to have said: 'An emperor has no family or ties of blood or friendship. He must not be moved by affection.'

Compared to the likes of him and to Taimur, am I a villain? There are Jahangirs in your country. But is there an Aurangzeb?

I wonder if this actor couple of yours would have named their child Aurangzeb.

～

At the next seance, the writer found the spirit rather less aggrieved.

'Through all these seances, Honourable Katib,' he said, 'I have spoken about everything but my own story. But I do have to give you context. Have you noticed, by the way, that I have begun to speak like you? I wonder whether the final story will be mine or yours. I transmit to your readers by relay, through this medium and then through you. May I ask, Honourable Katib, you have done your research and have read the *Baburnama* – what is your opinion of this work?'

'You've said all I could possibly say, Shahenshah. I find the poetry in the *Baburnama* quite intoxicating. It overwhelms my senses. Every word is poetry. Such was your ancestor Babur's linguistic skill that his autobiography seems to have been crafted in verse. He was all of seventeen when he wrote this:

I wander as a vagabond
through forest and over hills
all by myself.
Bowers of flowers
and crowded alleys
are all the same
to these weary feet.
It is not I who decide where they go,
or when they move,
or when they stop,
or how they shall come to rest.

'And yet, he had none of the effeteness one typically associates with an emperor who spends his time on poetry. The accounts of the wars he has fought alternate with reflections on his deepest emotions, Shahenshah.

'In 1503, when Babur was a fugitive, running from the Uzbeks, having lost both Samarkand and Fergana, he found himself at war again. His uncles, Sultan Mahmud Khan and Sultan Ahmad Alaq Khan, who were the Chagatai Khans of western and eastern Moghulistan respectively, had taken on the Uzbeks and lost the Battle of Akhsi. Babur found himself alone with his fellow warrior, Mirza Kuli Kokaltash. They were being surrounded by enemy troops. Mirza Kuli's horse went down, and the man looked at Babur.

"'I won't leave your side," Babur said. "We will face them together. We will survive or die together."

"'No," Mirza Kuli said. "You leave. Save yourself."

"'Life and death are all the same to me. I won't abandon you to the enemy."

"'This is no time for debate and discourse. You are not a soldier like I am. You have a destiny to fulfil. You are meant to be the padishah of a great empire. You must live for your subjects, not die for me. Please leave."

'Babur could not object. As he left, he turned back over and over again, loath to abandon a commander of the army and trying to ensure he wasn't captured for as long as he could watch him. He was barely twenty years old when this happened.

'There would be many such occasions in Giti Sitani Padishah Babur's life, where he had to choose between life and death. He never saw himself as a cut above his men. He writes: "There is nothing more despicable than a man who fears for his life." Elsewhere, as if continuing the thread of thought, he says: "One day or another, the next instant or a hundred years from now, one must leave this palace forever and ascend to the skies, is it not?"

'And yet, every time he prepared to die, he was saved quite miraculously. He found himself alone in a tiny village called Karnaan, at death's door. A villager who had found him had brought him to a garden where he could hear a little stream. Giti Sitani Firdaus Makani decided he would pray for one last time before he died. He did his ablutions at the stream and did his namaz. He then fell into a deep sleep. In his dream, the Sufi Khwaja Ubaydullah al-Ahrar appeared. "Every time you think of me, I will come to you," he said.

'Babur was woken by whispers. The villager who had purported to help him was now talking to another man. Babur realized he had been bound. The two men were discussing the bounty on his head. For all this, the villager had sworn on the Quran that he was only seeking to help.

'"So much for your promises!" the great Babur shouted.

'The two men turned, startled.

'Right then, they could hear a horse neighing at the gate of the garden.

'"Well, looks like you have met your end," one of the men said to Babur. "Your captors are here."

'But it turned out the horse was among several that had arrived at the garden, carrying Babur's men. One of the traitors fled, while the other was caught.

'When he had been taken to the safety of the camp, Babur asked his men, "How did you know I was here, in this village?"

'Their commander said, "Khwaja Ubaydullah appeared in all our dreams and woke us, saying the padishah was in a village called Karnaan and needed our help right away."

'Shahenshah, one must acknowledge the great irony of your ancestor Babur's life. It was he who laid the foundations of the Mughal empire in India, an empire that would become one of the most expansive in history, and yet he couldn't live in the empire he had inherited, the one his own ancestors had held for over a hundred and fifty years – Samarkand – for even a hundred and fifty days in a row. It remained an unfulfilled dream, all his life, to regain that seat of power.

'He did gain control of Samarkand in 1501, aged only eighteen. It was a hard-fought, hard-won battle. His enemies laid siege to the fort of Samarkand, and with no allies to crowd in from the sides, no food or water, Babur found himself alone as the head of a limbless corpse. Things had reached such a pass that people were killing their dogs and donkeys for meat. Horses were being fed leaves. The soldiers of the army were clambering over the walls in an effort to escape. Babur did what he had to. He fled in secret.

'He writes of how he had a fall from his horse, and with a head injury to exacerbate his exhaustion and starvation, he couldn't quite tell reality from his dreams. He believed he and his entourage killed and ate a horse. They went to a village called Dikhkat, he says, where the village head introduced them to his hundred-and-eleven-year-old mother, a matron who had ninety-six descendants in that village alone. She was said to have more than two hundred in all, counting those who had died before her. The last, her great-great-grandson, had been twenty-five. She told Babur that one of her relatives had fought alongside Taimur a century ago, when she was a ten-year-old girl. 'When I read this section of the *Baburnama*, Shahenshah, it struck me that gender roles were rather well defined at the time: the men would die at war, and the women would die in childbirth.

'And how they died, and in what barbarous fashion. I once saw a painting, Shahenshah, of a mountain of heads stacked one over the other, as if to make the walls of a pyramid. There's nothing remarkable about that, it was a Mughal custom to have this done of their enemies' heads. But what struck me in the painting was that most of the heads in there had grass in their mouths. Later, I realized that it was a sign of surrender. The fact that the men surrendering to Babur had met this fate sent chills down my spine.'

'There is nothing chilling about this, Honourable Katib,' said Aurangzeb. 'I know the painting to which you refer. It was of the Hangu expedition, one of the phases of Giti Sitani's first journey across the river Indus, to India. He was marching from Kohat to Bangash – the Kurram Valley – via Hangu, which was about twenty-three miles from Kohat. The road took them through a narrow valley with high mountains on either side. The Afghans of Kohat had occupied the mountains. Babur's guide told him that if he allowed the Afghans to cross over to a hill that was slightly detached, his men could slip into the slim neck of ground between the mountains and the hill and surround them. This was the strategy Babur followed. The army then attacked the hill from both sides. A hundred and fifty Afghan warriors were killed in the blink of an eye. Those who remained approached Babur with grass in their mouths, which signifies, "I am your ox. Spare me, and I will work for you."

'Giti Sitani followed custom and had them beheaded and a pyramid of those relieved heads erected, in accordance with Timurid and Mongol tradition. What choice did he have? Spare your enemy, and you have invited him to take your life. Dara would have killed me if I hadn't killed him. If Trotsky had come to power in place of Stalin, what do you think would have happened to Stalin? Victory belongs to he whose military power is bolstered by political acumen and shrewdness. If the Afghans had won the day, the painting would have shown Mughal heads. But there would have been no grass in their mouths. A tiger will not feed on grass even if he were starving, you see.'

'I do see, Shahenshah. But the violence in the *Baburnama* is hard to stomach. Kings cut off the heads of their enemies as if they were the tops of coconuts, they chop off fingers as if they were trimming nails, they blind their sons with all the fuss of a doctor administering a routine injection. I mean, the number of royal orders for blinding ... I'm surprised anyone could see at all. Such barbarism. It bewilders me that someone like Babur, whose sensibilities and sensitivity would not be out of place in this century, could carry out such cruel acts.'

'Honourable Katib, what irony. You speak of the sensibilities and sensitivity of this century. Yes, a century where every country has well-defined borders which no one can invade. And yet what barbarism prevails in your century! Is there a single country which spends more on education and health than on defence? What civilization, what culture do you uphold then? One sits back for a moment, and his neighbour has taken over a patch of his land; his neighbour sits back for a moment, and one has crossed into the neighbour's territory. And by the time all this is resolved by the United Nations, the sun would have swallowed the earth. When China ate Tibet whole, what was the rest of the world doing? The two countries have nothing in common, not language, not religion, not culture, not beliefs. You speak of the barbarism of my ancestors, and seem not to think of that of your contemporaries.

'Why do you think Mohtaram Giti Sitani Firdaus Makani Padishah Babur Ghazi came to India? He wasn't a plunderer like those who had ravaged the land before him. Why did he not return to Kabul after the Battle of Panipat, as his generals and commanders and soldiers wanted to? That was what all your Chola kings did, wasn't it? They conquered territory, and then went back to their old thrones. It wasn't so much *they came, they saw, they conquered*, as *they went, they conquered, they returned*. We came, we conquered, we stayed, and became naturalized citizens of your soil. Why did we choose this path, rather than take the easy way out? Let me explain. I will have to allow you to hear the rousing speech Giti Sitani Firdaus Makani once made to his army.

'The date was 16 March 1527. The Mughal army was fighting against the Rajput confederacy of Rana Sanga of Mewar in the city of Khanwa, near Fatehpur Sikri.

'It was a spring evening, before the onset of summer. Giti Sitani Firdaus Makani tossed his evening snack of makhjun – a mix of opium, ghee, and sugar – into his mouth, left his tent, and called for his generals to gather their men. With his entire army before him, he recited the Surah al-Fatiha and then began to speak:

> *My generals, my soldiers, my men!*
>
> *I stand before you today, looking at you, your bleary eyes and your weary limbs, exhausted from the battles we have fought and won, your homesick hearts aching to go back from where we commenced this fateful journey, your battered bodies yearning for the beds they left behind, your starving souls longing for the company of your loved ones.*
>
> *I ask of you nothing but these hearts and bodies and souls, your sweat and blood, your faith and fidelity, your constancy and commitment, your devotion and dedication.*
>
> *For it is not I who have brought you here, but Allah who has brought us here. It was not ambition or greed or hate that drove us through these lands, but destiny.*
>
> *At one score and one years of age, I set out with twenty warriors. We had no horses, for who needs horses when the horses*

of God are with us, to fly us to the gates of paradise? We had no swords, but our sticks served twice the purpose. We had no armour against enemies or the wind; we wore the clothes on our back and our feet were soled with farmers' slippers.

And yet here we are, still standing after the Battle of Panipat, ten and six months after we first set out.

Here we stand, multiplied into legions of men, driven by the same destiny that pushed us out of our homes all that time ago.

Here we stand, the soldiers of God, the chosen ones, the men who will not return like their predecessors from the Khyber Pass with all the gold they could carry and all the loot they could stuff into their caravans.

Here we stand, an army of rulers, not of robbers.

Here we stand, the men who will rewrite the destiny of this land we are about to conquer.

Here we stand, ready to do or die, to lay down our lives if God so wills.

I see men who defeated Ibrahim Lodi's one-hundred-and-twenty-thousand-strong army, ten times the size of our own.[22]

I see men who are descended from Genghis Khan himself.

I see men who are destined to make a last stand.

The Battle of Khanwa alone stands between us and history. We are at the final gambit of this game of chess.

I am no more, and no less, a man than you. It has been seven months since news reached me of the birth of my son, the first

---

22 The reason for this defeat was that Hindustan had never, until then, seen or heard the guns that Babur's army had acquired from the firangis. The sound of gunfire frightened the elephants of Ibrahim Lodi's army into running amok. The ensuing stampede caused chaos in the ranks, and allowed Babur's army an advantage, which they pressed to win the battle and establish Mughal rule in the region.

child of my beloved Mahim Begum. They named him Farooq, and I couldn't wait to go back and see him. But even before these feet could wash off the blood of the soil they had conquered, news reached me that Farooq has preceded us to heaven. My son ascended to the skies before I could so much as see his face.

A basket of fruits from Kabul brought me to tears. Do I not yearn for the raisins and watermelon of Fergana, the apples of Samarkand, the pomegranates that I may never taste again?

Why then do we stand here, not ready to return?

Why do I refuse to return to the throne of Kabul, the throne I ruled for one year short of a score?

Why do I look into your eyes, and read the plea in them, and yet submit another plea to you?

I ask you to cross the Sindhu river with me not for lust of land or money, for no amount of land or money could make up for the brothers we have lost, the vagaries of weather we have braved, the headless corpses we have left in our wake as we cut our way through all that stood between us and Hindustan.

I ask you to cross into Hindustan with me, or die trying, for it is God's will. My lords and comrades in arms. There lies a journey of only some months between us and the land of our birth. If our army is defeated — God save us from that day! — where would we have died? Where is our place of birth? Where is the city we love? Where are the relatives who would beat their breasts in mourning? Where is the dust that would embrace our lifeless bodies, the soil that would absorb her sons into herself? If we die today, we die among strangers and foreigners. We will not be buried by loving hands, we will not be missed by grieving family.

But I exhort you now, to remember that God alone is eternal and unshakeable, that every mortal soul that enters the world is subject to destruction. He who commences the banquet of life must at length drain the cup of death.

Better it is to die in glory than live with a name disgraced.

It is God's will that we will not return to the soil of our birth, but that we will forge a destiny in this land. We will birth our sons in this land. We will rule for centuries over this land.

Allah has ordained for us this beautiful fortune, where if we die, we go as martyrs and if we live, we have won the Holy Cause, we are victors and conquerors, the soldiers chosen by God himself for His great purpose on earth.

You carry arms now, but you carry the greatest ammunition in your hearts – your fearlessness, your courage, your loyalty, your faith.

I ask you now, let us all swear in the name of Allah, that we shall never flee from a death so divine, that for so long as our souls are not separated from our bodies, our bodies shall not be separated from the field of battle!

'And it was as one that the ten thousand men of his army cried out:

We swear upon the Holy Quran, we swear upon the chastity of our wives and lives of our offspring, that we shall not spare ourselves in sacrifice and devotion for as long as breath and life are in our bodies!

'Their war cry split the skies.

'It was those few minutes that would forge the next few centuries of Hindustan's history.

'And that, Honourable Katib, is the difference between a plunderer and a conqueror – a conqueror is a true leader of men.

'And yet, this is not how my great-great-great-grandfather saw himself, Honourable Katib.

'Even though he was a conqueror and the founder of a great empire, Giti Sitani Firdaus Makani Padishah Babur thought of himself as a qalandar. He could never attach himself to any place and spent all his life as a wanderer. He thought longingly that surely this musafir must come to rest somewhere. Surely there would be a home for him in some part of the world?

'For Fergana, where he was born, did not offer him the comfort of home. He felt its people were avaricious. Kabul didn't appeal to him for he felt the Afghan people were not trustworthy. And for all he said to his men, he couldn't believe for long that Hindustan could be home either. The people were too worldly, too obsessed with material things.

'There was no sophistication or respect, he felt, in their language. Neither the tongue they spoke nor their body language had the tehzeeb he held so dear. He wrote that their sentences sounded like threats, their guttural tongue like stones rolling their way down mountains. He ached to speak his native Chagatai, which to him was the most musical in the world. There was no beauty or subtlety or poetry or melody or culture or potency in anything in Hindustan, he said. The artisans had no laya in their craft. The animals were so scrawny that there was little point in eating their meat. The raisins were sour, the tamarind sweet. There was no infrastructure, he wrote. No schools. No hammams. No candles even. All the country had was gold, mountains upon mountains of it.

'The day he made the speech was the day he conjured the Mughal empire into being.

'But it took him three years to go see his family again. And he did not visit Kabul then either. He spoke of himself as a wanderer. He said it never bothered him because all the tears he had to shed for home, he had shed on one particular day. It was when he had taken ill while fighting to hold on to Samarkand. News had reached his birthplace, Andijan, that he was on his deathbed, and the fort of Andijan fell. The padishah was not, of course, on his deathbed. He recovered, heard of the surrender at Andijan, and set out to regain control. Halfway there, he learnt that the fort of Samarkand had fallen. With a truncated army, he had no hope of regaining Andijan. He said in Chagatai, 'Ghafil az in ja randa, as aan ja manda.' *Leave in ignorance, and lose your place.* It was the moment he realized he had been completely severed from his people and his land. He cried his heart out, and he had no tears left for anything else. No land could be his, no people could be his any more.

'Yet, I believe his heart was in Kabul. The blazing heat and torrential rains of Hindustan made him resent its climate all year round. He could never recreate the beauty of his gardens from Kabul in this country. Everywhere he looked, he saw only dust. He disliked the landscape, the plains that made him yearn for the hills and valleys of Kabul. He only reached Kabul in death. As he lay dying, he decreed that he should be buried there.'

CHAPTER 5

'He Who Is Fit to Rule'

A while passed before the writer met the spirit again. He had been moved by Babur's speech. Little of it was to be found in the *Baburnama*. Had it been passed down from father to son, through all those generations, down to Aurangzeb? He wrote down the words and reread them several times. They never failed to move him.

At the next seance, the spirit was contemplative.

~

AURANGZEB SAID:

Honourable Katib, we were discussing the bloodthirstiness of the Mughals. You know what happens when one spares one's enemies? Giti Sitani Firdaus Makani decided that Ibrahim Lodi was not an enemy, but an obstacle in his path. He had removed the obstacle but felt obliged to protect Lodi's family. He gave them rooms in the palace. He told Lodi's mother that he had no quarrel with anyone but her son. He had buried the man with full

---

honours himself, and now sought to replace him not simply as king but also as her son.

'You are my mother,' he said to her.

Do you know what he got for his trouble? Poison. Ibrahim Lodi's mother Dilawar Begum arranged for the emperor's food to be poisoned. It was Allah who saved him. That day, the emperor had no appetite and ate but a morsel of meat. That alone made him violently sick. He survived but suffered the after-effects of that attempted assassination all his life. He was a warrior who could carry a pehelwan on either shoulder and run up a hill, a man who could swim across oceans. But he became a shadow of his former self and eventually died at the relatively young age of forty-seven.

So, you see, if you don't kill your enemy, you will die at his – or her – hands.

For all this, he did not order Dilawar Begum killed. It is not our custom to execute women. He had her sent to Kabul, which he rightly should have after the war. Terrified that she would die a nasty death there, the woman jumped into the Sindhu river on the way and that was the last anyone saw of her. If only Giti Sitani Firdaus Makani had not exercised such compassion a few months earlier, he would have retained his strength and lived a much longer life.

The Peacock Throne was the sole seat in a game of musical chairs. That is why fratricide was so rampant in our dynasty. There was no space for love and affection when such a prize was on offer. There have been times when fathers have killed sons and sons have killed fathers.

All said and done, I wasn't that bad an egg, you see. Of my five sons, I sent four to rule distant lands. Azam Shah was something of a favourite because he had taken after me in courage.

I made him crown prince. Mu'azzam – whom you might know as Bahadur Shah I – was ten years older than Azam, and aspired to the throne even when I was alive. He hatched various conspiracies, each of which I unravelled and derailed. He was sent to prison each time. His constant treason ought rightly to have seen him sentenced to death. But I was a fond father. I use *fond* in the sense King Lear does. I was foolish. I hoped he might be *rehabilitated*, as you say these days, but it was not to be. He had his ambitions, but not the efficiency to see them fulfilled. When Shivaji raided Aurangabad... – you see, Honourable Katib, I have done as you requested...

~

The writer owes his readers an explanation.

Once, Aurangzeb told the writer firmly that he would have to drop the '-ji' while referring to Chhatrapati Shivaji, since that indicated respect, and he felt no need to show respect for his worst enemy. The writer tried to persuade the spirit that the '-ji' in 'Shivaji' was part of his name and not a suffix that indicated respect. But the emperor was adamant.

At this point, the writer first brought his hands together in a plea, and then – deciding this was no time to skimp on ceremony – fell at the Aghori's feet. He felt a sudden kinship with the sycophant who had once crawled under a table to seek his party leader's slippers.

'Shahenshah, I beg of you,' the writer said. 'I have been writing for forty years, and this is the first time the English translation of a novel of mine is being brought out by a mainstream publishing house. So far, it has been small, independent presses who could barely convince bookstores to stock their output.

'I had a horrible experience just a few months ago. Baahubilli and I were given an award for a translation sample, and the prize was publication in the US. We were so excited that we scripted the future of the novel – it would win the National Book Award, and then would be published in the UK, and win the Booker, and then I would get a Nobel Prize. But the day before we were to be announced as winners, the jury asked for another chapter, and then said they had changed their minds because they were afraid of the perceived potential for controversy and legal action.

'Baahubilli and I told them we would remove everything they thought was problematic, but then they told us they didn't have the time and resources to enter an editorial process. Then, Baahubilli turned Bhadrakali and fumed on Twitter, and they finally wrote an explanation on their website and then sent us a legal threat asking us not to speak about the withdrawal of the award any more. I asked Baahubilli what she thought, and she said, "It looks like it's been written by artificial intelligence software, but then there are grammatical errors, so probably not."

'"I mean, what do you think of the legal threat?" I asked.

'"Oh, that's rubbish," Baahubilli said. "The only thing that's clear from this is that no publisher has a sense of humour, and lawyers never did. Also, we'll most likely never win a prize again."

'You see, the same people sit on every jury, so Baahubilli and I will be blacklisted for awards. But there is a chance our work might be published. These publishers – HarperCollins India – have been kind enough to give us feedback and flag sentences that could cause controversy. I have now started censoring everything I say even at home – to the detriment of my marriage, because my wife says she isn't able to handle my sudden tameness. She has begun to suspect that I am being unfaithful. You see, censorship has put my personal life in jeopardy. But, censorship is the only thing that can come to the rescue of my professional life. So, please, I beg of you, don't call this Maratha icon by any name that would seem disrespectful, or I will be doomed forever.'

Aurangzeb was silent for some time, as if reflecting on what the writer had said.

Finally, he sighed and said, 'I'm not used to being told what to do. But I feel sorry for you. So I shall accommodate this request.'

The writer looked up at the Aghori's eyes, grateful both for the emperor's benevolence and for the years of practising bhujangasana that had allowed him to make such a long speech in that position.

~

NOW, AURANGZEB'S SPIRIT SAID:

When Shivaji raided Aurangabad – you see, Honourable Katib, I have done as you requested – Mu'azzam was helpless. I had to send my commander Raja Jaisingh to quell the attack. I could never trust Mu'azzam, not till the end. I all but banished him, sent him to rule the far corners of the empire. And, at the instigation of the Rajputs, he tried to start a rebellion against me. Eventually, his mother Nawab Bai had to be sent to fetch him to the Red Fort. This happened in 1670. I went on to rule for another 37 years. I kept him close, as one must with enemies.

I must talk about my youngest boy, Akbar. Muhammad Akbar. He was the son of my beloved wife Dilras Banu. He was her fifth and last child, born in 1657. She died from complications of childbirth within a month of his being born. It was a loss like no other. She was barely thirty-five. I had done all I could to ensure she didn't go the way of my mother, Mumtaz Mahal. In the twenty years of our conjugal life, she only had five children. And yet I couldn't save her. When she died, the love in my life died too. No one could fill the void she left behind. I had a monument erected in her memory in Aurangabad, Bibi ka Maqbara. It is quite identical to the Taj Mahal, but of course no one knows of it. Emotions such as love and fealty are the domain of the hero. Romance doesn't become the villain, does it?

I knew no love after, not until Udaipuri Mahal ... do you realize, Honourable Katib, my grandfather had over five thousand wives and my father around three hundred. I had but three. Udaipuri Mahal was a slave girl, not a wife. She was from the region you now call Georgia. I saw her when she was fifteen and I, fifty. She lived forty years with me and loved me so much she said she would commit sati as the Rajputs did were I to die before her. She didn't do that, but she went within four months of my death. Well ... I have got rather carried away with all this talk of love and loss. I was telling you of my last son with Dilras Banu.

The death of his mother had driven our older boy Azam near insane. It was our eldest daughter Zeb-un-Nissa who took charge and restored balance in our lives. She was the mother Muhammad Akbar never had. She was nineteen at the time, old enough to be a mother herself. It strikes me, Honourable Katib, that the life of a Mughal prince is in the hands of his brothers, while the life of a Mughal princess is in the hands of fate.

I said earlier that I was a fond father, but never did I err as I did in the case of my Akbar. I, who had been so critical of my father's weakness for Dara Shikoh, was helpless to control my own weakness for the motherless infant. Not only did I allow my daughter to spoil him senseless, but I joined her in this tomfoolery.

In fact, I doted on him so much I considered bequeathing the Peacock Throne to him, although he was the youngest. But he hardly gave me the chance to make the announcement, not even to him, let alone to the world. He began to conspire with my enemies from pretty much the moment he learnt to speak. He was in cahoots with the Rajputs and the Marathas for years. The Maratha king Sambhaji Bhosale, Shivaji's son, you know, dispatched him to Persia in 1686, and he stayed there until 1706. I don't see why he preferred this over waiting his turn for the throne, no conspiracies or compromises called for, do you?

I heard he used to pray every single day of those twenty years in Persia that I should die, so he would have the throne. I began to think of him as Akbar-i-abtar... ('Abtaar, you said, Shahenshah?' the writer asked.)

No, it is a short second syllable. Abtar. A for Apple, B for Bombay, T for Tamil Nadu, A for Apple, R for Red. It means dissolute, worthless. This was the apple of my eye. And he wanted me dead. He thought he was moving the pieces on the board. He forgot that it was another hand that was rolling the dice. His piece fell long before mine did.

You can't blame him for his impatience. I was eighty-five years old. He was two score years behind me, forty-five. You'd want to sit on a throne long before that, I should imagine. And yet, I challenged him: 'Let's see who goes first, you or I,' I said.

I outlived him by a year, Honourable Katib. How did I know he would go first? I knew I was in the right and he was in the wrong, and Allah is by the side of those who are in the right. Muslims believe there are two malaikas – angels – seated on our shoulders, one on each. They keep count of our good deeds and bad. You know the adage 'As you sow, so shall you reap'. The

malaikas' books will be checked on the Day of Judgement. Why
do you look troubled, Honourable Katib?

(The writer cleared his throat, wondered whether he should
speak, and then realized the spirit could read minds anyway. He
might as well say it. 'All this talk of fathers and sons made me
think of your letters, and how you spoke with so much reverence
and affection about your father. Yet, you imprisoned him towards
the end of his life, and…')

I'm afraid you've used the wrong word, Honourable Katib.
It wasn't 'imprisonment' in the sense you use the word now. He
wasn't thrown into some decrepit dungeon. I suppose you might
describe it as 'house arrest', except he lived in a fort and therefore
it was 'fort arrest', all rather luxurious if you ask me. He continued
to live as an emperor within the fort. His beloved Taj Mahal was
right before his eyes. He could stare at it from several angles, all
day long.

The emperor rather lucked out with me. If Dara Shikoh
had succeeded instead, he would have had our father poisoned.
When the emperor lived with Dara Shikoh, our sister Jahanara
Begum would personally examine every meal that was sent to his
chambers. It was quite the joke within the palace. What an abject
state for an emperor! He was the ruler of all the world he knew,
and yet he couldn't eat a morsel in peace. What was on the plate?
Was it nutrition that would sustain his health, or poison that
would snuff out his life? In all, I think the house arrest, or fort
arrest, ought to have come as a relief.

Your historians write that the Mughal empire would have
disintegrated had any of my brothers mounted the throne. Dara
did not have the circumspection, wisdom, cunning or wiles that
a ruler needs. He was simply arrogant. He could not address

anyone with respect, for his erudition had enlarged his ego. Even his closest friends would be subjected to derision and insult. He surrounded himself with firangis, whom he must have believed were superior in some manner to our race. Christianity would have ruled from the Peacock Throne alongside him. It is not I who say this, but Niccolao Manucci. Although, of course, he says it wistfully.

Our brother Shah Shuja was more intelligent and braver than Dara. But he was an alcoholic. And a womanizer. You could sum up his life in three words – booze, breasts, bacchanalia. You couldn't trust an empire to a man who was buried in those. You could say he was a second Caligula where sexual perversity was concerned. Let me give you an example. He took a shine to the wife of a prominent trader and had her brought to the zenana. The trader rushed to the court and begged for her return. There could be no greater humiliation for a Rajput than his wife being taken to the home of another man. The trader even offered up his daughter in her stead. Shah Shuja agreed to this. When the trader surrendered his daughter, though, Shah Shuja did not keep up his end of the bargain. Mother and daughter were both locked in the zenana. With the help of the other Rajput women in the zenana, who understood what this would do to the honour of the trader, the two immolated themselves. When the news came, the trader rushed to the court and began to scream uncontrollably. Shah Shuja, in a fit of irritation, marched up to him and beheaded him with one stroke, right in the middle of court. If this was his behaviour even before ascension to the throne, can you imagine what such a psychopath would have done with the powers bestowed upon an emperor?

Murad Bakhsh was a braveheart if ever there was one. But I'm afraid he was a living example of the proverb 'Fools rush in where angels fear to tread'. He was quite as lecherous as Shah Shuja too. Our father was so concerned by all he heard of Murad's lasciviousness and high-handedness that he sent his diwan, Ali Naqi, to Ahmedabad to keep an eye on him.

It was the ineptitude of my brothers that forced me, a man built for simplicity and prayer, on to the Peacock Throne. It was my duty as a prince. I wrote to my father to say it is he who is fit to rule who lives and dies for his people, it is he who is fit to rule whose suzerain obligations subsume sensual temptation, it is he who is fit to rule who leads the vanguard, sword in hand, and I pointed out to him that he himself has not fulfilled any of these criteria but for the last.

When you speak of fathers and sons, Honourable Katib, I would urge you to consider Prince Noor-ud-din Muhammad Salim, better known to you by his honorific Jahangir, a name that inspires many among you to bestow it upon your children. In the year 1602, three full years before his father's death, the prince established a court in Allahabad and had the mint produce coins with his face engraved on them. He believed Abu'l-Fazl, who wrote the *Akbarnama* and was a dear friend and adviser to the emperor, was an obstacle to his being named successor. When Abu'l-Fazl was rushing to the capital in response to the emperor's summons, with only a skeletal crew of bodyguards stitched together in his hurry, Prince Salim planned to have him killed on the way. Assigned to this task was Veer Singh Deo, the Bundela Rajput chief who ruled the kingdom of Orchha. He did the deed when Abu'l-Fazl was in his territory and sent his head to Prince Salim. When Prince Salim became Emperor Jahangir, he appointed Abu'l-Fazl's son Shaikh Afzal Khan the governor of Bihar. For his pains, Veer Singh Deo was given enormous powers, and quite naturally, he abused the influence he had in the region.

His son Jhujhar Singh succeeded him but was not a patch on the astute warrior, admirable administrator and unscrupulous human being his father had been.

In 1634, I was assigned to cut him and his son Vikramjit down to size for having tried to assert their independence from my father's domain. My success saw me appointed to positions of responsibility. My years from the age of eighteen to twenty-four were relatively peaceful. I married a couple of times and had a few children, among them Zeb-un-Nissa, a poet born of a man who had no ear or patience for rhyme or rhythm.

Yet, Dara's burning jealousy of me – the seeds for which might have been sown on the day I forced an elephant in musth to beat a retreat – would not let me relish a single moment of my life. He connived and plotted and complained and whined until I wrote to our father in 1944 to say I was resigning my post and recusing myself from all royal duties. I could no longer take the ignominy of being taken to task by my father on hearsay from Dara. The final straw was his doing away, without informing me or explaining why, with my monthly allowance and royal prerogatives.

Do you know why? Dara had had an extravagant palace constructed by the banks of the Yamuna in Agra. He invited his father and brothers to stay. Having shown us around the palace, he led us to a subterranean hall, evidently to show us how cool it remained in spite of the summer heat. I couldn't help noticing that there was a single point of entry, which also served as the sole exit. The royal bodyguard was present in full force. I had a strong sense of foreboding, and so I excused myself from that part of the tour and remained outside with my weapons at the ready. The emperor saw this as a public insult to Dara.

My resignation must have come as a relief to him.

I couldn't care less. I had the ground beneath me and the skies over me. I could feed the mouths I had to feed from stitching prayer caps and selling the Qurans I calligraphed. They could take away my allowance and my perquisites, remove my authority and my prerogatives, but what could they do about my taqwa and my iman, my namaz and my ihsan?

I would have gone on as persona non grata for the rest of my life, but then fate intervened.

The Surah al-Hadid says, in verse 22:

Maa asaaba min museebatin fil ardi wa laa fee
anfusikum illaa fee kitaabim min qabli an
nabra ahaa innaa zaalika 'alal laahi yaseer

It means that no calamity or blessing strikes the earth or us human beings that is not preordained, written in the book. The book is the Lawh al-Mahfouz, the Preserved Tablet on which is etched all that has happened and all that will happen in this world.

On 10 November 1644, my father's beloved daughter, my oldest sister Jahanara, all but lost her life in a fire. It was barely a week after Diwali. You are surprised we celebrated Diwali at the Mughal royal palace, Honourable Katib, but remember that most of its occupants were Rajputs. Of the four-thousand-odd women in the palace, barely five hundred were Muslim. Most of the army was Rajput too. Jahanara was watching her favourite dancer perform one evening. It may have been the oil and camphor lamps, or it may have been a stray firework, but the dancer's clothes caught a spark and she was engulfed in flames. My sister instinctively ran to douse the fire, only for the flames to jump on to her. The dancer lost her life, and Jahanara would have too if she hadn't been pulled away in the nick of time and treated by the royal physician, who was a firangi. When she had recovered enough to be able to meet her father, the overwhelmed emperor asked her to name anything in the world that she desired and it would be hers. She asked that I be reinstated in the royal order. In two months, I had been appointed subedar of Gujarat. In 1652, I was dispatched to the Deccan to serve as subedar.

I often wonder how I might have lived if the epiphany I had in my dying days had come to me earlier – I realized on my deathbed that I had sinned a great deal in my ninety years on earth. The wars, the intrigues, the decapitations and the ransacking ... I couldn't undo any of it, could I? A pure soul was sent to earth and went back to the higher world burdened by sin.

Would I have done it differently if I could have done it all over again? I always had the welfare of the people in mind. But it occurred to me late in life that people preferred freedom to welfare. My ban on music and dance in 1668 was not the result of my personal dislike for these excesses, but because I felt the royal treasury would be better placed to alleviate the poverty of the people if we stopped pouring gold on dancers and musicians. It was a similar story with houses of pleasure. When I went to the Jama Masjid in the mornings, I would see the road littered with drunks sprawled like so many pigs. I was tempted to take a whip to them all. I suppose I did take a metaphorical whip to them...

There was retribution, of course. When I was climbing the steps of the mosque, I saw an object flying at me and ducked just in time. It was a heavy brick. If I hadn't evaded it, my story would have ended right there. Another day, someone aimed a wooden stick fashioned into a rough spear at me. Bricks and sticks in my time, AK-47s in yours. I didn't punish these fools. It is Allah who gives life and ordains death, as the second verse of the Surah al-Hadid says.

You are thinking of the beheading of Tegh Bahadur, aren't you? The story is more complex than you know, Honourable Katib. You only think of religion, not the politics of the time which was so very different from yours. You must look at the dynamics of my relationship with the Sikhs in the context of the alliances that were formed during the war against Dara Shikoh.

But let me finish what I was saying. My subjects did not see that I was bolstering the treasury by depriving them of the debauchery. The palace was crawling with astrologers armed with palm leaves. I sent all but one away. I banned the buying of jewellery in the palace. You should have seen the women and the hijras – why, even the men – on festive occasions. You couldn't see their faces for all the gold glittering on them. And there was an asinine custom, where every year on the date of the emperor's birth, he would be given his weight in gold by those who came to see him. I put a stop to that too. Do you see, Honourable Katib, where corruption begins? At the royal court. In the corridors of power. I was no menial, to be tipped every time I met someone. All I wanted was that the people pay their taxes. That would take care of the treasury.

Speaking of which, that is the other grand accusation. Kafirs complained then, and continue to complain now, that I imposed the jizya on Hindus. That is only half the story. I imposed jizya on Hindus and zakat on Muslims. Do you know how much the zakat is? Two and a half per cent of one's surplus wealth in a lunar year. I challenge any of your mathematical scholars to contradict me when I say that the jizya worked out to far less.

(The writer couldn't let that pass without saying, 'You must forgive my asking, Shahenshah, but it was you who imposed a fee of six and a half rupees for devotees who wanted to take a dip in the Triveni Sangam. That was a bit on the high side back in the day, wouldn't you say?' The writer was used to Aurangzeb's sophistry, and was fairly sure his interlocutor would rationalize and justify the fee. So imagine his surprise when Aurangzeb sighed and said what he did.)

A grave error, Honourable Katib, a most regrettable one. I should never have done that. But my treasury was empty. I ought to have thought of something else, something less polarizing. I was the reason the khazana was empty, wasn't I? I was the instigator of most of the wars of my time. Tell me, Honourable Katib, in the legendary Mahabharata war between good and evil, even the side that was fighting for justice and fairness had to resort to unfair means, didn't it?

My time has been documented most accurately by Bernier and Manucci. Bernier was all praise for me, whereas there wasn't much love lost between me and Manucci. Yet, he could fault me little; I would say his writings do truly contain the soul of Alamgir's Hindustan. Manucci was a brilliant physician, you know. Back in our time, piles was a fatal disease. He found a cure, using nothing but mallow leaves. His acumen made him influential with several qazis and wazirs and umaras. I had offered him the post of royal physician, but he always found a way to politely decline. He never said it outright, but I do think it was because I was compelled to send his previous employer to meet our maker. Manucci was a cunning politician, largely because he could read people so accurately. It was he who said Hindustanis valued money over all else, their lives included. He learnt this the hard way. A nobleman had lost his mind and nothing would cure him. Manucci took him in and gave him the psychiatric aid he needed. When the nobleman was well enough to return home, he sent as the physician's fee a horse that had seen its best days … well, had seen all its days, truth be told. Manucci told the messenger who brought the horse that his master ought to return, for it was evident his mind was still ailing. When I heard of this, I had the nobleman sent to the mental asylum. For all that Manucci and I had no great fondness for each other, there was much respect on either side. I always admired him for being a straight arrow.

That was a rare quality in my day, you know, confined to stories and song. The man who would give up his life for a friend. The man who never broke a promise. Manucci was that sort of man. When he was serving the royal family of Lahore, he fell in love with one of the women of the household. The only way they could be together was to flee to Europe through Surat. Her private allowance would allow her to buy a ship. Yet, he refused. He could not betray the family that had given him his sustenance, he said. He returned from Lahore without his love.

No one was exempt from the avarice and wiliness of the time, not Hindus, not Muslims, and certainly not the firangis. They were the worst of the lot, the firangis. Manucci was simply the exception that proves the rule. At a time when firangi physicians were happy to poison their patients for money – from relatives who stood to inherit, of course – Manucci alone stood tall. My son – the man who would be Shah Alam – once made this demand of him. Of course, you couldn't turn down a royal and stay on in the capital. Manucci all but fled to Madras. He served us well there too, for it was he who allowed us to negotiate with the governors Gyfford and Pitt and thus avoid a war which would have further depleted the treasury. And instead of Bahadur Shah Zafar, it would have been I who was best remembered for being the last Mughal.

Truth be told, I learnt more about my subjects from Manucci than I did from my spies. Which spy would dare tell me I was ruling an empire of thieves? Manucci did. He said he'd had no recourse to a single night's uninterrupted sleep in my empire because his reputation as a successful doctor had ensured that, no matter which city he moved to, a line of thieves was waiting to raid his house. He hadn't passed a night without an encounter with a thief, he said, not until he moved to Madras. I always wondered what you Madrasis were like. I never got the chance to meet any of you, let alone rule over you.

Manucci was quite the storyteller. It appeared he'd had an adventure every day. He would recount them to me in great detail, stories that you could craft entire novels out of, Honourable Katib. Once, he said, as he was returning from the market, he saw preparations under way for a woman's sati. It turned out that the woman had poisoned her husband so she could marry her lover, a musician. The husband did her the courtesy of dying, but her scheming must have put the fear of God in the musician, who now refused to marry her. Seeing no way out of her predicament, the woman decided to commit sati. As the pyre was being lit, the entire town gathered for the spectacle. Children were sitting on trees, some hanging from its branches like monkeys. The woman emerged, dressed as a bride as was the custom, wearing all her jewellery. Evidently, these satis would hand over their jewellery to those they loved most. The musician ensured he was right up front, where she couldn't miss him. She walked around the fire, approached him, and removed the heaviest gold chain from around her neck to tie around his. He bent his head, she fastened the chain, embraced him and then plunged into the fire with him. Manucci swore that, even when the two had been reduced to blackened corpses, the woman's arms held their deathly grip around her lover's neck.

Manucci told me you couldn't pass an entire morning on a journey without coming across at least two satis. Once, near Surat, he had seen a crowd of Brahmins trying to force a screaming woman into a pyre. She saw Manucci and shouted to him to save her. Happily for her, he had with him an Armenian friend. Both of them unsheathed their swords, and the sight of two flashing swords was all it took for the Brahmins to turn tail. The Armenian took the woman to wife. The Brahmins petitioned me and called it an interference in their customs and the laws of their religion, for which the firangi ought to be punished. Do you know what I did? I brought in a universal law banning sati. I knew it was political suicide, but the welfare of my subjects was far more important to me than popularity among them. But sadly, my decree did not stop sati. I was to learn that laws cannot force a change of heart.

Well, Honourable Katib, if spies kept the truth from us emperors, sycophants kept the truth from history. For you people to know what the reality of the Mughal empire was, you must read the firangis, not the *Humayunnama* or the *Akbarnama* which would have you believe my forebears had recreated heaven on earth.

Manucci told the court of an incident that left me shaken. On one of his journeys, he passed an upturned bullock cart. Its passengers were sprawled across the road, their limbs and heads and torsos all torn apart from each other. There were a couple of survivors, one of whom had lost an arm and was waving the other one desperately for help. What was most incredible was this – everyone was naked. Not only had the dacoits who'd waylaid them killed them and stolen their goods, they had stolen their clothes too. Hindustan was plagued by famine and disease and war; to top it all off, if you survived those three ills, you could be stripped and killed by highway robbers. You know, Honourable Katib, for all that I tell you the people's welfare was my greatest priority, even I wasn't able to contain war expenses.

The wars. It was the wars that haunted me, Honourable Katib, through my last days. Not just the expenses, but my acts in themselves. Back when I committed what I would later come to realize were sins, I rationalized them. I told myself that the one way to retain power was to retain the respect of the public, and that would not happen unless they feared me. And I put the fear of God and the emperor in them.

I do believe I was right, for within two centuries of my rule, the Mughal empire had reduced to nothing.

Our doom began with Shah Shuja, who set off to Agra from his seat in Bengal on the pretext that he had had news that our father had been killed by Dara Shikoh. The emperor sent him a missive, stating that he was well and that Shah Shuja was to return to Bengal. But Shah Shuja wrote back: 'I believe this letter has been forged. I will not believe the emperor is well until I have kissed his feet with my own lips.'

I had to make a play too. I wrote to my brother Murad Bakhsh, as great a fool as he was a braveheart, and said:

I have no desire for a seat on the Peacock Throne. You know as well as I do that all I ever wanted was to live the life of a fakir. I write to you for this reason – not only is our brother Dara Shikoh entirely unqualified for this coveted seat, he has also turned into a kafir. To allow him to mount the throne is to condemn all Muslims to hellfire. Shah Shuja is no better. They're peas in a pod. Among the sons of our father, you alone are worthy of the throne. I have always been fond of you and will always support you. All I seek is a promise from you that I will have place enough and peace enough to perform namaz five times a day. I will earn my daily bread, and do not ask that of you. In return, I shall be your ally in good times and bad. I would like to see you on the throne not simply from love of you, but fear that if one of our brothers were to succeed our father, the people of Hindustan would become the slaves of firangis. I send as a token of my support a sum of rupees one lakh for your forthcoming expenses. I would like you to leave for Surat at once to secure the fort there, for it has most of our treasures.

Murad Bakhsh took me at my word. How could such an innocent have become an emperor? The firangis would have had him for breakfast. He made a jubilant announcement of my support to his claim. He joined forces with me at Samugarh, and it was in fact his fierce cavalry charge that was instrumental in decimating Dara's army.

On 7 July 1658, I invited him to my tent to celebrate our victory and plan his coronation. When he came in, I noticed he was in a sweat.

'My dear brother,' I said, 'you look like you are still fighting a war.' I went up to him, took a muslin cloth and gently wiped his face myself. He was moved nearly to tears, the fool. I smiled at him and said, 'Let us have some wine now.'

'What, *us*?' he asked. 'Since when have you begun drinking wine, Biradar Joon?'

'Since you've given me reason to celebrate, my cherished brother,' I said. 'You've always known of the enmity between Dara and me. Shah Shuja has proven himself a fool. I have no intention to rule. It warms my heart that I have one brother to whom I can trust the empire of our ancestors. All I ask from you is a house for myself, where I can spend my days in prayer, where I can earn my living from the sale of handwritten Qurans and handmade prayer caps. The hand will be mine.'

I clapped for the servants to bring us wine – wine from Shiraz and Kabul, wine that Murad had not been able to source in Gujarat. I had also arranged for four beauties from Kashmir to serve the wine. Their scanty clothing left little to the imagination. Murad was intoxicated even before the wine was poured. Watching him look at them, I wondered whether he would pounce on them right in my presence.

The women poured out the wine into two goblets.

I raised mine and said, 'To my future padishah.'

Murad raised his goblet, too, and drank it all in one gulp. I clapped my hands, and his goblet was refilled. As he swallowed the Shirazi and Kabuli wine in turns, he didn't notice that I was emptying my goblet into the ground and not my throat. I kept up a steady chatter about his impending coronation.

'Biradar Joon, I will never forget this day,' he slurred.

'I intend for you to never forget this day,' I said.

'You know what my stupid khwajasara Shah Abbas said? That Aurangzeb – you, Biradar Joon – would never write to me in sincerity. That all this was a ploy to get rid of the one remaining heir to the throne. I told him his brain was as impotent as his body.' And the fool laughed long and loud at his own quip. 'Some of my courtiers had even stupider advice for me – they said, if

Aurangzeb was so keen to see me on the throne, why join forces with him ahead of the coronation? Why not ascend to the throne, and then send Aurangzeb as general of my army to dispose of the other two?'

I thought to myself that even his sycophants were sharper than he.

In some time, as my brother lay among his own vomit and saliva, his head lolling, I called my guards and had him arrested.

Once I'd had the souse removed from the tent and attar sprayed to rid the place of the smell of wine and vomit, I absorbed his armies into mine, and had one of his aides alone killed – his khwajasara.

Murad had no knowledge of what had happened until he woke in the Gwalior prison. He would spend the last three years of his life there until he was tried in 1661 for having killed my father's diwan, Ali Naqi, who had – on the orders of the emperor – dared question Murad's excesses. Murad was sentenced to death, and was beheaded on 14 December 1661, at the age of thirty-seven.

(At this point, Aurangzeb sighed.)

I ... I hesitate to tell you this, Honourable Katib, but my brother was not quite as much a fool as I make it out – it was not simply wishful thinking and gullibility that drove Murad Bakhsh. I considered keeping this from you, a secret I have kept all these centuries after all ... but then, this is my last appearance, my last speech, and I ought not to tell lies by omission or commission. And so I tell you this. I wrote in my letter: 'I swear on the Holy Quran, dearer to me than life itself, that I will never betray you.'

Those words haunt me to this day. They haunted me towards the end of my life in flesh and blood, too. I would see figures moving in my chambers. I would call out to ask who they were, but I couldn't speak. I would want to get up and question them, but I couldn't move. I couldn't call for my guards. I knew they were the ghosts of my sins, the lies, the wiles, the treachery. I told myself all was fair in love and war.

I think I was cut from the same cloth as the Krishna you kafirs worship, Honourable Katib. Don't look so shocked. You're the king of transgressive fiction in Tamil, are you not?

(At this, the writer said, 'There is enough controversy in what you say about yourself and the world, Shahenshah, without all this talk of me. If I were to write that you called me "the king of transgressive fiction", my fellow Tamil writers would never let me hear the end of it. Can we just modify it to "representative of transgressive fiction"?)

I leave the editing of it to you and your translator. But I would appreciate your refraining from interruption while I tell my story.

(At this, the writer considered apologizing, but then wondered whether that might be construed as an interruption and contented himself with a silent apology. The spirit had the ability to read his mind, after all.)

It might be a trifle unseemly for me to speak of myself thus, but only the firangis could divine just how cunning I was, and how manipulative. No one else has either understood or acknowledged my political acumen, although they did slander me.

I believe 'Shesha' in the language of the Hindus means 'he who remains'. The one who is left standing, I suppose, when all else is gone. You say Balarama, the brother of Krishna, was an avatar of Shesha, was he not? He stayed away from the war. But Krishna invested himself in it. He didn't have to. I think he simply enjoyed the mind games he could play. Why, he was the reason Balarama left on a pilgrimage rather than fight for the Kauravas, wasn't he? Balarama couldn't bear to fight against his beloved nephew Abhimanyu. Yet, it was Krishna who saw that their sister Subhadra eloped with Arjuna after she had been promised to Duryodhana. Why did Krishna ask Duryodhana for five villages for the Pandavas' share, knowing he would refuse? So that history would record that he had attempted to stop the war. He bluffed Duryodhana, who was too big a fool to call his bluff. Why did he tell Karna that he was Kunti's son, instead of telling Yudhishthira, who would then have crowned his older brother king, and evaded war with Duryodhana, who would never have grudged his closest friend the title of king? Because Krishna revelled in war. Perhaps I did too, Honourable Katib.

('Shahenshah,' the writer said, 'while I dare not comment on your theory about your resemblance to Krishna in the current political climate of the world, I daresay your story was written a century before you were born. Have you read *The Prince* by Machiavelli? You are quite the model of *The Prince*.)

I'll put that on my to-read list, Honourable Katib. I daresay it won't be a flattering resemblance, though. (The writer decided it would be prudent to avoid responding to that last sentence and said, instead, 'Shahenshah, you spoke earlier of the Mahabharata war. They attribute a quote to Josef Stalin. He is reported to have said, "If one man dies, it is a tragedy; if a million people die, it is a statistic."')

A misquote, I'm afraid. Those were fictitious words spoken by a fictitious diplomat in an essay by Kurt Tucholsky. But given your tragic history with German, perhaps we will not discuss that in any more detail now. You were, I'm sure, going to make a nuanced point.

('In that legendary war,' the writer said, 'it is believed 1,06,00,20,600 people died. A hundred and six crore and twenty thousand six hundred. Or one billion, sixty million and twenty thousand six hundred. Given that the population of the entire world could not have been quite so much at the time, let us make allowance for exaggeration and assume the count ran much lower. But surely, it must have been hundreds of thousands of deaths? It appears there were just as many during the Mughal rule, Shahenshah. All historical accounts speak of rivers of blood. Of blood turning the soil into marshland. Of there being no space for one to keep a foot on solid ground unsoiled by blood. Of dismembered bodies. Shahenshah, you're up to date with current affairs. I assume you've heard of Adolf Hitler's concentration camps?')

I've heard first-person accounts you never could have, inhabiting as I do the land of spirits. I can tell you stories you could not have seen in films about the Holocaust, stories you could not have heard from survivors.

('I'm haunted by the images I have seen,' said the writer. 'Of the shoes of children. Of golden teeth prised out from the mouths of the inmates. All this for what? Land? Principle? Power? It seems to me that all wars are pyrrhic. There is no winner. And yet, we fight, over and over again. History repeats itself through war.')

I came to see it that way during my last days, Honourable Katib. My last years, I should say. The final four years of my life were spent sleeplessly, thinking of the corpses I had left in my wake. I think often of a story from the Mahabharata. Everyone knows of it. The tale opens with the union of King Shantanu and the river Ganga, conveniently personified into a woman so they might marry. She has a single condition for the marriage – that he not question any of her acts. And what does she do? Give birth to child after child, only to throw the infant in the waters and send the babe to its death. The king keeps his peace – and his promise – seven times.

But the eighth time, he is not able to rein himself in. He stops her and demands to know why she has been killing their offspring. He knows she will leave him, but his need for the answer overwhelms his need for her. She tells him the story he has forgotten. 'My king,' she says, 'we were both celestial beings. I had once visited Brahmaloka, where the devas were assembled. To test their willpower, the god of wind, Vayu, directed a breeze so that the cloth covering my chest fluttered. All the devas turned their faces away, except one who could not stop staring at my chest – the god of water, Varuna. You, in another birth. Lord Brahma, in his fury, cursed us both. We would take mortal lives – the celestial who offended the modesty of a woman, and the woman who could not protect her own modesty. We were to be married in our time on this earth, and so we have been. I was making my way down to the earth, steeped in regret and sorrow, when the eight Vasus stopped me. They had been cursed too, thanks to one of them – Prabhasa – trying to satisfy his wife. The said wife had demanded – quite unreasonably – a beautiful cow she had spotted in the forest. With a little help from his friends, our man stole the cow for her. Of course, rather unhappily for them, it turned out that the cow belonged to the sage Vasishtha, who promptly cursed them with mortality. When they pleaded their case, the sage gave seven of them a way out – if they could find a woman who would consent to be their mother and release them from their mortal bodies at birth, they could make their way back to the celestial abode right away. The eighth, Prabhasa, would have to live out his life. I saw an opportunity to help them out and make some recompense. I thought I might be able to free Prabhasa too, but here he is, the eighth Vasu, the one I leave behind with you.'

For having been a 'joru ka ghulam' in his celestial life, he would be a celibate in his mortal one. He was to become Bhishma, of course. You know why this story moves me? It tells us that death is not unwelcome. It is a relief, a release from this terrible life. Perhaps I was only doing as Ganga did, Honourable Katib, alleviating souls from their curses? A carpet of blood, yes, but a red carpet still, leading them to eternal life?

Right, I see you want me to stop philosophizing and get back to my story.

I was going to tell you the story of Mir Jumla and my relationship with him. Mir Jumla had done rather well for himself in the Deccan and worked his way into the good books of the Sultan of Golconda. However, perhaps from greed or perhaps from a sense of justice, he felt entitled to all the goods he captured in running campaigns of conquest for Golconda, chiefly because he owned the ships and armies used in the battles. He was a diamond merchant, you see. He owned half the diamond mines in the Deccan, and it was said he counted his diamonds by the sack, not by the carat. His private army included foreign mercenaries, so you can conjecture just how rich he was.

Between rivals at court and the insecurity of the Deccan Sultans, Mir Jumla soon found himself in a sticky position. His family was all but under house arrest. Unless he obeyed the Sultan's every demand, they and he would be in grave danger. I saw an opportunity to make Golconda mine and started a secret correspondence with him. I was not yet emperor, of course. Our father was on the throne. I would need his cooperation to win Mir

Jumla over, but the emperor was at the mercy of Dara and was pretty much a puppet.

At the time our ties began, I was thirty-nine years old and Mir Jumla sixty-six. From respect for his seniority in age, I called him 'Babaji'. I was subedar of the Deccan at the time, living in Daulatabad. Babaji was a courtier at Golconda. The Sultan Abdullah Qutb Shah did not quite trust him. I heard from a spy that the Sultan might have been particularly suspicious of Babaji because he apparently had an illicit relationship with the Sultan's mother. Of course, this could not be verified. It might have simply been the Sultan's insecurity that one of his courtiers was richer than he.

The long and short of it is this: Babaji suggested I come to Golconda as a messenger from the emperor. They could not raise an army against me if I came waving a white flag. Babaji would supply me with an army and fifty thousand rupees to do battle. I could ambush the royal family of Golconda. It was all going to plan when the Sultan got to know of our correspondence. He fled his palace for the Golconda Fort. I captured the palace. I must tell you, Honourable Katib – it was the practice of our times for the army that captured a palace to send the women either to the harem or the zenana. They would either be in our service, or the service of our women. I did not do this. I would raid the palaces for the money alone and give the women back to their king. So, I had the women sent safely to the Golconda Fort before I laid siege on the fort itself. The siege lasted two months. The emperor would not let me extend it any longer. Dara was in panic, you see. He knew I would have proven myself the successor of our father, beyond doubt, if I were allowed to capture Golconda. I had to return. But before that, I made a peace accord with the Sultan – his daughter was married off to my son Muhammad Sultan, and he gave it to me in writing that Muhammad would be his heir.

My first collaboration with Mir Jumla, then, was a success.

As it happened, my son aspired not to the Golconda Fort but the Peacock Throne itself. He went so far as to conspire with Shah Shuja. When I got wind of it, I had little choice but to imprison Muhammad Sultan. The boy who would have sat on the throne of Golconda and eventually mine ended up dividing the remaining seventeen years of his life between the Salimgarh prison and the Gwalior prison.

The outcome of my foray into Golconda was my lifelong friendship with Mir Jumla. He came to Delhi with his armies. His family came along and was housed in Dara Shikoh's palace. It was a tricky situation, where Babaji could not afford to antagonize Dara or the emperor. His bond with me was strong. I needed his armies for my impending play for the Peacock Throne. But I could not let Dara suspect we had an understanding. I suppose you might say I did as Machiavelli's prince might have done. I told Babaji we would have to stage a drama – I would imprison him and seize his army. That would make Dara see him as a prospective ally. His family and he would be safe.

It was a tricky time. The emperor's health was failing, and his four sons were strengthening their armies and sharpening their knives in four different corners of the empire – Dara in Delhi and Agra, Murad Bakhsh in Gujarat, Shah Shuja in Bengal and I in the Deccan. Our father lived in constant terror of his food being poisoned by Dara. He wrote as much in a letter to me, which was unfortunately intercepted by Dara. I believe he took great offence and told our father, 'How could you have not only suspected me of plotting to poison you, but also gone so far as to tell that traitor Aurangzeb of your paranoia? I would give my life for you. I desisted from going to the land of the Pashtuns so I could be here for you, and this is the faith you have in me, dear Father? I read your words and am filled with such distress and rage that I wonder whether I should not really do as you would have me do.'

The emperor was too afraid to eat his meals for two days after this threat. From the third day on, he would have Begum Sahiba taste the meal first, wait out an hour to ensure she was all right, and only then eat himself. My sister then began to personally supervise the preparation of their meals.

CHAPTER 6

How to Humanize
History's Villains

At the next seance, the writer sensed the Aghori scrutinizing him.

'You seem troubled today, Honourable Katib,' Aurangzeb said. 'You seem unable to meet my eyes.'

'There has been a problem since we last spoke,' said the writer. 'My friend Savitri worries that what I said about Krishna's wiliness might upset the powers that be and create a controversy that might lead me to join the list of writers who must live in fear for their lives. She says after years of being considered a pornographic writer, I have finally found a place among litterateurs. And creating such a controversy, while elongating my stint in the canon, may shorten my stint on earth. I believe I should edit out the portion where I have compared a Hindu god's avatar to you. It can only offend. And it will offend everyone.'

'I suppose we did have a fair bit in common, this Krishna and I. We worked for the greater good of the greater number ... why does that line sound familiar?'

'It is the principle of utilitarianism, Shahenshah. Have you interacted with Jeremy Bentham in the spirit world?'

'I can't say the name sounds familiar. Was he a controversial figure too?'

'Not really, Shahenshah. But in the interest of humanizing you, perhaps we can speak of your family in some detail? Perhaps you can speak of those among your offspring you didn't imprison, for instance.'

'Ah, Honourable Katib, you would like me to speak of Zeb-un-Nissa. She was beloved of all in the empire. Quite the opposite of me where that was concerned. And where everything else was concerned. She was a poet, you know. She devoted herself entirely to words, and refused to marry so she could spend all her time lost in reading and writing. What a girl she was. She was all of seven years old when she became a hafiza, having learnt the Quran by heart. We celebrated this achievement over two days. Three thousand mohurs[23] were distributed among the poorest of the poor. The entire army was given a feast in the maidan across the Red Fort.

'I raised my daughter as a scholar. She had lessons in Arabic and mathematics and astronomy, in addition to Farsi. She wrote poetry in Arabic and Farsi from when she was a mere child. I suppose people will say that the apple fell rather far from the tree.'

'Not true, Shahenshah. You might have let go of the court's poets, but I don't think it means you despised poetry. Your letters are poetry in prose, according to the Farsi scholars I have consulted for my research for this novel. Even in English translation, your style reminds me of that of Saadi Shirazi, particularly his *Bustan*.

---

23 A gold coin valued at approximately fifteen rupees at the time.

And some of the stories in *Gulistan* come to mind too. You will remember Nausherwan-i-Adil tells his son as he is about to die, "The people are the roots, and the king the tree that draws its strength from those roots." I am reminded of scattered quotes from your letters – "The bond between earth and sky has been broken; the rain has been forgotten by the sky, and the tears of those on earth fail to ascend to the skies," you write. "He must fear poison who has no antidote," you write. "Fear the sighs of the downtrodden, for those will be heard loudest and with most sympathy in the kingdom of God," you write. And then there are times when you could have fooled me into thinking your words were written by Tiruvalluvar, that master of aphorism. "Corruption is not merely the collection of wealth," you write, "but the portrayal of truth as falsehood and lies as fact." In a letter, you say, "I treasure the words of Saadi Shirazi, who says the man who feeds a single one of the poor and needy is more beloved of God than the seer who seeks God in an empty desert." You might not acknowledge it, but I do believe poetry was in the blood of the Mughals, and couldn't escape your veins either. There are times when your letters bring the *Baburnama* to mind.'

'You flatter me, Honourable Katib. But those letters were written in my old age, as I crossed eighty-seven and eighty-eight and eighty-nine, and thought of how the story of my life had been written in blood. I was keen that my heirs do not make the same mistakes I did, and I wrote them desperate letters filled with advice that they – to their detriment and that of the people over whom they ruled – did not heed. Those apples did not fall far from the tree. They wanted the Peacock Throne, as I did.'

'This talk of Zeb-un-Nissa being a hafiza brings a question to mind, Shahenshah. Why did you, who quote poets in your letters, ban Hafiz Shamsuddin Muhammad's works?'

'Would you show Sunny Leone's films to schoolchildren, Honourable Katib? I can see you pale. I'm not saying Hafiz was quite the same as Sunny Leone, but his words were not meant to be read by schoolchildren. I only banned him from being taught in schools, not from being read in the empire. And from my palaces, whose women I did not want reading them. Surely you see my point, Honourable Katib, you who have written at length about how terrible it is that there are reality shows in which children sing item numbers and that their parents are praised and congratulated by the judges, with no thought of how cringe-inducing it is for children to be singing those vulgar lines? I thought in my last days that my censorship should not have been so severe, but then I would think that the idle mind is the devil's workshop, and I was right not to fill those with poetry they could misinterpret.

'A prime example of that adage is my sister Jahanara Begum, born to my parents four years before me. Honourable Katib, you will notice that all the characters of your novel, who once peopled my life, contain within them thousands of pages worth of stories and tears and enigmas and secrets, particularly the women.

'I have not spoken until now of why I imprisoned my father. Most believe it was to dethrone him. I thought it was best to let that opinion prevail. I will tell you the truth now. I could have kept him under house arrest in the Delhi palace as Dara did, and made him a puppet whose strings I pulled as Dara did. I could have evaded the epithet of "the man who imprisoned his father" which has remained my most enduring label over three centuries. But the reason I imprisoned him in Agra was that the emperor had weakened the moral axis of society. You can repair any flaw

in the rest of the machine, but when the fulcrum is gone, there
is no point.'

~

With that, Aurangzeb closed his eyes and remained still, his left
leg over his right. The writer and Rizwan looked at each other.
Then, the spirit opened his eyes, reached for the pot of water kept
at hand, dipped the kulhad into it and gulped down some water.
In the silence of the room, we could hear the water gush down his
throat. Finally, Aurangzeb opened his eyes and began his story,
avoiding the writer's glance.

~

AND THE SPIRIT SAID:

It was because of the illicit relations between the emperor and
Jahanara that I did as I did. In the year 1631, when my mother
ascended to jannat at the age of thirty-eight, my sister was
seventeen. My mother had lived exactly half her life with my
father. In those nineteen years, she birthed fourteen children –
eight boys and six girls. Of them, seven were either stillborn or
died within weeks or days or hours of birth. My mother had spent
the majority of her marital life in pregnancy. When she left this
earth, Jahanara became the padishah begum.

My father went mad with the grief of losing his beloved wife.
He too had spent half his life with her; he was only a year older
than my mother. His hair and beard grew unkempt. He could
not eat and could not sleep. Jahanara looked after him like a child

through this time. She resembled our mother strongly, and in his half-crazed state, my father began to see her as Mumtaz. My father outlived his wife by thirty-five years. He spent nineteen years with my mother, and thirty-five with my sister. She never married. Their relationship was an open secret. To speak of the emperor and his daughter engaging in ... what they were ... it would be treason.

Why did I feel compelled to do something about that which was known and not spoken of? Because people had begun to talk and joke. Some of the courtiers and mullahs were debating the issue. 'What is wrong with the man who planted the tree eating its fruit?' someone said. I could not let this become the norm. It would be the undoing of the societal moral compass.

If I were truly cruel, I would have separated the two in the emperor's last years. When I had him put away in Agra, he was sixty-six and my sister forty-four.

I had made several efforts to get her away from him. I tried to find a groom for her. My father rejected every proposal I brought.

She was not without her favourites, either. And he found a way to ... you see, Honourable Katib, my sister's beauty – only paralleled by our mother's – and her influence upon the emperor had won her plenty of enemies. Once, the women got to know that she had fallen in love with a man and saw to it that the whispers reached my father. He walked into my sister's chamber one day. It was not the done thing for the emperor to visit her without notice. Rightfully, she ought to have been summoned to his presence. But lust and jealousy and possessiveness have a way of turning the most regal mind sick. And so, he went with a small entourage to my sister's quarters. His spies had given him precise information – the man was in her chamber. The moment he heard the emperor's approach, he jumped into a vat. Luckily for him, it was empty of water.

The emperor entered the chamber and spoke to my sister at length about the daily mundanities of court.

Suddenly, he said, 'Your hands appear to be dirty. Shouldn't you have a bath?' He then called to the two khwajasaras who had accompanied him and ordered, 'Boil some water in that vat for the begum's bath.'

The vat in which the princess's lover was hiding was filled with water, and the firewood lit. The emperor remained seated, speaking to my sister of the court, and did not leave until the khwajasaras had nodded to indicate that the man was dead.

There was another man, a Persian noble called Nasar Khan, highly educated and highly accomplished. His intelligence attracted Jahanara Begum, and before long, the palace was rife with rumours. The emperor did not trouble himself or his entourage with boiling vats. He invited Nasar Khan to his chambers and offered him paan. The betel leaves were coated with poison. Nasar Khan partook of the paan without guessing why the emperor was in such a good mood. When Nasar Khan mounted his palanquin to leave the palace, he felt dizzy. He might have guessed then why the emperor had smiled. But before he could articulate his suspicions, he was dead.

These were two instances of which I heard. I wonder how many prospective suitors had been summarily sent to meet their maker without word getting out.

My sister did not seem overly troubled by this. You might wonder if the relationship between father and daughter was indeed consensual. There is little chance it wasn't. The women in the palace always had a right to say no – by killing themselves. My sister lived. And when I sent our father to Agra, she informed me that she would be leaving with him.

I believe they will get their just deserts on the Day of Judgement.

This man, who is believed to have created the grandest symbol of love by building that 'World Wonder', the Taj Mahal, had in fact taken his own daughter for a wife ... not for a year or two, but for thirty-five years. And yet, he is considered a romantic, far softer and kinder than this fakir who was crowned king.

You wonder what this has to do with Zeb-un-Nissa. Honourable Katib. I wish I didn't have to say the words, even to deny the charge. But the people believed I had taken after my father in that respect ... that my daughter and I ... I cannot complete the sentence. I could have had the rumour-mongers beheaded. But how many heads would it take to quell the whispers? If only I'd had my father indicted in public, and hanged him in the marketplace with his head perched on a stake as a warning, perhaps they would not have spoken of me in this manner. But I didn't want the Mughal empire founded by Giti Sitani Firdaus Makani to descend to such ugliness. I succeeded in one respect – neither I, who is innocent of the charge, nor my father, who is guilty, was spoken of as 'the man who took his daughter for his wife'. I would settle for the epithet of 'the man who jailed his father'.

(A long silence followed. The writer filled a tumbler with the nannari sherbet he had brought along, and offered it to Alamgir. Aurangzeb touched his right hand to his heart by way of thanking the writer, and then signalled that Rizwan and he partake of the sherbet too. The room was silent but for the sound of three men sipping from their glasses. And then, Alamgir resumed his speech.)

Perhaps the blame lay not only with the precedent, but also the fact that Zeb-un-Nissa was a poet, and that I gave her all the freedom a poet must have. If only she had been a man, she would have attained the fame of Hafiz. She was a fiercely independent woman, so much so that she insisted on a face to face and a tête-à-tête before she agreed to marriage with a suitor. She met a hundred and fifty-six suitors between the ages of seventeen and thirty, about one a month, and rejected them all.

Her beauty and brilliance won renown throughout the world. Men from far and wide came to try their luck, only to join the list of rejects. After each one, I would ask her the reason for her refusal. It was an interesting exchange. You might think I am a cold father. But I have never felt anxious over her spinsterhood. I have always been detached from the world and all it contains, even my own children. I enjoyed the intellectual exchange with Zeb-un-Nissa.

Once, a Persian prince, handsome as they come and a poet to boot, wrote her a letter. They say subtlety is the soul of poetry, but our man wrote quite explicitly – rather like you, Honourable Katib. Oh, please don't take offence … I was joking.

('It is not umbrage, but terror that distorts my face, Shahenshah,' the writer said. 'The world is such that one fears for one's life every time a hint of controversiality is spoken of. Do forgive my lack of humour.')

This world of yours does seem to treat litterateurs rather more shabbily than I did, Honourable Katib. Anyway, our Persian prince wrote something along the lines of 'I cannot wait to taste your lips'. As your Puratchiththalaivar has demonstrated, a man should make a show of not being interested in a woman in order to intrigue her. It was his heroines who chased him down as he went about saving the world, wasn't it? If only the prince had known this trick.

For all that Zeb-un-Nissa was a poet and a Sufi, for all that she held that men and women were equal and even sneaked out of the women's quarters to train with weapons – why, she even fought on the battlefield … she was also a believer. As devout as me, perhaps. She never removed her niqab. She had a poet friend, Nasir Ali, with whom she would indulge in repartee in verse. He once wrote, 'O Chandravadani, won't you let the clouds part and reveal your beautiful face to me?' She wrote back:

> *If I were to part those clouds,*
> *the koel may forget to sing,*
> *the Brahmins who worship Lakshmi*
> *may forget their gods and pray at my altar.*
> *But you may conjure up my face*
> *in your poetic imagination.*
> *For like the fragrance of a rose,*
> *like the soul of a body,*
> *like the waters in a cloud,*
> *like the cold in the moonrays,*
> *like the compassion in a saint,*
> *my beauty hides in my niqab.*

Remember, her takhallus was 'Makhfi' – she who is hidden. And to such a woman, our Persian prince proposes a kiss. Need I tell you the outcome of that proposal?

There was another prince, to whom she posed the question: 'I am the daughter of Alamgir, the richest man in the world. If you were to marry me, you would have a mountain of wealth at your disposal. What would you do with it?'

'I would become a diamond merchant like Mir Jumla,' the prince said, perhaps hoping his admiration of her father's friend would impress her.

The poet baulked at the idea of living with a merchant.

Do you know, Honourable Katib, I gave her an allowance of four lakh rupees a year. She spent it on two things – aiding the poor and stocking her library. She sent more people on the Hajj pilgrimage than anyone else in history could have. And her library was the grandest and most admired in the world. It made no sense to me, of course, to build a library. But I had no care for money or for what people did with it. The point I was making is – could a woman like this marry a merchant?

Another suitor was asked: 'What is rarest in this world?'

He said: 'Your father's Kohinoor diamond.'

He was sent on his way. When I asked her what answer would have satisfied her, she said: 'Simplicity. He could have said "Your father's simplicity".'

She asked another: 'What do you plan to do once we're married?'

He said: 'I will give you as many children as I can.'

She told me there was little point in aspiring to something so very pedestrian. 'One must innovate,' she said. 'What pride could I possibly take in doing what so many queens have already done?'

And then there was the final suitor. He was asked the same question.

He said: 'I will follow the path your father has forged. After his time, there is bound to be a war of succession. We must nip it in the bud. I dream of seeing you on the throne, ruling as Razia Sultana once did.'

'And how will you nip this war in the bud?'

'With poison.'

He was the son of a subedar. He had found the temerity to come to the capital and apprise my daughter of his plans to poison me. Need I tell you what happened once he was back home?

Now, a poet must fall in love every now and again, must she not? Zeb-un-Nissa was no exception. In 1662, I moved my capital to Lahore because I was unwell. The subedar of Lahore was Aqeel Khan, a heroic warrior and the image of male beauty. As I have already said, Zeb-un-Nissa carried my blood in her veins. She knew no fear and was not shy of the battlefield. She would have outshone Razia Sultana had she mounted the throne. She admired Aqeel Khan's exploits in war. And in love. For he met her in the garden, in the guise of a gardener. My spies reported the exchange.

'I have muddied myself just to set eyes upon you,' he said. 'Look at the form I have assumed. I am of this earth.'

'You could be of the air, and I still wouldn't allow you to caress a strand of my hair,' she quipped back.

It was the start of a romance. She seemed to have met her match. I invited Aqeel Khan to Delhi. But the fool decided I was going to behead him for his besottedness and wrote me a letter, swearing, 'I have no designs on your daughter, Shahenshah.' To top it all off, he resigned his post of subedar too.

Perhaps it was Zeb-un-Nissa's fate to remain single all her life. Perhaps if she had been of a less illustrious house, the daughter of a courtier or qazi rather than of an emperor, it would all have been different. Perhaps if she had been possessed of a less brilliant brain, it would all have been different.

She was engaged to be married to my brother Dara Shikoh's son Suleiman. She was even dearer to Dara than she was to me. He had a weakness for poets, after all. They say I killed Suleiman so they wouldn't be married. What calumny! We were at war. Did it make any sense to dispose of Dara and leave his heir alive?

It is compassion that kills the brave. Take the rebels of your time. Che Guevara, the poster boy for both rebellion and style. Why was he killed? Because he didn't practise what he preached in his *La Guerra de Guerrillas* – he says everyone a guerrilla encounters on his way must be killed. Everyone is a potential mole. A man or woman could be the greatest revolutionary on earth, but connect electrodes to his or her genitals, and the mouth will relay all that the brain remembers. Farmer or factory worker, he must be killed before he can sing. He must be killed so other farmers and factory workers can live better, for they will live better only if the revolution lives. Long before he wrote those words, I knew them to be true. In order for one to live, one's obstacles – one's potential obstacles – must die.

If Che Guevara hadn't spared the farmers and workers he encountered, he might have lived a far longer life. Dara Shikoh wouldn't have disposed of his son Suleiman in my stead, and would have been killed by Suleiman for his softness.

(At this point, the writer interrupted to ask, 'Shahenshah, I wonder whether you have seen the film *13 Tzameti*? Your recounting of the patricide and fratricide and filicide and sororicide in your family quite reminds me of the game in the film, something like Russian roulette.')

Except Russian roulette is a game of chance, Honourable Katib. Ours was a game of deliberation and strategy.

(The writer took some time to recover from the chilling statement.)

Do you know what the al-Quran, Surah an-Nisa, 4:135, says, Honourable Katib?

'O believers! Stand firm for justice as witnesses for Allah even if it is against yourselves, your parents, or close relatives, against the rich or against the poor, for Allah is more concerned with their well-being than you are. Do not, then, allow your desires to sway you from the path of justice. If you distort your testimony or refuse to give it, then know that Allah is aware of what you do.'

I simply followed this mandate, you see.

On 29 May 1658, Dara lost the Battle of Samugarh, and his son Suleiman fled to Garhwal where he begged for the protection of the king Prithvi Shah. The king granted him protection and refused to give him up. My threats fell on deaf ears. Prithvi Shah would lay down his life before he surrendered Suleiman.

You know, Honourable Katib, I ascended the Peacock Throne not just from my own astuteness, in war and in rule, but due largely to the support of my umaras and the Rajputs. Dara, who had assumed he would be emperor, had treated everyone with arrogance, and his behaviour made him several powerful enemies in the court.

Raja Prithvi Shah was not among my supporters. The rulers of Garhwal had, for long, nursed hatred for us Mughals. When my father was emperor, Mahipati Shah was the ruler of Garhwal. He died young, and his wife Rani Karnavati ruled as regent until their son Prithvi Shah came of age. Sensing an opportunity, my father sent his army on a mission of conquest. The Mughal invaders were

soundly defeated. Rani Karnavati had earned the epithet Nakti
Rani, a corruption of Naak-kaati Rani. She would have the noses
of defeated invaders cut off before she sent them back. She took
no prisoners and ordered no deaths. She simply took noses.

I did not seek all-out war with Garhwal. I sent my general
Raja Jaisingh to speak to Raja Prithvi Shah. But the Raja of
Garhwal only sent me a note: 'The emperor must keep in mind
that the hand that lopped off noses could well have lopped
off heads.'

He left me with little choice. I sent my armies forward. But
I was to realize the reason for his temerity. The Garhwal range of
the Himalayas. My soldiers could not cross them, and the armies
turned back, noses intact and heads bowed.

I could not win the straightforward way. And so, I arranged
for Suleiman to be poisoned in the Garhwal palace. But our mole
was found out and killed, while Suleiman survived. The attempt
terrified Suleiman, however, and he fled for Tibet. This was to be
his undoing. He was intercepted and brought before me in chains.

He was beloved of many in court. There were those who shed
tears upon seeing him in chains. Several pleaded with me to forgive
him. I wondered whether they would have pleaded my cause had
I been the one in chains and Suleiman or Dara on the throne.

I have already told you how Giti Sitani Firdaus Makani
nearly lost his life at the hands of Ibrahim Lodi's mother. Even
though he survived, he was so weakened by the poison that it
altered his life entirely, and indeed shortened his lifespan. When
Suleiman was brought before me in chains, this was the precedent
that came to mind. I spared the daughters of Dara Shikoh and
some of his younger sons. But I could not let Suleiman live if I
intended to live.

When he stood before me, arms and legs bound in chains, though, I thought of the baby he had been, the baby who crawled across the floor before me, the baby who punched the air with his pudgy fists as he lay on my lap, the baby who had grown up to be engaged to my own little girl. I thought to myself that I would rather risk death at his hands than kill him with my own. I would give him his life as my daughter's dowry. And yet, Allah willed otherwise. Suleiman would have lived if he had stayed silent. But he chose to speak.

'If you see me as a threat to your life, kill me. But do not imprison me.'

Those words echoed through the silent court. They struck me as sparks of fire, and my ego became their tinder. I ordered him imprisoned in Gwalior. No house arrest or fort arrest, this. It was a regular dungeon. This was 1662. I would think of him every day, languishing in prison. I couldn't bring myself to kill him. He could stay alive for as long as he was no threat to me. I ordered opium and poison administered in his food every day. He wouldn't lose his life. But he would lose his memory. He would forget even who he was. But for some reason, this concoction didn't work. Finally, I had no choice but to order him executed by strangulation.

Suleiman's death had nothing to do with my daughter and everything to do with empire, you see.

(At this point, the writer had to confront the emperor. He said, 'Shahenshah, you speak so very fondly of your daughter. And yet … yet you had her imprisoned. I read that she was jailed at the age of forty-three and spent the last two decades of her life in her cell. You had such love and admiration for her, and yet…')

I was compelled to do so for what she did. She may not
have conspired against me herself, but she was an accomplice to
her brother Muhammad Akbar. Why, you ask? I told you, she
loved him as her own son. The year of his birth, the year of his
mother's death, the year of my ascension to the throne were all
the same – 1657. I was too busy climbing over corpses to reach
the throne to stop and pick up my motherless baby boy and kiss
him and caress him. Zeb-un-Nissa was all the parent he knew,
then and forever. This blind love for him eventually pushed
her into prison. A mother would know when her son must be
checked; but she was a foster mother, and she simply gave him
all he asked for.

Honourable Katib, I have already told you, prison was not a
dungeon. It was a palace. It was house arrest. She did not have
her annual allowance of four lakh rupees at her disposal any more.
And she was not allowed to leave the fort. But her life went on as
it always had. Why, she continued to write poetry till her death.

And her poetry, how I encouraged it! I knew nothing of
poetry, of course. It was the scholar Chandrabhan Brahman who
spoke of her poetry. Unlike other emperors in my lineage, I did
not surround myself with sycophants. In fact, my closest circle
was one of critics, men who were unafraid to speak to me of
my shortcomings. Of course, I would not brook any debate or
question on religion. But that does not make me a bigot. Why, I
have read both your epics, the Ramayana and the Mahabharata
in the original Sanskrit.

Chandrabhan was as catholic in his tastes as I. He was a Farsi
scholar, as you know. He once told me that my daughter's poetry
was of the highest standard and should be heard throughout the
world. Unlike the other Brahmins in court, he would never flatter.

He would speak the truth as he saw it. What was on his mind spilled on to his tongue. And so, I knew he must be a sincere admirer of Makhfi's poetry.

I read her work. While the structure of the verse and the quality of language was as good as any I had read, I did find a shade of haram in it, perhaps thanks to Dara's influence. There were words and imagery that I couldn't accept. Yet, Chandrabhan defended their use, and I trusted him. Upon his urging, I invited poets from across the world to Delhi. Mushairas would go on every day, from evening to midnight. Chandrabhan and Nasir Ali of Sirhind organized these, and Zeb-un-Nissa revelled in them. I didn't attend them, of course.

There is more I could tell you of her life, things that would contradict what the firangis say. My being dead has made it easy for them to fictionalize my life and my deeds. I must tell you, first of all, that Zeb-un-Nissa did not die in her palatial prison. She was released two years before her death, in 1699. But I must confess that she had lost her joie de vivre. She felt and looked her age. She had lost touch with her friends, her fellow poets. All except Nasir Ali. Perhaps because of him, she continued to write poetry. It was only after her death that I discovered some of the poems she had hidden away. Some of them were quite blasphemous. Take, for instance, this:

> *Why should you, O Makhfi,*
> *complain of friends, or even of enemies?*
> *Fate has frowned upon you*
> *from the beginning of time.*
> *Let no one know the secrets of your love.*
> *On the path of love, O Makhfi, walk alone,*

even if Jesus were to seek to be your companion
tell him you have no desire for his friendship.

She would often compare the mosque and the temple, and even go so far as to say God was present in both, or even too great to be worshipped in either.

I am no Muslim,
but an idolater.
I bow before
the sculpture that is love
and worship her.
I am no Brahmin,
for I tear away
my sacred thread
and wear instead
the strands of her plaited hair
around my neck.

I see that reference to the sacred thread has made you nervous. Are you afraid you'll be taken to court? Let me recite one, then, that will warm the hearts of the men who now rule Hindustan.

In the mosque, I seek my idol
on the Day of Judgement,
we would have had much trouble
in proving we too were believers,
had we not thought to bring along
our beloved Kafir idol as witness.

Do you realize, Honourable Katib, that Zeb-un-Nissa and her poetry only live on because of me? That it was I who had it compiled and published?

Let us speak no more of her imprisonment and those rumours that hurt me. She must be remembered for her poetry, for her grace and goodness, for her kindness to the poor, for her love of her library. That is my Zeb-un-Nissa.

CHAPTER 7

Fathers, Sons &
the Peacock Throne

The seances in which poetry had taken precedence had made it impossible for the writer to ask a question that had been niggling at his mind. At the first opportunity that arose, he gathered his courage, cleared his throat and said, 'Shahenshah, I ask you this in the confidence that we have been speaking like old friends for some time, and that several centuries have passed since you last ordered a beheading. You have spoken often about the harems of your predecessors. Perhaps I ought rightfully to ask Padishah Akbar this question, but you will forgive me for seeking an answer from you. It's just that I am better acquainted with your spirit than with his. My question is: How did they manage to impregnate hundreds, sometimes thousands, of women and sire countless children, when most of them were slave to alcohol and afeem? It is said that those who are experts at hatha yoga can last hours with a woman, but I've heard tell that Emperor Jahangir could barely hold a cup in hand for his nerves were so wrecked that his fingers would constantly tremble. How then, could he…? I mean, in the present time, this is one of the great challenges facing humanity – lowered virility, lowered potency. Pharmacies are better stocked with Viagra than with medication. But back then…'

Aurangzeb laughed. He laughed until tears streamed from his eyes. He laughed until he nearly choked.

The writer was both relieved and bewildered.

And then the spirit said, 'Has your research not led you to a single book where this was discussed, Honourable Katib? Or did it not occur to you that in a court with medicine men so skilled that they could concoct poisons that physicians could not detect, it could not have been hard to concoct a more potent drug for potency than your modern-day Viagra? The emperor Jahangir did not worry about his fingers trembling because he had servants to hold the cup to his lip. But since a servant could not be engaged for similar services in his private chambers, he ensured that the part of his body that most mattered there remained rigid.'

'May I ask how you, who had fewer wives than any other Mughal emperor and little interest in harems, know this, Shahenshah?'

'You have been to Chile, haven't you, Honourable Katib? Yet, for some reason, you have never been to Mexico. But do you not know of its culture? Have you not read its literature? What I mean to say is, one does not have to undergo an experience in order to know that it exists. But this discussion is getting rather frivolous. You said your friend Savitri was concerned that you were considered a writer of pornography. We are venturing rather close now. Perhaps we should move on to her other concern, the one about controversy? For there *are* certain elements of the Mahabharata war I should like to discuss with you.

'It isn't simply Krishna, but everyone else – with the exception of Yudhishthira – who seemed to twist the notion of fairness in that great war. Apparently, that was why Yudhishthira was the only human of the lot allowed into the gates of heaven, accompanied by a dog. When I read of that war, my cruellest deeds appear as nothing before it.

'Could anyone pierce the womb of a pregnant woman to kill the foetus within? No, I'm not referring to the riots of 2002 and Kausar Bano Sheikh. The politics of your present day are but a sequel to the politics of my day. I speak of Uttara.

'They say the Mahabharata war was the fight between good and evil, justice and injustice. But what kind of justice was followed during the war? On the thirteenth day of the war, Abhimanyu was caught in the chakravyuha. He had single-handedly killed more than ten thousand warriors. Not even Drona was able to handle him. And yet he was killed. How?

'The rules of war state that one must not assault an enemy without warning. But Karna did precisely that to Abhimanyu. The rules of war state that one must only take on an opponent who is armed as one is – cavalry to cavalry, infantry to infantry, and so on. The rules of war state that an unarmed man must not be attacked. And yet, six maharathis[24] took him on; six maharathis attacked this one warrior from six different directions. He had no bow, no arrows, no chariot. Drona broke his sword. Karna broke his shield. He used the wheel of his chariot as his shield. The rules of war state that a hero who has fallen to the ground and been shorn of his weapons must be allowed to get replacements before

---

24 In Indian mythology, a warrior with the skill to fight 7,20,000 other warriors simultaneously.

he is attacked by an opponent. And yet, Drumasena, the son of Dushasana, killed Abhimanyu as he lay on the battlefield. The rules of war state that the bodies of felled soldiers must be treated with respect. And yet, Jayadratha kicked the head of Abhimanyu's corpse to check whether he was truly dead.

'And then there is the story of Drona. Drona – who had turned the battlefield into a river of blood, where the headdresses of fallen warriors frothed and bubbled as foam, where corpses floated as logs, chariots as tortoises, decapitated heads as stones on the riverbank, piles of bodies as bunds that dammed the river, spears and lances as water snakes, maces as little fish – was unstoppable. His river of blood ferried warriors by the hundreds, by the thousands, from this earth to the heavens.

'For as long as he had his bow and arrows, the Pandavas stood no chance. Yudhishthira knew this. Krishna, as always, had a way out. The one thing that would make the great warrior, the master of archery, lay down his weapons would be news of his son Ashwatthama's death. And the one person of whom he would believe that his son had been killed was Yudhishthira himself, Yudhishthira who would never tell a lie. And so, Bhima killed an elephant named Ashwatthama and roared, "Ashwatthama is dead!"

'Drona approached Yudhishthira to ask if this was true.

'"Ashwatthama is indeed dead," Yudhishthira said. "Ashwatthama, the elephant." Of these words, he muttered "the elephant" alone under his breath.

'Drona was so stunned that he dropped his bow and collapsed to the ground. Dhrishtadyumna arrived at the spot, and decapitated Drona who was all but a corpse. He then threw the head of this great man at the Kaurava army.

'Ashwatthama saw his father's head fly through the air. His blood boiled. In the dead of the night, he killed the progeny of the Pandavas. The rules of war state that there will be no fighting after sunset. And yet he slipped into the enemy's camp and killed the sleeping sons of the Pandavas. But that didn't satisfy him. There was a baby in the womb of Abhimanyu's wife, Uttara, a baby who carried Pandava blood. And so, he pierced her womb and cut the baby to pieces. Yes, yes, there is yet another story about how Krishna brought this baby back to life. But could there be a deed that is of greater haram than killing a foetus with a sword? All is fair in love and war, they say.

'To you, these are stories. To me, this is life. War is life. History might say my capital was Agra, my capital was Delhi, and so on. But then, I spent nearly all my life on the battlefield. Of those ninety long years, at least fifty were spent entirely in war. It was my court. It was my treasury. The Surah al-Ma'idah of the Holy Quran says that any man who kills but to avenge one soul with another or to prevent great injustice has essentially killed all of mankind, and any man who saves one life has saved all of mankind.

'And yet I, who took the Holy Quran for my lifeblood, killed many on the battlefield. Why did I do so? I was following what Saadi said – that if the shepherd were to sleep, the wolves would steal away the lambs. If I hadn't fought those wars, the empire would have been swallowed by British wolves.

'But I made a grave error. It was foolishness on my part to waste decades on the Marathas. I should have let Golconda and Bijapur be. Their rulers were Muslim too. I should have let them engage the Marathas in war for those decades, and my treasury would have been the healthier for it.

'I see you're wondering why I spoke of the Mahabharata war. You see, Honourable Katib, the point I'm trying to make is that in a country whose gods are not exempt from human folly, why must a human prove himself as flawless as a god in order not to be cast as a villain?

'I know you'll have to censor much of what I say. But even the little you can report would perhaps change the minds of a few people who have learnt a distorted history of my life.

'Honourable Katib, you requested a diversion from talk of war so you could show your readers I was a loving father. And look where we have ended up, discussing the great war of your epics, comparing the deaths of Abhimanyu and Suleiman Shikoh. How can a warrior not talk of war? I beseech you, then, to allow me to continue my narrative, in chronological order.

'We last left my father in the palace of Dara Shikoh, with my sister supervising his meals from fear that he would be poisoned by my brother, his chosen heir.

'Let me take you to 6 September 1657. The emperor had taken ill. He was sixty-five years old at the time. Dara had all the roads to Delhi blocked at once. The emperor had no news from the outside world. Murad Bakhsh, subedar of Gujarat, declared himself king of the region. Shah Shuja did the same in Bengal. When the emperor was given news of this, in spite of Dara's best efforts, he ordered armies sent to my aid, the lone son he trusted to quash the other two. Dara Shikoh realized my father had begun to change his mind regarding the inheritance of the throne. The emperor had realized I alone was fit to rule the Mughal empire after him. Dara couldn't poison my father's body, but he could poison his mind. He had the armies stalled and diverted. His personal army, headed by his son Suleiman, and the emperor's army under Raja Jaisingh were sent to fight Shah Shuja. He instigated my father to arrest those loyal to me in court and have their properties confiscated. My letters asking to meet my father on account of his ill health went unanswered, perhaps undelivered.

'The response I got arrived on 15 April 1658 – not a letter, but an army. My father's army, along with the forces of Murad Bakhsh, arrived with a command to decimate my own forces and arrest me. I made short work of them and they fled.

'On 23 May 1658, as I broke my fast on the first day of Ramzan, my spies informed me that Dara was on his way with his own army. On the sixth day of Ramzan, I led my own army to within a furlong of Dara's advancing force. It was a Friday, and I did not intend to indulge in battle.

'Dara's forces were very close. It was a searingly hot summer, and it seemed the wind itself was on fire. Dara's men, wearing full armour and ready for battle, collapsed that day from waiting in that heat. Some died of sunstroke. Why did Dara not advance on that day and take me on? Fear. He was terrified of me. He was a coward, bereft of a warrior's courage and steadfastness and decisiveness. He was meant for wine and women and evenings of music and delights, not for war and days of battle and deprivation. He waited for me until sunset, and then retreated.

'There was another reason too. Khalilullah Khan, his most trusted adviser, was working for me. I had bribed him and everyone in Dara's immediate circle. Khalilullah Khan used astrology to sway Dara's mind. I've already told you, the Mughals were obsessed with astrology. He said he had seen ominous signs, and Dara should not wage war until the next day. Our father sent a missive from Agra, ordering Dara's return. But my brother, for the first time in his life, disobeyed our father. He believed he could defeat me the next day, when the signs were in his favour.

'What signs? I was orchestrating it all. If only he had attacked that day, my travel-weary men would have succumbed. If only he had listened to the emperor, he would have escaped the terrible fate lying in store. If only he had known better than to trust every flatterer, he would have been less gullible. The gullibility, fostered by his years of comfort in our father's palace, listening to the sycophantic ramblings of courtiers, even as my mind and body were hardened on the battlefield, would be his undoing. He was as a plant that had received too much water; he had wilted from overnourishment.

'On the seventh day of Ramzan, his men opened fire with guns and muskets. My men had been primed for this. But it was as if hell had arrived on earth. Flames blazed through the air. Everywhere you looked, you saw heads without bodies and bodies without heads, limbs lying asunder and men wailing as their insides spilled out of their bodies. Rustam Khan, Rao Raja Chhatrasal, Raja Rai Singh Rathore and all the other generals of Dara's army were killed that day. And then that fool made his biggest mistake. He dismounted from his war elephant and got on a horse.

'This was Khalilullah Khan's doing too. He had gone up to Dara and said, as I had instructed, "The war is over, Your Highness. All that remains is to arrest that traitor and march him to your father. I will come with you, escorted by my cavalry. Let us rush to him on our horses and surround him even as he lies stooped in defeat!"

'And so, Dara got down from the elephant. Those who saw their king switch the elephant for a horse thought he was fleeing for his life. And those who didn't see him were told by Khalilullah Khan's men that he had been killed in war, and the riderless elephant became evidence of it.

'I had once dismounted from my elephant too, in the thick of war. But that was because it was time to pray. When my men saw me step down from my elephant, set aside my arms and kneel to pray, they took courage from the sight. Here was their leader, with no care for his life, trusting in God, confident that the war was won, so confident he had no need for elephant or arms.

'But let us go back to Dara. The soldiers now either believed their leader was dead, or that he was fleeing the battle. And they began to flee too.

'It was all over in three hours. Their morale was gone with the leader's dismounting. And the horses, pampered as they had been in the royal stables, could not handle the heat. Neither could the soldiers.

'I only lost one of my generals that day, Azam Khan, and he died from sunstroke, not war wounds.

'The next day, I led my armies to Samugarh. The emperor was in Agra. I had a letter sent to him, explaining all that had happened and begging his forgiveness for setting out against his armies. He sent a reply at once, along with a sword named Alamgir as his gift to me. What further validation could I have asked for? I set out for Agra at once, and reached Dara's palace on 11 June 1658, the twentieth day of Ramzan.

'But I could not meet my father. Dara had been sending him letters from Delhi, turning him against me. I was denied permission to enter his chambers. I left for Delhi to confront my brother, who promptly fled. I sent Bahadur Khan after him.

'I learnt that Dara had reached Lahore, along with his wife Nadira Banu, daughter Jahanzeb Banu Begum and son Sipihr Shikoh.

'My astrologers had said the twenty-seventh day of Shaban, 1658 – 21 June according to your calendar – would be the most auspicious day for my coronation. We had a simple ceremony. The khutbah could not be read by the qazi of Delhi, the Supreme Censor, for the emperor was still alive, his chosen heir still at large, and Shah Shuja reigning in Bengal. The khutbah was read by the court qazi instead. It was a hasty coronation, with the formalities and festivities kept for later, down to the minting of fresh coins.

'I then had to dispose of the others. I sent Khalilullah Khan's armies to support the forces led by Bahadur Khan. They had to cross the river Sutlej. We received news that Suleiman Shikoh had set off for Haridwar in order to aid his father. On 4 August, we learnt that our forces had crossed the Sutlej and Suleiman had gone into hiding in Kashmir. While we were trying to ferret him out, we learnt that Dara had banded together an army of 20,000 and had them waiting at the banks of the river Beas to counter my commanders Bahadur Khan and Khalilullah Khan. This army was under the command of his son Sipihr Shikoh. Raja Jaisingh had reconciled with me in this time, and I sent another army under his command to aid my commanders. Dara then ran from Lahore to Multan. I sent my vizier Saf-shikan Khan and nine thousand soldiers under the command of Sheikh Mir to confront him. 'And that was when I got news that Shah Shuja had set out from Bengal with an army to battle mine.

'It was under these circumstances that I arrived in Delhi on 20 November 1658.'

'Shahenshah, Dara Shikoh's actions remind me of Mario Vargas Llosa's The Feast of the Goat. Have you read it?'

'I don't believe this Mario Vargas Llosa Sahib has entered the spirit world yet.'

'Oh, yes, that is indeed the case. Well, I'm reminded of what follows the assassination of the dictator Rafael Trujillo and the downfall of his regime in the Dominican Republic. General Rose Román could have taken over control. All he had to do was dispose of Trujillo's family and then announce that elections would be held. He made the same mistake as Dara, and that changed the course of history. Why did he hesitate, I wonder?'

'I can't speak for your general, but I can for my brother. It was fear. Lack of confidence. And his desire to pander to the emperor's advice not to commit fratricide. Every ancestor of mine doled out this advice to his sons, but only one ever practised what he preached, and that was Humayun.'

'But not you, Shahenshah. You told your sons that killing each other in order to win the Peacock Throne would only result in not a single one of the brothers surviving. You wrote that they would lose their hold on the empire. It was an accurate prediction. An empty treasury, corrupt officials, communal hatred ... you had warned them of all these, but your sons wouldn't listen.'

'Sons are never good at listening to advice, Honourable Katib.'

CHAPTER 8

Three Alamgirs

The writer knew it was time to leave when the spirit spoke an aphorism. So, it was at the next seance that Aurangzeb made an announcement.

~

AURANGZEB SAID:

I would divide my royal life into three sections, in accordance with my age, Honourable Katib – forty to fifty, fifty to eighty-five, and eighty-five to ninety. Having read my letters, you know that the last Alamgir repudiated much of what the first two had done.

And now, I will tell you the story of the first Alamgir.

Once I'd captured the Delhi Fort, my worries about Dara ceased. His own generals had washed their hands of his interests. But Shah Shuja's intentions were worrying. Was he headed for Delhi or for Patna? If it was the latter, I had no cause for concern. I sent Prince Muhammad Sultan from Agra towards Bengal. I also sent a detailed letter to Shah Shuja, saying I had no quarrel with him and would be happy for him to rule over Bengal. We could have a truce, and peace.

But when has peace ever been respected in this world? Shah Shuja's armies continued to march on Delhi. Prince Muhammad Sultan was waiting on the outskirts of the village of Khajuha. On 2 January 1659, Prince Mu'azzam Khan joined him and they waited, three-quarters of a kilometre from Shah Shuja's armies. On the fourth of January, I reached the spot. I chose not to send the musketeers at the vanguard, and instead sent forth my 90,000-strong cavalry.

My unconventional decision paid off. We won the battle for the day and returned to camp. That night would prove an unforgettable one.

Raja Jaswant Singh, who had begged my forgiveness, and whom I had enlisted in my army and given charge of the entire right front, assaulted the armies of Muhammad Sultan in their sleep. His Rajput warriors made away with all the goods of that sleeping army. Back in the day, since our return was not guaranteed, we would take most of the treasury to the battlefield to liquidate for our daily expenses.

Worse, they had killed all the warriors from the Mughal armies that they chanced upon. The warriors were asleep, exhausted from the day's exploits. They slipped from dreams to death without a moment of consciousness. My army had been halved, and Muhammad Sultan's routed, overnight. The man had played us.

Yet, I was unfazed. Wars are won and lost not from firepower or skill with weapons – they are won by mental strength and steadfastness. Dara would have fled had he been in my place. When my panicked generals came running to me, I was in the middle of my voluntary tahajjud prayer. You must know from reading accounts of me by firangis that I slept only three hours a night. I dedicated the rest of the night to the tahajjud prayer, and this kept me vital for my waking twenty-one hours. When I rose from that night's tahajjud, I saw Mir Jumla, white-faced, waiting with the news.

In response, I said, 'Let us thank our stars that he fled in the middle of the night and not in full view of the enemy, on the battlefield. You must rest. Go to sleep, and we will take stock in the morning.' I had faith Allah was with us, and we would dig deep and find the strength we needed.

In the morning, I realized I was left with a cavalry of just two thousand. But my men were inspired. Cannonballs flew through the day. War elephants were kept at bay. The cavalry advanced. The day ended with Shah Shuja climbing down from his howdah and fleeing for his life. I set Prince Muhammad Sultan on his heels. It was a long chase. Shah Shuja went to Satgaon, where my wazir gave him shelter, and then to Arakan, where the ruler took him in. The fool that he was, Shah Shuja began to conspire to overthrow the Raja of Arakan and take his place. Learning of this, the king had him and his family killed. And how? By setting the palace in which they'd been accommodated on fire. Can you imagine a more painful death than being burned alive? We have no evidence of this, though, and no knowledge of what happened to the immensely valuable treasures he carried with him. Some say he did not even make it to Arakan and died in Satgaon. Others say he and his family fled to Mecca. Whatever it was, we had seen the last of Shah Shuja when he ran from the battlefield.

Things could have turned out very differently. Raja Jaswant Singh had written a letter to Shah Shuja, apprising him of his plan and saying they could join forces to overthrow me. But my brothers were so used to my writing false letters to trick them that Shah Shuja believed this was another of my tricks. If only he had believed that one, genuine letter, my depleted army would have had to take on his and Raja Jaswant Singh's. I doubt we would have won the day. But Allah was on our side.

You might wonder at my leniency to Raja Jaswant Singh, my repeated forgiveness of him. Any other ruler in my place would have had him impaled and watched him die slowly and painfully over eight days. But how I treated those who betrayed me and those who helped me was part of my strategy. There were times when I had to do away with those who had rendered me great help when most needed. There were other times when I had to spare blackguards like Jaswant Singh. An emperor's ego must always concede to pragmatism. I knew I would need him to defeat Dara, and so I spared him.

With the war of succession at an end, and only the job of ferreting out the runaways left, I could focus on my grand coronation. The date was set for 5 June 1659.

I had everything done as convention dictated. The khutbah was read. I was crowned with pomp and ceremony. All that remained was the minting of coins. I forbade the use of the kalima in the coins, to prevent its being defiled by the touch of non-believers. Instead, a poetic verse in praise of my rule would be imprinted on the obverse side of the coins, and the regnal year and location of the mint on the reverse side. In Persian, it read, 'Sikka zad dar jahan chu badr munir shah Aurangzeb Alamgir.' Meaning, this coin was brought to the world by Emperor Aurangzeb Alamgir, like a full moon.

In the meanwhile, Dara continued to run from capture. With him was his wife, Nadira Banu. He reached Lahore, hoping to band together an army. Raja Swarup Singh, with whom he had sought refuge, gave him a four-thousand-strong cavalry and a ten-thousand-strong infantry. He promised him three hundred thousand foot soldiers and fifteen thousand horsemen. Would anyone believe such a promise? Dara was fool enough to do so. Raja Swarup Singh charged him ten lakh rupees for this service, which he paid.

What I am about to tell you now is a love story. A love not seen in Shakespeare, whom you praise so much. The love of Nadira Banu for her husband. Haven't I told you, it is the story of the women of the Mughal empire you must write? Nadira Banu was among those women, an astute lady. She was suspicious of Raja Swarup Singh. She decided she would find a way to guarantee her husband's safety.

She went to Raja Swarup Singh and said, 'I take you as my son. If I had milk in my breast, I would feed it to you now. But I haven't been with child lately. And so, I give you this water, with which I have washed my breasts. To drink it is to drink my breastmilk. To drink it is to accept me as your mother, and my husband as your father. Do not let my husband down.'

Raja Swarup Singh drank the water. He accepted the payment of ten lakh rupees. And then he came straight to me.

This is not a world for poets, Honourable Katib. Not a world for Daras. What a sacrifice his wife had made! Do you know, their love was true. So true that Dara never married another woman. She was his one and only consort and companion.

Anyway, Dara had to run again. He went to Multan, and then to Sindh. He was hoping to go to Persia, but Nadira Banu feared further betrayal. What if the ruler of Persia took her and her daughter for his slaves? And so, Dara went to Kathiawar instead, where the governor of Gujarat, Shah Nawaz Khan – my father-in-law and Murad Bakhsh's – opened his khazana and gave him an army.

Having mustered together a force, he went to Ajmer, hoping to enlist Raja Jaswant Singh's support. This was a critical juncture. It was why I had spared Jaswant Singh at the time. I would need him to turn the tide. I also needed my wits about me. I knew Dara was a coward. Like all cowards, he was paranoid. While he trusted the flattery of sycophants, he mistrusted the fealty of his supporters. It was easy for me to create a rift between him and his most capable generals. I had a forger write letters in their hand to me and ensured that Dara's spies intercepted them. Khalilullah Khan's betrayal had driven Dara to near lunacy. He didn't know whom he could trust any longer. I now targeted his right-hand man, the most loyal Dawood Khan. I acted thus – I wrote a letter to Dawood Khan, which I intended to have Dara Shikoh intercept. This is what the letter said: 'I received your letter. I am grateful for your support, and approve of your decision. As you suggest, I shall lead an army towards you. Inshallah, we will meet soon. Under such trying circumstances, it is those who are true – like you – that make me take heart. You are true to our faith, and true to me. All those who forsake religion, be it Sipihr Shikoh or anyone else, will be duly punished.'

No one but Dara could have fallen for this. Dawood Khan would have laid down his life for Dara Shikoh. But Dara had no sense of judgement. He had never seen war before. He hadn't seen dismembered bodies that were still alive and screaming. He hadn't seen animal limbs and human limbs strewn so one could not tell them apart. He hadn't seen the soil turn red, saturated with blood. He could judge music and books and poetry. He could not judge people.

This was why he looked for help from a turncoat like Jaswant Singh, and believed him when he promised to send twenty thousand men to bolster the army. I had already got to Jaswant Singh, you see. I had sent a Brahmin, Ravi Rai, to him with a message. If he were to surrender to me at this time instead of joining forces with Dara, I would forgive him. I had also instructed Ravi Rai to speak thus, as if it were his opinion and not mine – 'Why does it matter to you which of the four princes sits on the Peacock Throne? Why must you lose your Rajput warriors in this fight among the Muslims? What if the prince you back were to be defeated? Won't the one who ascends the throne take his revenge on you?'

That was all it took for Raja Jaswant Singh to weigh his options, decide I was the likeliest to ascend the throne, and come crawling to me, begging for forgiveness.

And so it was that Dara Shikoh was cornered by my men at Deorai and had to run for his life yet again.

He went back to Sindh and sought refuge with Malik Jiwan Junaid Khan Barozai, whom he had saved from death twice. Twice, Emperor Shah Jahan had ordered that the man's head be trampled on by elephants for treason, and twice Dara had intervened.

It was fated that the man whom Dara had saved would be the reason Dara was killed. Dara intended to reach Kabul with the treasures he had collected from our father's khazana. If only he reached Kabul, Mahbad Khan would protect him. His son Sipihr Shikoh, his wife Nadira Banu and his daughter told him it was

folly to trust Malik Jiwan. And yet he did not listen. He believed
he knew it all. Nadira saw the end coming and drank poison to kill
herself before a death was chosen for her. Contrary to her last wish
to be buried in Delhi, Dara had her buried in Lahore. It would be
his last act as a free man.

François Bernier claims that it was I who had Dara Shikoh
chained and paraded on an elephant through the town. No, that
is not it at all. It was that thieving scoundrel Malik Jiwan who
did it. He knew my brother did not have enough men to protect
the bundles of gold ornaments his horses carried. He confiscated
the treasures and treated my brother to the honour of an elephant
parade in chains. And he brought him via Lahore to Delhi, still
on that elephant and still in chains.

My advisers were divided on what to do with him. Should he
be brought to the palace in that pitiful state for all to see? What if
there was rebellion, for he was so beloved of the people? Or would
it serve as a lesson, show what would come of taking on Alamgir?
I decided it would instil fear in the people, and I needed them to
be afraid of me. And so he was brought to the palace – chained,
and on an elephant so scrawny it was an insult to its species and
its rider. The people wept but did not rebel.

And I had another dilemma. Should I imprison Dara or kill
him? I chose the latter, and an ignominious manner of death
too. He was decapitated in the chamber in which he was being
held. No glorious public death for him. It was such a poor hack
job that I had to have the head that was brought to me washed
before I could tell for sure that it was Dara. I looked at the head
of that erstwhile poet, the lover of books, and shed tears. I then
ordered the head put in an ornamented box and sent to Agra, to be
presented to the emperor just as he sat down to his evening meal.

Sipihr Shikoh was sent to the prison at Gwalior. I rewarded Junaid Khan Barozai for his service. But he met his just deserts on his way back home. He was accosted by bandits, robbed and killed.

~

At this point, Aurangzeb paused for some time. When he spoke again, it was to say:

'Honourable Katib, Brother Rizwan, I have reflected on memories that cause me much pain. Could you give me some time alone?'

Rizwan and the writer made their way out.

'I don't understand Alamgir,' Rizwan said. 'History's version and his are in conflict, quite like Akira Kurosawa's Rashomon. Bernier equates Aurangzeb's rule to Rama Rajyam, really. Niccolao Manucci writes as if he were the villain of the film *I Saw the Devil*. Aurangzeb calls himself a fakir, and says he wept when he saw his brother's head, but then says he had that same head sent to his father to be opened before the poor man sat down to his evening meal. Which version of Aurangzeb is the real one?'

This reminded the writer of something else – a question he posed to Aurangzeb the moment they returned to the seance.

~

'Shahenshah,' said the writer, 'you have often said it is the Mughal women one should write about. But then you don't do so yourself. You write pages about your father, but not one about your mother. Why is that?'

'Because, Honourable Katib, I did not know her. She died in my eleventh year. It would be accurate to say none of us knew our mothers. We were sent to the battlefield the moment we could hold a sword. "Babes in arms" acquires a whole new meaning where the Mughals were concerned. "Arms" to us meant weapons, not our mothers' caresses. From 1536, when Giti Sitani Firdaus Makani made his seat in Delhi, to 1858, when Bahadur Shah Zafar was banished to Rangoon for treason, through the intervening three hundred and thirty-two years, no Mughal emperor had known the love of a mother. Our mothers were either in the bedchamber, getting impregnated, or on the delivery bed, sending forth prospective heirs.

'Perhaps this is why so many of the Mughals sought the comfort of women's arms and bosoms. They had never known the feminine touch of a mother, not since they had been sentient. And perhaps it was an aching for femininity that made so many of them poets, too. Bahadur Shah Zafar, starved on the streets of Rangoon, yet contrived to write poetry, didn't he?

'I believe you all still make a great fuss over *"Bhari hai dil mein jo hasrat kahoon"*? Even the self-pity of my descendants and ancestors seems to have taken on poetic metre.'

'He is our tragic hero, Shahenshah,' said the writer. 'He was a wonderful poet. Hindi cinema is obsessed with him. The Emperor of Almost Nothing, just Delhi and Palam. And yet, so fascinating. Such tragedy in the life of a ruler so unimportant. The scion of a lineage whose table European visitors would gawk at, descendant of emperors who had precious stones inlaid and embedded in their food plates, died in a Rangoon prison without a morsel of roti to satiate his hunger, without a drop of water to quench his thirst.'

'There was another such, Honourable Katib, long before Bahadur Shah Zafar. At least Zafar died with his eyes intact. The Emperor of Almost Nothing of whom I speak didn't even have those. He sat on the bare floor of the Red Fort like a blind beggar. He had erected four sticks and spread a cloth on those, and believed he was sitting on the Peacock Throne. My story will end with his story. It will make a fitting finale to your book. Let us not distract ourselves now.'

'Let us leave aside all these weaklings and speak of a man I much admire, admire no less than I do Giti Sitani Firdaus Makani Babur, in fact. His name may surprise you – it is Sher Shah Suri, our sworn enemy, the man who drove Arsh Ashyani Humayun from the throne, the man who only ruled for five years but left an indelible mark on the history of the subcontinent.

'We Mughals and the Pashtuns have never seen eye to eye. From the beginning of time, they have wanted to drive us out and rule in our stead. When Sher Shah Suri entered the employ of Emperor Babur, those were his thoughts too. "These Mughals are slave to the three Ms – maidens, moonshine and majoun. How are they fit to rule an empire? They have no courage, no valour, no strength, no sense of cleanliness or constraint, no intention to sacrifice for a greater cause. It is fortune which aids them," he thought. He was right in his reading of the Mughals, of all but Emperor Babur. However, while he did not lack for courage or valour or strength, he was still a lover of the three Ms. If he hadn't been softened by alcohol and narcotics, he would not have spared Ibrahim Lodi's family, and he would have lived and ruled a lot longer.

'Perhaps it was this softening of personality that brought literature and music and dance and painting to the Mughal court. And that is why, to the tiger that was Sher Shah Suri, we appeared as goats begging to be eaten alive. When he was subedar of Bengal, he had been invited to a feast thrown by Padishah Babur. He was served a plate of meat he did not recognize. He wasn't sure how to hold it or eat it. He thought for a moment, reached for the dagger at his belt, tore it to shreds and made small work of it. Padishah Babur, seeing this, had a sense of foreboding. A man whose dagger was always at the ready was dangerous, he thought. He whispered the thought to his wazir Mir Khalifa, and said the man, whoever he was, must be arrested. Mir Khalifa said it would be giving the man too much importance to do so. If only the padishah hadn't listened to him, the fate of Hindustan and indeed of his own son Humayun would have been rather different. But he realized his error too late. Sher Shah Suri had seen the emperor scrutinize him and then speak to the wazir. Guessing what might have been said, he slipped away before the next course was served. It was when he saw the empty seat that Padishah Babur realized he had been right.

'Sher Shah Suri, in the meanwhile, went to his home town Sasaram, where he began to gather an army to invade India and unseat the Mughals. He knew the task was formidable. Do you know what inspired him? A sleepy beggar. Yes, truly. He was out on his rounds of the city at midnight, in disguise. It was his custom to leave gold coins under the bundles of belongings that the city's beggars rested their heads on to sleep. One such beggar woke, saw the coin, and thinking he was dreaming, slurred, "The Sultan of Delhi has paid me a visit." Sher Shah Suri interpreted this as the Word of God, an auspicious sign. Emboldened by a man's possibly drunken, sleep-induced statement, he did become the Sultan of Delhi. He earned the sobriquet Ustad-i-Padishahan, the Teacher of Kings. This was how my ancestor Padishah Humayun referred to him, the very Humayun who was driven from his throne and palace and spent fourteen years in banishment before returning to rule.

'Sher Shah Suri, for all his courage and astuteness, would yet not have come to power if it had not been for the Mughals' weakening by alcohol.

'I tried to change that trend. I once met a man like myself, from your own state – Sasi Perumal – who used to stage protests against the sale of alcohol, right up to his dying day. And it struck me that, centuries later, we remain unpopular, we who counsel against this deadly brew. It killed that poor man, and it killed my image.'

'While it kills, it grounds too, Shahenshah. The average Indian earns a monthly salary of five thousand rupees. Our Superstar gets paid a hundred crore rupees for each film. Two hundred thousand times the average salary. And the fame that comes with it. Forget the Superstar. My own friend, a poet, became a film lyricist. He didn't know how to handle the fame and the success. He turned to drink. He died at the age of thirty-five. The alcohol becomes a hold, something that anchors them to a past life in the hurricane-like sweep of a new one.'

'Hmm, you may have a point, Honourable Katib. In the case of my dynasty, it was practically our legacy. Firdaus Makani writes often of his father Umar Sheikh Mirza's addiction to alcohol. It was considered a celebration, something quite mandatory for a joyous occasion. His father would throw weekly feasts for his friends in which the meal was entirely varieties of alcohol. His father Abu Sayed, Abu Sayed's father Sultan Muhammad, Sultan Muhammad's father Miran Shah, Miran Shah's father Taimur, after whom our Timurid dynasty takes its name … they were all connoisseurs of alcohol. Why, Taimur died of an arrack overdose, didn't he?

'My maternal lineage didn't lag far behind. Genghis Khan may not have been a souse, but his sons Tolui and Ogedei certainly were. If they had spent less time marinating in wine, my ancestors might have flown the Mongolian flag from every port of Europe.

'I believe it was this alcoholism that is to be blamed for the insanity that led to the mass rape of Oirat women – girls, I should say, children aged between seven and ten. Four thousand children who were brought to an open field, stripped in full view of their fathers and brothers and uncles, and then sent off either to Ogedei's harem or to the army caravans along the way.

'Genghis Khan had forbidden his armies from ever capturing women, even when they had routed their enemies. The famous quote attributed to the Father of your Nation, Mahatma Gandhi as you call him, that a country was truly free when a woman could walk alone at night bedecked in jewellery, was actually in evidence when Genghis Khan ruled. And yet his own son was driven to this heinous act by the alcohol that flowed through his veins. It is alcohol and nothing else that can make a man so vile, so low.'

~

After a pause, Aurangzeb asked the writer, 'I'm curious, Honourable Katib. I know the Hindu kings were not monogamous either. They had their own harems, only these were called "antahpur". I wonder about the women. Were they monandrous?'

The writer, who had long been wanting to speak about this, found the opportunity to say, 'Oh, Shahenshah, that is a long and sad story. Once upon a time, there lived a sage called Utathya, the older brother of Brihaspati, the guru of the devas. His wife Mamata was blindingly beautiful. His younger brother Brihaspati lusted after her. When he approached Mamata, she said she couldn't oblige him because she was pregnant from her husband and there was no place in her womb for two. That was her only qualm.

'But Brihaspati was quite like the dog of which Bhartrihari writes in his verse that begins *"Krishah kaanah khanjah…"* – even old, blind, deaf, lame, starved, tailless, plagued by sores and worms festering in those sores, with its neck stuck in a broken bowl, a dog will find new life in its genitalia when it sets its sights upon a bitch in heat. He was not willing to listen to reason. The foetus in Mamata's womb begged him for mercy. "There is no place for another here, uncle," said the unborn child. "Please don't impose upon me." And yet, Brihaspati thrust himself inside Mamata. The foetus kicked desperately, and one of its kicks fell on Brihaspati's penis. Upon this, the devaguru flew into a rage and cursed, "You who interrupted my orgasm, you will only know darkness."

'And so the child was born blind, and named Dirghatamas. His chief role in the history of the world appears to be his curse on womankind, for which we must credit his frustrated wife Pradeshwari who once said, "Of what use is a blind husband? Far from supporting his wife, he depends upon her. I have to support you. I find no pleasure from you." Incensed, Dirghatamas said, "I curse all womankind. May you be stuck with a single husband all your life, even if he were to die before the marriage is consummated. Any woman who goes against this mandate will be considered a whore." And women have been thus cursed since.'

'Oh, really, Honourable Katib? So Hindu women don't marry again even if their husbands die before the marriage is consummated?'

'You're going to get me into trouble with feminists, Shahenshah. All three of us here are men. My translator Baahubilli has already warned me that I'm walking a fine line.

As it is, much of my earlier work has been termed pornographic. I've turned to history now. Once I finish this novel about you, I'm going to start working on two others – about the saint Tyagaraja, and the king Ashoka.'

'The marketing genius, Ashoka.'

'Be that as it may, allow me to shift the discussion back to history once I give you the short answer, Huzoor. The concept of "relationships" has largely replaced marriage. I know a woman who is twenty-two years old and has already had thirteen break-ups. I asked her if all those relationships had been consummated. She said if they hadn't, she would refer to them as "friendships" and not "relationships".'

'A break-up?'

'It is like talaq, Shahenshah, but without marriage.'

'I heard in the spirit world of people giving talaq on mobile phones. A break-up is like that? Thirteen men have done that to this poor woman?'

'No, she has done that to thirteen men.'

'Women are allowed to give talaq nowadays? What has the world come to?'

'It's much worse, Shahenshah. Now, I live in perpetual fear of sting operations and honeytraps. Time was when I could begin my response to a letter from a girl called, let's say, Shreya, with "Dear Shreya". Now, I'm so scared of being accused of sexual harassment that I begin with "Dear sister".'

'A honeytrap?'

'Let me explain with an example. I have a friend, a marine engineer. He has travelled the world, and even at nearly seventy years of age, had a girl in every port. He fell for an email from a woman who said she was from the royal family of Nigeria and fighting for property worth a billion dollars. She would be happy to give him half, if only he could help her bear legal costs. She left a phone number, which this fool called. He has lost fifteen lakh rupees to her so far and intends to transfer another fifteen that she has asked for. What is thirty lakh rupees in the face of five hundred million dollars, he says. He showed me her photograph. She was white. How could she belong to the Nigerian royal family? When I asked him, he said, "I'm no fool. I asked her. She told me it was because, when Nigeria was a British colony, her great-great-grandmother had slept with a British officer. Everyone in the family has been white since." You must forgive my saying this, Shahenshah, but I'm so afraid of women nowadays that I've decided every time I feel the urge to have sex, I'm best off watching porn and then jerking off. I blame this on Dirghatamas.'

'It must be said that there is a fair bit of violence in your epics.'

'Yes, indeed, Shahenshah. In fact, Kisari Mohan Ganguli, the first to translate the Mahabharata into English, left this particular section in the original Sanskrit because he could not bear to translate the story of Dirghatamas, a victim of lust before he was even born. Another translator, Manmatha Nath Dutt, went a step further and excised it.'

'But this is not the only incident of violence, Honourable Katib. Take Ashwatthama. He who, seeking to destroy the Pandava line, cut out the foetus from Abhimanyu's wife Uttara's womb!'

'Yes, Shahenshah. Fortunately for the foetus, Lord Krishna was his great-uncle and managed to bring him back to life. On top of this, he cursed Ashwatthama with eternal life and no carnal satisfaction. As if to ensure this, he blessed Ashwatthama with boils all over his body which would spew blood and pus and repel any woman who might oblige him.'

'I'm not sure how we've come to this discussion from what I was saying about my Mongol ancestors nearly conquering Europe.'

'It is one of the accusations against me, Shahenshah, that I bring sex into everything.'

'I think we will end the seance here, Honourable Katib. Today we have spoken of too much that is haram. It would be sacrilege to speak of my ancestors after all this.'

~

At the next seance, Rizwan had an additional duty. He was to cough twice if the writer said something that would veer towards sex. Among other things, he hadn't entirely lost his nervousness about the ghosts of trampling elephants taking over the Aghori's body.

The spirit made no references to the transgressions of the past, though, and began to speak of his ancestors without fuss.

~

AURANGZEB SAID:

In Genghis Khan's time, Mongolia ruled over a quarter of the world's population. A land of seven lakh people, and their rulers had killed four crore people at war. Rivers of blood ran through every land their horses entered. Do you know why my Mongolian ancestors were such ferocious conquerors, why they assaulted the entire world with such rage? Was it insanity? Satanic tendencies? The bloodlust of cannibals? None of these. It was simply want. Nothing grew in Mongolia. Nothing could. The vagaries of the weather were such. One day, there would be a hailstorm. The second, the sun would shine so fiercely all the hailstones would melt. The third day, the melting of the hailstones would cause avalanches and floods, and men and animals would be washed away. What choice did they have but to go and conquer?

It was Genghis Khan who unified the tribes and turned the arid land into an empire. It was he who made the economy thrive too. He never killed the talent – he brought back artists and scholars to Mongolia. Do you know what makes a superpower? People believe it is the size of the army that defines an empire. No. It is the size of the economy. Today, you see Hindustanis migrating in droves to foreign lands. Handing over their entire life's savings to brokers who will get them a place on a crowded boat or a van smuggling humans. And what do they do there? They are coolies. Every single Hindustani who leaves the country is a coolie, down to those Indian-origin Americans who are CEOs of multinational companies and earn more than your film stars. They are white-collar coolies, but still coolies. Why do they leave? Because Hindustan can no longer support them. They cannot earn the money back home that they would elsewhere. In our time, the firangis migrated to India. They were our coolies. They boarded ships in their teens, hoping to make the journey to India in one piece, and then make their livelihoods here. We had an entire contingent of white people, mercenaries, in our armies. And they were given about the same respect brown and black people are given in countries ruled by Caucasians. That is, none at all.

An incident comes to mind. Once, the head of the East India Company fell at my feet in the middle of my court. He begged forgiveness for the Company's transgressions and said they would do anything I asked to make up. Would I please allow them to trade? He begged me not to turn him back. I took pity on him. I changed the course of history. If only I had turned a deaf ear to his pleas, India would have remained under Mughal rule.

Let us get back to the Mongols, then. Once alcohol finally killed Ogedei, his son Guyuk Khan became the next emperor. His mother Toregene was instrumental in this. She was regent from 1241 to 1246, between the death of her husband and the coronation of her son. Although Ogedei had named another son, Kochu, his successor, Toregene successfully manipulated the court and had her son crowned king. As befits the king of a superpower, the coronation was attended by every head of state from Europe. Later, that creature would kill his own mother. This would never have happened among the Mughals. We killed our male relatives but never harmed the women. Then again, the Mongol women were not like ours. They ruled kingdoms, and they faced all the peril that came with that. One such peril was assassination.

At the time of which we speak, the Europeans hadn't yet learned to abase themselves. They had been soundly defeated in the Battle of Legnica by the Mongols in 1241, and yet Pope Innocent IV sent a missive through the traveller Giovanni da Pian del Carpine to Guyuk in 1246, having sent another missive to the Mongol ruler Baichu in 1245 through a delegation led by Ascelin of Lombardia, appealing to them to stop their violence against Christians and – would you believe it? – to embrace Christianity instead. It took them two years to deliver the letter to Baichu, by which time Guyuk had already sent a reply to the Pope – he must accept the Mongol Khagan as his lord and master, and appear in person at the royal seat of Karakorum so that he could hear 'every command there is of the yassa' – the code of law that Genghis Khan had decreed as the de facto law of the Mongol empire.

Do you see from this, Honourable Katib, the power Asia enjoyed over Europe? It was a good thing the code didn't allow for the killing of messengers, or Giovanni would have been sliced into bits before he could write his famous travelogues.

～

At this, Aurangzeb looked at the writer contemplatively for some time. Then, he said, 'I'm curious about something, Honourable Katib. Do you mind my asking you a personal question – which religion do you follow? Are you a believer at all, in anything?'

'Shahenshah, I'm a believer that religion must be personal. I go by the Tamil saying, "*Yaadum oore, yaavarum kelir*", which means "Every city is home, and everyone is family". The greatest of seers did not ask to be worshipped. They recognized the transience of life and considered it but an illusion. They did not want to be memorialized in grand tombs. My own belief is: *Aham brahmasmi*. I am Brahmam. The goats and cows and hens and worms and stone and sand and metal and sun and moon and sky are all Brahmam. They are all God, as am I, and as are you and as is Rizwan. At a young age, perhaps because I was raised in Nagore, I happened to read the *Book of al-Tawasin* by the Sufi saint al-Hallaj. I remember this line from it: "I saw God in my mind's eye, and asked who He was. 'You,' He replied." People believe his famous claim "Ana'l Haqq" – I am the truth – suggests that he thought of himself as divine. But others say it was the annihilation of the self, it was the acknowledgement of oneself as part of God and nothing else.'

'I get where you're coming from, Honourable Katib. I have no quarrel with the Sufis. All I say is that they must not confuse the idea of one God with the idea of everything being a manifestation of God. For Allah alone is to be worshipped, and not His creations. I take issue with the notion of religious unity

being interpreted as "You and I are one". No. It was Padishah
Akbar who started it all, and the confusion prevails until today.
Religious unity is simply acknowledgement that you and I are
different and can yet coexist.

'Which brings to me another point, Honourable Katib. In
order to tell you my story, I will have to summarize the journeys
of my ancestors. And in telling their stories, I will also take you to
the banks of a river – a river of tears, Honourable Katib, the tears
of the queens and princesses, a river that would dwarf the Yamuna,
a river of which I was unaware for as long as I was alive. For such
is the life of an emperor. One's sole interaction with women is to
foster a lineage.'

~

WITH THAT PRONOUNCEMENT, THE SPIRIT BEGAN
TO SPEAK:

We last left Jahanbani Jannat Ashyani Humayun running for his
life after Sher Shah Suri took over the empire. Giti Sitani Firdaus
Makani had left one last piece of advice for his son – 'Don't ever
kill your brothers, even if they merit death.' Humayun lost to Sher
Shah Suri largely because his brothers had betrayed him. Having
fled Delhi for Lahore, he appealed to Sher Shah Suri to leave
Lahore to him. Sher Shah Suri replied that he would leave Kabul
for him instead. At the time, Kabul was administered by Kamran
Mirza, half-brother to Humayun. Kamran wrote to Sher Shah
Suri, promising to hand over Humayun in return for Punjab. Sher
Shah Suri ignored the letter, but Humayun was made aware of its
contents thanks to his spies.

At the time, Humayun and his wife Hamida Begum, eight months pregnant, were crossing the Thar desert with a small entourage. There was no food and no water. Hamida Begum's horse collapsed in the heat. There was only one other horse in the entourage – that of her husband Humayun. He gave up the horse for his beloved wife and became the first and possibly last emperor in history to journey upon a camel.

They arrived at Amarkot, where Hamida Begum nearly collapsed from fatigue. The Rajput ruler of Amarkot, Rana Prasad, rushed to offer them succour and refuge. It was in the Amarkot Fort that Arsh Ashyani Emperor Akbar was born, on the fifth day of Rajab, in the Hijri year 949 – 1542 by your firangi calendar.

They rested at the fort for several months. But Askari Mirza, brother of Kamran, was on the heels of Humayun. The entourage had to leave again, in December 1543. The toddler Akbar was left behind, and eventually raised in Kabul by the wives of Askari Mirza and Kamran Mirza, the very men who were the reason for his separation from his own parents.

One winter's night, assaulted by hailstones and freezing with cold, with no wood for fire and no food to eat, Humayun and his miserable caravan of under thirty people took shelter under a mountain.

The story of the Mughal empire would have ended that night if not for the headman of a Balochi tribe. Having shivered through the night, the caravan made for what appeared to be a Balochi settlement the next morning. The wife of Humayun's aide Hasan Ali was Balochi and spoke their language. When she explained the situation, she was told they would have to wait for the headman.

Not long after, the headman hurried to the former emperor and bowed low.

'We have received orders from Kamran Mirza and Askari Mirza that if we are to set eyes upon you, we are to take possession of all your goods and gold and hand them and you over to Kandahar. But having seen you, Padishah, I would give up my life and those of my children and those of my people to save you. Please accept my apologies for having detained you.'

Humayun rewarded him with rubies and pearls, and made for Persia, where he would gather an army and regain Hindustan after ten years. But do you realize, Honourable Katib, that he would not have lost the empire in the first place had he not been so addicted to afeem and women? If he had not spared his brothers in line with his father's wishes, and therefore not been betrayed by them? To wander the deserts with a young wife, leaving behind an infant to be raised by one's enemies ... what a terrible destiny!

Of course, the infant grew up to become Padishah Akbar. While his father and grandfather had not proven the greatest emperors because of their addictions, Padishah Akbar would have been worth emulating, had it not been for his weakness for women. It makes me seethe to think women were officially traded in Meena Bazaar. Where does Islam allow for such a disgusting practice?

His heir inherited all his vices and hardly any of his virtues.

Salim, who became Emperor Jahangir, was pampered since birth. Not only did he grow up hearing that he was to inherit one of the largest and most powerful empires in the world, he was also born after years of prayer and angst. Fatima, the first child of Emperor Akbar, died in infancy. After her were born the twins Hassan and Hussein, who both died suddenly forty days after birth – killed by poison, it was said. It appears poison flowed more abundantly than water in the Mughal court.

Years passed by and none of Emperor Akbar's wives produced a child. The emperor walked barefoot from Agra to Dargah Ajmer Sharif, praying for an heir. The next year, his wife Mariam – alias Jodha Bai – conceived the baby who would become Prince Salim. But he proved such a disappointment, slave as he was to intoxicants and sycophants, that Emperor Akbar had all but decided to hand over the empire to his grandson Prince Khusrau. We already know what happened to that ill-fated boy.

You should write a novel about *him*, Honourable Katib. The boy who would have been emperor, if only he hadn't believed he already was one. It was insecurity which led Emperor Jahangir, when he did ascend the throne, to see his own son as a rival, and insecurity which drove him to order Prince Khusrau and his wife arrested – 'fort arrest' in Agra. Prince Khusrau might have simply waited his turn, but he escaped the fort and tried to lead an army against his father, who had by then one of the greatest armies of the world at his disposal. Prince Khusrau was brought to the court, tried for treason, blinded and thrown into a dungeon. His supporters had it worse. They were sentenced to vertical impalement, and their cries were heard through a long night.

Soon enough, Emperor Jahangir became so addicted to afeem and alcohol that his wife Nur Jahan all but reigned in his stead.

I'm sure you think my father, lover of music and art, ascended to power quite naturally. But no. He killed six prospective heirs, including two of his own brothers, in order to inherit the Peacock Throne. He ordered Prince Khusrau killed, imprisoned and powerless though he was. The next in line was Sultan Pervez Mirza, father of Nadira Banu, who was fated to marry the son of her father's killer. For Emperor Shah Jahan had Sultan Pervez

Mirza poisoned. Nadira Banu's mother was the daughter of Shahzada Mirza Murad, the second son of Emperor Akbar.

It might come as a surprise, but I do think my father was an admirable ruler. I had to imprison him due to circumstances. But I ensured he was given his favourite foods, without fear of being poisoned, for as long as he was under ... fort arrest, we're calling it, aren't we? And he was treated with the utmost respect. For his sins of the flesh, he would be punished by Allah. It wasn't up to me.

I told you of how I believe the Portuguese massacre was a rosette to his memory. Now let me tell you why. Since Vasco da Gama alighted upon these shores, the Portuguese had played one ruler against another, and extended their influence from the Coromandel coast to the lands of Bengal. Not only did they convert anyone upon whom their eyes fell to Christianity, they also sold anyone they could lay their hands on into slavery. This went unchecked by the Mughals until my father's time.

There was an incident that roused my father. The Portuguese had begun to kidnap women and sell them into slavery too. One day, two relatives of my mother's were apprehended when they had stepped out of the palace with their bodyguards. The Portuguese would not listen to the palace guards' protests. The two women were taken captive. Another time, they captured a child, an eleven-year-old from the Agra Fort. She was known in the fort as Mirra. She would go on to become Catarina de San Juan.

The last straw was their establishing a trading centre at Hooghly, close to our own trading port at Satgaon. Emperor Shah Jahan sent armies led by Qasim Khan, the subedar of Bengal, to lay siege to the town of Hooghly. The siege lasted three months. Ten thousand people were killed and four thousand arrested.

My father gave them a choice – convert to Islam or die. Most chose death. When I read Fray Sebastião Manrique's account of it, I wondered at the writer's grief – if religious conversion is such an ordeal for Christians, how did they see fit to impose it on Muslims?

And now we come to my own story, or part of it, Honourable Katib. I'd like to tell you of the nights of the last phase of my life, the nights that were haunted by the ghosts of the past, the ghosts of the victims of my doings and the doings of my ancestors. The last three years of my life were spent almost entirely in the company of these spirits.

The moment I closed my eyes, my room would fill with these spirits. I would hear the cries of men and the screams of women. Oh, those screams! Hundreds, no thousands, of women, screaming as if they were burning to death! And I would feel the heat of a fire, a fire that could engulf an entire forest, I would feel the flames on my skin, and I would wake up burning from inside. I could not open my eyes, but my skin would feel smooth. And yet, I smelt acrid flesh, human flesh bursting into its constituent molecules in the fire. The next morning, I would wake from an exhausting sleep to find no one in the room and no sign of fire, no sign on my body or furniture.

Three years I suffered this. I would ask my daughter Zinat-un-Nissa and my beloved Udaipuri Mahal if I looked any different. They always said I didn't. They were the ones who took care of me in my last days, you know. Zinat-un-Nissa, another much-loved daughter, who like her sister Zeb-un-Nissa chose not to marry. She was ten years older than Udaipuri Mahal, and the two were great friends. Well, that's a story for another day. I even asked my khwajasara whether I looked ill, whether there were burns on my body, and he said, 'No, Huzoor.' I saw him cast a sidelong glance at me. He was assessing my sanity. 'The emperor has gone mad in his dotage,' he must have thought. The Alamgir of old would have had him blinded for daring to look at the emperor from the corner of his eye. But not the Alamgir who heard human screams through those dark nights. Mad or not, I'd gone soft in my dotage. People whispered about it within my earshot. Why, my letters to my sons are evidence of this softness.

What was the cure for those terrible nights? Should I ask the Sufis? Call Hindu astrologers as my ancestors had done? But somewhere inside, I knew that I was but reaping as I had sowed. And so, I would plug my ears with my fingers and try to block out those cries.

One night though, through my fingers, I heard a female voice – so close to me I started and looked for the woman – say, 'Don't open your eyes, Alamgir. I am from the time of your great-grandfather. His lust for land caused the women of my land to commit jauhar. I am Rani Durgavati.'

～

At this time, the writer's heart began to beat fast. His eyes widened, unblinking. He broke into a cold sweat and sat frozen, stunned by what he had heard. For the Aghori had suddenly spoken not in Aurangzeb's voice, but in a woman's. Had Rani Durgavati entered the Aghori's body then?

～

THE WOMAN'S VOICE ANSWERED:

Yes, indeed, Honourable Lekhak, it is I, Rani Durgavati. Do excuse my intrusion, but I felt it was important to tell you the story of the jauhar and the saka myself. It was we, my people and I, who haunted Alamgir those last three years of his life. Why him, you may ask, why not Akbar? For Akbar deserved to pay for his sins in multiple lifetimes. We thought Aurangzeb was deserving of the mercy of paying for them once and for all, in that very lifetime. ·

They speak of Akbar's *tolerance*, Honourable Lekhak. His *religious tolerance*. But he was no different from your politicians who wait for Ramzan and attend iftar parties just for the photo ops. He knew he would gain popularity, a first step to complete domination, if he pretended to religious tolerance. He only saw religion for its profitability. He struck deals with the Rajputs so he could marry their beautiful women and enlist their large armies in his wars. Akbar's story is a story of lust – for women, for land, for all things worldly.

And I, Durgavati, queen of Gondwana, was among the victims of that lust. He attacked us because he coveted our lands and the elephants we had, of which his army was in dire need. My husband Dalpat Shah had died in 1550, and our son Veer Narayan was all of five years old. In 1564, our land was attacked by Mughal armies led by Asaf Khan, the subedar of Ilahabad. The Mughals had thought they would walk over us, but the battle lasted three years. We knew we could not withstand the brute force of the Mughal army, but we were determined to die trying. Not a soul would be captured alive. We had a choice – jauhar or saka. Most of the women chose jauhar. Some of us chose saka and fought alongside our menfolk.

We wore our saffron, to symbolize our readiness for our
suicide mission, and went to meet the Mughals. They would take
us, but they would not take us easily, and they would not take us
alive. Not one body would they have that was not a corpse. Men
who had never even held knives to shave their beards, women who
had only held knives to cut vegetables, people who knew nothing
of war, laypeople who had never seen the battlefield – all went out
as one to make a final stand against Akbar's marauding army. We
Gonds place our pride above our lives.

Three thousand women, knowing they would be taken straight
to the harem if they were captured alive, chose jauhar the night
before we took to the battlefield.

Where, in all this, is justice or fairness? How is it deemed
right for a well-trained army to lay siege to common folk from
lust of land? How is it acceptable to condemn three thousand
women to choose between becoming corpses or concubines? How
is it fair for swordsmen to kill unarmed civilians? Krishna said he
would return to the earth to restore justice. Perhaps, just as ants
don't understand human justice, we humans don't understand
divine justice.

I was cornered on the battlefield. I could make a run for it.
Or I could plunge a knife into my heart. I embraced death on the
battlefield, Honourable Lekhak. Alamgir has told you his side of
the story. Now, listen to my side. Listen to the things you might
not want to know.

Listen to my assertion that Akbar was no hero. Did you
know that Gondwana had some of the few kingdoms that were
never subject to British rule? We didn't win independence with
the rest of India in 1947. We had always been independent. Not
even the British, with their wiles and willpower and war strategy,

could conquer us all. True, my kingdom fell to the Mughals, but there were other Gond kingdoms that resisted all attempts at subjugation.

And there's more, Honourable Lekhak, there's a reason I've taken over the Aghori's body today. I want you to rewrite history. I want you to look at the things you believe because you want to believe them, and I want you to acknowledge that those are not true. From Babur's time to that of Aurangzeb – acting on behalf of his father, but still leading the army – women have committed jauhar to escape the harem. Your liberals would like to believe that Rani Padmini – Padmavati, as she is sometimes called – was a fictional character. But she lived, Honourable Lekhak, she lived. The walls of the Chittor Fort echo with the wails of the women who died that night. You know the role of Alauddin Khilji in this. But do you know the role of Amir Khusrau, Sufi beloved of you liberals, direct disciple of Nizamuddin Auliya, Khusrau the Spiritual?

Do you know how he delighted in describing what he saw that night?

If I were to tell you, if all of India were to read this, your country would erupt in communal feud like never before. You would wonder how his book, the *Khaza'in ul-Futuh*, is not banned in this country that is so in love with censorship. Because no one reads him. No one reads anything of him but his devotional poetry. His writing shows us that Rani Padmavati was no fictional character, that the seven-month siege was no fictional twist, that on 26 August 1303, the queen and thousands of other women immolated themselves so they would not be enslaved.

He writes that when Khilji's army stormed the fort the day after the jauhar, thirty thousand Hindu heads were taken. He writes that the women who burnt themselves with their children went straight to hell. He writes that this is the rightful reward for infidels. He writes that the hellfire brought light to the fort. He writes that Khilji's army examined the piles of corpses and stabbed to death those who were not yet dead. He writes that, because the general was fond of polo, the men got on their horses and played polo with the heads of the fallen Hindus. He writes that, because there were so many fallen Hindus, the army had to divide itself into multiple teams to play polo. He writes that the blood spewing out of those heads as they were tossed around the improvised polo field made mesmerizing patterns in the air.

Those mesmerizing patterns contain the ink in which our bloody history is written, Honourable Lekhak.

The night of our jauhar, the night before I stabbed myself, the rest of the country celebrated Holi. A twenty-five-year-old Akbar celebrated his own Holi, with just one colour – red, blood red. Our blood spattered on their clothes, our blood ran into the soil, our blood turned into rivers.

Think now, Lekhak, how tolerant was that emperor?

Think now, Lekhak, how spiritual was that Sufi whom you so celebrate?

I come not to haunt you, but to share my pain.

And I ask you to listen now.

~

With this, Rani Durgavati fell silent. As the writer and Rizwan watched, spellbound, the Aghori opened his mouth and the wails of thousands upon thousands of women, the hiss of a fire that could have felled a forest, rent the air. The writer's blood froze. His nerves jangled.

The wails finally stopped. Rani Durgavati did not return. Neither did Aurangzeb. After a long wait, the writer and Rizwan made their silent way home.

A week passed before the next seance.

～

WHEN THEY MET AGAIN, AURANGZEB SAID:

Honourable Katib, I heard all that Rani Durgavati said. Please don't ask me for answers. I have none. I shall have none on the Day of Judgement either, and shall face my just deserts.

All I ask of you is this – tell my side of the story. Tell your readers that I did all that I did in order to set right the excesses of my father's rule. His obsession with capturing Kandahar had emptied the treasury. And yet the soirées in the palace went on as before, with golden goblets for wine from foreign lands. The expense grew to four times that of his predecessors. And where did he find the money? He taxed the citizens. The collections from tax grew threefold. Can you imagine how many people would have killed themselves from penury?

The zenana was full of women who never knew the touch of a king, because how would any mortal, royal or otherwise, find the time to sleep with five thousand women? They were sometimes serviced by the khwajasaras. The court eunuchs, you say, how did they know to service them? Because they would have been men if not for forced castration. It was I who put an end to the zenanas and the forced castrations. It was I who got rid of the hakims who would give the rulers the equivalent of your Viagra so they could use their concubines.

And I am the villain of this piece.

My father once wrote to me saying I was too polite for a prince. I ought to be more high-handed, he said.

I wrote back quoting Anas ibn Malik, most loyal disciple of the Prophet, who said Allah will favour those who know politeness and modesty.

So much for the romantic Shah Jahan who built the Taj Mahal. Did you know it was he who, in 1634, brought in a law saying any Hindu man who wedded a Muslim woman should convert to Islam? It was that which drove a wedge between the two religions. Inter-religious marriages were common before this. As you know, there is a higher percentage of Rajput blood than Mongol in us Mughals, by virtue of our mothers.

Jadunath Sarkar writes that my life was a Greek tragedy. I concur. My first forty years were spent in preparation for the throne and in building the empire over which I would rule. My forty-first year was spent winning that throne. The next twenty years went better than those preceding. But the final phase of my life, which began with the birth of my son Muhammad Akbar in 1681, made up for that golden period. I spent all my years either on the battlefield or in preparing for battle against my own sons. I waged war in my eighties, and I was haunted by...

~

The writer looked at the Aghori, whose face was frozen.

'Huzoor?' he said.

Silence.

'Shahenshah?'

The Aghori opened his mouth. His face had changed slightly. The frown lines had disappeared. His eyes were wide open, suggestive of naiveté, if not innocence.

~

IN A DIFFERENT VOICE, HE SAID:

Honourable Katib, you must know from my voice that this is
not Aurangzeb. I am the one variously called the fool, the souse,
the braveheart, the lascivious – Murad Bakhsh. The man whose
history no one has written because he was neither an emperor
like his father or his brother Aurangzeb, nor a scholar and poet
like Dara Shikoh. My great-grandfather's lasciviousness was of
no consequence, nor was my grandfather's addiction to alcohol
and narcotics, nor my father's various weaknesses, for they were
emperors, and I was not.

　　I ought to have been. The man who speaks of being a fakir
who cared only for country and Quran made a false promise on
the latter that cost me the former. Or I would have ascended the
throne and done as my forefathers had taught me – kill all your
kith and kin that could claim your kingdom. Humayun was the
only one of my ancestors who spared his father, brothers and sons
– and for his pains, he wandered the desert and lived in exile for
a decade and a half, while his son and heir was being raised by
the wives of the men who had set out to kill him. My grandfather
Jahangir conspired against his own father and blinded his own
son Khusrau. He sent an army after my father, saying he should
either be brought before him in chains or driven out of the empire.
When my father was captured, he was separated from his sons
Aurangzeb and Dara Shikoh on the orders of Emperor Jahangir,
who demanded that they be raised in his own palace as the price
for my father's liberty. My brother Aurangzeb sent my father our
brother Dara Shikoh's head with his dinner. And let us talk of his
treatment of me.

　　No, let us first talk of me, of my role in Samugarh. By all
accounts, it was no equal war. The armies attacking us were far

stronger than those on our side. We emerged victorious because of this fool, this souse, this lascivious braveheart. 'He fought like a lone lion on the battlefield,' they say of me. You wouldn't find a square inch on the body of my elephant, on the body of yours truly, on the body of our howdah that did not have a spear through it. It was raining spears on the battlefield. The howdah, with its appearance of a porcupine, was taken to the Red Fort in grand ceremony after we won the war, and was on display until 1719. When someone asked whose howdah it was, he would be told the story of the lone lion on the battlefield of Samugarh.

And what became of that lone lion? Here is what my brother said to me, in that tent:

> *I will never forget 15 April 1637, the day I wedded Dilras. You led the groom's procession, followed by our maternal grandfather Asaf Khan. Do you remember the henna function of the day before, my beloved brother?*
>
> *A curtain was raised between me and the women of the zenana. There was a hole through which I was asked to thrust my hands and my feet in turn.*
>
> *One of the older women began to tease me. 'Thrust a little further, dear prince, or how can you reach the place you must?'*
>
> *The women broke into peals of laughter. I was unused to ribaldry and I turned red. It had not crossed my mind that women could pun thus. It was despicable enough when men did it.*
>
> *Another woman said, 'The prince's arms could pass for his legs. What do you think his legs would look like?'*
>
> *Another replied, 'Why, his legs must be as long as Hanuman's tail!' Many of the womenfolk in the zenana were Rajputanis, and so they would refer to the Hindu gods, don't you remember?*

'And if that is the case,' yet another said, 'what of the prince's tail?'

That is when you stepped in, my dear brother.

You said, 'The prince's tail could pass for his sword, ladies. It is just as sharp. It could pierce three bodies in one stroke and tear its way through each!'

The women were stunned. And then they began to laugh.

You didn't stop there. 'Don't wag your tails with the prince. If the prince were to wag his tail, remember that it will make an entry and exit from the other side!'

This time, I couldn't help laughing myself. You were a child of thirteen back then, and you could take on words as easily as you took on swords.

I heard those words, and my heart melted. No one had touched me with the warmth with which he had when he wiped off my sweat with a muslin cloth. No one had spoken to me with such warmth as when he spoke of his wedding day. And all this for a throne.

I might be a fool and a souse, but my soul is pure. My brother's soul is black. Not all the penance and prayer in the world can wash away its darkness. I wonder what thoughts went through his mind every time he saw that howdah in Delhi? Did he feel remorse? Or did he feel triumph at having fooled its occupant?

Remember, Honourable Katib, that history is always written by the victors. Even when they feel wronged, it is they who have the right to rewrite history. Tell me, would your publishers have been interested in this translation, would your friends be worried about the consequences of a controversy, if it were titled *Conversations with Murad Bakhsh?*

I, who never shed a tear in life, had only tears left in my soul after death. But without a body, I had no eyes with which to shed them.

~

The Aghori now stopped talking. We would not hear Murad Bakhsh's words again. But we heard his tears. The soul had finally found a body with eyes to shed those tears, and he shed them for a half hour, running in rivulets down the Aghori's cheeks and soaking his clothes in sorrow.

CHAPTER 9

Kokkarakko

The last two guests whom Aurangzeb had introduced to the writer had left the room echoing with their wails. The writer felt everyone needed a change of vibe. And so he turned to the man who left many a room echoing with … well, 'Kokkarakko'.

The writer had hoped to spare at least this novel from Kokkarakko. It was the latter's wont to sneak into every single one of the writer's novels and distort it. You might ask why the writer allows this. Fair enough. This calls for some history and context.

You see, our writer does not make for easy company. But all writers are socially awkward, you might say. Our man is exceptionally so. Let me explain with some examples.

The writer had a friend who once sent him a WhatsApp forward that annoyed him. He sent a voice message to the friend. 'You're talking like a dick with venereal disease,' he said.

The illogic of the comparison did not amuse the friend, who chose instead to be hurt by the writer's words. The writer was entitled to his opinions, but did he have to express them in such unsavoury language? The friend didn't dare ask. The question would provoke even more graphic swearing.

'You're driving away friend after friend with your destructive impulses. You're going to be left all alone in the end,' said Torture Govindan, who had earned the epithet thanks to his proclivity for carrying salt in search of wounds to rub it into.

The writer had another friend in Pondicherry, whom he visited regularly. Meeting his friend was a pretext. It was Pondicherry he wanted. And its alcohol. The friend was rich. He'd put the writer up in an exclusive hotel and have Remy Martin sent to his room. The writer would spend Friday, Saturday and Sunday in an intoxicated daze and disappear on Monday without so much as a 'seeya'. This was a monthly ritual which went on for ten years. And then the Pondicherry friend turned teetotal.

This made him entirely useless to the writer. It also sent the writer into an existential crisis. He realized he had no real friends. He'd contrived to make friends with a bunch of crorepatis, thanks to which wine and women were plentiful in his life. Yet, this was not quite enough. The writer wanted dissolute friends, yes, but dissolute friends with literary sensibilities. It was at this point that Kokkarakko entered his life.

Kokkarakko was no reader. He was like any other man on the street, except he was smart. You could wake him up from sleep and ask him about Michel Foucault. He would excuse himself for a moment and stagger to the toilet, look up the internet while pissing into the bowl, and come back prepared with a lecture that would not have been out of place at the Sorbonne in the peak of its glory.

The writer deemed him interesting enough to give Kokkarakko a guest appearance in his novel *Exile*. He then gave the manuscript to Kokkarakko for his opinion. Kokkarakko's response was unprecedented. He edited the manuscript, providing counter-texts to each reference the writer had made to him, and mailed it back to the writer, copying the latter's stunned publisher on the email.

Now, the writer believes in democracy. He has also bought into the points Roland Barthes puts forward in his essay *The Death of the Author*. But it seemed a bit much for a character to go so rogue as to kill the author. Probably worse, Kokkarakko had killed the relationship the writer's persona in the novel had with his fictitious girlfriend, a relationship on which the writer had a tenuous hold at best.

'You have wound the writer around your little finger by using your fake sob stories on this gullible man,' Kokkarakko had raged at her character. Her character responded by saying Kokkarakko was a cynic, and the writer's jovial, positive self would be irreparably affected by friendship with this lunatic.

Chivalry demanded that the writer step in again. Kokkarakko ended up on the chopping board. The writer's girlfriend was given ever more prominence. The writer believed her character would outdo both Anna Karenina and Madame Bovary.

Yet, when the book was published, Kokkarakko became a fan favourite, and social media burst with hate against the writer's fictional girlfriend, who – because autofiction is the writer's thing – was based on his real-life wife. The writer is not one to accept defeat even when he has crossed its jaws and throat and is being churned in its stomach, and so he wrote a second version of *Exile*, in which the girlfriend had twice the screen time … tchah, text space. This provoked twice the ardour from his fans, which had two consequences.

One, the writer and his wife had a fallout over what the latter called the former's 'literary treason'.

Two, Kokkarakko became an icon across Tamil Nadu, whose readers began to clamour for a novel from the character. Kokkarakko obliged, and his novels have all been bestsellers. His latest fetched him five lakh rupees after he made it a literary NFT.

Perhaps you should also know why he is called 'Kokkarakko'. At the stroke of the witching hour, when the world sleeps, it is the rooster's wont to wake everyone with its cacophonous screams of 'Kokkarakko'. There seems enormous gravitas and urgency to this 'Kokkarakko', while it carries no sense. So it is with the writer's friend Kokkarakko. He began to sneak into every one of the writer's works.

Torture Govindan could not stand Kokkarakko. He had once asked the writer, 'Why can't you ever write a novel without Kokkarakko making an appearance? Write one, just one, let me see?'

Conversations with Aurangzeb was his attempt to prove to Torture that he was capable of writing one such novel. But Kokkarakko had contrived to work his way into this one too. The reason for this was the writer's weakness.

You see, the writer ached for feedback. He felt joyful when he was told the story worked. He felt just as joyful when he was told it didn't, provided he was also told why. You're flummoxed, I see. Well, there's not much I can say. Our writer is simply that sort of person.

He doesn't always follow the counsel of those who give him feedback, though. Torture Govindan had once said of a manuscript, 'There is too much swearing in this. It's only now that you're beginning to be seen as a literary writer, not a creator of porn. Don't ruin your reputation.' This moved the writer to ask his publishers to hold the novel – he had some edits to make. He added a chapter consisting entirely of swear words. The novel was published, and a copy sent to Torture.

With the writer already frazzled by all the havoc Kokkarakko had wreaked in his life, his wife made things worse. She and Kokkarakko have barely ever met. Once or twice at lit fests, perhaps. But one fine day, she answered the writer's mobile when Kokkarakko called and said, 'Don't call him again.'

This didn't affect Kokkarakko's relationship with the writer.

The writer did ask his wife why she had said such a thing.

'You've come to this state only because of Kokkarakko.'

'This state' referred to two aspects – he drank, and he was prone to rage. Kokkarakko was the one fuelling both, she said. 'If you drink, you'll die. The government warns that alcohol can claim lives.'

'That is the alcohol you get in government shops. I drink Remy Martin and thirty-year-old wine. That does not claim lives. It is the very elixir of life.'

'Alcohol is alcohol.'

'Right, let that be. What does Kokkarakko have to do with my temper, though?'

'Bad vibes. He sends those out. It affects you, and it affects your layam.'

He ought never to have taught her Tamil. She was using the word 'layam' against him now.

Torture added his tuppence. 'If it weren't for your wife, Kokkarakko would have killed you by now.'

'No. He's the reason I'm still alive.'

'No. He's fuelling your ills.'

There's something else I have to tell you.

Once, the writer's wife said, 'You're sixty-nine years old, aren't you?'

'Yes. I have contrived to reach that quite lovely number, one way if not the other.'

'You twist everything I say to make some vulgar comment. My point is, even at this age, why must you turn to that kid Kokkarakko for advice? Can't you write a story on your own? Why do you need his feedback and input for your ideas?'

'My brain has its limits. Let it go, won't you?'

The writer must acknowledge, though, that his wife and Torture Govindan have a point. This novel, which has been squeaky clean thus far, has already seen some swearing since Kokkarakko made his entry.

Anyway, let's get back to the story.

The writer took Kokkarakko with him for the next seance. He had sought the emperor's permission in advance, for among other things, this meant Aurangzeb would no longer dictate entire chapters – at least, not for as long as Kokkarakko was in the room. It was not in Kokkarakko's nature to stay for long without interrupting. The spirit said he would prefer interruptions from Kokkarakko to interruptions from his victims. A change of audience inspired a change of subject, and Aurangzeb said that in honour of the newcomer from Tamil Nadu, he would turn his attention to the Deccan.

'The story of the Marathas and the Deccan is not new to you,' Aurangzeb began. 'After all, the music and dance of Thanjavur are...'

'Huzoor, Huzoor, stop right there,' Kokkarakko said.

The writer sighed. The spirit looked startled. Kokkarakko was the kind who yelled sweet nothings into the ears of his lovers, and so there was no point asking him to talk to the emperor as he would to a lover. The writer had asked him to speak softly and with respect, but the two concepts were entirely lost on Kokkarakko. Even his 'Huzoor' sounded like a swear word.

The writer had already warned Aurangzeb and told him Kokkarakko might ask offensive questions. Alamgir had said that was his main interest in meeting him. There was little the writer could do but take him along.

'Look at the writer, he's thrilled because he thinks he can use your reference to Thanjavur to throw in all the research he can't fit into his Tyagaraja book,' Kokkarakko went on.

Aurangzeb looked baffled. He was not used to either interruption or stream of consciousness rambling.

'It's nothing, Shahenshah,' the writer said. 'I have been writing a book on Tyagaraja, the saint and singer. I have been researching the musical history of Thanjavur. This has been going on for a while, and I've been writing that novel alongside this one.'

'And I have told him he can't simply throw in all his research into a novel just so he will feel he has used his time to good effect,' Kokkarakko said. 'The readers will die of boredom. Everything is on Google and Wikipedia.'

'I have scoured libraries. I have got Farsi scholars to translate texts that are not available in…' the writer began to protest.

'The reader will *die* of boredom and haunt him. He's already haunted by two people, you and Tyagaraja.'

'This is true, Shahenshah,' the writer admitted. 'At times, I fear I will go insane. It is my wont to turn into my characters when I write novels. I am you at night, surrounded by the forms from your nightmares, the people you have killed. I swim in blood and walk on corpses. During the day, I turn into Tyagaraja, wandering the streets with the name of Rama on my lips. I could have survived if I'd had one of these personalities within me. But the two together are impossible to manage. One wants to bring the entire world under his rule, even if it means killing his own brothers and throwing his own father in jail. The other wants nothing at all. He casts away everything he owns. He doesn't even seek to eat. His food is alms. How can one body accommodate these two souls?'

'Yes, Huzoor, we have never seen him like this,' Kokkarakko said. 'He usually spends one week in intense work, and then takes off to Europe or South Asia with us friends for four days. We paint the town red, and then he returns and works for four days. And then it's party time, and then work, and so on. But now, he acts like you must have, making a living from stitching prayer caps. Except, he's working. All the time. He refuses to leave the house. I usually don't like speaking about or asking after anyone's health. If someone asks me whether I'm well, I tend to respond with, "No, I have been diagnosed with cancer," or "I might have AIDS," to see their reaction. But I've been so worried about our writer that I was moved to ask him when he would finish the novel. He responded with, "You've started off like Torture Govindan now."

'You're already familiar with Torture Govindan. He calls daily to ask the writer when he will finish the novel. How can he finish it unless you finish telling your story? When I asked him to tell Torture this, Torture retorted with, "Don't hang out with that Kokkarakko. You'll go to hell. You're not as street-smart as he is. You'll end up with some woman doing a MeToo on you."

He's said this so often that our writer is now afraid to speak to women. Anyway, offended as I was by the comparison, I persisted. He responded with, "Writing is my therapy." What could I say to that?'

'I'm afraid I see nothing wrong with the situation in which our Honourable Katib finds himself. To be this fakir at night and to be a saint in the morning, isn't that a stroke of luck? I don't know much about this Tyagaraja, but he sounds like a Sufi to me. You would do well to write about him. But, all right, we will not bore the reader. We will go on to the story of Rani Mangammal. She impressed me as no other woman has. Her husband Chokkanatha Nayagan was ruling over the kingdom of Madurai when he died suddenly. Their son Rangakrishna Muthu Veeran was too young to rule by himself, and so his mother served as the regent. No sooner had he started off on his wars of conquest than he fell gravely ill from the pox and died. His wife was pregnant with their first child. Rani Mangammal then took the throne and the title of "Rani". It appears she was destined for the throne. I heard from my spies that she was a wonderful ruler. As Jahanara Begum had done, she worked for the people too. She built roads, dug irrigation canals, constructed temples and planted trees.

'When we laid siege to the Gingee Fort, we demanded that the southern rulers accept our suzerainty. They had a choice – they could either pay us a tribute, or they could take us on in war. The Raja of Mysore and the Maratha ruler of Thanjavur agreed to pay the tribute we demanded. I expected Rani Mangammal would go to war. She wouldn't be able to afford the tribute we had demanded. I hadn't accounted for her cleverness. She knew it would be suicidal to take on the Mughals. She sent numerous gifts and promised to pay tribute, if only we would be as kind and just as befitted the descendants of Padishah Akbar and Padishah Babur before him, and give her some time to gather the amount. If she had done as I'd expected, Trichy would have been ours. That was all I really wanted. But how could I go back on my word? She had called my bluff. It was I who lost that battle, as I never would have on the ground. Courage is not simply going to the battlefield and fighting unto death. Sometimes, courage is choosing not to spill blood too, choosing to safeguard one's people. It takes great courage to put diplomacy before pride, pragmatism before pipe dreams.

'Let me contrast this with the Deccan famine of 1630–32. It was largely my father's fault that seventy-four lakh people died on his watch. At the time, the population of the Mughal empire was thirteen crore. More than a twentieth of the population was wiped out. And instead of alleviating the situation, he made it worse by going to war and diverting the meagre crop yield to feed his army instead of the very people who were growing those crops. This is the man who gave away tens of lakhs worth of gold and gems when his beloved daughter survived a fire accident. And yet he didn't hesitate to rob the poor. Rani Mangammal, on the other hand, only ever used the treasury funds to better the lives of the people. But she didn't hesitate to empty the treasury to appease a formidable prospective enemy and forge a useful friendship instead. Such wisdom! She knew I had set out to conquer her territory, and she responded with a cunning gambit. A heroic death would have been far stupider. I was manipulated into leaving her people unharmed. She is a true hero, don't you think?'

'This reminds me of something, Shahenshah. A grand event in the history of us Tamilians. It was ethnic cleansing, really. What "cleansing"? Genocide. But the person who was responsible for it was a Tamil leader. He went on about ethnic pride and dignity, and ended up sacrificing everyone of his ethnicity.'

'Who is this you speak of, Honourable Katib?'

'It is best I don't say his name, Huzoor. I didn't mention it in the Tamil version. And the chapters in which I speak of him were censored when the novel first came out in serialized form on an app in Tamil. It was heartbreaking, because these were exclusive accounts of war veterans with whom I have personally interacted. I will narrate these now, of course. But my translator Baahubilli feels it's better I mention his name. Controversy is never a bad thing, she says. One of her own books began to sell at ten times the rate after some group burnt a copy of it. The only thing is, I'm afraid they'll kill me.'

'You don't worry about all that,' said Kokkarakko, whom the writer had not addressed. 'If you're writing in Tamil and getting death threats, you will live and die in anonymity. But if you write in English and get death threats, they will make you a Twitter hero. You might even get asylum in some country where all the women would want selfies with you. Some might even want children with you. You keep saying you envy the people who get death threats. Now is your chance. You know, that writer who had a bounty on his head, he got married thrice after he first went into hiding, and each wife was younger and more glamorous than the previous one. What a life!'

'Yes, if one lives. But what if I die?'

'You're nearly seventy. What do you have to lose?'

The writer had to concede Kokkarakko had a point. 'All right, his name is Prabhakaran. Velupillai Prabhakaran.'

'James Bond style,' said Kokkarakko, killing the effect.

The writer hurried on before Aurangzeb could ask who James Bond was. 'This occurred in Sri Lanka, a tiny country to the south of India, and so close to Tamil Nadu it takes less time to travel there from Chennai than to travel to other places in our state.

There are two ethnicities there, two religions, two languages. The minority is Tamil, most of whom are Hindu, a sizeable number Christian, and very few of whom are Muslim. Almost none of them is Buddhist, which the Sinhala majority is. The Tamils felt they were sidelined. The heads of the two groups held talks. A young leader emerged on the Tamil side and said the only way the problem could be solved was by taking up arms. He formed a militant outfit and began to kill off the moderate leaders who favoured talks. This young man was Velupillai Prabhakaran. The group was the LTTE, the Liberation Tigers of Tamil Eezham. He killed not only the moderates, but other militant leaders too. And yet, he was seen as the saviour of the Tamils, not so much by Sri Lankan Tamils as by us in Tamil Nadu.'

'You too, Honourable Katib?'

'Didn't philosophers and writers and musicians and intellectuals believe Hitler was their saviour? How am I superior to them? But I must say I grew slowly disillusioned. Yet, he was considered the icon of the Tamils. Politicians in Tamil Nadu used his name for their own ends. They still do, all these years after his death. Tamils across the world consider him their hero.

'In the early years of this millennium, a moderate leader emerged on the Lankan side. She reached out to the Tamils and their militant leader. She said we could find a solution through elections. She offered a deal – the region could be autonomous, except for certain departments such as defence and finance. Others, such as education, sanitation, even home affairs could be with the state. Quite like in your times, Shahenshah. The nawabs and kings who would accept you as their suzerain and pay tributes. There were peace talks in Norway between the two parties. An accord was on the horizon, but then Prabhakaran ruined it all.

He was afraid he would lose his iconic status, and with that his power and authority.'

Kokkarakko cut in here. 'I'll tell you how this works. When my family was looking for a bride for me, my father had his heart set on one girl for his daughter-in-law. He insisted I should marry no one else but her. I was not interested. Not in her, not in marriage. But because my father was raving so much, I agreed to meet her. I planned to come up with some excuse and avoid marriage. But we got along right away. I said I was willing to marry her. My father immediately insisted that could not happen, she was all wrong for me, I could remain a bachelor all my life, but I should not marry her. Later, our writer told me I should have called my father aside and said, "I came here because you insisted. I have seen the girl. Now it's your decision. You want me to marry her, I will. If you don't want me to, I won't." My father would have been pleased at this total surrender. But when I exercised my agency, he felt he had lost his authority and power. He did as Prabhakaran did.'

This novel was suddenly becoming all about Kokkarakko. The writer ignored the interruption and said, 'So what could possibly come of this? The peace talks ended in stalemate. Militancy was back. Bomb explosions, suicide squads, army offensives, a nation burning. When elections were held, the LTTE called on the Tamils to boycott them. If they didn't obey, they would be called traitors and summarily executed. The moderate leader lost. The Sinhalas considered *her* a traitor to *their* cause. Her successor was as rabid as his militant counterpart. He promised to bring thirty years of civil war to an end and started an army offensive to rout the LTTE.

'The Tamil leader used innocent civilians as human shields for his army. The marauding army killed them all. The leader was killed too. And with his death, the Tamil cause was lost. There are varying reports of what happened to his family. Some say all his children were killed. Some say his daughter escaped, along with her mother. What we do know for sure is that one of his sons was killed at close quarters. He was a child, barely thirteen. All Tamils cried at the pictures of his body. He had also been photographed in an army camp, eating biscuits offered by his father's enemies, his face a picture of innocence, a little boy wearing shorts and a lungi around his shoulders. The next image that emerged of him was as a child lying on his back, three bullet holes in his chest. They were afraid he would become his father's heir and successor if left alive. This was all quite as Lenin did unto the Tsar's family after the Russian Revolution. Except that has been documented in great detail, in spite of the paucity of available media to capture evidence at the time. And the killing of Prabhakaran's family, of that little child, remains almost undocumented in spite of all kinds of media and instant access to news being the norm today.

'The end of the war must have come as a relief to the Tamils who lived. There were two things that were most essential for the war – money and manpower. The money was procured by smuggling narcotics. The manpower was procured by force. How many fools would willingly sacrifice their lives for a notional nation? They recruited child soldiers. They would show up at homes and take the children away. They would show up at schools and take the children away. What could the parents do? If they objected, they would be called traitors and sentenced to execution. "Here we are, sacrificing life and limb for you, and all you care about is living it up without making a contribution!" the soldiers would say. The contribution – a child. Many hid their children away. Those who could afford it, sent them to relatives abroad. Those who couldn't, got their teenage children married off outside the LTTE-controlled areas.

'In the final days of the war, in May 2009, Mullaivaikkaal – a tiny area in Mullaitheevu island – had been declared a no-fire zone. Three hundred and thirty thousand people were squeezed into this pocket of land. All civilians. They were assaulted by the Lankan army from one side and the Tamil militia from the other. Sea, land, air ... attack and ambush from everywhere. A hundred thousand people were killed. All because the LTTE decided to use them as human shields. There was no jauhar and no saka. There was only murder. A hundred thousand corpses in a bid for freedom, a hundred thousand testimonies to one man's craze for power. What is struggle? Death. What is dignity? Death. What is freedom? Death. That was Mullaivaikkaal's message to the world.

'The militants would not let their own people escape to safety. They had hoped human shields would force the army to withdraw. The army did not see the shields as human.

'There was a prominent lawyer who had to argue every case for the LTTE. He would be kidnapped every so often and produced in court along with the accused. He sent his sons off to Canada. His wife and he stayed behind, not sure how they would manage in the cold. When things got dangerous, they decided to leave for the capital of the country, Colombo. As they were about to leave town, two men showed up. "Don't move, or we'll shoot," one said. The lawyer's wife looked at him. She knew his father. She had seen the father as a boy. Here was that boy's son, about as old as her grandson, threatening to shoot her and her husband, the man who had saved so many of his fellow combatants. "Shoot me if you want, I don't care," she said. She took her husband's hand and walked past them. They did not shoot. I heard this story from the lady herself when I was on a trip to France. That is where the couple lives now.

'This is how the civilians were attacked from both sides. It was the worst for Tamil Muslims. All the Tamil Muslims who lived in LTTE-controlled lands had to leave everything behind. They were made to move out of their homes with just the clothes on their backs and a bundle or two of belongings. In some cases, even thermos flasks were seized from them. This left Tamils outside Sri Lanka entirely disillusioned.

'This was one of two incidents that began to sound the death knell for the LTTE. It is said, "He who lives by the sword, dies by the sword." This particular "he" simply turned the sword on himself.

'The other incident, of course, was the assassination of Rajiv Gandhi, former prime minister and likely future prime minister of India at the time. That gruesome killing, which left so many other innocents dead, turned many Indian Tamils against the LTTE.

'Having lost so much support over the years, the leader grew slowly mad. His madness cost hundreds of thousands of lives.'

'Honourable Katib, after his death, what is the situation? Do the Tamils and Sinhalas live peacefully under one flag?'

'Who can tell, Shahenshah? This generation is all about TikTok and Instagram. They don't care about ethnicity and identity and language. As for the Tamils who are ready to kill themselves for their language, they can barely speak it with the right enunciation. Most can't write Tamil. Where is the pride in all this?

'Let us talk of something else, Shahenshah. The Lankan war and its fallout are too painful to revisit. And I'm exhausted from having given you this account. This novel is about you, after all. We got into this diversion because you mentioned Rani Mangammal. You were also going to speak about your wars with the Marathas…'

'True, and I did intend to give you a detailed account. But after what your friend Kokkarakko said about people dying of boredom, I'm worried. What if, in addition to everyone I killed on the battlefield and sentenced to death in court, I'm haunted by those who died of boredom from reading my retelling of the wars between us Mughals and Shivaji's Marathas? Let me hear from you instead. For some time, I sense that you have been thinking of Chile. May I ask why?'

'Oh, whenever talk of heroism comes up, I think of a particular incident in the history of Chile, Shahenshah.

'11 September has become synonymous with that date from 2001. But it was equally, perhaps even more, significant for Chile for decades. On 11 September 1973, Dr Salvador Allende, who had been elected by the people, was ousted in a military coup by Augusto Pinochet Ugarte, who would rule as dictator for seventeen years. As usual, the American CIA was behind this sort of interference.

'Even as the junta attacked the Palacio de La Moneda, the presidential residence in Santiago, the commander announced on a loudspeaker that Allende would be spared if he surrendered. And that was when Allende spoke on the radio for the last time, addressing the people of his nation. This is what he said:

This will undoubtedly be the last opportunity for me to be able to address you. The Air Force has bombarded the antennas of Radio Magallanes. My words hold no bitterness; I speak from disappointment. May my words be a moral punishment for those who have betrayed their oath: soldiers of Chile, titular commanders in chief, Admiral Merino, who has designated himself commander of the navy, and Mr Mendoza, the contemptible snake of a general who only yesterday pledged his fidelity and loyalty to the government, and who also has appointed himself chief of the carabineros.[25] Given these facts, the only thing left for me is to say to workers: I am not going to renounce my title!

Finding myself in a moment of historic transition, I will pay with my life for my loyalty to the public. And I say to them that I am certain that the seeds which we have planted in the good conscience of thousands and thousands of Chileans will not be mowed down forever. [The leaders of the coup] have power and will be able to overwhelm us [now], but social change can be arrested by neither crime nor force. History is ours, and is made by people.

Workers of my country: I want to thank you for the loyalty that you have always had, the confidence that you placed in a man who was only an interpreter of the [collective] grand desire for justice, who gave his word that he would respect the constitution and the law and stood by his word.

At this final moment, the last moment when I can address you, I wish you to make the most of this lesson: foreign capital, imperialism, together with the response to it, created the climate in which the armed forces broke with tradition, the tradition

---

25 Paramilitary police.

*taught by General Schneider and reinforced by Commander
Araya, victims of the same social sector who today are hoping,
with the help of yet another hand, to reclaim the power to hold
on to their illicit gains and their privileges.*

*I address you, above all, the modest woman of our land, the
campesina*[26] *who believed in us, the mother who understood our
concern for children. I address the professionals of Chile, patriotic
professionals who continued working against the insurrection
that was supported by professional associations, classist
associations that also defended the benefits of capitalist society.*

*I address the youth, those who sang and sowed in us their joy
and their fighting spirit. I address the Chilean man, the worker,
the peasant, the intellectual, those who will be persecuted, because
fascism has already been reigning in our country for hours –
[evidenced] in acts of terrorism, blowing up the bridges, cutting
the railroad tracks, destroying the oil and gas pipelines, in the
face of silence from those who were under obligation to act [to
stop these attacks].*

They had made a promise. History will judge them.

*Radio Magallanes will be silenced for sure, and the tranquil
metallic notes of my voice will no longer reach you. It does not
matter. You will continue hearing it. I will always be by your
side. For, at the very least, I will be remembered as a man of
dignity who was loyal to his country.*

*The people must defend themselves, but they must not sacrifice
themselves. The people cannot allow themselves to be laid low or
besieged or shot, but they cannot be humiliated either.*

*Workers of my country, I have faith in Chile and its destiny.
Other men will overcome this dark and bitter moment when*

---

26 Peasant woman.

*treason seeks to prevail. Keep in mind that, much sooner than
later, the grand avenues will open again, and man will walk
free through those paths to construct a better society.*

Long live Chile! Long live the people! Long live the workers!

*These are my last words, and I am certain that my sacrifice
will not be in vain. I am certain that, at the very least, it will
be a moral lesson that will punish felony, cowardice and treason.*

'And having said this, he killed himself before they could
capture him.'

The writer spoke like a man possessed. His face was wet with
tears. 'When I went to the Santiago Museum for the first time
and heard this recorded speech, I fainted right away. I feel such a
close connection to Chile, Shahenshah.

'And Allende is not the only hero. One of the greatest, to me,
is Victor Jara.

'The moment Pinochet captured power, he rounded up the
writers, intellectuals, student leaders and artists who had supported
Allende and had them brought to the city's sports stadium.

'Victor Jara was all of the above and more – a poet, singer,
teacher, theatre director, guitarist, leftist. He was among the
thousands arrested that day. Jara was recognized as soon as he
entered the stadium. He was immediately taken away to the locker
room.

'There were many men who tortured Jara, and among those
who would be charged with the crime more than thirty years later
was Lieutenant Pedro Barrientos. It was he who, after four days
of torture, finally broke Victor Jara's wrist and then asked him to
play his guitar.

'Jara laughed, and even as his hand hung uselessly from his
wrist, he broke into the song 'Venceremos' – We Shall Prevail –

the song he had composed for the election campaign of President
Allende three years earlier.

'And he sang his last song too, which begins:

> *There are five thousand of us here,*
> *in this small part of the city.*
> *We are five thousand.*
> *I wonder how many we are*
> *in all the cities and in the whole country?*

'And ends:

> *How hard it is to sing*
> *when I must sing of horror.*
> *Horror which I am living,*
> *horror which I am dying.*
> *To see myself among so much*
> *and so many moments of infinity*
> *in which silence and screams*
> *are the end of my song.*
> *What I see, I have never seen.*
> *What I felt and what I feel*
> *will give birth to the moment.*

'That final act of resistance infuriated Barrientos so much that
he began to play Russian roulette with Victor Jara. Only, he kept
firing the pistol until the bullet was released. And then he shot
Victor Jara yet again. And again. And asked his men to shoot too.
Jara's body had forty bullet wounds.

'But his death was not in vain. He was memorialized. The
stadium was named after him. Contrast this, Shahenshah, with the

fate of Tamil writers. Most people outside Tamil Nadu don't even know of Bharatiyar, the poet whose work fuelled and mobilized thousands of freedom fighters. Rabindranath Tagore won the Nobel Prize and is celebrated as a poet laureate. Subramania Bharatiyar has one street in Delhi named after him. There were eight people at his funeral. He died at the age of thirty-two.

'This is our homeland, Shahenshah. Tamil Nadu. When a film star dies, the world comes to a standstill. Cameras rush to telecast the funeral live. People throng the streets and cry. Superstar arrives with a bouquet. So does Ulaga Nayagan. Kavipperarasar and Isai Thilagam arrive. The chief minister arrives. The leader of the opposition. The leader of the party that rants about caste.

'But when a writer dies, he attracts all the fuss of a dead sewer rat.

'Let me tell you of three writers. Ashokamitran, who writes better than many a Nobel winner. There were twenty-five people at his funeral. Of them, fifteen were his relatives. Then there was the poet Gnanakoothan. Sixteen people at his funeral. Twice the number that had attended Bharatiyar's. Some progress in a hundred years, I suppose.

'Do you know what sort of man Bharatiyar was? He would spend all day with intellectuals, planning protests and printing pamphlets. He would return home, where his wife would be waiting anxiously, hoping he had bought provisions. Seeing him walk down the street empty-handed, she would go to the neighbour's and ask for a tumbler of rice grains. She would then go to boil water to cook the rice. When she came for the rice, the tumbler would be empty. Bharatiyar would have thrown the rice to the crows and sparrows that had gathered at their home, and would be smiling with delight as they ate. And he would spontaneously compose a song about how the crow and sparrow were of his ilk.

'Once, Gandhi had come down to Madras to discuss the upcoming Congress session. A man with a well-groomed moustache and a turban on his head stormed into the room and sat beside Gandhi on his cot. "Mr Gandhi," he said, "there is a gathering at the Marina that I have organized today. Would you be able to do us the honour of being our chief guest?" Gandhi checked his itinerary. That day was packed, he said, could he come the next day? The man said he could not postpone it to the next day. "I take your leave, Mr Gandhi," he said, "you and your protest have my blessings." And he disappeared as fast as he had arrived. Gandhi turned to Rajaji, who was leaning against a post, and asked who the man was. Rajaji did not like Bharatiyar. He saw him as a junkie and a dissolute poet. Gandhi sensed this and said, "This man is a treasure. You and your language ought to be proud of him. You must protect him and provide for him." What Gandhi could see, the Tamils could not.

'Nothing has changed, Shahenshah. I too shall die a sewer rat.

'The third writer whom I was going to speak to you about is Pudhumaipithan. He lived in Chennai, and his wife in Tirunelveli. He wrote letters to her. I read his compiled letters. There is not one that doesn't contain a promise to send money. And not one that fails to beg forgiveness for not sending money. His wife responds to each, saying she is starving. A woman, starving! In one of her letters, she writes that she has heard from his friend Sengalvarayan, who has just returned from Chennai, that Pudhumaipithan has been in an accident. Was that true, she asked. "Madwoman," Pudhumaipithan writes back, "if I had been in an accident, wouldn't it have appeared in the papers?" So famous a writer that an accident would merit a news report, and his wife was starving. He had to turn to cinema to make money as a scriptwriter. And while working on one such film, he contracted tuberculosis. He died at the age of forty-two, trying to earn a living.

'Things haven't changed much. A writer friend of mine lives in one room of his son's flat. Opposite the apartment complex is a house bigger than the compound in which the apartments are housed. That belongs to a film music composer. My friend prides himself on his poverty. We writers do this disservice to ourselves. We believe we should be poor. As we were speaking, his granddaughter ran into the room and spoke to him in English. The irony. One of the greatest writers of Tamil, and he had to speak to his granddaughter in English.

'Even worse, there is the writer Mowni. I know his grandson well. We were speaking about him, when the grandson's ten-year-old daughter asked us, "Who is this Mowni you keep speaking about?" Her father said, "Your Mani Thatha wrote under the pen name Mowni." She looked at him in surprise. "What!" she said. "Mani Thatha was a writer?"

'A writer, I think, ought to be born in Chile. If one is killed, one is memorialized. If one lives, one is celebrated. Take the poet Nicanor Parra. He lived to the grand old age of a hundred and three. He was able to live because of how much money he made. You'd think he was a Hollywood icon. And then there was Pablo Neruda. Who hasn't heard of him? Pinochet considered him a threat and stationed guards around his house. Once, when they searched his house, as was routine, he said, "There is only one thing of danger to you here – poetry." He had already received the Nobel Prize by then. Look how South America treats its writers, even when the president is against them. Look how the world treats South American writers. Tamil Nadu, though ... thoooo!

'Aiyo, I'm sorry, Shahenshah. I let myself get carried away. Do forgive my rudeness.'

'I'm no longer an emperor, Honourable Katib. Think of me as a friend. You can swear, and you can spit. But I must tell you, all this talk of Chile and your obsession with it has made me curious. What a country, where the ruler is against poets and writers, but the people celebrate them! I wonder if we should make a trip there.'

'I'm afraid it's easier said than done, Huzoor,' the writer sighed. 'I had to wait twenty-five years to make that trip. I was aching to go. I wondered if I would ever have enough money to go. I would often tell my wife that if I died without going to Chile, I would haunt her and bite her throat to remind her of my unrealized dream.'

'How is your wife responsible for your not making enough money to go to Chile?' Aurangzeb asked.

'It's not that I didn't make the money, Shahenshah. One of my friends was depositing a considerable sum in my bank account every month to help me save for the trip. But it was all spent on my dogs.'

'What sort of dog eats that much?'

'A Great Dane. Only film stars can afford such a dog. I had one. My wife and son had gifted him to me as evidence of their love. And not just him. A Labrador too. They felt compelled to express their boundless love for the writer twice over. The cost of each puppy is a fraction of the monthly cost of maintenance.

Their love didn't cover the maintenance. How could I save any money to...'

'Don't worry, Honourable Katib. The three of us are in Santiago right now.'

What insanity was this! Yes. They were in Santiago, on Andrés Bello Avenue. It was a forty-eight-hour journey by flight. There was a stop at Dubai, another at São Paulo, and then they would finally arrive exhausted at Santiago. But they seemed to have been teleported as if in a dream.

The writer felt in his pocket for his passport. It was right there. He opened the pages and found a valid visa. There were immigration stamps at the Dubai and São Paulo and Santiago airports too. He checked Kokkarakko's passport. That had all the paperwork too. He hesitated before asking Aurangzeb for his passport. But Aurangzeb handed it over to him before he could verbalize the request. That had the same stamps. Only, the name on the passport was 'Gangaram Mohanram'. The writer then remembered that the Aghori's name was Gangaram. Oh, right. The body needed the passport.

Now, people might slot this novel under 'magical realism'. But that wouldn't be right. The writer was living in this world. He, Aurangzeb and Kokkarakko had truly travelled here. Kokkarakko seemed both unsurprised and unimpressed by the teleportation or whatever it was. He stood smoking nonchalantly.

If I were to detail what these three characters did in Chile, where they went, and what they saw and spoke of, this would turn into a travelogue. And so, I will only give you reports of a few key incidents.

The first day passed in the writer walking around in a daze, trying to figure out how they had arrived there, and with all the paperwork. Where had the passport and visa come from? Was this some magic? Catarina de San Juan was reported to have performed miracles in faraway villages even as she remained cloistered in the cathedral. Could this be bilocation of that sort?

'No, Honourable Katib,' said Aurangzeb, reading his thoughts as usual. 'Do not seek answers that will quell your sense of wonder.' And with that aphorism, he left the writer to his thoughts.

The next morning, the writer took them to the Palacio de La Moneda.

'Palace?' scoffed Aurangzeb. 'Why, this is barely the size of the kitchen of our zamindars' mansions! Is this how communists live?'

'No, Shahenshah. This used to be a factory, a mint, before it was converted into the presidential residence. I dread to take you to the Victor Jara Stadium now. The entire street smells of urine. That's the problem with memorials. They pain those to whom they are of significance. They stir nostalgia. To others, they mean nothing.

'My grandparents fled Burma during the Second World War, like many Indians. They were second-generation immigrants, so they knew they belonged to Tamil Nadu, but nothing else. For some reason, they chose Nagore to settle in. My grandfather drank himself to poverty and eventually death, like most migrants. But when he first arrived, they had money. And he built a house for my grandmother. In the middle of the house, he had an area set up for the dice game dayakattai. My grandmother and I, and later my mother and I, used to play dayakattai. My grandfather was long dead by then. My grandmother would tell the story of their move, the bagful of jewellery they had, the house my grandfather built, and the alcohol addiction that claimed his life. She would recite the story as if it had happened to someone else, with no emotion. She had raised twelve children on her own. Perhaps she had run out of tears.

'Eventually, all of us left Nagore. I visit every three or four years, to see the dargah. The cool stone of the floor, the smell of the mud, it is infused in my blood. I need to go to the dargah every few years. Every time I go, I visit the house. The people who bought it from us haven't changed a thing. The dayakattai nook still stands. The lady of the house serves me sweet tea with a sweet smile and tells me my readers often visit. They ask to see the dayakattai set-up. They tell her my grandfather built the house for my grandmother. Seeing my eyes wander to the dayakattai nook, she smiles again.

'Nostalgia is a mental illness. "Nostos" means to return home. "Algos" means pain. The pain of being unable to return home. Because time machines exist only in science fiction, the past is no longer accessible to us. We can't return to something that is no longer accessible. And that causes us pain. Those who cannot bear that pain turn to drink. Perhaps that is why so many migrants are alcoholics. I once realized what would happen if one didn't drink. I can never forget that incident.

'Delhi's Mandi House, winter walks on Barakhamba Road, the throngs of people at Sadar Bazar, the Hungarian Centre on Curzon Road where one would watch films and then wait for an auto or bus to go home, India International Centre ... these memories are etched into my brain. Barakhamba Road is lined with jamun trees whose fruits fall on the roads and turn into a veritable slush under the feet of passers-by. Occasionally, one chances upon an untarnished jamun that can be eaten. Winter walks on that road are an experience in themselves. When I think back to them, my mind goes into turmoil. It's as if a tsunami has been unleashed within me. I can't read or write or eat or sleep or listen to music or even think. It's as if I'm being dragged into a vortex. There are only two ways out – drinking oneself into oblivion, or fucking someone else into oblivion. Neither is usually an option.

'I've written of Majnu-ka-tilla in one of my novels. The Majnu-ka-tilla of the 1980s. The Tibetan market, run by refugees, was a line of open shops back then. You'd get chhang and buffalo curry. Most importantly, there was a forested area nearby, where even day was dark as night. The market has now modernized. I don't know if you can get chhang or buffalo curry there. But I wanted to see the forest when I went there after years.

'I got off the metro and looked for a ride. A cycle rickshaw approached. It stuns me that, even today, cycle rickshaws operate in Delhi. One man labours to carry another. Actually, it's usually two customers sharing a rickshaw. And North Indians tend to be fat. They ride with their buttocks spilling out of the seat even as the rickshaw puller huffs and puffs. Having reached their destination, they bargain too, over five and ten rupees. There are ten lakh rickshaw pullers in Delhi, operating six lakh vehicles between them, night and day. None of them is from Delhi. They are migrants, usually from Bihar or Chhattisgarh. I was moved to do some research on them, you see. On migrants. There were fifteen lakh unskilled migrants in 1991. By 2011, they numbered twenty-two lakh. Domestic help, corporation workers, security guards, drivers, pushcart operators, rickshaw pullers, dhobis, istriwallahs, barbers, ear-cleaners, water carriers … twenty-two lakh in all.

'Shahenshah, the man who took me to the forest told me his name was Ram Singh. He made three hundred rupees a day. On good days. There was no money to be made on rainy days. He kept fifty for his expenses and saved the rest to send home. His old mother, his wife and four children were dependent on him. He would eat at temples and gurdwaras and Jain mandirs so he didn't have to spend money on food. If he had a customer at mealtimes, he had to go without. But hunger he could bear. It was breathing that was hard, in winter. Diwali made it all worse. A week before and a week after, Delhi's smog became even thicker. The people who burst crackers would go back to their air-conditioned, air-purified homes. "But we have only the streets for home, don't we, Babuji?" he said. The rest is his story now, Shahenshah. Let me simply quote him for you:

The smoke teases our insides, Babuji. We cough, we cough up blood. The girls from the college nearby come to us in the mornings and lecture us about spitting on the streets. What do you mean, don't spit? If one has to spit, one has to spit. They should be glad we don't spit on their faces, with their earnest expressions and polished skins and exposed thighs and bouncing breasts.

Sex is in short supply too, Babuji. I go home once a year. For fifteen days. I intend to stay for a month, but my family only says one thing to me — money, money, we need money, we need money for clothes, we need money for a roof, look at the roof, you can see the sky through the roof, we need a new roof, we need money, we need money for medicines ... It strikes me that this hell is better than the repetition of that phrase, and I leave home for Delhi.

What does one do for sex? There is no shortage of randis. But there is a shortage of money. Those whores want a day's collection to spread their legs. An hour's work for them. I work from six in the morning to eleven at night, with no rest except for one hour at lunch, and that one hour is spent searching for a place of prayer that is serving food at the time. But for the randis? One hour, three hundred rupees. It makes you want to line them up and whip them.

There are two options if you can't find a girl – you either use your hand, or you find a boy and fuck his gaand. A hole is a hole.

But nothing helps in winter. We cough and bleed. We spit the blood. 'Don't spit on the roads,' say the girls, earnest faces, exposed thighs, polished skin, bouncing breasts.

The journalists come and speak to us. The photographers make their money from capturing us shiver and quake under our flea-ridden, hole-riddled blankets. Nothing changes. No one gives us money, no one gives us shelter, no one gives us blankets.

The city fucks us up, Babuji. It makes us monsters. Go to my village and ask them, they would say there is no better man than Ram Singh, he is a golden boy, no bad habits.

One day, you know what happened, Babuji? In Majnu-ka-tilla, by the very forest you want to visit, two girls from the college were standing at night. This was not uncommon. We usually passed them by, ignoring their "don't spit" lectures. But that night, we were high on charas that one of us had procured. Six of us. Two of them. Starved dogs, luscious meat. We fell on them. We dragged them to the forest. They resisted us, but they could not fight us. They did not scream. City girls, you see, scared and unprepared. If this had happened to my wife, she would have killed her attacker by biting his neck to pulp. He would have killed her with his bare hands even as he lay dying. The village kills. The city spares. We did not kill them. But we did not spare them. All our pent-up desire was fulfilled, our thirst slaked, our hunger satiated, a feast for the starving.

We left them unconscious, undead.

The next day, we did not find them in the forest. We wondered what would happen. Would the police come looking for us? Would they come back to point us out to the authorities? For several days, we waited and watched. Nothing happened. The girls did not appear again in the group that lectured us about spitting. I never touched charas again.

Here we are, Babuji, here is the forest.

'That, Shahenshah, is what he said.'

With that, the writer fell silent.

No one else spoke either, and then the writer said, 'This was strange, Shahenshah. All this while, you have been speaking through the Aghori. And now Ram Singh spoke through me.'

'No,' said Kokkarakko. 'Ram Singh did not speak through you. He spoke *to* you. He told you he raped two girls because they had earnest faces and polished skin and exposed thighs and bouncing breasts and an education and standards of hygiene. And you let him talk and got off at the forest and paid him his fare and maybe a tip because you felt sorry for him, sorry for that rapist bastard.

'You're a writer, you're an intellectual, and your heart bleeds for a rapist because he is shivering in the cold. That bastard speaks as if the charas and the circumstances gave him a right to rape those girls. He left them *unconscious*. And you said nothing.

'And you, Alamgir, you who speak of honour and women's honour, you said nothing about his saying nothing. Exposed thighs? She could expose her entire body, and yet no man has a right to rape her! Have you forgotten the Delhi bus rape of 2012? Jyoti Singh said the most violent of the six was the "juvenile", the anonymous juvenile who got away with three years of detention and was sent on his way with ten thousand rupees and a sewing machine, the person who had inserted an iron rod into her vagina. *The city fucks us up*, he says, your Ram Singh. Every Ram Singh says that. Every rapist says that. Ask my village, ask my mother, ask my sister. It was the city, it was the charas, it was the clothes she was wearing. *No.* It was you, you're the monster, you're the rapist! The defence lawyer appointed by the court for those six men claims he would have burnt his daughter alive if she had been out at night, watching films with her boyfriend. The court listens.

'In Chennai, a man rapes and kills a six-year-old girl. His father takes him out on bail. He asks his mother for money, she refuses, he kills her and flees. This is the state of criminal law of India. And you don't even tell that rapist who blamed the city and the charas and the lectures that he was a criminal!'

The writer had to acknowledge that Kokkarakko was right. He had once gone to Tihar Jail to visit a friend who had been incarcerated.

'What are your roommates like?' he had grinned to the friend.

The friend had laughed. 'They all believe they are innocent. Every one of them.'

The writer has never forgotten that sentence. Doesn't their conscience hurt them, he wanted to ask. But he already knew the answer. It was their conscience that rationalized it. It was the charas, it was the city, it was the circumstances, it was the clothes. It wasn't me. You'd have done the same thing in my place.

The rickshaw puller rationalized it. The emperor rationalized it. Rapes across centuries. Raids across centuries. Riots across centuries. Torture. Extortion. Siege. Jauhar. Jail. Saka. Suicide.

'All right, now,' said Kokkarakko, stubbing his cigarette. 'We're in Santiago. Why are we talking of rickshaw pullers and rapes? Let's go see where Neruda lived.'

That is Kokkarakko for you.

CHAPTER 10

Escape from Santiago

Pablo Neruda had three houses in Chile, all of which Alamgir had to be shown. Looking at the one in Isla Negra, he marvelled, 'What kind of country is this? The writers' houses are the size of palaces, and the rulers' houses the size of their kitchens.'

'A country that celebrates its writers,' sighed the writer.

The writer has promised you not to turn this into a travelogue, and so we won't go into the details of the houses, or what Pablo Neruda had filled their rooms with. As Kokkarakko said earlier, those things can be googled. Pablo Neruda is better documented than the Mughals, and the writer found his secondary research on the poet fairly easy.

Alamgir asked, as they sat in a cafe, 'How is it no one drinks water here? They don't even serve water at these feasts you bring me to. They drink fruit juice or green tea or coffee or beer or wine with their food, but never water. Have you noticed, Honourable Katib?'

'Yes, Shahenshah, I suffered much on that account when I first came here too. It's the same in Europe. I would end up drinking tap water there, because no one seemed to even sell water.'

241

Kokkarakko was behaving like someone born and bred in Chile, drinking fruit juice and beer and wine in turns with his meals. He looked at the writer and said, 'What's your problem, though? You like your wine.'

Yes, the writer did like his wine. But could he substitute water for wine? It was his habit to drink one litre of water every morning, right after he brushed his teeth. Could he finish a bottle of wine instead?

You could try buying water, but they'd give you soda in the shops. 'Agua' meant 'water', didn't it? Why soda? The writer later discovered the water they sold was 'agua con gas'. The writer would be half dead from thirst and gratefully reach for the agua, only to find it was agua con gas. The soda nauseated him. Worse, since no one ever drank agua, with or without gas, the bottle had spent days in the fridge and the aerated water was a block of ice.

'Why has no writer spoken of this problem?' Alamgir asked.

Because no Indian writer has come to South America, the writer thought. The need for water seemed to be a uniquely Indian phenomenon. During his travels in Europe, his friends thought it peculiar that he drank water with food. They found it ridiculous that he carried a bottle of water with him wherever they went.

Water was like air, wasn't it? How did non-Indians live without it, the writer wondered. Back in India, the government – which rarely does anything when elections are not around the corner – had set up water stands for the public. Not just the central government, but the state governments too. Offices had a peon designated the 'waterman'. His job was to ensure all the employees had a glass of water at hand every few minutes. Restaurants in India would serve water before the waiter even brought the menu. When Indian restaurants began to sell bottled water, Indians complained that Kali Yuga was well and truly here, the Great Flood that heralded Doomsday was going to inundate the earth. Eventually, they caved and began to buy water, because one had to drink water. Not if you were Chilean. Not if you were anything but Indian.

When the writer had first arrived in South America, with grand plans of a multi-country visit, starting with a climb to Machu Picchu from the Bolivian side, their guide had suggested they take bottles of water along, since the thinner air could trigger altitude sickness and thirst. Only small bottles, with a quarter of a litre of water, were available. The writer had bought a single bottle, assuming there would be more shops along the way. He'd got through it in five minutes. So had the rest of his group.

Worse was waiting for him. Their next stop was Cusco, at an even higher elevation than Machu Picchu. The temperature had dropped below zero. That night, he hadn't been able to breathe. When he spoke, his mouth made only a 'zh' sound. 'Ezhaale moozhu vizha muzhizha,' he said, meaning 'Ennale moochu vida mudila' – I cannot breathe. He prided himself on being among the very few Tamilians who could pronounce 'zh', the sound unique to Tamil and Malayalam. Every Malayali could pronounce it. And almost no Tamilian could. Now, his very travel group did not understand what he was trying to say. He'd stumbled his way to the hotel reception, where his condition rather than his speech prompted the manager to bring him an oxygen cylinder. This was apparently par for the course here. The writer wondered how the rest of his group was entirely unaffected.

When dawn broke, the writer fled to Santiago. He wanted to be at sea level. As he waited for the taxi that would take him to the airport, he saw a group of men in their eighties, smoking cigars in the lounge. They were absolutely fine. He himself was yet to reach seventy. And he prided himself on his European outlook. Yet, his body had proven itself Indian.

Cusco had been the capital of the Incan empire. The writer had planned to spend a good while looking around. It was he who had drawn up the itinerary for the group, and now the rest of them would see it while he cut his trip short. Perhaps he could hang on for a day or two? And then go to Bolivia, where his hero Che Guevara had started a revolution? Nope. He wouldn't last another night, let alone two.

He thought of all the Indians who had been brought home in coffins from trips abroad. A young film director had gone to Tashkent to shoot a sequence. He had apparently had a heart attack from the cold. But rumour had it that he had overdosed on a cocktail of narcotics and vodka and Viagra, and had the said heart attack in the middle of an orgy in a brothel. Perhaps. But Lal Bahadur Shastri, the Indian prime minister who could not possibly have touched vodka or women or Viagra on his own trip to Tashkent, had not made it out alive either. Right now, Cusco seemed even more dangerous than Tashkent. And so, the writer left for Santiago, where…

'For God's sake, must you hijack your own novel? This was Alamgir's story, and now it's yours,' Kokkarakko interrupted. 'And here you are, with a sob story. I'm not saying it's uninteresting. But you need to stop these meanderings. It makes the novel less crisp.'

The writer stopped there, but in honour of his nostalgia, he decided to have pisco instead of wine that night. Alamgir wanted water, but they only got agua con gas, which he did not like. The hotel reception said there was no water in the hotel. The writer decided to shelve these mundane concerns and focused on his pisco instead.

~

All of a sudden, the writer saw a macaw sitting on one corner of his mattress. It was the size of an eagle. And it spoke fluent Urdu. The writer had watched YouTube videos of talking parrots. But this macaw enunciated its words in a manner that was undoubtedly human. Yet its voice was that of a parrot.

More surprisingly, its first words were, 'Honourable Katib, it is I, Aurangzeb.'

The writer's mouth fell open.

'You look stunned,' said the macaw. 'Well, I can't blame you. The pisco knocked you out pretty badly some hours ago. You see, I was terribly thirsty and didn't know what to do. Then I remembered your saying one could drink water from the tap...'

'Aiyo! That's in Europe! Not in third world countries like this!'

'Well, I drank water from the tap, and my voice turned into this parrot-like squawk. It seemed ignominious for the Aghori to speak in such a voice, and so I took the form of a macaw.'

'Oh God, what will I do now? I have no clue what's going on in my own novel. First, we landed up in Santiago without ever getting into a flight but with passports stamped with visas and immigration approvals. There is even a permit to take up residence in Chile. My readers will claim it is all lies. Or they will call it magical realism. But then, the question arises: Alamgir, who was able to swing such an impossible task...'

'No, it was not I but the Aghori who did it, really.'

'All modesty aside, Shahenshah … one of you swung that. Having the ability to pull off such miracles, must you go and drink tap water? Why not turn soda into water instead?'

'Have you got me mixed up with Aladdin's genie, Honourable Katib?'

'But if you could…' the writer trailed off. He was beginning to sound like a broken record, and Kokkarakko might wake from his alcoholic stupor and materialize in his room to lecture him on repetition in writing. 'Never mind, Shahenshah. But why choose a macaw? Why not a peacock?'

'Why, Honourable Katib, I thought you had transcended identities such as caste and religion and language and nation. And yet you would have me turn into your national bird and…'

'Oh, no, no. This was because the peacock is Lord Muruga's vahana, and I thought it might make for a nice DP for my social media accounts if I could get one seated on a peacock…'

'You'd like to sit on me, Honourable Katib?'

The conversation was taking an unpleasant turn. The writer was wondering how to handle the situation when Kokkarakko entered suddenly, knife in hand. He swept up the macaw, slit its throat, plucked its feathers, basted it in several sauces and then threw it on to the grill. All this in the fraction of a second. The writer hadn't noticed the grill, all set up for a barbecue, earlier.

Then, the full horror of the situation hit him. Kokkarakko had just barbecued the Aghori. What would happen now? Had they killed the Aghori? And what about the spirit of Alamgir? Would the two of them wreak revenge on the writer and Kokkarakko for this humiliation? Kokkarakko removed the bird from the grill, sliced it and served it in three portions. He held one out to the writer. It smelled wonderful, but how could the writer partake of it without knowing whom he was eating?

Perhaps this was all a dream?`

The writer looked about himself, only to jump out of his skin.

Aurangzeb was seated on a chair in the room, smiling cheerfully. 'Honourable Katib, see what a wonderful meal Kokkarakko has barbecued for us! Don't worry, this is not the macaw. This is chicken. No beef on your account, no pork on mine. Barbecued chicken. Please join us,' he said, pointing to the writer's plate.

Kokkarakko had already begun to eat.

The writer would never figure out quite what happened in the suite that night.

But something happened the next day that rendered the events of the night fairly insignificant.

Although Santiago wasn't as famed for its nightlife as Rio de Janeiro was, the writer did have a bucket list. For one, he wanted to walk the streets and look at the women. The women wore almost nothing. Unfortunately, a man did not have the right to ogle women anywhere outside the subcontinent. So, he had to be discreet. Often, he thought he saw naked women. It was only on closer scrutiny that he spied the strap of a thong or a bra. Aurangzeb was muttering about qayamat.

The writer followed his gaze. A woman in her fifties was walking their way. She wore a thong. But there were holes in the scanty cloth that made up the thong. One could see her pubic hair through it.

'Don't look, Alamgir, it's considered ill-mannered,' the writer said, although he was somewhat fascinated himself.

'I don't see why. There are Hollywood films where the camera focuses on women's backsides and thighs. There is a Bruce Willis film in which a woman bends over and two men have a conversation about whether she is wearing chaddis or not...' Alamgir began.

'Not chaddis, Shahenshah, the word is *panties*,' Kokkarakko said usefully.

'Whatever it is, here's a woman with her pubic hair on display. If a man went about with his dick on display, wouldn't he be arrested for obscenity? When women want equality, why are they spared that fate?' demanded Alamgir.

While the writer was tempted to agree with him, he caught Kokkarakko's eye and said instead, 'You see, Alamgir, it is like this. Women speak of centuries of male gaze, and this is their reclamation of their bodies. For instance, there is a movement called "Free the Nipple", which...'

'Enough! I have heard enough! I must shut my ears and my eyes, both!' Alamgir cried. 'Qayamat is here!'

This prompted the writer to make up his mind about something ... but we'll come to that shortly.

What I'm going to tell you about first is La Piojera. The writer had wanted to see this dive bar for himself desperately and hadn't had the chance during his previous visit.

'What kind of miserable place is this?' Aurangzeb said.

'It is meant to look like this, Alamgir,' said the writer. 'It is a no-frills place. It started in 1896, and from back then to now, it has been affordable to the poorest of the poor – blue-collar workers and intellectuals. In fact, its official name was Santiago Antiguo. And it was also known as Bar Democrático. But when the then president of Chile, Arturo Alessandri Palma, visited in 1922, wanting to see for himself why this was such a beloved bar, he looked at it just as you did and exclaimed with the same dismay you did, "You brought me to this piojera?" "Piojera" means fleahouse. In 1981, the owner made the name official. The speciality of this dive bar is terremoto, which means earthquake. It's ice cream with pipeño, and you simply have to try it, Shahenshah. By the way, they don't accept cards here. Only cash.'

In response, Aurangzeb pulled out a fat purse from his pocket. The writer looked inside. It was bulging with American dollars. They crossed the courtyard, and passed through the entrance of the garish building, with its half-ochre, half-red walls. They looked around for a place to sit among the wooden tables, their tops wet with spilled alcohol. The air was heavy with human breath and uncensored swearing.

'Hijo de puta!'

'Puta madre!'

'Cabron!'

It was as if a murder could occur at any moment. The writer was reminded of tea shacks in the villages of Tamil Nadu.

'Why, this sounds like *Narcos*!' Alamgir said.

'Shahenshah! You never told me you watch *Narcos*!'

'Watch? I scanned it. It takes only seconds. I've watched a whole lot of your web series since you first mentioned the concept, Honourable Katib. *Inmate, Gotham, Lucifer, La Reina del Sur, Breaking Bad* … you name it. While I'm glad I'm up to date, I lose out. I don't experience the thrill and tension of anticipation. Let me give you an example. When the High Sparrow announced on *Game of Thrones* that Cersei would pay penance by walking naked through the town, the rest of you had a week of torment and joy. Would she be paraded naked? Would something happen that would preclude the parade? Was her brother-slash-lover going to rescue her? You waited, and you lived through several prospects during that week of waiting. And then the climax came, quite fittingly. I lost out.'

'You seem to be quite the avid fan of *Game of Thrones*, Shahenshah.'

'Yes, indeed I am. The reason is Ramsay. He's my favourite character.'

'Aiyo! He's the world's worst villain. He's a step ahead of your family, Shahenshah. Worried that he might lose his hard-won title, he killed his father and fed his stepmother and her infant son alive to his dogs!'

'What is this, Honourable Katib! Can you, who have read Lacan and Foucault and Derrida, speak of binary oppositions such as good and bad, hero and villain? One of my favourite things about *Game of Thrones* is the relationship between Ramsay and Theon, the way the dynamics are explored. Ramsay tortures Theon in ways even I cannot imagine. He cuts off Theon's penis. And then he eats a sausage and makes Theon wonder whether that is his penis on the plate. One could go on. But the most nuanced moment is this – Ramsay asks Theon to give him a shave and dozes off. Theon has a sharp razor in hand. He places it against Ramsay's neck. He is a trained warrior. He could slit the man's throat. And yet he doesn't. Because he is no longer Theon. He is the same body. But the immense torture he has undergone has allowed Ramsay to tear his mind into pieces and put it back together. In the intervals between sessions of torture, he lives in fear of what will come next. He is not even able to bring himself to kill the cause from worry over the consequences. The same thing happens in *Feast of the Goat*, does it not, when the journalist appears to interview Trujillo? He is not even screened by the bodyguards. The pistol is with him even as Trujillo talks, and yet … he is too afraid to pull the trigger.'

'Yes, Shahenshah. Fear informs the decisions – or the lack thereof – in these two instances. But I'd like to draw your attention to a short story by Hernando Tellez, "Espumo y nada más" – Lather and Nothing More. The decision made in that story is unlike the ones in these two. It is a decision informed by honour, a brave decision. I don't want to give this away, because my readers will find the story online and you can scan it in seconds. But it's a story that stunned me. Which brings me to Vladimir Nabokov's "Razor". You know…'

It struck the writer that Kokkarakko hadn't interrupted him in a while. So he interrupted himself to look at his friend, who was drowning himself in terremoto.

'What's the matter, why are you silent?' Alamgir asked Kokkarakko, reading the writer's mind as usual.

'I've never watched a web series. Besides, the two of you are intellectualizing pulp. This is what the writer always does.'

'But to dismiss all web series as pulp and refrain from watching any, don't you see you're losing out on a whole world?' Alamgir said.

'To dismiss all intoxicants as evil and refrain from drinking terremoto, don't you see you and we and the readers are losing out on a whole world?' Kokkarakko responded.

Alamgir fell silent.

～

Some pages ago, the writer told you Alamgir's reaction to the women of Santiago – and particularly to the woman with the torn thong – had prompted a decision. This is what it was – he had made up his mind to take the emperor to a cafe con piernas. There were cafes con piernas of various persuasions and various degrees of undress. The one they chose had waitresses with G-strings to hide their vaginas and a ribbon across their nipples. How the two stayed in place was a thing of wonder.

The emperor started with an intellectual question. 'I'd like to know the difference between chaddis, panties, G-strings and thongs.'

'He has written about this in detail in one of his other novels,' Kokkarakko said. 'You can scan it in your head, Alamgir, so his readers are spared the repetition.'

Just then, three women came towards their group. The writer surmised that none of the women was Chilean. They were probably from Venezuela.

Two of the women wrapped their arms around the writer's and Kokkarakko's shoulders and began to whisper, 'Mi amor…'

'What is myamore?' Kokkarakko asked.

'Mi amor. It means "my love"…' the writer said weakly.

The third woman seemed to hesitate before Aurangzeb. That was the emperor's vibe, the writer thought. She must have sensed she was unwelcome. Alamgir raised a hand and indicated to her that she should move away. She did.

One of the remaining two took Kokkarakko's hand and placed it on her tattooed thigh. She then slid on to his thigh and negotiated one leg over so she was astride it.

'If only I'd known this would happen, I'd have worn shorts,' Kokkarakko said.

The other woman climbed on to the stool by the writer and began to murmur seductively into his ear in Spanish.

'What will you have to drink?' the writer asked.

'Juice,' she said.

The writer ordered coffee and juice. He realized why she'd asked for juice when he tasted the coffee. It was arguably the worst he had ever had.

'Why is the coffee in a *cafe* so awful?' he asked.

'Who comes here for coffee?' the woman said with a laugh, touching his hand to her thigh.

True. They were here for the piernas, not the cafe. One drank in the women, not the coffee. By this time, Kokkarakko's waitress had led him to the bowels of the bar.

But Kokkarakko emerged even faster than he had gone.

'She wanted me to fuck her in the stalls!' he yelled. 'What the fuck! Let's get out of here!'

The three of them left the bar, only to see a man and a woman fighting at the corner of the street.

They went closer and eavesdropped. It turned out she was a part-time sex worker. She had a day job as a waitress and would supplement her income with prostitution. One of her clients had paid her extra money to take a nude picture of her. He had shown it to his friends. It turned out one of those friends was her brother who had had no clue about his sister's part-time vocation. He was arguing with her, asking how she could have slept with his friend. This was rather irrational, since neither the client nor she had known he was her brother's friend. But her response blew the writer's mind.

'De puta madre, if you gave me money, I'd fuck you too,' she said. 'But you're so fucking useless, you'd borrow the money to pay me, from *me*.'

She stormed off. The writer hurried after her. He told her in broken Spanish that the three of them were writers and they would like to know her story.

'How am I a writer?' Alamgir asked, when the writer returned with the woman.

'Your letters are sheer poetry,' the writer replied.

The woman's story was mundane enough. Her name was Alejandra. She did not know who her father was. Her mother had given birth to her at thirteen years of age. Her brother had a different father. Their mother finally married, and the stepfather began to abuse Alejandra. Her mother knew about it. She would sometimes argue with her husband about the abuse until the walls shook, and then they would have make-up sex until the panels of those walls came loose. Alejandra ran away when she was seventeen years old. She put her brother through school and college. And now...

'Never mind,' said Kokkarakko. 'Hang out with us through the night. We don't want to sleep with you. We want to talk to you.'

Alejandra agreed. She told them of clients with kinks. One would sob all night, pay her and leave. He would not lay a hand on her, he would simply sob. Another would kiss her feet all night. Nothing else. The older men usually asked her to 'behave like a whore'. Their wives would not do the things they wanted them to. The younger men were mostly impotent, she said. It probably had to do with typing too much, too much exposure to the rays of computers. One of them just asked to cuddle. But he paid up. It was the worst if one was married to such a man, as her friend was. Anyway, yet another ... at this moment, they stopped short.

They had come to a street corner where two heavily made-up women stood, clearly soliciting. The younger one was perhaps in her early twenties and immensely beautiful. The older one must have been in her mid-forties. The writer had seen prostitutes in their sixties in Paris. He had initially been horrified, but later learnt that some men had a fetish for senior citizens. What kind of world was this, where children and old women were paid for sex, he'd thought then. It made no sense, though, for two women of such different ages to stand together. They could not possibly be proposing a threesome. And how would it aid either?

'Oh,' said Alejandra casually. 'They're mother and daughter. The mother will bluff. She'll ask for fifty dollars. The daughter, they'll expect to charge twice as much, but she will ask for only sixty. Any client would agree. So everyone's happy.'

'What is this?' cried Alamgir. 'A mother helping her daughter make money off her own body. This is absurd! We must put an end to this!'

Kokkarakko was unmoved. One of his novels was all about the sexual kinks of people. He stood smoking, while Alamgir spun around as if every corner held some new danger and cried, 'What shall we do, what shall we do, Honourable Katib?'

'Why don't you become the ruler of this country, Shahenshah?' the writer said. 'But then don't be like Pinochet. You must be a good and just ruler.'

'That is an oxymoron,' grunted Kokkarakko.

'Why, there was Dr Allende, wasn't there?' the writer said.

'All right, I'm going to go occupy the head of this country's emperor,' Aurangzeb announced. 'Let's see what happens.'

'What is this, Shahenshah? You're talking like this is one of our Tamil films. You're going to go occupy the president's head, and then what?' the writer said.

'Well, it's night now. Take a look at the papers tomorrow,' said Alamgir enigmatically.

~

The next morning, an announcement from the presidential palace was beamed across news channels and flashed across dailies. Only three people – Alamgir, the writer and Kokkarakko – were aware of the context and backstory. It stunned the nation. Some analysts wondered whether the president had gone insane. Political experts on news channels tore their hair as they held heated debates on the announcement. Leftists said another Pinochet was emerging. Some said American imperialism was behind the whole thing. These were the announcements:

a) No longer could cafes con piernas operate within the city limits. New ones must be established outside, and the existing ones removed from their premises and shifted to the outskirts immediately.

b) Women were no longer permitted to wander around with G-strings as their only piece of clothing. (Clarification: The government had no quarrel with the G-string. It was only with the G-string being used as a garment in itself that the nation took issue.)

c) All restaurants must serve still water free with coffee.

d) Tourists from India, Afghanistan, Pakistan and Bangladesh must be allowed to visit without a visa.

Doctors were all praise for the third point in this list. Indian prime minister Narendra Modi called the Chilean president to thank him for this amicable gesture. Many Indians believed this had been wrought by Modi's efforts and celebrated their dear leader for yet another political feat.

However, the first two points set off a wave of opposition in Chile. Feminists and students were the first to protest. The president sent the police and army to quell the rebellion. He wanted history to remember his government's 'iron hand'. The protesters, though, set government buildings on fire. The president declared an emergency, imposed curfew and issued shoot-on-sight orders. The public defied these orders. One million and two hundred thousand people streamed on to the streets, challenging the authorities to shoot them.

International media screamed, 'CHILE BURNS!'

Within days of its inception, the protest changed shades. It began as 'The G-String Rebellion' but soon became about socio-economic disparity and corruption in high offices. The public demanded a revision of educational norms. Only the super-rich could dream of a good education. The middle class, let alone the poor, were being edged out of advanced learning.

The streets rang out with calls for the president's resignation.

Kokkarakko and the writer convinced Alamgir it would be perilous to remain in Chile any longer. They returned the way they had come and found themselves in the Aghori's room, their passports stamped by immigration officials they had never encountered.

Voices from the Past

Perhaps it was the ignominy of a stint in the macaw's body, or perhaps it was the G-strings, but Aurangzeb said he needed a break to process their time in Chile. Kokkarakko took his leave too, saying he would be back if he was so inclined.

Rizwan had not accompanied them to Chile, and the writer was wondering what he must do, when the Aghori changed his posture. He crossed his legs and held his staff like a walking stick. He then spoke, but in a different voice.

~

THE SPIRIT SAID:

Why, my dear sir, I am Jadunath Sarkar. You have gone so far as to quote me in your conversation, and I would have manifested myself earlier, but then you appear to have been making some history yourself.

Well, Aurangzeb mentioned that I had said his life was rather a Greek tragedy, and it is true.

Asia had never before seen a more intelligent, fastidious, disciplined, scholarly, simple, teetotal, hard-working or wise emperor. And yet, his fifty-year rule would sound the death knell for the Mughal empire. Why? I fear you have exaggerated his broad-mindedness thus far. He has come across as a misunderstood hero. I must set you right on this score. His tragic flaw was his bigotry.

He may not have imposed his religion on everyone, but he saw everyone through the lens of his religion. It was not just the Hindus he hated, but the Shias too. When the qazi of Delhi Sheikh ul-Islam warned him against creating an intra-religious rift, the emperor began to criticize the qazi, which drove the latter to a life of seclusion.

And while he did construct the odd temple, he destroyed many and desecrated many more. The Kashi Vishwanath temple was demolished in August 1669. The Keshava Raj temple was pulverized in January 1670 – a temple constructed at a cost of thirty-three lakh rupees at the time – and a mosque erected in its stead; its statues were ferried to Agra, where they were used on the steps leading to a mosque Jahanara Begum had commissioned. The Somnath temple, the Someshwar temple, the three great temples of Udaipur, two hundred and forty temples in Mewar and sixty-seven temples in Jaipur were reduced to dust.

The jizya tax is spoken of in most accounts; but his order that no Hindu who was not a Rajput should keep arms or mount elephants, palanquins, or Arab or Persian horses is largely forgotten. In 1672, he issued a letter to his satraps saying Hindus must be phased out of positions in government. When protests rose against his bigoted diktats, they were put down mercilessly. Thousands were killed.

And he offended the Rajputs greatly. When one of his vassal kings, Raja Jaswant Singh, passed away in 1678, Aurangzeb took over his Jodhpur palace, and had his two wives and their two sons, the heirs of the raja, brought to his palace. He installed a puppet king in Jodhpur and took thirty-six lakh rupees from him for the title. Some of the Rajputs in Aurangzeb's palace secreted the two Rathore heirs away to Marwar. But Aurangzeb insulted them by bringing in some beggar boy, claiming he was the son of Raja Jaswant Singh and the scion of the Rathore dynasty. This beggar was raised in Aurangzeb's palace. The Rajputs never forgot the affront. They plagued Aurangzeb all his life. The number of Rajputs in the army reduced drastically too.

His attacks on Bijapur and Golconda were driven by his hatred for the Shias. The sieges on these forts cost thousands of lives on both sides. Disease ran riot in the army camps, killing tens of thousands. At the age of eighty-one, he went to war against the Marathas and met the same fate as Sisyphus. The forts to which his army was laying siege were on hilltops, at vantage positions. The wind and the rain would drain the energy and morale of Aurangzeb's men. Time was when he used to pay heed to his army generals. But now, when they begged him to call off the pointless siege and return, he called them cowards and dotards.

The khazana was being emptied for pyrrhic wars. Tiny kingdoms whose addition to the empire made little difference were conquered at great cost, financial, emotional, physical and human. His subjects began to resent him.

I came here to warn you not to get carried away by your intimate conversations with the emperor. He was a bigot, deny it as he may. I now take your leave, sir, and shall return if I see fit to do so.

~

THEN THE SPIRIT SPOKE IN AURANGZEB'S VOICE, BUT
THE WRITER DETECTED A NOTE OF WEARINESS:

Honourable Katib, I am a man besieged. I wanted a break, but
I have returned to clarify certain things. It appears my absence,
my inability to defend myself is an excuse for slander. Well, not
'slander' exactly, but certainly misinterpretation of my actions.

It is not to deny what Sarkar Sahib says that I am here, but to
remind you and him that it was the custom of the time to destroy
all that was dear to the conquered, particularly the temples of
kafirs.

I have a question for you. Let's talk about Hiroshima and
Nagasaki. Didn't they know a hundred and fifty thousand
innocent civilians would die along with the twenty thousand
soldiers who wore enemy colours? Why, then, did they bomb
those cities? To end the world war, was it not? To me, at the time,
I felt I had an end in mind, and the means were irrelevant. I had
to give the people good governance. And it was to this end that
I spent my dotage on the battlefield. It was only on my deathbed
that I realized I was a sinner. There could be no forgiveness for
me. My letters in those last years were but pleas to the Almighty
for forgiveness.

From December 1699 when we began the Battle of Satara to
April 1705 when we tried to overcome Wagingera, we spent our
days laying siege to fort after fort in the Deccan. An eighty-seven-
year-old emperor leads an army of tens of thousands on these
expeditions, over eight decades after learning the Holy Quran
by heart. He learnt the words, but what did he learn from them?
Nothing at all. It was at the gates of death that he realized all he
had done was inflict death and suffering on innocents.

In Devpur, near Wagingera, I fell so ill I could no longer write my own decrees. I would simply sign off on them. It was then that I realized I was nearing death. I decided to return to Ahmednagar.

But before I speak of my death, let me speak of my life. Let me speak of the things of which most of your readers can't know. Let me speak of my food habits. I reduced my consumption of meat greatly once I took over as emperor. This does not mean I ate like rabbits and Brahmins. Nor did I advertise my vegetarianism as my forebear Padishah Akbar did. I was not vegetarian, but I did eat vegetables. And I did reduce meat, not because I believed it was evil, but because the oils and masalas used to season the meat in our cuisine would ruin one's health. I knew I needed to stay healthy, and so I forced myself to eat fruits and roots.

Yes, my health was one reason. The other reason was to deny myself all sensory pleasure. Did you know that I was quite the virtuoso on the veena? You look suitably stunned, Honourable Katib. But I denied myself the pleasure of music, as I denied myself the pleasure of muses. I had no harem. I never laid hands on a woman who wasn't a wife. Yes, well, there was Udaipuri Mahal, but she loved me as no other woman had.

She once told me she would kill herself were I to die. I once told her that was nonsense, she was no Rajput princess to fall into flames. She asked me if fire was the only way to die and grabbed her dagger. She screamed, raised an arm over her head and brought the dagger down at great speed so it would slice through her stomach, and stopped right as the point of the knife touched her skin. I was stunned, by her passion and her precision equally. And I felt truly grateful to Allah for having ensured that my last days were not spent away from this beautiful woman who was so in love with me. She was drunk as the devil, and yet she had such control over her movements. At that moment, something occurred for which I have no explanation. I felt a surge of desire, at the age of eighty-eight. And she, moments after nearly impaling herself on a dagger, felt just as much desire. We reached heights of pleasure that night which we never had before. I wonder, Honourable Katib, is there a connection between death and desire?

~

The writer responded, 'Yes, Shahenshah, Georges Bataille has a fair bit to say on the subject. But if I may ask you a question, how is it that you who abhorred alcohol loved a woman who was addicted to it? How did you permit her to consume alcohol?'

'I lived by the principles of my religion, Honourable Katib, but never sought to impose them on anyone else. I brought in regulations in order to avoid public nuisance, but I never banned a single intoxicant.'

'Shahenshah, while we're on the subject of passion and intoxicants, may I ask you something that has been troubling me for a while? Well ... while doing my research, I read of a sweetheart of yours called Zainabadi Mahal, a slave girl of your uncle Mir Khalil, a woman who lived in the zenana of your maternal aunt. That you once drank wine because she asked you to...'

'Hira Bai. Who became Zainabadi Mahal. Yes, it is true that I lost my heart to her the moment I set my eyes on her, leaping up to pick mangoes from a tree in the garden of the zenana in Burhanpur. They were out of reach, and she soon gave up and began to sing. Her voice, her face, her spirit ... I was in love. I knew she was the woman for me. I would marry her and only her, I said. I had never heard a voice like hers. You would not believe what I did the first time I heard that voice. I fainted. My aunt rushed to lay my head on her lap and fan me. I would not rise for two hours. She asked me what the matter was. I told her I was in love. I began to find occasion to visit Burhanpur. I spent days and weeks and months in the company of that one muse of mine, playing the veena as she sang. She was an ethereal dancer too. Even as her feet tattooed the earth, it appeared she was not of this world at all. The scenes played out like the films you describe of your hero for sringara, Honourable Katib, Puratchiththalaivar, I think you said?

'One day, she told me she had no wish to be the hundred and first member of a harem.

'There would be no harem, I said, for I would not break the rules of Islam and marry more than four women. And she would not be the hundred and first of them, but the first of my wives.

'She said she did not believe that.

'I asked what I could do to make her believe me.

'She held out a goblet of wine to me and asked me to drink it.

'I did not tarry a moment. I would have done anything for her. My mind and body and soul were all hers at the time. She haunted my thoughts. I paced with the rage of a hungry tiger, the fever of the churning oceans. She encroached upon my every moment, underlaid every breath. To see her in person gave me some relief. But the separation made my ache far worse. And when she held out the goblet, I told her boisson or poison, I would drink it for her.

'I put the goblet to my lips.

'Hira Bai reached out and knocked it away.

'The force with which she pushed away the goblet caused a drop to land on my lips. She brought her dupatta to my lips to wipe it away, but my tongue instinctively licked my lips. And so I did taste wine, just once in my life. I see, Honourable Katib, that you're reminded of Shakespeare's *Romeo and Juliet*. You're thinking of the lines:

> *I will kiss thy lips.*
> *Haply some poison yet doth hang on them,*
> *to make me die with a restorative.*

'Things did unfold as a tragedy for us. Hira Bai died suddenly and mysteriously not long after I had claimed her for my own. I suspect she had been poisoned by Mir Khalil. Her death was a turning point in my life. There would be no wine and no veena for me, ever. I wonder what might have happened had she lived. Perhaps I would have been a souse like my forefathers. And perhaps I would have played the veena through those nine decades of my life.

'Well, I must go now. I will leave you with others who have things to tell you. I am tired from all that I have lived as a corporeal being, and tired from all that I have relived as a spirit in our recent meetings.'

The Aghori closed his eyes, shook his head wearily, and then sat still.

He then opened his eyes and looked around, as if curious. He brought his hands together and bowed slightly.

~

AND NOW, ANOTHER VOICE SPOKE:

Namaskar.

Scholar, embodiment of simplicity, an emperor who shunned extravagance, teetotaller, the most fastidious and disciplined of men, with an impossible capacity for hard work ... and yet his rule was the death knell for the Mughal empire. Why? It was the curse of a Sufi that wrought this fate.

My dear lekhak, I'm Bhimsen Saxena, entrenched and embedded in Aurangzeb's army, tasked with documenting his wars in the Deccan, and perhaps the most interesting of Alamgir's biographers, if I say so myself – for I am the only Hindu who has written of his time. I am the only witness to the fact that he was no predecessor to the Taliban.

In the rivalry between Chhatrapati Shivaji and Aurangzeb Alamgir, it ought to be expected that a Hindu such as I would have aligned myself with the former. But I chose the latter, for he is a true devotee of his God and held in enormous regard those who sought God. Shivaji had no respect for holy men. The reason he died so young, barely in his fiftieth year, was this – turning a deaf ear to the dervish Jan Muhammad of Jalna, he raided the city. Knowing it was the custom for marauding armies of Hindus to spare religious sites, the people took shelter in the dervish's dargah. But Shivaji broke with custom to attack the dargah. This act of his would take his life. Aurangzeb, on the other hand, didn't go a day without taking the blessings of the Sufi saints. It was his will that he be laid to rest in an anonymous grave in the dargah of Hazrat Khwaja Syed Shah Maqdoom Zain-ud-din Dawood bin Hussain Shirazi at Khuldabad.

And yet, this emperor who so humbled himself before Sufis that he would go to their dargahs on foot and sit with folded hands before them, waiting to receive their blessings, once did the unthinkable.

This concerns the Sufi Sarmad Shaheed, and this is the story of how Muhammad Said Sarmad became a shaheed. Khwaja Harey Bharey was his preceptor, and this is the story of how they came to be laid to rest side by side, the tomb green on one side and blood red on the other. This is the story of the blood on the wall. The thing was, Sarmad shunned all things material, including clothes. His nakedness irked Aurangzeb. Although it must be said that his pendulous stomach did lend him a modicum of modesty, functioning as a screen for that which should not be seen.

There were other things he did that did not find favour with Alamgir. For one, during the rule of Padishah Shah Jahan, he predicted that it would be Dara Shikoh who came to power next. And then he took a lover, a Hindu and – perhaps worse – a man, Abhay Chand, the son of a rich merchant. The two of them wrote impassioned ghazals to each other, sensual on the surface and spiritual when one examined the layers. It must be said that homosexuality was not abhorred in our time as it is in yours. Take Mahmud Ghaznavi, who is arguably more famous for his companionship with the Georgian slave Malik Ayaz than for his attack on the Somnath temple. But anything that was not in tune with the tenets of his religion was anathema to Alamgir. And so it was that Sarmad was an exception to his rule that all Sufis were deserving of deference.

Three years into his reign, Alamgir sent Sarmad a warning. He was to clothe himself or face the consequences. Personal freedom could not impinge on societal mores.

One Friday, as Alamgir was climbing the steps of the Jama Masjid, he saw Sarmad sitting in all his glory before him, having ignored the warning.

The emperor personally went up to the Sufi and said, 'Don't you think you are flouting the sharia by walking around like this?'

'I have nothing to hide,' the Sufi replied. 'It is the sinners who must clothe their shame.'

He might as well have slapped the emperor and boxed both his ears. Now, there was no way forward – either Alamgir would have to die, or Sarmad would. But then, how could one lay a hand on Sarmad? He was so popular that the city would burn were he to be killed. In your time, a hitman could have been hired, or Sarmad could have been conveniently disappeared. But back in our time, things were more straightforward. It would have to be by the order of the emperor. And there would have to be a solid trial and verdict to justify the execution.

There was only one way out. There was only one sin for which one could be executed without question – apostasy.

And so, Sarmad was brought to court, whereupon the qazi first asked him: 'You said it would be Dara Shikoh who became emperor. But that did not come to pass. How do you justify it?'

'I did not speak of this empire, but the celestial empire. The afterlife.'

Whereupon the qazi said, 'Well, then, recite the kalima.'

'La ilaha,' said Sarmad. *There is no God.*

That was enough to prove that Sarmad was in fact Satan. And so he was dragged through the streets and paraded to prison.

He had denied the existence of God. He was a proven apostate, an infidel, a non-believer, and there was nothing for it but to execute him.

Sarmad was sentenced to beheading.

And then it happened. I saw it with my own eyes, so I can promise you it is no myth.

Once the head was severed from the body of Sarmad, the body remained standing upright and calmly picked up the rolling head which was still spouting blood. And then the mouth of the head, held in the Sufi's hands, spoke: '... il-Allahu, Muhammadur-Rasoolallah.'

He had completed the kalima.

'La ilaha il-Allahu, Muhammadur-Rasoolallah,' the head spoke again.

And again. And again. And again.

La ilaha il-Allahu, Muhammadur-Rasoolallah
La ilaha il-Allahu, Muhammadur-Rasoolallah
La ilaha il-Allahu, Muhammadur-Rasoolallah

Even as the head recited the kalima, the body broke into a dance of ecstasy and whirled out of the execution spot at great speed. We ran behind the body, struggling to keep up. It was just as impossible to conceive of such a corpulent body finding it in itself to move at that speed as it was to conceive of a fakir growing quite so corpulent. The body danced its way to the Jama Masjid, the head spilling its blood. I ran to the stream of blood, dipped my fingers in it and touched them to my forehead – a tika of blood, a blessing holier than any I had known. The body stood on the steps and began to dance – the tandava of Shiva, the dance of Kali, the most fearsome dance I had ever seen. It was like Kali Yuga had reached its climax. The streets would crumble, the city would burn, the floods would swallow us all. It was doomsday.

As we stood trembling, we heard a voice.

'Hey Sarmad! Hey Sarmad!'

It came from the tomb of Khwaja Harey Bharey.

'Hey Sarmad, do not do this, let nature take its course. Come here.'

The moment it heard that voice, the corpse stopped its dance of death and began to climb down the stairs. It walked out of the eastern gate and sat by the mazar of Khwaja Harey Bharey under a neem tree. It then placed its head upon its neck and lay down. There would be no further movement from the corpse.

From the next day on, Alamgir found blood on his plate every time he sat down to eat. Could one possibly eat? He was haunted by nightmares every time he closed his eyes. Unable to bear this any more, he turned to his diwan, Dayanat Khan.

Now, Dayanat Khan was a devotee of the Sufi Shah Noor Auliya. Once, when Alamgir was at the Aurangabad court, he had asked Dayanat Khan to bring him a document the next day. The diwan had said he would, despite knowing that the document had been left behind in Delhi, and that he would not be forgiven for this. He might be imprisoned, he might even be killed. It was a crucial document containing the details of taxes collected over the previous year.

Aware that he might not live to see another day, Dayanat Khan went to the khanqah to pay his last respects to Sufi Shah Noor Auliya.

'Your devoted disciple's life will end tomorrow, Huzoor,' Dayanat Khan said.

The Sufi asked him to return after the evening prayer.

When Dayanat Khan arrived, he found Shah Noor all set for a journey.

'Let us go,' the seer said, and walked towards Dayanat Khan's chariot.

Dayanat Khan followed him into it.

'Let's go towards Delhi,' the seer said.

They crossed the city gates.

'Where are we now?' the seer demanded.

'The road to Delhi,' Dayanat Khan said.

The Sufi smiled. 'Look again.'

And Dayanat Khan realized they were already in Delhi. He directed the chariot to his house, retrieved the document and took his seat on the chariot. In the blink of an eye, they were outside the city gates of Aurangabad.

When Alamgir asked to see the document the next day, Dayanat Khan brought it forward.

There's something you should know about the emperor – he had a strong sense of intuition. He could read faces. There was just one time he failed, and that was the case of Sarmad Shaheed. He couldn't see the holiness that manifested before his eyes. His rage had blinded him. Now, he knew Dayanat Khan was hiding something. He remembered his panicked look of the previous day when asked to produce the document. He had also divined the likely cause of that panic.

'Wasn't this document left behind in Delhi?' Alamgir asked.

'Yes, Shahenshah,' admitted Dayanat Khan.

He then told him of the events of the previous night. And Alamgir too became a devotee of Shah Noor Auliya.

Now, upon seeing blood on his plate, he spoke to his diwan, asking for an audience with the seer. He believed Shah Noor Auliya alone could resolve the situation. They went to the Sufi's khanqah.

'What does the emperor seek?' asked the seer.

Having recounted the story of Sarmad, the emperor said, 'I must ask forgiveness of Sarmad, or my nightmares will drive me insane.'

'Tell me of your dream from last night,' Shah Noor Auliya said.

'In my dream, I walked up to Sarmad and said, "Don't you think you are flouting the sharia by walking around like this?" Sarmad replied, "All right, then, fetch me the blanket from there." I went towards the blanket. I lifted it, only to see the heads of all the people I had ever killed rolling under it. And Sarmad began to recite:

> *Insanity is no crime.*
> *The crime is yours*
> *for detesting*
> *the insanity born of love.'*

'This dream implies that there is no redemption for your sin, and that your empire will disintegrate.'

'If that is punishment for my crime, I shall bear it, Hazrat. But all I ask is that you take pity on this sinner and call upon Sarmad's spirit.'

'Why?'

'I would like to beg his forgiveness.'

Shah Noor Auliya did call upon the spirit. Sarmad's spirit told Alamgir what his penance was to be – he must earn his keep. He could handwrite the Quran and sell it; he could sew prayer caps. He could do anything he wanted, but he must not live off the treasury. The shadow of the curse would never be lifted. But if he earned his meals, they would be free of blood.

And that is the true story of Alamgir's simplicity – this is why he ate off the money he earned. On the off chance that he was travelling and did not have recourse to his own funds and had to eat meals prepared from treasury funds, the blood would run on his plate.

However, thanks to the grace of Shah Noor Auliya, he had been able to ask forgiveness and eat the meals he earned. This is why Sufism took such a hold on Hindustan. Let me ask you, Honourable Lekhak, has any Hindu ascetic or saint allowed the common man to see him and receive his barkat for specific problems as the Sufi seers did? Has any of them been able to draw no distinction between prince and pauper, Brahmin and street sweeper? Has any of them offered redemption, rather than invoke karma? In my lifetime, I've been to Nagore, from where you hail. I noticed that the dargah offered vibhuti as prasad, just as temples do. I saw Hindus visit in droves.

'Why do you visit the dargah when there are temples dedicated to both Shiva and Vishnu here?' I once asked a fellow Hindu.

'Those gods must look after the entire world. They don't have the time for us simple folk,' he replied. 'Whereas the auliya is our god-in-residence. He has cured someone or the other from every single family in Nagore of ills, physical or mental.'

The Sufis, and not forced conversions, were the true reason for the spread of Islam in Hindustan. They lived among the people, always approachable, even those who chose to reside in caves in dense forests. They always made time for those who sought their blessings. Can the same be said of our Hindu seers, with the exception of your land's Ramalinga Swamigal?

Take, for instance, Palangposh Auliya.

Oh, before I tell you about him, I should tell you how Alamgir met him. Palangposh Auliya lived on the outskirts of Aurangabad and would habitually meditate on a desolate hill. The hill was also favoured by those who came to smoke ganja. None of them had heard of the great man. Three such ganja addicts made it their sport to drag the seer – who, to them, was an eccentric old man

– up the hill when they arrived, and then roll him down the hill when they were leaving. For a whole month, they did this. The seer would meditate as they smoked the chillum.

One fine day, Alamgir had come to pay his respects to the Sufi. Unable to find him anywhere in the forest, he finally arrived at the hill and climbed it with his entourage. Seeing the smokers with their chillum, he ordered that they be given fifty lashes and that their backs be marked with a spear to show that they had been thus punished.

Once they had been flogged and branded, they were brought before Alamgir.

He asked them where Palangposh Auliya was.

They had never heard the name.

Terrified that they would be punished for their ignorance, one said, 'There is an old man under that tree. He knows where the Sufi is.'

Alamgir went to the tree and realized that the old man with mud-stained clothes and bloodstained flesh was the seer himself. Not wanting to disturb him, the emperor went and sat quietly some distance away, his head bowed. He waited until Palangposh Auliya opened his eyes, and then sought his blessings, received his barkat and left.

The three degenerates had realized by now that the man they had tossed around like a rag doll was indeed the seer. If smoking chillum merited fifty lashes, what would assaulting the Sufi get them? They prepared to be divested of their heads. But the seer did not breathe a word to Alamgir. When the emperor had left, the fools fell at the seer's feet and devoted themselves to his service.

And what service it was! Back in our time, the money spent on a week's worth of gruel and tea in his khanqah was five thousand rupees. The fires in the kitchen were always burning. No one who came seeking the auliya's blessings was allowed to leave on an empty stomach. And the karamat – the miracles – he performed for his devotees ... Why, once while I was visiting the khanqah at Aurangabad, he went into a trance. It turned out he had manifested himself in Agra to argue a case in which his devotee Abdul Wahab had been falsely implicated. The problem with our Hindu ascetics is that they would tell those who sought them out that this was all karma and there was no way out. That was not the Sufi way.

But here's an interesting thing about Palangposh Auliya. He would ask for money for his barkat. And if one refused or hesitated, he would leave. And he would not ask them to give him what they wished. He would name a figure for his fee. He is known to have asked for two lakh rupees back then.

His disciple Musafir Baba once asked him, 'But is it not wrong to demand money for blessing a devotee?'

Without a word, Palangposh Auliya sat facing the qiblah and began to perform muraqabah. He sat frozen for three days, and with him, the world came to a standstill. With no one being able to approach him, desperate devotees were left to their own resources. Orphanages that depended on him for support and homes for war widows found themselves unable to feed their residents. When Palangposh Auliya finally came to, he bored his eyes into those of Musafir Baba. Musafir Baba nodded and said, 'I understand.'

And do you know what sort of person Musafir Baba himself was? He walked from Surat to Mecca. His devotees included the wealthiest and most influential of men. He could have sailed to Mecca on a ship fitted out especially for him. He could, at the very least, have travelled by camel. But no. He believed a fakir must go everywhere by foot.

His teacher and guide, Palangposh Auliya, had told him, 'You're a fool if you think being a Sufi is all about performing muraqabah and reciting dhikr and attaining a state of sukr. It is about taking on the burdens of one's fellow men. It is about being like the body in the hands of the person performing the ghusl al-mayyit.'[27]

As a young disciple, Musafir Baba's duties included seeing to the needs of those who visited the khanqah. Nearly all visitors had a fondness for smoking tobacco. Musafir Baba would have to procure and roll the leaves. By the end of the day, his hands would be blistered and he would feel sick. He wore no slippers, and only had a lungi to clothe himself. It had become so old and frayed that he was hard put to safeguard his modesty when he slept. And the few portions of the cloth that weren't worn housed lice by the score. The moment he dozed off, they would begin to bite. And so it was that Musafir Baba never had a full night's sleep. Observing this, one of the devotees gifted him a soft set of pyjamas. When Musafir Baba discarded the lungi and donned the pyjamas, he found his eyes closing at once. He curled up under a tree and fell into such a deep slumber that he didn't hear the Sufi return from his rounds.

When he woke, well into the evening, he dashed to the seer in a panic.

Palangposh Auliya smiled and said with a twinkle in his eyes, 'The Sufi who longs for comfort can hardly stand by the adage "Al

---

27 The tradition of washing a body before burial.

fakhr faqri" – that which is worthiest of pride is poverty – now, can he?'

Musafir Baba was given only one meal a day. Once, as he was sitting down to eat, a beggar came to the khanqah asking for alms. Palangposh Auliya asked his disciple to give the beggar his food. This happened three days in a row. And Musafir Baba realized he was being trained to be a dervish too. For a dervish could not approach anyone for food unless he had been starving for three days. If he had gone without nourishment for three days, he was allowed to visit three houses and stand outside. He must not beg. If the residents of those homes saw him and were moved to give him food, he could eat. If he failed, he had no choice but to wait out a further period of three days without food. Then, he was allowed to stand outside seven houses.

The true fakir, Musafir Baba said, must never own anything. Anything he obtained must be used and disposed of that very day. If he were to fall down dead at any moment, he must die without possessions. That is the way of the Sufi.

I tell you, Honourable Lekhak, it is my belief that the Sufis not only offered succour to the seekers, but served as the voice of the oppressed, representatives of the outcasts. They stood up to authority and spoke for the voiceless. I told you about the Sufis because you must understand that Islam spread in India not by the sword, but by love – it was their kindness and concern for fellow human beings that made the Sufis ambassadors of Islam. And that is how this monotheistic religion took hold in a nation with hundreds of millions of gods.

For all that is said about Alamgir, he wasn't an enemy of the Hindus. Like him, I was an ardent adherent of my religion, and neither I nor my family suffered for it through the generations we have served the Mughals.

What I am now about to tell you, I tell you in my capacity as a spy. Not many people know this, but I was one of Alamgir's most trusted spies. Before I leave, I shall tell you a secret that I had promised never to reveal in my lifetime.

You might wonder at my warmth, as a man of my religion, towards Alamgir when I should have rightly favoured Dara Shikoh. And my book has often been quoted for saying, 'Dara Shikoh's body was relieved of the burden of his head.' The fact remains that Dara could never have ruled an empire. He fled the battlefield when the Samugarh war was his to lose. Because he trusted the wrong people.

It's a sad thing, but the Mughals never knew whom to trust. This might be among the reasons why Alamgir most envied Shivaji – he could, at the very least, trust his own sons. When we laid siege to the Gingee Fort under the command of Zulfiqar Ali Khan – the longest siege in Mughal history, lasting eight whole years – we were humiliated more by our own than by the Marathas. Alamgir's son Kam Bakhsh, who briefly joined the camp and decided it was a lost cause, sent a secret missive to Rajaram, Chhatrapati Shivaji's son who held the Gingee Fort, suggesting that he join the Marathas against his own father's army. He ended up in chains and Alamgir had to send an envoy to negotiate his release. He all but beheaded his son for the betrayal.

And yet, this son would not be the relative of whom he was most ashamed. That honour must go to Roshanara. Honourable Lekhak, I see you fidget. You worry that any account of Roshanara must be necessarily pornographic, a charge which has earlier been levied against you. I will be brief, for much has been written about her, and your much-loved historian William Dalrymple has described her life and death in more graphic terms than I could hope to, but I did promise to tell you a secret. Alamgir had made me swear on my favourite deity, Smashan Tara, that I would never breathe a word of this for as long as there was breath in my body. Now that I have neither breath nor body, I am finally free to tell you.

This concerns a man named Lorenzo. He was a resident of the dungeons and had been accorded a unique punishment: his tongue had been ripped out, and he was in solitary confinement in a cell with no window, not even the barest skylight. True, he couldn't speak. But even if he could have, there would have been no one to hear. Two meals were sent to him each day. A hole in the ground served as his toilet. Typically, it was the qazi who would deliver the verdict and the sentence. But Lorenzo had not been tried. His crime was of such a nature.

Lorenzo ran the pleasure houses in one particular section of the firangi quarter. While Alamgir detested the very idea of brothels, there was less governance in that quarter. The firangis were seen as a necessary evil. It was their gunpowder that had helped Babur defeat Ibrahim Lodi, and they had a division all to themselves in the Mughal army. You must remember that these were not the firangis of the East India Company. They were not educated and sophisticated. They were largely criminals who had boarded ships to escape punishment for their crimes in their native countries. The lucky ones were drafted into the army. The rest were homeless. Some of those turned to crime in this land too. Lorenzo was among those, and this is how he came to meet the fate he did.

One day, Alamgir sent for me and asked me to find out what exactly happened in Lorenzo's pleasure houses. It didn't take me long to trace the links – men and women, often boys and girls, were sent from his pleasure houses to the palace of Roshanara Begum, Alamgir's sister and the woman he had appointed padishah begum once he came to power. The men returned. The girls didn't. There were rumours about this, but I had to see it for myself before I reported back to Alamgir. I confirmed that there was a weekly orgy at the palace of Roshanara. In attendance were the most important and influential courtiers, and no one dared speak of it for fear of their wrath.

It so happened that one of these attendees owed me for an enormous favour I had done him with Alamgir. He vouched for me, and I was allowed into this select gathering. The moment we entered, we were given masks so no one would know who was who. Roshanara Begum alone did not wear a mask. No one wore anything but the mask. All the bodies around me were naked, and I was asked to divest myself of my clothes too. The things I saw, Honourable Lekhak ... men and women were curling their bodies around each other with no care for age or gender. Some of the men strangled the girls as they climaxed – I believe it heightened the pleasure. The girls who died were buried in the garden. This was why none of Lorenzo's girls returned. Some of the men were asphyxiated too. Why, I was very nearly one of them. The begum herself, Roshanara Begum, who was fifty-four years old at the time, took a shine to me. We ... *coupled*, shall we say, four times that night. The last time, she wove her fingers around my neck and began to press hard. As I struggled to breathe, she screamed with pleasure. Thankfully, I was a hatha yoga practitioner and was able to retain my consciousness. When she was done, she collapsed.

A stone's throw away, Alamgir must have been at his prayers. I realized this was the beginning of the end of the Mughal empire.

I'm sure there were orgies as lavish and licentious in the eras of Padishah Akbar and Padishah Jahangir. But it is one thing to frolic under consent of the emperor, and another to do so behind his back and yet under his very nose. What humiliation for Alamgir! I was forced to report what I had seen ... and what I had done ... and what happened to Roshanara after that is public knowledge.

If this was the state of affairs in the royal family, you can imagine what life was like for the common man. Never had there been greater disparity between the rich and the poor. Here, you had people drinking imported wine out of goblets made of gold studded with diamonds and rubies. There, you had people foraging in the gutters for rats to kill and eat. One could barely walk ten feet without fear of being assaulted by robbers. People even killed children so that they could steal the jewels on their little ears and necks and hands and feet. This should come as no surprise when people were selling off their own children into prostitution and slavery so that they could feed themselves. The emperor had grown disconnected from the life of the empire, and it was the wazirs who dictated the law. Corruption was rampant. The emperor was away most of the time, fighting wars. Winning would leave him with little to gain, and losing would further hurt the treasury. Taxes were so high that people either fell prey to usurers and killed themselves, or had nothing to pawn and killed themselves from fear of arrest for failure to pay their duties.

Aurangzeb may have been an exception to the Mughal emperors' hereditary lust for flesh. But he was not an exception to their hereditary lust for land. And so it was that princes and nobles and their children were raised in the mud and slush of army encampments while their palaces lay empty. This was why Aurangzeb's rule sounded the death knell for the Mughal empire.

There is much I have yet to tell you, Honourable Lekhak. But I am forced to leave now. You will shortly know why. If I have occasion to return, we shall meet again.

~

With that, the Aghori fell silent. The writer and Rizwan waited for some time as usual, and eventually turned in for the night.

CHAPTER 12

The Truth about Jahanara

Aurangzeb was still on a break, the writer realized during the next seance.

The Aghori was smiling sweetly, and something about him suggested the feminine. The Aghori's thighs were pressed against each other, he had slumped slightly, and a shawl was thrown about his shoulders.

The voice of the Aghori was lilting and musical, the voice of a woman, the voice of a poet.

~

AND THIS IS WHAT SHE SAID:

Alhamdulillah! Not in all the eighteen thousand worlds can one find one equal to Allah ... Honourable Katib, you seem surprised to hear a woman's voice. I am not Alamgir, but his sister Jahanara. I, who became padishah begum of the Mughal empire aged only seventeen, who lived as a fakira and a devotee of Hazrat Mullah Shah, who was so beloved of the people that her brother invited her back to the palace after a term of house arrest ... I am here, for my story has never been told. The stories and films of your time focus on Nur Jahan, who wrapped her husband around her little finger and had her own coinage even when he was alive, and on Roshanara, whose lasciviousness and licentiousness you celebrate as symbolic of women's liberation. And I, who stayed true to my faith and my family, I am forgotten. This is why I pushed Bhimsen Saxena out of the Aghori's body. I could have spoken right away, but I have a lot to say, and perhaps the Aghori needed some rest. It comes naturally to us women to look to the comfort of those around us, even the bodies we possess. Since you're a postmodern writer, I assume your audience will understand that your novel must necessarily break form. Here I am now, to tell you *my* story. I am tired of my history being written by other people. Here you have it, for the first time, from the horse's mouth.

Empress of the World – Jahan Ara, Jahanara. And yet what life did I live, with all the riches of the world at my disposal, servants at my beck and call, and eight elephants of my own? My mother, in all the seventeen years I knew her, walked about the palace with a full womb and heavy breasts. I never knew the joy of the burden of milk-laden breasts and a childbearing womb. My body never knew the pleasure of a man's love. All I had to caress my flesh were jewels. Sometimes, I would see the royal horses and elephants, fitted out with golden ornaments and opulent silks for their parades, and I would wonder how different I was from them. I, too, had my royal masters, and I was only safe for as long as I did as they bade me do.

The men of the family could fill their zenanas with Rajputanis until their offspring had but a pint of Mughal blood, and yet God forbid that a woman should fall in love with a Rajput. It was the liberal Akbar who brought this rule in, you know. The *tolerant* emperor who invited pandits and priests and fakirs and digambars to spiritual debates at the palace passed a law stating that no Mughal woman could marry a Hindu. So much for religious unity. The men could have their inter-religious unions, of course. Thirty wives, three hundred concubines, religion no bar. And we women must guard their izzat by remaining virgins or marrying the men they chose. I was in love, Honourable Katib. I loved a man intensely, a Rajput warrior. But in order for him to keep his life, we had to keep our secret. I could not know the comfort of home and hearth.

Once, as my palanquin was passing Chandni Chowk, I saw a beggar woman feeding her children. Two infants pumped their fists as they lay on her lap and suckled, one at each breast. Her rags left little to the imagination. Seeing her, I was so struck with envy that it felt as if a hot rod had pierced through my womb, clawed through my breasts and struck my heart.

My body became the reason for the men to ask me to lock myself up. But I had a key – citing spirituality and social work, I got out of the zenana. I pursued Sufism under the guidance of Hazrat Mullah Shah. It all began with a dream. A nightmare. I was all alone in a snowfield. There was white everywhere, and not a soul to be seen. There was no path in the snow, no food, no water. I would die there all alone, I thought. No, there had to be a way out. It was a metaphor of my life, I thought. This is how I live and die, all alone in a snowfield. Just then, I spied a pond in the distance. A lone lotus blossomed in the pond. Was *that* the metaphor? Would I blossom even in the snowfield?

Just then, I heard Mullah Shah's voice. 'The grass on which the deer graze, the monasteries in which the brothers live, the temples in which the sculptures dance, the Kaaba upon which the hajis gaze, the Holy Quran itself … the heart takes many forms when the religion it follows is love. You will come to your home very soon.'

And with that, I woke and found myself in my own room.

('Begum Sahiba,' the writer said, 'I'm reminded of a story. In Shirdi, there lived a baba. A Sufi of sorts. A devotee once beseeched him to grace his home for lunch. After months of pleading, he finally got a nod from the baba. The devotee rushed home and prepared a feast. He waited anxiously for the baba to come. The hours rolled on. The baba was reputed never to miss an appointment. And yet, he did not show up all day. The next day, the devotee went to meet the baba. He had to wait hours for the other devotees to finish their audiences with him. Exhausted, he finally went to the baba's chamber. "Baba, you promised to come home yesterday but didn't. Why?" he asked. The baba looked at him in surprise. "But I did!" he said. "I tasted everything and it was excellent. That jangiri was particularly wonderful!" "When did you come?" the devotee asked in surprise. "I came first as a stray dog, and you chased me away," the baba said. "And then I came as a beggar, and you said there was no food. So finally, I decided I was best off being a mouse. I went to the kitchen and ate my fill, and came back happy." This was how the baba taught the devotee a lesson – to see holiness in everything.')

This was exactly what Mullah Shah was telling me too, Honourable Katib. The thing is, people believe those in the zenana were either idiots or concubines or both. It was Akbar who made 'zenana' synonymous with 'harem'. There were strong women in the Mughal empire, women who all but ruled from the zenana.

It is well known that if it had not been for his maternal grandmother Aisan Daulat Begum, the man who was to become the first Mughal emperor of India, Babur, would have lost even Fergana to the conspiracies of his relatives. In her younger days, she was captured multiple times by enemies but always restored to her husband with honour. Do you know why? When, once, a guard of Sheikh Jamaluddin – whose prisoner she was – approached her to take her to the sheikh, she grabbed his dagger, killed him and threw him over her shoulder. The sheikh praised her courage and sent her home. Babur's mother Qutlugh Nigar Khanum and his sister Khanzada Begum were enormous sources of support to him as well. Humayun had just as strong a mother in Maham Begum. As for Akbar, who was deprived of his parents in infancy, he was raised by Maham Anga. It was she who sidelined Bairam Khan.

But, you see, Honourable Katib, none of these women was selfless. They all sought to further their political influence and power. I never did. I trod the path of the Sufi. The first time I was drawn to Sufism was when I heard the story of my grandfather Jahangir seeking an audience with Hazrat Mian Mir. He had to wait his turn, and then wait some more as the auliya saw to the poor and sick.

When at last he met the seer, he asked him why he had made him wait.

'The shahenshah and the fakir are one to me,' said Hazrat Mian Mir.

Jahangir had come to ask for his barkat. He was going to war in the Deccan and wanted the seer's blessings.

Mian Mir was silent. At that moment, one of the hazrat's impoverished visitors came up to him with a coin.

'There is a man here who is poorer than you and I,' the hazrat told him. 'Please give the coin to him.' And he pointed at Emperor

Jahangir. Seeing the emperor struggle to control his rage, the seer smiled and said, 'Do you believe you are so poor that you must wage war in an alien land to make a life for yourself?'

It was Hazrat Mian Mir's disciple Mullah Shah whom my father approached when Dara Shikoh was driven mad with grief after the death of his firstborn. A single touch of the hazrat cured him. It was then that I decided I would become his murid – his disciple and follower. I stayed on in Lahore and lived in his khanqah for six months. Hazrat Mullah Shah truly lived the Sufi's life. He wore only a lungi, irrespective of the weather. There were no comforts in his khanqah. And yet, all the promised delights of heaven were mine in the bliss I knew there.

Aha! Honourable Katib, you forget I too can read your thoughts.

My God, you were thinking, *this must be my first novel with more spirituality than sex. And it would be far better to be accused of writing pornography than of pontificating. How many men and women who ate off golden plates will ramble on about being fakirs before I finally get to hear something interesting? What I really want to know is, did you sleep with your father or not? Get to the point, dammit!*

You look a little shocked. Are you not used to women being explicit? Ah, you have been conversing with my brother, ever subtle and diplomatic, in word if not in deed.

You want me to cut to the chase. But surely you realize the value of build-up?

Yes, but the publishers will complain about the length of the book, you're thinking. *And my translator Baahubilli will ask for an extension of the deadline, and this novel might become ineligible for awards for this year, and ... oh, no, stop thinking, stop thinking, she can read your mind.*

('I beg your pardon, Begum Sahiba, I...' the writer stammered. At this, Jahanara threw her head back and laughed loud and long, even as the writer felt mortified.)

Do not worry, Honourable Katib, I can do with a laugh.

I shall answer your question, but permit me a while in this corporeal form. It has been a long time since I was able to laugh or cry, since I was able to inhabit a body capable of those functions.

You see, my father and grandfather – Shah Jahan and Jahangir – had one thing in common. They ensured they would always be seen in the context of love. All their brutality, on their own sons and subjects, would pale before the Salim–Anarkali romance and the Taj Mahal. And so would the loves of other kings and queens of the Mughal empire.

But are *you* not interested, Honourable Katib, in the tale of my own romance? You who pride yourself on thinking differently from the hoi polloi? Do you not want to know who that Rajput warrior was? He was none other than Raja Chhatrasal. There I was, aged seventeen and the padishah begum of the empire. My father's other wives had been cast aside, and I was chosen for the title. I was motherless, and had to raise a motherless infant. My father was dazed by his grief. Dara and I took over the reins of the empire. I had no time to think of myself. This romance would have to end.

It all began when Raja Chhatrasal came to court to pay his respects to my father. He had brought with him forty war elephants and innumerable treasures as gifts. His grandfather Rao Ratan Singh had been an important mansabdar in the time of Padishah Jahangir. He was a descendant of Rudra Pratap Singh of Orchha. When I realized I was in love, and knew it had to end before it began, I sent a rakhi to Raja Chhatrasal – a custom fostered by Padishah Akbar. He responded with a letter:

Raksha Bandhan does not speak of fraternal love alone. The rakhi is symbolically tied on the wrist of a man whom a woman trusts to guard her honour. It is my privilege to be entrusted with your honour. I shall not hesitate to lay down my life to protect it.

He would visit the palace every now and again, and we would engage in long conversations. There were times when I detected a sense of mistrust and unease with him. The Rajputs had ceded to the Mughals, he once said, but the animosity between them on account of religion would ensure there was always a rift.

'Why do you speak thus?' I asked him. 'Wasn't it to avoid this very rift that Padishah Akbar put himself to such trouble? Not only did he organize religious conferences and spiritual discussions, but he also set an example by his social conduct. He married Rajput women. Why, half the blood in my veins is Rajput, isn't it?'

'And yet, Begum Sahiba, did he not ensure that you could never marry a Rajput?' the raja said.

I hesitated, and then responded, 'The fight for the crown is bloody enough among the sons of sons. Perhaps they did not want the daughters to have offspring who could lay claim to the throne too. Perhaps that was why...'

'I beg the Begum Sahiba's forgiveness. But there is another reason the Rajputs will never forgive the Mughals. What happened at Chittorgarh. What was Padishah Akbar's train of thought, I wonder. It must have been this: *When all the other Rajputs have ceded to me without forcing me to spill blood, why does the Rana of Mewar alone put his ego before his people? He claims it*

*is the Rajput's way to lay down his life before giving up his freedom.
Are the other kings of Rajputana not Rajputs, then? If they had stayed
united, we could never have got in. And yet, they speak of pride. What
is the point of this king alone thumping his chest?* He might have been
the epitome of tolerance to you, Begum Sahiba, but he could not
brook the idea of anyone else holding land. It is my strong belief
that no one but Dara Shikoh can save Hindustan from boiling
over with communal hatred.'

There was no anger in his voice, just sadness. His eyes were
downcast and his shoulders slumped, from what little I could see
through the muslin screen that separated us. He could not discern
my expression at all, for I wore a niqab too. There were khwajasaras
standing guard around us, so we had to measure our words when
we spoke. But he had made two confessions – his love for me, and
his support for Dara. He would fight fifty-two battles for Dara.
In the fifty-third, he would lose his life – Samugarh. He would
live for more than a decade after this conversation, but our love
would remain unacknowledged to the public and unconsummated
in private. As I saw his chiselled face and studied his tender
expression, it struck me that if only I had been a man and he a
woman, he would have been in my zenana by now.

'Will the Begum Sahiba give me leave to depart?' he asked
at last.

That night, I couldn't sleep a wink. My body ached for him.
I feverishly longed for his touch. But if his fingertips so much as
brushed mine, his fate would be sealed. I will never forget the
hours of torment I underwent that night, reliving our encounter
of the afternoon. I finally began to meditate on Hazrat Mullah
Shah and then sat down to perform tahajjud.

I prayed for peace, for myself and the empire. I prayed that this lust for land – a curse that the men of my dynasty inherit – should not end in fanaa. But how could a dynasty made up entirely of perpetrators of fratricide and patricide and filicide, and the odd survivors of attempts at fratricide and patricide and filicide, end in anything but fanaa?

I will never forget how my father reacted when he was sent his beloved Dara's head in a box. He opened it and screamed, 'Khusrau! This is Khusrau! My brother Khusrau, whom I killed, has come to haunt me!'

Perhaps your democracy is the way forward, Honourable Katib. It is too much for one man to rule over an entire people all by himself. He is bound to go insane. And yet, the hunger for power is so much that he will kill even his own children in order to protect his throne.

My father spent years fleeing from the wrath of his own father Padishah Jahangir. It was only by surrendering Dara and Aurangzeb into our grandfather's care and paying ten lakh rupees as a fine for making a bid for the throne that he was allowed to live. And when the padishah was on his deathbed, all hell broke loose.

Nur Jahan had intended to rule through her own son Shahryar. But Prince Shahryar was only twenty years old. Parvez Mirza, the padishah's first son, was thirty-eight. He had the support of a powerful general, Mahabat Khan. But Nur Jahan would outwit him yet. She had a missive sent with the royal seal, proclaiming that Mahabat Khan – who was on his way to join Parvez Mirza with his army – had been made subedar of Bengal. Mahabat Khan was obliged to join the post. Right away, a second missive was sent – he was to return to the empire all the elephants and riches he had amassed during the three-year internal strife between Padishah Jahangir and my father. Now he was in a fix. If he obeyed, he would be penniless. If he didn't, he would be accused of thieving, and perhaps of treason.

But Mahabat Khan was wily too. He sent the elephants but kept the goods. He took with him an army of five thousand soldiers, along with their families so they couldn't think of defecting. And then he laid a trap. When Padishah Jahangir had camped by the banks of the Jhelum en route to Kabul, Mahabat Khan stationed two thousand warriors on the opposite bank and ordered them to set fire to anyone who crossed the bridge. Accompanied by just a hundred soldiers, he went right into the padishah's tent and said these arrangements were for the emperor's security. If the padishah wished, he could punish Mahabat Khan for it, he said, and bent low before the emperor. The emperor had his sword at the ready. But killing the man would be pointless. The camp was surrounded by his soldiers. And so, Mahabat Khan's requests were, perforce, acceded to. He asked that the emperor accompany him on an elephant ride, showing the townspeople that he was in royal favour. Nur Jahan tried her best to attack him from the other bank with her brother's forces, but it was of no use. They had to surrender in the end. Mahabat Khan accompanied the emperor to Kabul, and the subjects believed he was a close confidant of the padishah.

Yet, Nur Jahan would not admit defeat. She quietly gathered forces among the many generals who were furious with Mahabat Khan for the humiliation. She persuaded her perpetually intoxicated husband – intoxicated by substance, not by her now, mind you – to tell Mahabat Khan he had been conned by Nur Jahan's chicanery and he was glad he now had a trusted lieutenant in him. Perhaps it is the conceit of the clever, but Mahabat

Khan fell for it. He let his guard down when he accompanied the emperor to Lahore, and it was his turn to be surrounded by enemy troops.

In the meanwhile, Parvez Mirza who had inherited his father's addiction to afeem and alcohol but not his longevity died. Although it was his liver that killed him, my father's track record of fratricide ensured the blame fell on him. My father had considered making another play for the throne, but with this blemish on him, he knew the time wasn't right.

In less than a year, the padishah had passed away. Nur Jahan was banking on her brother Asaf Khan to put her son Shahryar on the throne, but Asaf Khan's daughter was my mother Mumtaz Mahal, and he defected to support my father.

And yet, the moment Padishah Jahangir had been buried, Shahryar announced himself emperor. He opened the khazana and distributed seventy lakh rupees among the courtiers to buy their support.

However, his army was no match for that of his uncle Asaf Khan's. It ended in a rout, and with Shahryar having to escape through the zenana. But he was caught, too, and blinded on Asaf Khan's orders. The misfortune didn't last long. He was put out of his misery by my father, who ordered all his surviving brothers and their descendants relieved of their earthly existence. When all this was unfolding, I had only one thought – thousands of men had died, fighting for potential emperors. The best-case scenario was that they would win and be spared their lives. The most likely scenario was that they would die, leaving their wives and children destitute – all for someone else to ascend the Peacock Throne.

When I heard the story of the Ramayana, I used to wonder at the prince who left for the forest on the day he was to be crowned king, all because his father had granted his stepmother her wish. I determined I would be like him, not like my ancestors and brothers, jumping over the corpses of fathers and sons and brothers.

And this was why, when Aurangzeb told me I could stay on as the padishah begum, I turned him down and went to Agra to serve my father as he spent his last days in house arrest.

('There have been rumours about that, Begum Sahiba...' the writer ventured.)

You are misguided by the accounts of firangis, Honourable Katib. The firangis' idea of love begins and ends with the body, just as their idea of relationships begins and ends with trade. To them, everything is material. They know nothing of spirituality. They immortalized those rumours in their accounts. Do you think my brother Aurangzeb would have reinstated me as the padishah begum after our father's death if he believed those rumours? He welcomed me with gold and jewellery worth fourteen lakh rupees and granted me an allowance of seventeen lakh rupees a year. I spent it all on the people – on building mosques, on creating Chandni Chowk.

Honourable Katib, there are two paths open to us – the path of love, and the path of hate. I chose the former; my brother chose the latter. He did not set eyes on our father for the last fourteen years of Padishah Shah Jahan's life. He simmered with hatred and burnt himself from within. He did not set foot in Agra through the eight years our father was imprisoned in the palace.

The rumour was started by my father's wives and courtiers, who were jealous of the affection he showered on me and the trust he placed in me.

I know my brother has told you he believed these rumours. Perhaps he wanted to believe them but knew deep inside that they were untrue. It would suit him for the people to believe these rumours, to be disgusted with the padishah, for the usurper of the throne occupied by an emperor who merited contempt was more likely to be popular.

Why is it, I wonder, Honourable Katib, that women's bodies are always the battlefields for men's egos? I was victimized in a way – my body was made a character in a story, a vicious rumour to bolster my brother's usurping of the throne. And then there are other bodies which would be made into weapons ... women's bodies, for the victor to take from the vanquished.

I was here when Rani Durgavati told her story. It was a story Raja Chhatrasal would recount often. The hurt carried on through the generations, his and mine, hers and Padishah Akbar's, the three hundred Gond men's and the ten thousand Mughal men's. Jauhar. Saka. Men with loincloths and yellow bands around their waists, signalling they were ready for death. Mughal warriors with their weapons and training, cutting them to pieces. Once Rani Durgavati killed herself, they went for her son Veer Narayan in Sauragarh. Veer Narayan sent two of his lieutenants to supervise the jauhar.

Think about this, Honourable Katib. They say three thousand women immolated themselves. How big a fire would they have had to light? How many trees and dried leaves, how much cotton and ghee? As the blaze went up, wouldn't some of the women have been scared? Their faces burning from the heat alone, didn't they think perhaps they should not jump into it? But because they carried the izzat of the men in their bodies, it would have to be ensured that they did jump in. If they ran, they had to be chased down and thrown in. That was why the supervisors were there.

The blaze raged on for four days. When, at last, it had smouldered and died down, they discovered a miracle had occurred. Two women had survived, sheltered by a teak tree. One was Kamalavati, Durgavati's sister. The other was Veer Narayan's betrothed. Both women were taken to Padishah Akbar's zenana, a fate three thousand believed was worse than a fiery death.

I wonder, sometimes, whether it was the curses of these generations of women that saw the Mughal empire disintegrate. Here was my brother Aurangzeb, that most capable of rulers. And yet, corruption and espionage were never so rampant as in his time. Although our descendants ruled for another couple of centuries, the Mughal emperor was no longer the emperor of Hindustan after my brother's time; his dominion dwindled to Delhi alone.

The East India Company bolstered the Marathas' strength by giving them arms and allowances. My brother could never conquer the Deccan because of this strategy. Sea piracy was at its peak. When the East India Company refused to compensate the subjects of the Mughal empire for their losses, Aurangzeb nullified all the agreements he had signed with them and sent his commanders to supervise blockades of the company's operations in Surat and Patna, and even lay siege to Fort St George in Madras.

My brother made short-term gains, but forged enmity with the firangis too. The poor had become poorer, the rich were living on loans. The treasury was empty, and yet my brother was in the battlefield, fighting until he was nearly ninety years old. His rage was directed against the Hindus, and this was reflected in taxes, in the judgements of the qazi, in the punishments meted out to

Hindu convicts. While Europe was witnessing the Renaissance, while the sciences were being given more importance than ever, Hindustan saw the most regressive of stances and most pointless of battles. A cancer had taken root within the Mughal empire. It would destroy the empire from within.

Perhaps the one thing that remains from those days, almost as it used to be when it was first built, is Chandni Chowk. When I returned to Delhi after my father's death, after the isolation of eight years, I went to see this place that I had created eighteen years earlier. It was just the same – the same shops, the same people, the same sounds, the same sights. Right at the entryway was a paan shop under a banyan tree, whose proprietor was Chandan Singh. He remained in place, nearly eighty years old now, but beaming all the same. I'm sure the banyan still stands today. I wonder whether the paan shop is now run by a descendant of Chandan Singh, wearing the same tika on his forehead and Rajput-style turban around his head, and smiling through betel-stained teeth.

I would like to tell you about Chandni Chowk, Honourable Katib. I'd like to speak of how I planned it, how I built it. However, it was considered unseemly in my time to speak about one's own brainchild, one's own achievements. Marketing was not our forte, you see.

I'd like to leave you with this vision, of myself as a fakira.

A fakira is one who has nothing, who lets go of all that is material. When I survived the fire that nearly killed me, my father gave away my weight in gold to the poor. This was an honour reserved for emperors. And yet, this is how he expressed his joy at my having survived. He also decreed that all profits from the Surat port would come to me. At the time, the annual income from the port was fifteen lakh rupees, and it soon doubled.

But I didn't spend a paisa of that on myself. I spent it on the people. I built mosques in Agra and Delhi and Srinagar. I commissioned hajj ships to take those who could not afford the journey to Mecca. And I had the tomb of my pir Mullah Shah constructed, choosing every stone myself, so it would be as simple as he would have liked and yet withstand centuries of sun and rain, wind and hail. Do you know, Honourable Katib, he once said he would have chosen me as his spiritual heir if only I had been a man?

I have spent some time with you, telling you my story as I would like it told. The few writers and filmmakers who have documented my life have made me out to be a Laila pining for her Majnun. I was no Laila, and there was no Majnun in my life.

I would like to leave you with this image. It was the month of Ramzan, and I had the good fortune to be at the Ajmer Sharif dargah, looking upon Khwaja Moinuddin Chishti's tomb. I stood barefoot as I prayed, and then I did a full seven circles around the tomb, sometimes crawling on the floor and kissing it. I sat at the dargah, finishing my prayers before I broke my fast that day. The dargah of a saint whose spiritual lineage goes back to the Prophet himself! How blessed I was to have been there in the holy month of Ramzan!

I'd like you to see me, sitting there, my eyes closed and my spirit soaring, ecstatic and peaceful all at once. The fakira, alone, meditating. She now takes leave of you, Honourable Katib. Khuda hafiz.

CHAPTER 13

'An Other to the Self, a Shakuni for a Krishna'

It was evident from the way the Aghori sat during the next seance that the emperor was back. The writer was tempted to hug him with the joy of an old friend, but decided that might be a breach of protocol.

'I am most glad to see you, Shahenshah,' he said instead.

The spirit smiled.

~

AURANGZEB SAID:

I have been away for a long time, Honourable Katib. I'm glad to be back, now. There is much I have to say, and while I do not object to the longing so many of my contemporaries – and siblings – have for their history to be rewritten, I must gently remind them and you of the title of this book.

Dara hasn't shown up. Perhaps he's already satisfied with his portrayal in history. I didn't know in my lifetime just how popular his Farsi translation of the Upanishads was. It offended me deeply that he claimed the *Kitab al-Maknun* mentioned in the Quran is, in fact, a reference to the Upanishads. I later learnt that the Latin translation of Dara's *Sirr-i-Akbar* was a favourite of the philosopher Schopenhauer's. He apparently kept the book by his bedside. Dara was a bridge between cultures, and is recognized for it. But my mind goes back over and over again to his foolishness at Samugarh. What could have possessed him to jump off his elephant at such a critical time? To have waited a day rather than attack my beleaguered forces?

Did you know, Dara had an affair with Khalilullah Khan's wife. And yet he chose to trust her husband. She warned him that her husband would prove a traitor. Poor Dara, he believed he could read people. His education and scholarship gave him an arrogance and high-handedness that earned him more enemies than his intellect earned him friends. I hope you won't take offence, but all writers are like that, are they not?

In the time I've been away, I've read some of your recommendations, Honourable Katib. And so, I find myself able to quote Mark Antony from *Julius Caesar*. 'The evil that men do lives after them; the good is oft interred with their bones,' he says. In Dara's case, the converse is true. The evil he wrought was interred with his bones, while he is remembered as Akbar's heir in tolerance. He *was*, indeed, Akbar's heir in a sense. I trust you have read the Birbal stories, Honourable Katib? In those, the padishah comes across as a fool. I used to wonder if it was the Hindus, resentful of being ruled by Muslims, who came up with those plot lines. But I later learned that those incidents had certainly occurred. Padishah Akbar was, then, a fool. So was Dara. It suits your current ruling government to portray them as tolerant Muslims.

The Akbar–Birbal stories would remind me of a similar pairing in the *Arabian Nights* – Haroun al-Rashid and Abu Nuwas. Every emperor, it appears, had a poet companion who would make him out to be a fool. I was spared the ignominy, possibly because I followed the advice of the Surah Ash-Shu'ara of the Holy Quran, which says: 'As for the poets, it is only those lost in error that follow them. Do you not see that they wander aimlessly in every valley, and that they never practise as they preach, nor preach as they practise?'

The Sufis, I did not consider poets. To me, saints were philosophers. Dara once met Baba Lal Bairagi in Lahore and recorded the conversation in a book titled *Mukalama Baba Lal wa Dara Shikoh*. The baba was said to be two hundred and ninety-eight years old. When he came back to the court, Dara showed the emperor his book. Our father invited Baba Lal to the palace right away, wanting to see a three-hundred-year-old man for himself. Baba Lal barely looked thirty, let alone three hundred. When he spoke, he held everyone as if in a trance. He said something I would never forget: 'He whom God decides is a fakir may be the richest man in the world; and yet, he will be a fakir.' I sought to meet him often. He turned down my invitations. When I finally made the journey to his khanqah myself, I found I could not enter. When my men and I tried to go in, our world went dark – it was as if we had all been suddenly blinded. When we turned away, we could see again. And then when we turned to go in, we were blind again. I sat outside the khanqah, determined not to leave until the baba saw me. At long last, he came out and asked me what I wanted. I told him I wanted to be a good emperor. What should I do, I asked.

'Remember what I said,' he answered.

He whom God decides is a fakir may be the richest man in the world; and yet, he will be a fakir.

I remembered that often during my last days. I believed I lived as a fakir, but which fakir goes to battle when he is nearly ninety years old, Honourable Katib?

~

And with that, he lapsed into silence. The writer and Rizwan waited a while. When it was clear Alamgir had left the Aghori's body, they left too.

They were not sure what to expect from the next meeting. Would the emperor go off on another break?

As it happened, he did not.

~

THE SPIRIT SAID:

I was thinking, Honourable Katib, how historians and novelists are largely interested in the royals. No one seems to care much how the common man lived. You look surprised. When did Aurangzeb become a communist, you wonder.

Well, there is much I learnt about my own empire, the one I had inherited, from reading *Ardhakathanaka*, the autobiography of Banarasi Das, a jeweller by trade and a poet by aspiration. I learnt that Kilich Khan, one of my most trusted commanders and, in fact, the one who taught me how to wield a sword, was a psychopath who beat a group of jewellers – including Banarasi Das's father Kharagsen – to within an inch of their lives. I had seen Kilich Khan as a judicious and pious man, and it took this account for me to see the other side.

Let us reverse roles this once. Allow me to recommend this book to you. Reading of the riots that followed the death of Padishah Akbar, a poem that begins '*Ghar-ghar dar-dar kiye kapaat*', I realized how terrible it must have been for our subjects when an emperor died. There were those who sank into grief, but it was mostly fear. This is not too different from what happens when the politicians of your day die, is it, Honourable Katib? Except, back then, the riots would stop once the next emperor was crowned. In the case of Padishah Akbar, no one knew who would be crowned king next. It is the horror of that moment which Banarasi Das brings out so well.

And yet, he is not really a common man, is he? His father engaged palanquins to carry the entire family, four men to carry two ornate wooden palanquins bearing five people each, over a distance of a hundred and twenty-five kilometres, from Jaunpur to Fatehpur. It was palanquin bearers like these, who lived like cattle, who were the real common men, the ones whose lives unravelled as the treasury emptied. We don't know their stories, for they were illiterate and did not write.

Nevertheless, I think you might enjoy this book, *Ardhakathanaka*. It reads like a thriller combined with a confessional. You might be more sympathetic than me to Banarasi Das's account of how he was equally obsessed with learning and ladies, and how his father tried to divert his attention to the family trade. Encounters with thieves, encounters with crafty townspeople, an account of the plague, an analysis of three

marriages that yielded nine children, none of whom survived ...
perhaps it might make for an interesting film for your times?

What is the purpose of an autobiography? Is it an eyewitness
account? Or an attempt to sanitize a life lived? Or self-
interrogation? In the case of Banarasi Das, it is none of the above.
But I do feel he lacks the daring of Babur – while my ancestor
confessed that he couldn't be as sexually aroused by his wife as he
was by little boys, Banarasi Das only gives us a vague 'I indulged
in base activities'. No autobiography written by a Hindu, with
the exception of your Mahatma Gandhi, displays daring. Well,
perhaps 'daring' is not the right word. I should say 'candour'.

If one were to bring Derrida into this, we must look at how
the Self cannot exist without the Other. Now, you're writing
my autobiography, aren't you? Who, then, is Aurangzeb? You?
Or me? You've often said you become your characters when you
write from their points of view. Then, whose voice is that of your
character Aurangzeb? If there is no Self without the Other, who
is the Other in my case? It is only Allah who is the pure Self with
no Other, isn't it?

('If you'll forgive me, Huzoor,' the writer said, 'Allah has an
Other too. Shaitan.')

Shabhash, shabhash! One can't outdo a writer, can one? I
don't have the scholarship or the standing to debate you on this
subject. Dara might have been up for it.

I can tell you of another Other to my Self, though – the
Maratha warrior, the man whom you so obsequiously refer to as
'Chhatrapati Shivaji'. Perhaps he is the Other that completes my
Self. Who, then, is writing this book? What would your Derrida say?

('Huzoor,' said the writer, 'I believe he might see the narrator
as the confluence of three voices – yours, mine and Chhatrapati

Shivaji's. We have not spoken much of him, but you have often said you wish to speak of him. I sense that you were so obsessed with him through your life that he has infiltrated your very being. Derrida would say that the Self, self-identity and narrative equally inform an autobiography. In our case, this becomes an oxymoron, for your autobiography is punctuated by the accounts of others – perhaps they are Others to your Self too. It strikes me, Huzoor, that if you had chosen two voices alone – yours and Chhatrapati Shivaji's – and alternated those, or used those at random, leaving the writer and the reader to guess who is speaking in each chapter, it might have made for quite a path-breaking postmodern novel.')

As far as etymology goes, 'auto' refers to the Self, 'bio' to a life lived, and 'graphy' to writing. But if the Other is involved in this, there is no such thing as an *auto*biography, is there?

('Well,' said the writer, 'I believe the annihilation of the Self to which Derrida refers may be compared to us erasing writing on paper. We never erase completely. The imprints of what we wrote remain on the paper. And then we use those as foundations on which we perch our rewriting. So it is with recasting our lives. The Self that narrates the story climbs out of the story and collapses some distance away.')

There's a more interesting Other than Shivaji, I think. Shakuni. The man from your Mahabharata. The youngest of a hundred sons born to the king of Gandhara, whose only daughter was Gandhari. One among a hundred princes to a tiny kingdom that had to acquiesce when Bhishma knocked on the doors and asked for a bride for his blind nephew. The man who embraced brahmacharya for his father, who kidnapped princesses for his brothers, and who now demanded a nurse for his nephew. The man disgusts me. Bhishma, not Shakuni, I mean.

In another one of your inexplicable Hindu rituals, Gandhari was secretly married off to a goat because her astrology charts indicated her first husband would die. When Bhishma came to know of this, he accused her father of cheating him and fobbing off a widow on his nephew. He refused to listen to reason and imprisoned the lot, I believe, the father and his hundred sons.

Shakuni alone protested. 'Did he not keep it secret that his nephew was blind? My sister, who is so afraid of the dark that she would hold my hand for strength when dusk fell, was so devastated by the realization of her husband's eternal darkness that she too embraced the dark for good. How is that just? How is that fair?'

Bhishma was unmoved. He intended to kill all of them, but without spilling a drop of blood. Their daily meal in jail was one grain of rice each. They would all be fed, and they would all die. The clan would perish.

But the prisoners had other plans. They would ensure one, just one, of them ate the hundred and one grains and survived. He would sire heirs, and he would destroy Bhishma's precious Kuru dynasty. How were they to choose the One? Their father set them a task. Which of them could thread a grain of rice through the cavity of a tiny bone? Ninety-nine tried and failed. The hundredth was Shakuni. He tied the grain of rice to an ant with a piece of string and placed the bone before the ant. The ant climbed into the cavity and emerged on the other side.

This would become a metaphor for the manipulations of Shakuni in later days. I need hardly tell you the story of Shakuni. Your morning and evening entertainment since the 1980s have been versions of the Mahabharata. Entire generations have grown up on those, and a host of those actors have crafted political careers in your saffron state by using their television roles as campaign vehicles.

But let us speak of Shakuni, who watched his brothers die so he may live. Shakuni, who ate their flesh as they died, for those hundred and one grains of rice were enough to survive but not to live. Shakuni, who cut off his father's fingers one by one on the latter's command and fashioned them into dice that would one day spell the doom of the Kurus. Shakuni, who limped all his life because his father – as his last act – plunged a knife into his foot with fingerless hands so that Shakuni would remember forever his duty towards his clan. Shakuni, whose beloved sister lived in darkness. Shakuni, who too lived in darkness.

Shakuni is like me, Honourable Katib. Except I carried false blame for three hundred years. He, for three thousand. Or is it more?

> *'No, no. This won't do. Your Alamgir has it wrong. Under no circumstances should he be allowed to draw this ridiculous parallel between Shakuni and himself. For the first time, this book jars.'*

~

Kokkarakko was back. The writer sighed. Thankfully, Kokkarakko had made his appearance when the writer was working on his manuscript. The spirit was not around to listen in.

'The book jars, you said. Why?' the writer demanded.

'Look,' said Kokkarakko. 'Shakuni was a gambler, an avenger. Aurangzeb was an emperor. A despot and a tyrant. Shakuni set out to wipe out a dynasty that had tried to wipe out his own. He plotted to this end. And he was justified in doing as he did. His was arguably the saddest story in the world. If only he hadn't succeeded in his mission, he would have been seen as a mahatma.

The idea of revenge would have disappeared from the world if he hadn't set out to exact his own, because if such a wronged man could forgive, how could anyone else not? But in Aurangzeb's case, every deed and every decree of his affected the common man, affected the poorest of the poor in Hindustan.

'Secondly, Shakuni's actions were in fact *reactions*. If only Bhishma had not done as he had, Shakuni might have been a perfectly amenable man. We speak of him as a gambler. But he was no gambling addict. The game of dice was simply his means to an end. He was obeying his father's orders. Shakuni was, thus, a tool and nothing more. Blaming him is like blaming a computer that has been programmed to carry out a task, for carrying out that very task. If the task is to release missiles, it will do so, won't it? If the task is altruistic, it will be carried out too. Shakuni was programmed as a child. You can hack a computer program. You can remove viruses. What happened to Shakuni was far more insidious than a vile computer program. He cannot be held responsible for what he did.

'Aurangzeb, on the other hand, did everything he did of his own accord. From his own desire for the throne. He might refute this charge. He may claim he did not *desire* anything. Well, then, it was his ambition, his aim. Whatever it was, it was of his own making. No one had betrayed him or caused him immense suffering. He had no reason to avenge himself against anyone. He might claim the firangis would have taken over Hindustan, that pirates would have robbed its riches, that the empire would have broken up into fragments. But let me ask this question openly: Did he nurse such great affection for his subjects, then? Was it for love of them that he killed his own brothers? For this great love that he imprisoned his father? For this love that he spent the

last twenty-six years of his life on the battlefields of the Deccan?
For this love that he packed Dara's head in a box and had it sent
to their father?

'Right. And then he had his *beloved* daughter Zeb-un-Nissa
imprisoned when she was forty-three years old. Yes, yes, I know,
I know, not a dungeon, house arrest, fort arrest, whatever. But
she was ostracized by society, wasn't she? She was forced to live
in isolation, wasn't she, with only a handful of servants? And her
interactions with even those servants were spied upon, weren't
they? She lived like this until her very death, as her grandfather
had. Life imprisonment was, in this case, truly imprisonment for
life. Shah Jahan was condemned to this for only eight years. She,
on the other hand, spent *twenty-one* years in prison. No one knows
why. Aurangzeb hasn't given you an explanation. If she hadn't
had recourse to the written word, her life would have been hell.
Her prolific poetry from those years is evidence that it was her
writing that came to her rescue. The greatest irony is this – after
her death, Aurangzeb was so struck by sorrow that he had a grand
tomb constructed for her. Imprisoned in life, memorialized in a
palatial monument in death.

'There are a great number who believe Dara might have saved
the soul of Hindustan if he had ascended the throne instead. The
tolerance between religions would have been far better. At the
very least, communal hatred would not have simmered as it did in
Aurangzeb's time. All those hundreds of reasons Aurangzeb offers
up as justification for his usurping the throne, Dara had as many
and more justifications.

'Under such circumstances, he has no business drawing
a comparison between Shakuni and himself. Now, it must be
acknowledged that, at the individual level, he lived an austere

and straightforward life. I do have questions and doubts and suspicions and objections regarding the nature of his purported straightforwardness, but I have no quarrel with him. His stitching of prayer caps to earn his living has gone down in history. Even today, the highest-ranking judges and civil servants and politicians are known to give away their salaries and earn their living with the equivalent of stitching those prayer caps, so he did set an example, and the trend did not die with him.

'Therefore, it is my demand that he be honest and straightforward in telling us why he really wanted the throne. And don't go on about how all this is permissible in a postmodern novel. You can't write everything he says without questioning him and challenging him. That would be a disgrace. Are you his steno, or a writer?'

'All right. But what are you referring to when you speak of why he really wanted the throne? What is this reason, according to you?' the writer asked.

'Ambition. Love of power. What else? He might not have realized it at the time. He might have rationalized the mass murders and dishonourable betrayals as necessary evils in order to safeguard his religion. But has he admitted it was ambition and desire for power that motivated him to usurp the throne, even as he is "writing" his story through a postmodernist? And one like you, who has openly spoken of his own flaws, his obsession with women, his weakness for...'

'Listen, I didn't...'

'It would be only appropriate for him to follow your confessional style. That would be the USP of your interaction.'

'Dei, Kokkarakko, I didn't say I was obsessed with women.'

'Don't obsess over words now. Your philosophy in life is "I love wine, women and gods". How is that different from what I said?'

The writer gave up on debating with Kokkarakko at this point. He would end up convincing the writer that he was indeed obsessed with women. But the writer did convey Kokkarakko's point to Aurangzeb, quoting him verbatim.

Having heard him out, Aurangzeb said, 'I don't refute anything that our honourable friend Kokkarakko has said. I don't think he has ever read my will. I reproduce it for you and him now:

> *I, Aurangzeb, have ruled this enormous swathe of land known as Hindustan and served as its emperor. In my personal life, I have followed the path of the lord. However, in my public life, I have sinned greatly. I failed to do any of the good deeds I sought to do for my subjects. My soul curses me constantly, calls me a sinner. As I lie on my deathbed, what is the point in my worrying about this?*
>
> *My khwajasara, Aaya Beg, has my purse. It contains four rupees and two annas, money I have earned with my own hands, stitching prayer caps. I would like my coffin purchased with that. Nothing else must be spent on storing the corpse of this sinner. This is my will. I earned three hundred and five rupees from selling my handwritten scrolls of the Holy Quran. Aaya Beg has that too. I would like this sum used to buy kheer for poor Muslims.*
>
> *My clothes, inkstand, quill and books must be given to my son Azam. He must bear the cost of the digging of my grave. I would like to be buried deep in the forest. Do not cover my face when you bury me. I would like to meet my maker without a*

screen before my face. I have heard that he who stands unclothed and naked before his maker will be forgiven for his trespasses.

My body must be wrapped in rough cloth, not in fine silks. Do not throw petals on the path my corpse travels. No flowers or garlands should be placed on my corpse. No music should play. I despise music.

No memorial shall mark the spot of my burial. Not even my name shall mark my grave. No tree shall be planted over it, for a sinner like me does not deserve shade in death.

I have not been able to pay my soldiers and servants for months on end. The treasury lies empty. But I command the next emperor to find the funds to pay these debts. Niyamat Ali must be commended for his service to me. It was he who sponged me every day, and kept me and my bed clean.

My son Azam should rule from Delhi, while Kam Bakhsh must be given Bijapur and Calcutta.

No one should be emperor. The emperor is the most unfortunate of men. No religious debates should invoke me or my deeds. My story shall never be told.

My back is curved from weakness now. My legs are tired. I came to this earth a stranger, and I leave a stranger.

'What more evidence does your friend need of my remorse than this, Honourable Katib? But let me clarify my stance on the similarity between Shakuni and me.'

'Before you get there, I have a question, Shahenshah. Having written in your will that your story must never be told, why did you choose to tell it through me now?'

'Three hundred years have passed, haven't they? Besides, has any aspect of my will been fulfilled? My burial alone was carried out as I asked. All these hundreds of years later, religious debate in your political arena continues to invoke my name. I had no option but to tell my story. The reason I spoke of Shakuni was that I have oft heard him referred to as the Other to Krishna's Self. They make a pair in Derrida's theory.

'I have heard this too: Duryodhana once gifted Balarama a magic mirror. When one looked into it, it would reflect not one's face but the face of the person who was dearest to one. Everyone tried it out. Finally, it was given to Krishna. Krishna refused to look at it. But when the rest persisted, he gave in. He held the mirror to his face. The sabha expected to see Arjuna reflected in it. However, the face in the mirror was that of Shakuni.

'I believe it was to reduce the burden of Bhoomadevi by halving the population that the avatar of Krishna came down to the earth. This was Draupadi's purpose too. By the time they were done, the population had more than halved. To ensure war happened, though, Krishna needed an Other, a counterpart. This was none other than Shakuni. Yes, Arjuna did as Krishna said. But it was Shakuni who did as Krishna willed. His thoughts were constantly on Krishna, anticipating his every move.

'When the last rites of the dead were to be performed, the priest asked whose name ought to be said first. Everyone chorused "Bhishma". But Krishna alone said "Shakuni". The Pandavas were shocked. How could a scheming, plotting cheat be honoured before the man who lived by his conscience all his life? And that was when Krishna told them the story. Shakuni's soul could finally be at peace. The Kurus were destroyed. The Pandavas said, "But we're still standing. We have won the war. How can you say the clan is destroyed?"

'Krishna smiled and said, "Which war have you won? Which of your loved ones is left alive? And which of you has Kuru blood in his veins?" The Pandavas fell silent. None of them had a father from the Kuru clan, did he?

'Krishna went on, "Shakuni's thoughts were always on me, far more often than yours were. It is he who fulfilled my purpose on earth – to reduce Bhoomadevi's burden. For that is why I am here."

'Just as Shakuni was Krishna's Other, your Chhatrapati was my Other.

'In 1681, twenty-three years after I was crowned emperor of Hindustan, I headed towards the Deccan from Ajmer. I was sixty-three years old. I did not think then that I would never see Delhi or Agra again. I did not think I would spend the next twenty-six years of my life on the battlefield. I travelled a thousand four hundred kilometres to the banks of the river Krishna. My commanders travelled a further seven hundred kilometres to the banks of the river Kaveri. When I took ill at the age of eighty-seven, I decided to leave for Delhi. I couldn't travel beyond Ahmednagar.

'My predecessors spent half of every year relaxing in Kashmir. I wandered the battlefields. Why? I left for the Deccan a year after Shivaji's death. He haunted me. His strategies haunted me. His men moved as shadows. They would sneak into towns at night, and raid the houses and rape the women and loot the town and disappear into the dark. My soldiers were helpless. They were used to confrontation, not to ambushes in civil zones. Our spies proved incapable too. And that was why I set off myself. It was a fool's errand, as we already know.

'Shivaji completed me. He was my other half. Do you know why? He lost to me, and yet I was jealous of him. As you have

already divined, it had to do with his sons. What would I not give
to have sons like Sambhaji and Rajaram?

'You spoke of Allende and Victor Jara. These sons of Shivaji
were no less. I remember when Sambhaji stood before me in
chains. He stood erect, his chest out. I had never encountered eyes
that knew no mortal fear. He expected to be sentenced to death,
and he was ready to go with dignity. I have never seen anyone
make no move to beg for another chance, to beg me to spare him.
He stood strong and silent. He had been flogged all night and his
skin was in shreds. Blisters and boils shone on his flesh. And yet
he stood tall.

'I told him I would spare his life if he would convert.

'He told me he would convert if I would marry him to my
daughter.

'I have never had anyone tortured as I had him tortured that
night. I couldn't sleep. I paced. I could hear him, shouting, no,
roaring the names of his stone gods as he was being flogged, even
with no skin on his back.

'I could take it no more. *Cut off his tongue,* I said. What would
a man do when his tongue was cut off? He would scream and wail.
Sambhaji laughed. *Cut off his ears,* I said. With no tongue and no
ears, Sambhaji laughed. *Cut off his nose.* He laughed. *Cut off his
fingers.* He laughed. *Cut off his hands.* He laughed. *Cut off his arms.*
He laughed. *Cut off his legs.* He laughed. Every time, he laughed
louder and louder, a tongueless laugh that made the entire palace
quake and shake and shudder and quiver. His eyes met mine,
proud and fearless. *Dig out his eyes.* His eyes were dug out and
thrown away. And yet he laughed. Was he a man or a demon, I
wondered. That day, my court witnessed humiliation, true defeat.
I had been defeated. He was my slave, a man who should have
begged me for mercy. And he laughed in my face. I could only

punish his body. His mind was his own. His pride shone through every sinew of that tormented body. His eyes showed no fear, not even when they were scooped out of their hollows. How I envied Shivaji this son. My own sons were all cowards. For seventy years, I danced with death. And yet my sons were all cowards. You already know all that they have done. We have spoken of it earlier, and it pains me too much to revisit those betrayals now, although I relive them in my head constantly.

'What a nightmare the Marathas proved! They were as fierce as their lands, as raw and ferocious and savage. With the Vindhya and Satpura hill ranges to the north, the Arabian Sea to the west, criss-crossing rivers and vicious forests to the south and east, the land was hard to access. When it rained, it poured for five months at a stretch. It was hell on earth. And it was on this hell that I spent the last two and a half decades of my life, only to return empty-handed, broken of body and spirit. For when we did access the lands, we found the warriors far superior to our own, because their commanders were straightforward. Do you know, Honourable Katib, I've noticed that the Rajputs did not ever care about the end; it was the means that were important. They lived and died by their code of honour. The Marathas were the opposite. To them, the means were simply the *means to an end*. The end was all that mattered. Whereas we Mughals, we were … what can one even say? It is said of the Marathas that they never forgot their friends and never forgave their foes. We betrayed our fathers by trying to turn their foes into our friends. We blinded our sons. We lied to our brothers. William Norris writes that a bottle of good wine could prompt a Mughal to give up his own children. Sometimes, I think he was right.'

~

With that, the spirit fell silent.

A long time passed.

The writer nodded at Rizwan and was about to get up, when the Aghori raised his hand to stop them.

'The next time you come, bring Kokkarakko with you.'

~

At the next seance, with Kokkarakko seated in his audience, Aurangzeb said, 'I believe my mirroring of Shivaji began when we were children. He grew up in a fatherless home, with his mother Jija Bai sinking herself into worship as she pined for her husband's return. He, too, learned to seek refuge in religion. I grew up in a house so full of family, one could barely walk two feet without bumping into a relative. Yet, I felt all alone. Rajputs everywhere. Idol worship in every nook. I felt like a Muslim child trapped in a Hindu home. I, too, sought refuge in religion.

'And there was an important difference. Except for Padishah Akbar, all the Timurid emperors were given an intense education. As a child, I was taught Farsi, Hindi and Sanskrit, and had a working knowledge of French and English. The Marathas believed it was the gomastha's job to read and write. Like Padishah Akbar, Shivaji did not know how to write even his own name. Perhaps this was an advantage to him in some ways. He was not educated, and therefore not cultured. He never stood on ceremony, never respected codes – not even the codes of war. He would use guerrilla warfare to attack weak forts, he would make false promises to win allies, and he would go back on his word with no pinch of conscience. There's strategy, and then there's chicanery. Could you respect the latter if you had some education, some exposure to history and honourable martial practice? And yet ... he had children who stood tall and proud, who laughed as they were vivisected, while mine betrayed me and each other and offered to become sell-swords to the very enemy against whom they were leading a charge!

'Shivaji had no morals and no qualms. When his father was captured by the Sultan of Bijapur, he all but grovelled to Murad Bakhsh, promising to accept Mughal suzerainty and pay tributes, if only he would help him release his father. Seven years later, he led an army against the Mughals. When he wanted to capture this little town called Jaoli in the Satara region of Maharashtra, he sent a crew of a hundred and twenty-five men under the guise of asking the clan leader Krishna Bhaji for his daughter's hand in marriage to Shivaji. When they were in Krishna Bhaji's chambers, Raghunath – the leader of the crew – stabbed him. They were ambushed in their own home. That was Shivaji for you. The Morè clan of Jaoli had done him no harm. And yet...'

'Shahenshah, I must interrupt.' That was Kokkarakko. 'When you started speaking of your childhood and Shivaji's, I thought you were going to evoke some trauma which would make for interesting psychoanalysis for the readers. But this is just another mundane account – well, potentially a graphic account of a mundane war. Bloodshed, battlefields, betrayal ... how much more talk of history before you turn this novel into a snooze fest? I can guess what you're about to say. Your so-called "Other" was a cheat and scoundrel. He told lies, no different from you when you swore falsely on the Holy Quran. And yet he is a hero, and you're a villain. You've said this too many times now. You don't want to become a figure of pathos. Worse, many stories have been told about you and Shivaji. Why, we have illustrated children's books that show Shivaji and his son escaping in fruit baskets from right under your nose when they were captives in Agra. That could only make you a comic figure, unless you make a case for why you allowed that escape. You ... why are *you* looking at me like that?'

The last question was addressed to the writer, who could only imagine how he looked. He was horrified, terrified and mortified in equal measure.

At the last seance, Aurangzeb's spirit had given him graphic details of what he had done to Sambhaji in a temper. For all this, Sambhaji hadn't even spoken to him as Kokkarakko had. And the spirit was no formless one. It had a body, that of the Aghori. Aghoris were reputed to eat human flesh. What if he ate them alive?

'You need have no such fear, Honourable Katib,' said Aurangzeb.

Oh God. And it could read minds. He ... *he* could read minds. Or should he say 'they', the royal plural for the royal guest...? No, no, he should just stop thinking.

Aurangzeb smiled, and then laughed.

'Do not worry. It was precisely your friend Kokkarakko's inability to mince words that prompted my suggestion that you bring him along. We do need his feedback on these conversations. I've heard his own writing is quite salacious. While I can't aspire to salaciousness for mine, perhaps we can stray from scholarship to sensationalism once in a while. I apologize for having disappointed you, Kokkarakko Sahib. How may I make it up to you?'

'I'll leave you to think about it,' Kokkarakko said. 'Anyway, I'll read the novel once it is published. I have other things to do now.'

And he left as unceremoniously as he had arrived.

CHAPTER 14

The Emperor of Almost Nothing

Even as Rizwan and he entered the room, the writer knew that this would be the last time he met Aurangzeb.

The spirit nodded, having read his mind.

'You are right, Honourable Katib. I'm here to tie up the loose ends,' Aurangzeb said. 'You began this novel asking me about Mirra. If a girl of the royal household could be sold into slavery and thrown into a den of prostitution, imagine the safety situation for the commoners, Honourable Katib! It was to remove these social evils that I dedicated myself to discipline – in my own personal life, and in the empire itself. But I realized in my last years that I had failed entirely. I wish to rewrite my life, Honourable Katib. I'd like to do away with those last years, those years when the women who had committed jauhar screamed into my ears through the night. Do write that Aurangzeb killed himself at the age of eighty-six.'

'But how can I do that, Huzoor? Yes, one does have the right to fictionalize events in a novel. But putting your death down to suicide is a stretch – who could possibly believe that?'

321

'Why, in the novel *The Emperor's Writings,* Dirk Collier attributed Padishah Akbar's death to suicide. Why can't you do the same?'

'The intrepid Aurangzeb, who spent his eighties on various battlefields, and suicide? The two don't go together. Besides, how can you ask me to use another writer's plot device?'

'Well, in that case, I have another request. Please make sure you dedicate a fair bit of space to my sister Jahanara Begum's account. I owe her so much. It was she who got my father to reinstate me in the service of the empire. She was a Sufi in royal clothing. She sent me letters of advice, speaking of Islam and how a good Muslim should conduct himself. If only I had paid heed to them as I should have, I wouldn't have been haunted by those nightmares in my last days.'

'Shahenshah, you speak of the padishah begum with such affection and admiration. And yet, it was you who spoke of her … umm … her father and … your father, I mean…'

'Let the padishah begum have the last word on that, Honourable Katib. It is like the film you mentioned once, *Rashomon.* Everyone has a different perspective on events to which one has been witness.

'We are approaching the end of my story. Do you remember the Emperor of Almost Nothing whom I mentioned a few seances ago? I told you he sat on the bare floor of the Red Fort like a blind beggar. I told you my story would end with his story.

'His name was Shah Alam. Shah Alam II. He ruled towards the dusk of the Mughal empire's reign in this land. In 1788, the head of the Afghan Rohilla army, Ghulam Qadir, approached the Red Fort. The gates were opened for him. This was orchestrated by the head of the guard, in betrayal of the emperor. The emperor Shah Alam II was helpless. What was the backstory?

'To understand the fall of India's greatest empire, we must go beyond my time. Ghulam Qadir's father, Zabita Khan, had led a series of rebellions against the Mughal empire. Shah Alam II launched a campaign against Zabita Khan, led by the Maratha leader Mahadaji Shinde. Zabita Khan managed to evade capture, but his family was not so lucky. Ghulam Qadir was a child, perhaps eight or ten years of age, and Shah Alam was besotted with the boy. Some say he adopted him, calling him his 'farzand'. Others say he castrated him and used him as his catamite. The one thing on which everyone agrees is that he was treated like a prince.

'Every time the child cried that he wanted to go back to his parents, the emperor would read him a poem he had composed. He composed one for every instance the child cried. There were times when he considered sending him back home to his parents, but the courtiers told the emperor not to. He wrote another poem, which said:

> For as long as Aftab looks upon you, my child,
> you will be protected.

'"Aftab" refers to the sun in the sky. It was also the takhallus of Shah Alam.

It is also said that there were two reasons for the castration – Shah Alam's own desire for him, and his wanting to ensure the women of the harem did not have secret relations with Ghulam Qadir, for he knew the boy would grow into a stunningly handsome man.

'People speak of the great betrayal Ghulam Qadir wrought on the emperor, tormenting his family as he did when he entered the Red Fort. They say a bloodier incident than the massacre of 1787–88 was never seen. A slave is a slave, however much love is showered upon him by his captor. A gilded cage is a cage. Mutilation is mutilation, and it must be avenged. And it was. Two eyeballs for a pair of balls.

'True, Honourable Katib, I might have become somewhat influenced by the banter between you and Kokkarakko. I shall try to return to my earlier tongue. But no ... what is the point? My empire went to dust. My language may as well go too. This might be construed as a literary device that illustrates the point. The seeds of the Mughal empire's downfall were sown in Alamgir's time, and in Alamgir's tongue. Here he is, speaking of balls.

'I told you earlier of Nader Shah's massacre in Delhi, how he turned the city into a cemetery.

'And yet that would pale in comparison to what Ghulam Qadir did from the month of July 1788 through to October of that year. That is perhaps what led to the absolute and final abasement and debasement of my descendants, who were reduced in the 1800s to living in an alley known as the Saltani Quarter, a series of blocks where men of the Timurid dynasty lived as beggars and pounced on packets of food and penurious privy purses that the East India Company threw at them.

'Ten emperors sat on the Peacock Throne in the years between my death in 1707 and the coronation of Shah Alam II in 1760. Some ruled only for days. I believe your parliament saw one such crisis in the 1990s? Well, I suppose it sounds the death knell for government when multiple rulers play musical chairs.

'Shah Alam ruled for forty-seven years, and I for forty-nine. But the difference was this – he was a mirage in the desert, and I the oasis. He spent six years in Allahabad, as the firangis' puppet. What humiliation! His servants were whipped, his musicians were arrested, his letters were intercepted, his requests to meet the king of England ignored.

'He could never have got back on the Peacock Throne if it were not for the Marathas. And he barely had a chance to sit on that throne before Zabita Khan began to plague him. If I had been in Shah Alam's place, I'd have lopped off the heads of both Zabita Khan and his beautiful son. Shah Alam did not act as an emperor, as a warrior, as a victor, as a Muslim. He acted as a poet, besotted with beauty, perhaps predisposed to sparing lives. I think this may be why the Quran comes down so hard on poets. They're fools, and they're immoral. Charity or lust, whatever drove him to do as he did, would be his undoing.

'Ghulam Qadir claimed his post as the leader of the Rohillas after his father's death. And he had much to avenge. When Zabita Khan was routed, he was only allowed to flee the fort in exchange for everything else within. The men and women were stripped, their clothes and jewels confiscated, the people sent out naked. The women were raped by the Mughals and the Marathas. The graves, including that of Zabita Khan's father, were dug up, the bodies exhumed and shorn of the jewellery with which they had been buried. The plunder was worth a hundred and twenty lakh rupees. Today, that would work out to two thousand crore rupees. Of this, Shah Alam was only given a tenth. He tried to save the women of Zabita Khan's family from the Maratha soldiers, but even his own soldiers wouldn't obey his orders, let alone the Marathas.

'When Ghulam Qadir arrived at the Red Fort, he intended to enact it all again. Except, the defeat of Zabita Khan had had a fallout of days. The invasion of the Red Fort and the subsequent reign of terror lasted months. Three months.

'He had promised to take revenge, you see.

'The courtiers and advisers to Shah Alam II had always been suspicious of Ghulam Qadir. Many had lost close family to Zabita Khan. Once, Shah Alam heard that one of the noblemen, Majid ud-Daula, whose brother Abul Qasim had been beheaded by Zabita Khan, intended to kill his son as payback. Terrified for his beloved, Shah Alam sent Ghulam Qadir back to his family with a retinue of bodyguards for protection. That night, Ghulam Qadir shook his fist and said, "I will get my own back at the madman who held me captive and sang songs to me. I will ensure the Red Fort sinks into the Ganga."

'In 1787, he began his offensive. As he neared Delhi with his men, various noblemen with spy networks began to warn Shah Alam.

'"Why do all of you nurse such venom against that poor orphan? My sons, my courtiers, my advisers, my noblemen … none of you knows either the rules of governance or the bonds of affection. Ghulam Qadir has eaten under my roof. He will never betray me."

'Who raises a tribal as a prince? Who goes to bed with a snake and expects to wake up alive the next morning?

'Ghulam Qadir marched on the Red Fort in 1787. He wasn't able to enter because Mahadaji Shinde came to Shah Alam's aid. Shah Alam's army was reduced to his bodyguards. He hadn't paid the rest for months. The treasury was empty. Once Mahadaji returned home, Ghulam Qadir marched on the fort again. This time, he bribed Shah Alam's innermost circle of guards. He led an army of two thousand men into the fort.

'What happened next outdoes both our most terrible visions of hell, and the writings of Marquis de Sade whom you mention so often.

'Some of those things have been documented, others have been rumoured, but the worst have been withheld. Things happened there that no one could see except us spirits, and that is what I will speak of now. What I saw in those weeks told me what I should have realized a hundred years earlier – that war is meaningless; that its victims are the helpless; that its victors will eventually become victims too. I will tell you what I saw.

'The women were all stripped and raped. The men were stripped and flogged. But this wasn't enough. He wanted money. There was no money. Everyone said there was no money. His soldiers searched not only the treasury, but every part of the Red Fort. The treasure must be buried somewhere, he thought, and interrogated everyone more and more cruelly. They would crack eventually. But there was nothing to say. They were hiding nothing. There was no money.

'He lined up Shah Alam's nineteen sons and stripped them. He flogged them until their skin hung in shreds, then made them stand on all fours like dogs. He made them chew on his servants' slippers, and flogged their buttocks. We could see bone. They said there was no money. No one could have borne such torture without breaking unless he was truly innocent. Ghulam Qadir refused to believe them. Perhaps he didn't want to. He asked for the chamber pots to be brought to the courtyard, dragged one of the princes to it, and killed him by plunging his head into faeces until he suffocated and died.

'One of the princesses saw this, screamed and fainted. Suddenly remembering that the princesses had only been apprehended, Ghulam Qadir ordered that they be stripped.

'"Tell me where the treasures are buried and you can have your clothes back," he said to them.

'"We don't know, there's nothing in the treasury, no one hid anything." They all said the same thing.

'Ghulam Qadir ordered his men to rape them. They fell on the princesses like a pack of wolves. Not even Shah Alam's queens escaped this fate. They were stripped and raped in public. Then they were made to dance for Ghulam Qadir.

'One fine day, he turned his attentions on Shah Alam himself. He pushed Shah Alam, who was by then old and frail before his time, to the floor. Then Ghulam Qadir blinded the emperor with his own hands, digging his eyeballs out with the Afghani knife he wore on his belt. The servants who tried to staunch the bleeding from the emperor's eyes were killed.

'Ghulam Qadir went on until the beginning of October, visiting new horrors and unimaginable humiliations upon the royal family – my descendants, Honourable Katib. Then, news reached him that the formidable Maratha king Mahadaji Shinde was in Delhi with his troops. Ghulam Qadir made his escape through the Yamuna. Mahadaji Shinde sent part of his army after the Rohilla chieftain.

'On 11 October 1788, the Marathas captured the Red Fort and reinstated Shah Alam as the emperor. The men who were chasing Ghulam Qadir followed him to Aligarh and then Meerut and finally a village called Bamnauli. Ghulam Qadir had lost all his men and horses to the Marathas and sought refuge in the house of a Brahmin. The Brahmin told the Marathas right away, and Ghulam Qadir was taken into custody.

'On 31 December 1788, he was brought before Mahadaji Shinde. He was caged like an animal, but otherwise left unharmed until February 1789, when Shinde received a letter from Shah Alam. *Send me Ghulam Qadir's eyes, or I will have no choice but to leave for Mecca and live as a beggar in that holy land.*

'On 3 March 1789, Shinde marched up to Ghulam Qadir's cage, and began by cutting off his ears and nose. Then, he pulled out his tongue and tore out his lips. Finally, he gouged out Ghulam Qadir's eyes and put them in a box. Qadir was killed along with his men.

'It was said of Shah Alam II, "Sultanat-i Shah Alam, az Dilli ta Palam" – the empire of Shah Alam stretched from Delhi to Palam. "Delhi" meant Lal Qila, the Red Fort. Twelve miles. The empire which once spread from Afghanistan to Bengal, the Himalayas to the Deccan, was now reduced to twelve miles of land. If only he had done as his advisers counselled. When Mirza Najaf Khan, who was responsible for capturing Zabita Khan, passed away, he ought to have appointed Najaf Khan's nephew Mirza Shafi as the commander-in-chief of the army. Instead, he went with his own instincts, trusting sycophants and traitors until he had reduced the Mughal empire to a stretch of twelve miles.

'One day, a British official came to meet the emperor. No one at the Red Fort appeared to know where he was. The official would later write in his notes that everyone appeared to be dazed and sleepwalking. There were no guards and no khwajasaras. He looked for the king through the expanse of the Red Fort, a quest that took hours, without success. The Peacock Throne was not in its place. Had that been stolen too, he wondered.

'Exhausted, he was about to leave when his attention was drawn to what seemed to be a flag on one of the numerous balconies of the fort. He made for the balcony, and realized what he had seen was not a flag but a cloth tied down as if to offer shade.

'A miserable-looking blind man sat on a worn blanket beneath it. The poor beggar must have lost his way, the official thought, as he watched him reach into his coin box to caress something. The official went closer, wondering who this beggar was who had set up shop in a place that no one would visit. From where did he expect his coin to arrive?

'"Who goes there?" said the beggar in a commanding voice. "Who goes there without saluting the emperor?"

'The official looked into the coin box to see what the blind man was caressing. From his palms, a pair of human eyes glared at the official.'

Selected Bibliography

- Alam, Muzaffar and Sanjay Subrahmanyam. *Writing the Mughal World: Studies on Culture and Politics*. Columbia University Press, 2011.

- Begum, Gulbadan and Annette Susannah Beveridge, translators. *Humayun-nama: The History of Humayun*. Royal Asiatic Society, 1902.

- Bernier, François. *Travels in the Mogul Empire, A.D. 1656–1668*. Translated by Irving Brock and Archibald Constable. Archibald Constable and Co., 1892.

- Beveridge, Annette Susannah, translator. *The Babur-nama (Memoirs of Babur)*. Luzac and Co., 1912–22.

- Bilimoria, Jamshid H., translator. *Ruka'at-i-Alamgiri Or Letters of Aurangzebe*. Luzac and Co., 1908.

- Bokhari, Afshan. *Imperial Women in Mughal India: The Piety and Patronage of Jahanara Begum*. Tauris Academic Studies, 2019.

- Dalrymple, William. *City of Djinns: A Year in Delhi*. Penguin Books, 1993.

- Das, Banarasi. *The Ardhakathanaka* (1641). Translated by Chowdhury, Rohini. Penguin Books India, 2009.

- De, B., translator. *The Tabaqat-i-Akbari of Khwajah Nizamuddin Ahmad (A History of India from the Early Musalman Invasions to the Thirty-Sixth year of the Reign of Akbar)*. Asiatic Society, 1939.

- Digby, Simon. *Sufis and Soldiers in Awrangzeb's Deccan*. Oxford University Press, 2001.

- Findly, Ellison Banks. *Nur Jahan: Empress of Mughal India*. Oxford University Press, 1993.

- Hambly, Gavin R. G., editor. *Women in the Medieval Islamic World*. Palgrave Macmillan, 1998.

- Hosten, H. and C.E. Luard, translators. *Travels of Fray Sebastien Manrique 1629–1643*. Hakluyt Society, 1927.

- Ikram, S.M. *Muslim Civilization in India*. Columbia University Press, 1964.

- Kinra, Rajeev. *Writing Self, Writing Empire: Chandar Bhan Brahman and the Cultural World of the Indo-Persian State Secretary*. University of California Press, 2015.

- Koch, Ebba, editor. *The Mughal Empire from Jahangir to Shah Jahan*. Marg Foundation, 2019.

- Lal, Magan and Jessie Duncan Westbook. *The Diwan of Zeb-un-Nissa, The First Fifty Ghazals rendered from the Persian, with an Introduction and Notes*. John Murray, 1913.

- Lal, Ruby. *Domesticity and Power in the Early Mughal World*. Cambridge University Press, 2005.

- Loti, Pierre. *India*. Translated by George A.F. Inman. T. Werner Laurie, 1906.
- Manucci, Niccolao. *A Pepys of Mogul India: 1653–1708*. Translated by William Irvine. E.P. Dutton and Company, 1913.
- Mukhoty, Ira. *Daughters of the Sun: Empresses, Queens and Begums of the Mughal Empire*. Aleph Book Company, 2018.
- Sarkar, Jadunath. *History of Aurangzib*. M.C. Sarker and Sons, 1912–24.
- Saxena, Bhimsen. *Tarikh-i-Dilkasha: Memoirs of Bhimsen Relating to Aurangzeb's Deccan Campaigns*. Translated by Jadunath Sarkar. Department of Archives (Bombay), 1972.
- Sharma, Sunil. *Mughal Arcadia: Persian Literature in an Indian Court*. Harvard University Press, 2017.
- Strong, John S. *The Legend of Aśoka: A Study and Translation of the Aśokāvadāna*. Princeton University Press, 1983.
- Thackston, Wheeler M., editor and translator. *The History of Akbar* by Abu'l-Fazl ibn Mubarak. Murty Classical Library of India, Harvard University Press. 2015.
- Thackston, Wheeler M., editor and translator. *The Jahangirnama: Memoirs of Jahangir, Emperor of India*. Oxford University Press, 1999.

About the Author

CHARU NIVEDITA is the author of more than sixty works in Tamil, ranging from collections of essays to novels, anthologies of poetry to short stories. Known as a postmodern, transgressive writer, he is most interested in autofiction and metafiction. He is best known for the novel *Zero Degree*, which was longlisted for the 2013 edition of the Jan Michalski Prize for Literature and has found a place in several academic syllabi in India and overseas. His books *Marginal Man, To Byzantium: A Turkey Travelogue, Unfaithfully Yours, Morgue Keeper* and *Towards a Third Cinema* have been translated into English and published by independent presses. Charu Nivedita lives in Chennai with his human and animal family.

About the Translator

NANDINI KRISHNAN is the author of *Hitched: The Modern Woman and Arranged Marriage* and *Invisible Men: Inside India's Transmasculine Networks*. She is also the award-winning translator of *Estuary* and *Four Strokes of Luck* by Perumal Murugan, and *Ponniyin Selvan* by Kalki Krishnamurthy. Nandini's novel-in-manuscript won the Caravan and Writers of India Festival contest 2014. Her translation of Sajjad Haider Yaldram's short story, 'Save Me from My Friends', was shortlisted for the Jawad Memorial Prize for Urdu–English Translation 2022. Nandini lives in Madras, with dozens of animals, thousands of books and a varying number of humans.

30 Years *of*

![HarperCollins logo] HarperCollins *Publishers* India

At HarperCollins, we believe in telling the best stories and finding the widest possible readership for our books in every format possible. We started publishing 30 years ago; a great deal has changed since then, but what has remained constant is the passion with which our authors write their books, the love with which readers receive them, and the sheer joy and excitement that we as publishers feel in being a part of the publishing process.

Over the years, we've had the pleasure of publishing some of the finest writing from the subcontinent and around the world, and some of the biggest bestsellers in India's publishing history. Our books and authors have won a phenomenal range of awards, and we ourselves have been named Publisher of the Year the greatest number of times. But nothing has meant more to us than the fact that millions of people have read the books we published, and somewhere, a book of ours might have made a difference.

As we step into our fourth decade, we go back to that one word – a word which has been a driving force for us all these years.

Read.